Praise for

Blood and Honey

'Hurley's decent, persistent cop is cementing his reputation as one of Britain's most credible official sleuths, crisscrossing the mean streets of a city that is a brilliantly depicted microcosm of contemporary Britain ... The unfolding panorama of Blair's England is both edifying and shameful, and a sterling demonstration of the way crime writing can target society's woes'
Guardian

'There is no doubt that his series of police-procedural novels is one of the best since the genre was invented more than half a century ago'   *Literary Review*

Cut to Black

'The book has everything required of a first-rate police procedural and Hurley is now firmly at the top, with few rivals in this genre'   *Sunday Telegraph*

'Hurley is one of my favourite Brit crime writers of the last few years, and long may he continue to chronicle Portsmouth's seedier side'   *Independent on Sunday*

'This series gets stronger and stronger, and there is obviously space for more'   *Crimetime*

Deadlight

'I officially declare myself a fan of Graham Hurley. His attention to detail (without slowing the pace of the novel) and realistic display of police work mark him as a most accomplished purveyor of the British police procedural' *Deadly Pleasures*

'Graham Hurley's *Deadlight* is excellent modern British crime writing. Hurley demonstrates great attention to detail in regard to police procedure, as well as highlighting the conflicts of ideology that exist within the police force' *Independent on Sunday*

'Uncompromisingly realistic and often depressing in its view of the battle against crime, this series grows in stature with each book' *Sunday Telegraph*

'*Deadlight* is a complex and skilfully plotted book and Hurley has a rare knack for understated characterisation that is extremely effective in building up people's lives. *Deadlight* is acutely observed and Hurley is quite simply a superb storyteller' *Sherlock*

'This is a bravura piece of downbeat crime writing; Hurley just seems to get better and better with each Faraday book' *Crime Time*

Angels Passing

'An ambitious police procedural epic ... The often sordid life of a large British city is caught with pinpoint accuracy, together with a host of realistic characters on both sides of the law ... A splendid achievement'
Guardian

'Splendidly gritty ... most enjoyable' *FHM*

'This impressive series ... With the grimness of his concerns and the liveliness of his writing, Hurley is in some ways a South Coast answer to Ian Rankin – before long, I suspect, he'll be just as famous'

Morning Star

'A realistic depiction of modern police work . . . strong stuff, and it makes gripping and, at times, grim reading' *Sunday Telegraph*

'With this, his third novel in the Joe Faraday series, Graham Hurley has taken another step forward and merits comparison with some of the best writers in that branch of the genre . . . It is the sense of Panda cars going down mean streets in Portsmouth which makes this novel so good' *Crime Time*

This is Graham Hurley's sixth novel to feature DI Joe Faraday and DC Paul Winter. An award-winning TV documentary maker, Graham now writes full time. He lives with his wife, Lin, in the West Country. Visit his website at www.grahamhurley.co.uk.

By Graham Hurley

FEATURING DI JOE FARADAY
The Price of Darkness
One Under
Blood and Honey
Cut to Black
Deadlight
Angels Passing
The Take
Turnstone

OTHER NOVELS
Permissible Limits
Nocturne
Heaven's Light
The Perfect Soldier
Sabbathman
Thunder in the Blood
The Devil's Breath
Reaper
Rules of Engagement

NON-FICTION
Airshow

BLOOD AND HONEY

Graham Hurley

An Orion paperback

First published in Great Britain in 2006
by Orion
This paperback edition published in 2006
by Orion Books Ltd,
Orion House, 5 Upper St Martin's Lane,
London WC2H 9EA

An Hachette Livre UK company

A CIP catalogue record for this book is available
from the British Library.

Typeset by Deltatype Ltd, Birkenhead, Merseyside

Printed and bound in Great Britain by
Clays Ltd, St Ives plc

The Orion Publishing Group's policy is to use papers that
are natural, renewable and recyclable products and
made from wood grown in sustainable forests. The logging
and manufacturing processes are expected to conform to
the environmental regulations of the country of origin.

www.orionbooks.co.uk

For Lin
again and always

Acknowledgements

My thanks to the following for their time and advice: John Ashworth, John Banfield, Glen Barham, Robert Bradley, Steven Burton, John Campbell, Mike Dobson, Roly Dumont, Pat Forsyth, Diana Franklin, Jason Goodwin, Simon Goss, Colin Griffiths, Andy Harrington, Mark Hickson, Richard John, Ken Littlewood, Clare Mason, Dave McKinney, Chris Meadus, Clive Merritt, Lucy Pickering, Nick Pugh, John Roberts, Dave Sackman, Morag Scott, Pete Shand, Sarah Skelton, Colin Smith, Debbie Spurlock, Sean Strevens, Tara Walker, Pat Wedick and Nicola Wragg. Simon Spanton offered the book the softest of editorial landings, while my wife Lin shamed us all by doing something practical for Pompey's many asylum seekers. Actions, not mere words.

To the victor, the bones.
– *Milos Stankovic*

Prelude

Monday, 16 February 2004

Flat on her belly on the freezing turf, she sucked in a tiny lungful of air and then steadied the binoculars and tried again. Hundreds of feet below, a flooding tide washed over the tumble of chalky boulders at the foot of the cliff, wave after wave curtaining the shape she thought she'd glimpsed. The shape worried at her. It couldn't be, just couldn't be. Not the way she'd seen it. Not in that kind of state.

Shifting her weight in the bulky anorak, she tracked slowly left, waiting for the next wave to fold, collapse and die. Sluicing back, it revealed only the pale whites of the broken chalk latticed with the rich greens and browns of half a winter's growth of seaweed. She swallowed hard, wondering whether she might have imagined it, this split-second image that refused to go away. Maybe it was a mirage, a trick of the light. Maybe getting up at six in the morning and shipping across to the island on the rumour of an abnormally early nesting season did funny things to the inside of your head.

On the point of giving up and finding a new location, she eased the binoculars a little further to the left, trying to go with the grain of the tide. For an instant came the blur of a black-headed gull riding the column of wind blasting up the cliff face, then – all too distinct – she found herself looking at the shape again, unmistakable this time, momentarily trapped against a sizeable boulder. She watched, fascinated, appalled, then fumbled for her mobile, one hand still locked on the binoculars. For a second, presented by the operator with a brisk list of options, she didn't quite know what to say.

'Police,' she managed at last.

But it was the coastguard who arrived first, bumping over the frosty turf in a new-looking Land Rover. Pausing for a brief account of what had happened, he accompanied the woman to the edge of the cliff, using his own binoculars to confirm the presence of the body beneath. Back at the Land Rover, he leaned into the cab and reached for the radio. The woman caught mention of 'Bembridge' and 'lifeboat' before the clatter of a big helicopter drowned out the rest of the conversation. The helicopter seemed to appear from nowhere, tracking low over the down, then banking steeply as it left the cliff face behind it. The coastguard motioned the woman away from the edge of the cliff as the rotor wash swirled around them.

'Cliff rescue team should be here any minute,' he said. 'Police, too.'

The policeman was young. He took the woman through what she had seen and asked her if she was prepared to make a statement later. Beyond them, on the clifftop, the rescue team were lowering four men and a stretcher on a skein of ropes while the helicopter hovered offshore, the face of the watching pilot clearly visible. Abruptly, he waved to someone down below; gave him the thumbs up. Then, as if this was something they did every day of their working lives, the team on the clifftop were hauling their cargo in.

The woman edged back to the cliff, absorbed by this

small drama, by the way that the shape in her binoculars had surrendered to this smooth exercise in retrieval. Peering over, she had time to register two of the men steadying a stretcher, halfway up the cliff. Strapped to the stretcher was a plastic body bag, grey, bulky. From this distance it looked like a parcel they'd found on the beach.

The woman shifted, unable to tear herself away. The blast of the wind. The steady *whump-whump* of the helicopter. The angry scream of disturbed gulls. And the deadweight of that strange grey package, bumping against the cliff face. Then came a hand on her shoulder and she turned to find herself eye to eye with the coastguard. He was tall, blue jumpsuit, tightly cropped grey hair.

'Best not to look, madam. This wind. Don't want two of you down there, do we?'

Chastened, the woman stepped away from the edge. But, try as she might, she couldn't rid herself of that first glimpse of the body now on the stretcher, the image that had registered for a split second in her binoculars and triggered this extraordinary operation. The mottled naked greyness of the flesh. The huge distended belly. The floppy limbs flailing in the tide. And how strange a body looked without a head.

One

Faraday stood at the window in the Southsea hover-craft terminal, staring out. The gale anticipated on last night's TV weather forecast had arrived at last, low ragged skirts of cloud and a hard, driving rain that had soaked him in the brief dash across the road from the seafront car park. Now, half-expecting the service to be suspended, he peered through the blurry, salt-caked glass.

The low, dark swell of the Isle of Wight had long disappeared. Beyond the angry lunge of the waves and a glimpse of the heaving buoy that marked the deep-water channel, he could see nothing. Even the seaweed, long brown ribbons of the stuff, was blowing like litter across the glistening concrete ramp that plunged down towards the boiling tideline.

The woman at the ticket office, to his faint disappointment, met his enquiry about cancellation with a shake of her head. Conditions weren't perfect, she admitted, but the weather was still within operating limits. If the inbound service was a minute or two later than scheduled, she counselled patience.

Faraday returned to his sodden briefcase and extracted a thin manila envelope. Settling damply in the moulded plastic chair, he reread the file that had been sent back to Major Crimes a couple of days ago.

The details were sparse. A twenty-five-year-old

4

white male, name of Aaron Tolly, had been found dead at the back of a block of flats off Ryde seafront. The body had been discovered before dawn by a local runner in early training for the London marathon. His 999 call had brought both an ambulance and a patrol car to the scene and by mid-morning Detective Superintendent Willard had dispatched Detective Inspector Nick Hayder plus two DCs from Major Crimes to spearhead what the local DI was already calling a murder investigation.

Faraday flipped quickly through the file. Same-day inquiries had established that Tolly was an alcoholic and occasional heroin user with a long record of convictions for shoplifting and benefit fraud. He'd shipped over to the island from Pompey and now lived in a heavily secured squat on the third floor of the premises. On the night of his death, according to a witness who knew him by sight, he'd been drinking alone in a shelter on the seafront. Later that evening he'd evidently tried to cadge money for more drinks in a local pub. His keys had been found inside the squalid flat he called home. To someone with a head for heights and plenty of nerve, a fire escape to a locked door at the rear of the flat offered access to an adjacent bedroom window. One of the other vagrants who dossed there thought he might have heard a bang or two at the door and then a brief scraping noise at the window. At the post-mortem the pathologist identified injuries consistent with a fall. Recorded body temperatures put the time of death at around midnight. In Nick Hayder's judgement Tolly had got pissed again, found his way up the fire escape, tried for the half-open bedroom window, and missed.

At the back of the file Faraday found a sheaf of colour stills from the Scenes of Crime photographer.

He lingered for a moment on the last of the shots. Tolly lay sprawled beside a line of brimming dustbins, his arms outstretched, one leg buckled beneath the other. There was a glimpse of white flesh through a tear in his jeans and Faraday noticed that one of his battered runners was unlaced. Faraday gazed at the thin, gaunt face, the eyes wide open, the mouth shaping the beginnings of a scream. Tolly hadn't shaved for a day or two and a brown trickle of congealed blood tracked through the stubble below his left ear. The post-mortem report had spoken of multiple skull fractures with haemorrhages in the underlying brain tissue. With injuries like these, according to the pathologist, Tolly would have been killed on impact.

Faraday leafed back through the file, checking every link in the sequence of events Hayder and his team had put together. The stretch of unswept concrete where Tolly had met his death lay directly beneath the bedroom window. With his keys inside a locked flat, there was every possibility he'd tried to find an alternative way in. No witnesses had spoken of any kind of altercation earlier in the evening. Drunk and alone, Tolly had tumbled into oblivion.

Faraday looked up, hearing the approaching roar of the hovercraft. Hayder and his team had stayed on the island for another couple of days. Unearthing no evidence to convince him otherwise, he'd returned the file to the local DI with a note confirming an absence of suspicious circumstances. By now the Coroner should have held an inquest and returned a verdict. Yet here was Faraday, en route to CID headquarters in Newport. The DI was insisting on a full review. And Willard, whose responsibility for Major Crimes extended to the Isle of Wight, wanted to know why.

Faraday got to his feet, slipping the file into his briefcase. The hovercraft was a dark shadow fifty metres offshore. Emerging through the grey curtain of rain, it yawed violently from side to side, clawed its way out of the waves, climbed the weed-strewn ramp, and then settled unsteadily on the wet concrete.

The departures hall had mysteriously emptied. The youth on the exit door inspected Faraday's ticket.

'You ready for this, sir?' he muttered.

The trip across was mercifully brief. Never had he been closer to losing his breakfast. On landfall at Ryde, half-expecting a waiting CID car, Faraday was obliged to take a taxi. Half an hour to Newport with the heater on full blast was enough to dry out, and by the time he'd settled himself in the DI's office he felt a good deal better.

Detective Inspector Colin Irving had been in charge of the island's CID for longer than anyone could remember. A tall, bespectacled, slightly bookish figure, he guarded his independence with the kind of fierce pride that went with an Aldershot youth and three years in uniform patrolling the badlands of Basingstoke. As someone who himself had once lived on the island, Faraday was the first to acknowledge that the most passionate islanders were always the ones who'd blown in from somewhere else.

'Busy?'

Irving took the question at face value. He was still describing a recent series of encounters with the Animal Liberation Front when a kindly-looking management assistant appeared with coffee. Faraday took his chance to change the subject.

'Tolly . . .' he began. 'What else do we know about him?'

'Not a lot. He's Pompey born and bred. Shame he didn't stay, really. Saved us all a lot of bother.'

'Is that what this is about?'

Irving shook his head but said nothing. Both men understood the reality of divisional CID work only too well. Successful detections on dwelling burglaries or thefts from vehicles won lots of brownie points from the Home Office but serious offences – stranger rape, homicide – brought you nothing but grief and a heavy overtime bill. Hence the bid to offload onto Major Crimes.

'So why isn't he done and dusted?' Faraday tapped the file. 'What's happened?'

'We've picked up good intelligence. Stuff we can't ignore.'

'About Tolly?'

'Of course. That's why I phoned Mr Willard.'

An informant, he said, had come forward with information about a prisoner on the island, a Scouse drug dealer serving seven years for supply. The Scouser had a girlfriend who made regular prison visits and it seemed she'd run into Tolly. After a couple of meetings they'd started some kind of relationship.

'Which prison?'

'Albany.'

Faraday nodded. HMP Albany was one of a complex of three prisons on the road to Cowes. The Isle of Wight had long become a temporary home for relatives of convicts, especially those banged up for years on end. Wives and mothers liked the island so much they often stayed forever.

'So what happened?' Faraday asked again.

'We think the Scouser may have put the word out. There'd be no shortage of takers if he was talking decent money. Maybe he only paid for a beating but

8

these things get out of hand.' Irving offered a bleak smile. 'Know what I mean?'

Faraday nodded. On the face of it Irving's theory sounded plausible enough but the total absence of supporting evidence argued for caution. According to Hayder's investigation, no one had seen Tolly in company. Neither were there any physical signs of assault prior to Tolly's death. Not that Irving cared. The recent intelligence had become part of the file and that meant he had to cover his arse.

'How good is this intelligence?'

'It exists.'

'That's not my question. I'm asking you where it came from.'

'You'll have to talk to his handler. You know the score.'

'Of course I know the score. I'm simply asking what else you've done before you lifted the phone. Have you checked this guy out? Is he a regular? Has he got debts of his own to settle? You know Willard's views on crap intelligence.'

Mention of Willard brought colour to Irving's face.

'You're telling me I'm jumping the gun?'

'I'm suggesting you might need to do a little more footwork.'

'Like how?'

'Like getting one of your blokes to poke around a bit, find out what this informant of yours is really up to. There'll be a story in there somewhere, you know there will.'

'And you think I've got the bodies to waste on something like that?'

Irving had abandoned any pretence of indignation. He was angry now, the anger of a hard-pressed divisional DI, but Faraday could cope with that.

'I know there's no brownie points in homicide,' he said gently. 'But I've got a boss you wouldn't believe and he thinks you're cuffing it.'

'Willard said that?'

'Good as.'

'And you're the messenger?'

'Not at all. But I know the way he works, what he thinks, and on the evidence of this –' Faraday tapped the file '– he'll tell you you're taking the piss. What are your PIs looking like?'

'Bloody good. Best on the force. Plus a clear-up rate most DIs would die for.'

'And you want to keep it that way.'

'Of course we bloody do.'

'But you're stretched, like we're all stretched.'

'Too right.'

'So the more running around we do on your behalf . . .'

Irving began to shake his head, then abandoned his seat at the little conference table and stepped across to the window. Home Office Performance Indicators had become the bane of divisional life. Devoting precious CID resources to Aaron Tolly would do absolutely nothing when it came to ranking Irving's PIs against other Basic Command Units, a merciless comparison tool that was driving good coppers insane.

'It's barmy, isn't it?' Irving might have been talking to himself. 'No fucking way to run a whelk stall.'

'I agree.' Faraday drained his coffee. 'Does your canteen still do toast?'

The canteen was virtually empty, just a single figure bent over a magazine at the table beside the micro-wave. Faraday found himself a jar of coffee and refilled the electric kettle. The remains of a loaf of sliced white lay in an open cake tin and Faraday was still looking for something to put on it when a voice prompted him to try in the cupboard beside the fridge.

'There's peanut butter and some of those sachets of jam. Uniform finished the marmalade first thing. Animals.'

Faraday turned round. The figure at the table hadn't stirred. The mail beside the hang-gliding magazine was addressed to DC Darren Webster.

'DI Faraday. Major Crimes.' Faraday extended a hand. 'Any butter?'

'In the fridge.' Webster at last looked up. 'Sir.'

His handshake was firm and the smile came as a slight surprise. Webster had a stubble-cheeked, outdoor face. There were hints of strength in the set of the jaw, and the newness of his suit was offset by the loosened tie. Here was a young detective, thought Faraday, who knows exactly who he is.

'Over from Pompey?' Webster enquired.

'Yes.'

'Anything else you need?' His eyes had returned to the magazine.

Faraday shook his head. He made himself a couple of slices of toast, then decanted boiling water onto a spoonful of Happy Shopper instant.

'Mind if I join you?'

Faraday sat down without waiting for an answer. Webster was deep in a feature article about hang-gliding in New Zealand. With some reluctance he finally closed the magazine and put it to one side.

'These guys fly over glaciers.' He sounded wistful. 'Can you imagine what that must be like?'

Faraday thought about the question over a mouthful of toast. He hadn't tasted peanut butter in years.

'You do it yourself?' He wiped his mouth. 'Hang-gliding?'

'Yep.'

'Here? On the island?'

'Yep. Last weekend we were down at St Catherine's.'

'Good?'

'Crap. They were giving a steady force four, south-south-west, but the wind was all over the place. Bloody cold, too. We never got off the cliff.' He hesitated, uncertain about the real strength of Faraday's interest.

'I watch birds,' Faraday said simply. 'I've been at it for years. Fascinates me.'

'The flying or the birds?'

'Both.'

Webster hesitated for a moment longer, then plunged into what the last couple of months had yielded for him and his mates. They'd flown most of the cliffs along the south coast of the island, and spent a dodgy weekend trying to stay airborne from a new launch site on Culver Down, the looming chalk shoulder that fell into Sandown Bay. Winter flying wasn't to everybody's taste but you could normally rely on a good blow, and if you had the right kit, and the bottle to go with it, the views could be awesome.

'You've got a favourite?'

'Needles, without a doubt. We kick off from a little bowl above the emplacements. There's a bay below it, a cove really, and you can't see it from the landward side which I suppose makes it even more special. The colours can be incredible, especially those times when a front's on the way and the wind's spot on the nose and the vis is so good you just know it's going to piss down before very long.'

Faraday answered Webster's grin with one of his own. He'd lost count of the days when he'd been up before dawn, tucked into a niche on a cliff top or a woodland copse with his binoculars and his Thermos and the much-thumbed notebook he carried to record bird sightings, waiting to read the weather from the clues scrolled across the slowly lightening sky. Miles from the nearest road life took on a totally different feel. You'd feel exposed, yes, but infinitely less vulnerable.

'I used to live down in Freshwater,' he murmured. 'Years back.'

'You grew up here?'

'No. Bournemouth. After school I went off to the States for a bit. By the time I came back my folks had moved onto the island. Dad had a health problem, couple of strokes. Mum ran a B. and B. in Freshwater Bay. They had to put up with us for a couple of months before we found a place to rent.'

'Us?'

'Me and my wife.' Faraday looked at him for a moment, surprised by the directness of the question, wondering whether to elaborate, but decided against it. Instead he talked about those first days on the island, the mornings he'd abandon the hunt for a job and simply walk on Tennyson Down, out towards the Needles.

'I'd never been anywhere like it,' he said. 'Not then, not now. God's country.'

'You mean that?'

'Absolutely. And the birds make it better. Ever catch a lark – May, June, way up in the blue – belting its little heart out?'

'Yeah.' Webster was grinning again. 'Yeah . . . and those bloody gulls, giving us grief when we launch.

13

Listen to them and you'd think they owned the bloody cliff.'

'But they do. Nesting time, they've got parental rights. Ever think about that?'

'Never.' Webster pushed his chair back and stretched. 'What's Major Crimes like then? Hectic?'

'Comes and goes. Just now it's quiet . . . which is why I've got time to pop over.' Faraday's fingers strayed to the last corner of toast.

'You've come on a specific job?'

'Yes.'

'One of ours?'

'Yes.'

'Mind if I ask which one?'

'Not at all. Aaron Tolly? Name ring any bells?'

'Of course. The Ryde Skydiver.' He glanced towards Faraday. 'You bring a car over, sir?'

Faraday shook his head. 'Cab from the hovercraft.'

'OK.' Webster checked his watch again. 'I'm off to Freshwater on a load of calls. Should take a couple of hours. I don't know how you're placed time-wise but I could drop you down by the Albion if you fancied it. Pick you up again afterwards.'

Faraday thought about the invitation for a second or two, then glanced towards the window. The rain seemed to have stopped and the first daubs of watery blue were beginning to appear above the rooftops across the car park. At Freshwater Bay a footpath climbed up from the Albion Hotel onto Tennyson Down. It might be a touch muddy, and there'd doubtless be the odd shower, but just now he couldn't think of a better way of preparing himself for the file review.

'Great idea,' he said, getting to his feet.

*

In the privacy of the unmarked squad Fiesta Webster opened up about Aaron Tolly. The man had been, he said, a pain in the arse. He'd fled to Ryde after a run-in with a Pompey drug dealer. He had no friends, no visible means of support, and a thirst for White Lightning cider that had put him in front of the magistrates on a shoplifting charge within a month. Over the first couple of pints Tolly could string together a sentence or two, even manage the beginnings of a conversation, but after that he talked the purest nonsense. Webster knew women in Ryde for whom twat was too kind a judgement. Tolly, they said, was fit for nothing.

'No one special in his life?'

'You mean ladies?' Webster shot Faraday a look. 'You have to be joking. Bloke was a disgrace. On a windy night you could smell him from the end of the pier.'

Faraday nodded, settling back in the seat as a row of bungalows gave way to bare fields and the distant swell of Brighstone Down. The crime scene photos of Tolly sprawled by the dustbins had lodged deep in his brain. It was an image that seemed to sum up so many of the case histories that passed through Major Crimes. Young men trapped in cul-de-sacs of their own making, lost, adrift, wasted. At length he mentioned the possibility of some kind of contract.

'On Tolly?' Webster laughed. 'Who'd bother?'

'Someone he'd pissed off, obviously.' Faraday was watching the faraway silhouette of a hawk, maybe a falcon, circling high above a copse of trees. 'How about some Scouser banged up in Albany?'

'Who told you that?'

'Doesn't matter.'

'It's bollocks, sir. With respect.'

'How do you know?'

'Because I heard the same whisper. It comes from a local guy in Ryde, fancies himself as a bit of a dealer. He's putting the word around about some kind of contract to see the opposition off. Didn't want Tolly's death to go to waste.'

'Opposition?'

'Scousers. They're running serious gear in. Mondays usually, off the Fast Cat. Set your clock by it.'

'Does DI Irving know about this?'

'Of course he does. He's as keen on stitching up the Scousers as everyone else, our Ryde dealer included. This used to be a nice island once. Can't have scum like that around.'

Faraday grinned, watching the hawk swoop earthwards. Twenty years in the job already told him that Hayder had been right about Tolly but it was still good to have his instincts confirmed. Irving wanted to rev up Major Crimes to take a run or two at the Scousers. That way they might fold their tents and bugger off. Nice try, he thought.

Webster was making good time. In a mile or so they'd be down on the island's south coast, a couple of minutes drive from Freshwater Bay. The sodden fields beside the road were splashed with sunshine and Faraday could feel the thin warmth on the side of his face. He glanced across at Webster.

'You like CID?'

'Love it. Some days are a pain but there's lots going on if you know where to look. People think this place is toytown – acres of bungalows, old blokes in Morris Minors, nothing happening – but they couldn't be more wrong. Like I've said, we've got a drug problem you wouldn't believe. Bits of Ryde are Smack City, Ventnor too; all these old Victorian spas, overrun with lowlife. You get blokes down from the north, not just Scousers but all sorts, Manchester, Glasgow, you name it. They drift in for the summer, work in the camps, the hotels, pubs, whatever; then come the winter they sign on, draw housing benefit, and end up selling decent amounts of gear. The DI put an operation together recently – *Edith*. Charge list runs to a dozen or so blokes, all of them up for supply. Not bad, eh?'

He shot a sideways look across the car but they were on the coast road by now and Faraday was gazing out at the startling whiteness of the chalk cliffs stretching away towards the Needles. In conditions like these – racing clouds, sudden bursts of sunshine – the view still took his breath away.

'You're happy here?' He finally turned back to Webster.

'Of course. But I can't stay here forever, can I? Not if I want to get anywhere. That's the problem with the island. Shut your eyes, count to ten, and you're suddenly forty years old with a wife and three kids and absolutely no chance of ever doing anything else.'

'What do you fancy then?'

'Major Crimes would be nice.' He glanced at Faraday again. 'Sir.'

'You think so?'

'Definitely.'

'You wouldn't miss being your own boss? Making your own decisions? You think you could hack it in a bigger team?'

'If the jobs were half-decent, of course I could.'

Faraday nodded, twisting in the seat and craning his neck backwards as a clifftop path he'd often used flashed by. The Major Crimes set-up had recently been reorganised and there was now a permanent team of

DCs, sorting jobs county-wide, with two years rotation.

'Vacancies certainly come up,' he admitted, 'but not that often.'

'I know, sir. I keep checking.'

They were in Freshwater Bay by now, driving towards the hotel that flanked the beach. Beyond the low stone wall sunlight danced on the choppy green water. Faraday eyed a tidy-looking fishing launch secured to a buoy, bucking and rolling on the incoming waves, and he wondered what it might be like, measuring out your life to the rhythm of the tides and the seasons.

'Here, sir?'

Beyond the Albion Hotel Webster had come to a halt beside the path that wound up through the trees to the foot of Tennyson Down. In a couple of hours he'd be back, same place, say half two. Then he paused, reaching back for a file from the briefcase on the back seat.

'One thing I forgot.'

'What's that?' Faraday had the door open. The wind was cold.

'We had a G28 this week. Monday it was. Up there.' He nodded towards the down. 'Woman from the mainland called it in. Came over to check out the wildlife.'

Faraday shut the door for a moment. A G28 was the Coroner's form for a sudden death. He'd been away on Monday and Tuesday, and thus missed the incident on the daily force-wide update.

'What happened?'

'This woman saw the body at the foot of the cliff. Happens more often than you might think. May have jumped, may have fallen off a boat, God knows. There must be something about this stretch of coast. That's four in a year now.'

'Man or woman?'

'Bloke. ID's tricky. Prints are useless because he'd had been in the water a while and the crabs had eaten the flesh off his fingers. We've got no clothing to go on either; no tattoos, rings, piercings, nothing.'

'Dental records?'

'No chance.'

'Why not?'

'There wasn't a head.'

'No *head*?'

'Afraid not. The pathologist's got a theory about impact forces. If he'd jumped, hit the rocks at a certain angle, it could have snapped the spinal column. The waves would have done the rest. It's just a theory, that's all.'

'But you're still making inquiries?'

'Of course, sir. And the RNLI boys are going to take a look with the inshore RIB when the weather quietens down.'

'Look for what?'

'The head.'

'Of course.'

Faraday opened the door again, sobered by the thought of what may have preceded this gruesome discovery. A three-hundred-foot fall from the top would take more than three seconds, a statistic he'd tucked away from a previous inquiry, and three seconds was plenty of time for serious regrets. Standing on the pavement, zipping up his anorak, he was suddenly struck by another thought.

'Tell me.' He ducked his head back into the car. 'What was this woman looking for?'

'Peregrine falcons, sir.' Webster had the file open on his lap. 'I knew you'd ask.'

After the first hour, DC Suttle was beginning to fidget. He and DC Winter had been sitting in the darkened Skoda since eight o'clock, perfect line of sight on the apartment. This time of night, late February, Old Portsmouth was deserted. Barely a decade ago, as Winter had already pointed out, this finger of land that curled into Portsmouth Harbour would have been thick with drinkers making a Friday night of it at the Spice Island pubs. Now, it served as a parking lot for top-of-the-range Mercedes and BMWs, the kind of motors that went with a fancy postcode, a quiet retirement and a glimpse or two of the sea.

Winter was watching a figure in a raincoat across the road, bent against the wind, dragging what looked like a spaniel behind him.

'Last crap before bye-byes.' He nodded towards the nearby beach. 'Another reason you'd never swim from here.'

Suttle was wrestling with the last of the crossword from yesterday's *Sun*. In Winter's eyes he was still a boy, barely out of his teens, but a year partnering the older detective in the busy chaos of the Portsmouth Crime Squad had given him an easy self-confidence. He laughed a great deal at some of the madder jobs, and Winter appreciated that, though the current operation – codenamed *Plover* – had so far failed to engage his full attention.

'Season of mists and mellow fruitfulness.' Suttle tapped his teeth with the end of the biro. 'Begins with A. Six letters.'

'Autumn.'

'Yeah, but how do you spell it?'

'A-U-T-U—' Winter broke off, his hand reaching for the radio. 'Kilo Foxtrot, Papa India, over.'

A burst of static, then an acknowledgement. Suttle had abandoned the crossword.

'Stand by, stand by, stand by. Target vehicle a Saab convertible is *left, left* into High Street, Old Portsmouth. Confirmed the subject is driving. Over to you, backup.'

'Yes, yes.'

Winter watched the sleek Saab convertible pause at the exit from the apartment block, signal left, then pull out onto the empty road. The beauty of this little ambush was the subject's lack of options. Turn right, and two hundred metres later Singer would be in the harbour.

'Sweet,' Winter muttered to himself.

The Saab accelerated past the shadowed casemates of the seaward fortifications. Singer, alone in the car, seemed to be checking his face in the rear-view mirror. Already, one hand on the wheel, he was talking on a mobile.

'That'd be the wife, then.' Suttle laughed. 'Working late at the office. Nightmare day. Completely knackered. Who'd be a solicitor, eh?'

Winter ignored him. The blokes from Traffic were parked beyond the cathedral. He'd worked with them before and he knew they were up for it. They'd sit on Singer's arse for a couple of hundred metres, then pull him before he got to the roundabout. Winter was laying short odds on a decent stash of charlie, one last toot before Singer drove up to Clanfield to face the missus, and he knew the solicitor wouldn't have bothered to do anything elaborate in the way of hiding it. In his frame of mind the last thing he'd expect was a

21

random shake-down. That's the way these guys led their lives. Total self-belief.

'How long then?' Suttle was eyeing the apartments across the road.

'Couple of minutes, tops.'

'What about his mobile? What if he rings chummy?' He nodded at the apartment block.

'No chance. First off, he'll bluster, give them grief about unjustified intrusion, all that bollocks. By that time they'll have his mobile off him. That and the gear.'

They waited in silence, Winter trying to picture the word 'autumn' in his mind's eye. Lately, along with the headaches and the problem with his eyes, had come a series of alarming holes in what used to be his memory, and spelling the simplest words was one of them.

'Papa India, Kilo Foxtrot, over.'

'Kilo Foxtrot.' Winter was still holding the radio. 'Go ahead.'

'Affirmative suss cocaine. Subject is under arrest. Out.'

There was a click and a buzz of static before Winter turned the radio off. He opened the door and sat back for a moment or two, listening to the rasp of surf from the nearby beach. His eyes were closed, and he was smiling.

'Try U-M-N,' he said at last.

The apartment block, Camber Court, was a brand new addition to this increasingly select corner of Old Portsmouth. There were ten flats in all. Half of them overlooked the thick stone curtain of the Hot Walls towards Spithead and the Isle of Wight. The rest, to the rear, offered a perfect view of the ancient Camber

Dock, home to a picturesque jumble of tugboats, pilot launches, fishing smacks and the odd motor cruiser. Part with a large cheque, and you could get up early and watch the scallop boats slipping out on the morning tide. Alternatively, as Winter had patiently explained to DI Cathy Lamb, you could arrive at half six on a dark winter's night, neck a glass or two of decent red, pull the curtains and fuck yourself stupid.

Five flights of newly carpeted stairs led to the penthouse in the rear flats. The door opened at Winter's second knock. In the surveillance photos Richardson had been huddled in a full-length cashmere coat. Now he was wearing designer jeans, a collarless white shirt, and sported a tiny pony tail secured with a twist of blue and red beads. For a puffy-faced overweight gay in his early fifties, this outfit suggested a wistful yearning to turn back the clock.

'Gentlemen?' The eyes were glassy behind the wire-rimmed specs.

'DC Winter. Portsmouth Crime Squad. This is DC Suttle. We'd like a word if we may.'

'Now?'

'Yes.'

'My goodness. Well . . .' Winter realised the man was pissed '. . . why not?'

He held the door open as Winter stepped past. Safely inside the apartment, he confirmed the owner's ID. Stephen Wallace Richardson.

'But I'm not the owner,' Richardson added. 'Would that I was. You need to talk to Mr Hakim.'

'And where would we find him?'

'This week? Maybe Beirut. Maybe Dubai. Maybe Monte Carlo. I can give you a mobile number if it makes things easier.'

'So what do you do . . . Mr Richardson?'

'I'm a guest, really. No, more a lodger. It's a grace and favour thing. Mr Hakim and I go back a long way. You might say I keep an eye on the place.' He did his best to look helpful. 'Is there a problem?'

The question brought a grin to Suttle's face. The entrance hall was big, almost a room in itself. A fluted vase on an antique occasional table held what looked like a hand-painted dildo – a whorl of yellows ribbed with scarlet – and a collection of photos on the wall, beautifully lit, artfully composed, offered an arresting level of anatomical detail. On closer inspection, the photos were all of the same woman and Suttle couldn't remember seeing a body so exposed since a stag-night weekend in the fleshpots of Antwerp.

'That music . . .?' Winter had cocked an ear. It sounded classical, maybe opera, and it was coming from a room at the end.

'Friend of mine,' Richardson mumbled. 'Adores Verdi.'

'Yeah?'

Winter was already trying another of the five doors. Richardson watched him, seemingly helpless.

'Our salon.' He answered Winter's enquiring look. 'Please. Be my guest.'

Suttle followed Winter through the door. The room was huge, extending the full width of the apartment. Three of the four picture windows were masked with venetian blinds but through the tall window at the kitchen end of the room Suttle could see the black gleam of water in the Camber Dock and the lights of the houses and apartments beyond.

Winter was standing beside a dining table in the central part of the room. The table was set for four places. Plates and cutlery for the early courses had been cleared away but the remains of a rack of lamb

24

lay in the centre of the tablecloth, flanked by a gravy boat and a little hillock of mint sauce in a Chinese bowl. A trail of gravy drops led to one of the place mats and spoons and forks still awaited the dessert course. Two of the wine bottles on a trolley beside the table were upended in coolers.

Winter turned in time to see Richardson stepping back into the hall.

'If you don't mind, sir.' He motioned him into the sitting room again. 'So who does the cooking?'

'I do.'

'All part of the service, is it? Bed and board?'

Without waiting for an answer, Winter shepherded Richardson towards the vast crescent of leather sofa that dominated the left-hand end of the room. The corners of the sofa were padded with heavy tapestry pillows, and a newly opened box of Montecristo cigars had been abandoned beside a copy of the *Daily Telegraph*. There was a bottle of Krug and more glasses on the low occasional table, plus a selection of magazines. Winter gazed down at them. Nesting amongst the copies of *Tatler, Country Living* and *Yachts and Yachting* were a number of porn magazines, mainly Italian and Spanish. He reached for the nearest and began to flick through it. With a waiting room like this, Winter thought, visits to the doctor might become a real pleasure.

From the kitchen came a yelp of delight. Suttle had been checking the line of cupboards over the neat stack of dishes on the granite-veined work surface. A shelf full of spices beside the six-ring ceramic hob had yielded a roughly crafted wooden box divided into three compartments. Winter inspected it, then invited Richardson to lift it down. One of the three compartments was brimming with a snowy-white powder.

Suttle's grin spread even wider. Couple of grand's worth. At least.

'What's that, then?' Winter nodded at the box. 'Bicarb of soda?'

Richardson was looking pained. A couple of minutes ago he'd been on the point of loading the dishwasher. Now this.

Winter told Suttle to call in for a Scenes of Crime team, then escorted Richardson back to the other end of the room. Before he even thought of contemplating an arrest, he wanted the full tour.

The last time Winter had been on this page in the Pompey book of villainy, he'd had to climb endless flights of greasy steps in almost total darkness to bust a couple of middle-aged toms doing the business in some top-floor doss off the seafront. The punters were being serviced side by side on rubber blow-up mattresses, there was a pit bull chained up in the corner, and you couldn't move for empty cider bottles from the Happy Shopper down the road. At the time it had felt like a kind of victory – at least the dog went to a good home – but even hours later, taking statements from the women back at the Bridewell, he hadn't been able to rid himself of the smell: White Lightning, body fluids, plus gristly bits of discarded kebab from the van round the corner. Three good arguments, thought Winter at the time, for staying in with a bottle of Scotch and a lifetime's repeats of *The Sopranos*.

Camber Court, thank God, belonged on a different planet.

'What's this, then?'

'A television.'

'I know that, but what's on it?'

Winter invited Richardson to press the PLAY button on the DVD. Two men appeared on the huge wall-mounted plasma screen. A third man – tanned, young, supple, inventive – was obliging them both. Winter watched for a moment, his head cocked left and right as he tried to follow the action, warmed by the sheer class of what he'd stepped into.

'These perverts for your benefit?'

Richardson nodded, drawn in by a sequence he'd probably enjoyed a thousand times before.

'Cook's nips,' he agreed. 'Keeps an old man very happy.'

'What else have you got?'

'Pretty much everything.' He indicated a line of DVDs on a shelf beneath the player. 'Depends what you're after. Sado. Foot fetish. Wee-wee. Animals.' He looked pained again. 'Black men with ten-foot willies.'

'Your punters have a favourite?'

'Of course. But it wasn't me who told you.'

He shot Winter a quick, conspiratorial look then bent to the DVDs and extracted a disc. Slipping it into the player, he stepped back, evidently resigned to whatever followed. Winter summoned Suttle with a nod at the screen. A man in his forties was flat on his back, straddled by a tall white girl with a string of pearls round her neck. The man's head hung over the end of the bed, his upside-down face a foot or so away from the camera lens. His eyes were closed and blood was pulsing into his big, jowly face as he paced the rhythm of her body above him. 'Slower,' he kept telling her. 'Slower.'

The girl was moving almost imperceptibly now, an inch up and down, exquisite control. Her long white fingers tipped with black nail varnish were cupping her breasts, and when the command finally came she reached sideways for a bulging plastic bag, then half twisted backwards as she pressed the bag down between the man's legs. The mouth in the camera lens opened wide, then wider still, a strangled cry, pain and pleasure; then the girl's other hand sank down across her belly and she began to masturbate, very slowly, still straddling a flagging erection.

Winter reached for the DVD control, pressed PAUSE. 'What's in the bag?'

'Ice. Never fails.'

'This is one of your punters?' Winter was still looking at the screen.

'I like to think of them as friends.'

'And he gets off on looking at himself?'

Suttle stirred beside Winter. He couldn't take his eyes off the image frozen on the plasma screen, the girl on the edge of her climax, the fingers half buried, the emerald-green eyes half closed.

'That's the girl in the photos,' he murmured. 'Outside in the hall.'

There were two bedrooms in the apartment. The first one, empty, was a mess. In the flickering light from a semicircle of candles on a cabinet beside the bed Winter tried to make sense of the tumble of sheets and bolsters. At the foot of the bed the heel of a black stiletto was wedged in an empty bottle of Krug. Beside it, an abandoned scarlet basque and a packet of Rizlas. Most of the ceiling was occupied by a huge oval mirror with a gilt surround, and shadows danced across the walls as the draught from the hall stirred the bedside candles. An hour or so earlier, thought Winter, Singer would have been spreadeagled on this enormous rumpled playground, stirred to his umpteenth orgasm by one of Richardson's girlies.

Through the open door to the en suite bathroom Winter could hear the splash of falling water. He stepped into the steam, glimpsing a small naked body squatting on the loo, legs spread, inspecting a mark on her inside thigh. Winter hooked a towel from the nearby rail, threw it across.

'Company, love,' he said briefly. 'Get yourself decent.'

Back in the hall he headed for the bedroom with the music. This time there were no candles. A middle-aged man was lying on his back on a nest of pillows, his eyes closed, his body tented by the top sheet. The headboard behind him was a mosaic of tiny mirrors, and Winter watched as another body under the sheet obeyed his muttered instructions. He recognised the face from the plasma screen in the lounge at once, the grey indoor complexion, the heavy jowls, the mouth that so easily shaped itself into a snarl. The man on the bed had his right arm flung out, the fingers riding the volume control on the CD machine, and the music swelled and died in time with the nodding head beneath the sheet.

Winter let the scene develop for a second or two, then switched on the overhead chandelier. The blaze of light emptied the room of intimacy but it was a while before the eyes on the pillow opened. The man grunted, got up on one elbow, exposing the sagging pale flesh of his chest.

'Who the hell are you?' It was the voice of someone used to command and respect, a boardroom voice, the kind of voice that spelled trouble. Late forties at least, thought Winter. Maybe older.

'DC Winter. Portsmouth Crime Squad. I must ask you to get dressed, sir.'

'Why?'

'Because I have reason to suspect you may be using Class A narcotics.'

'Nonsense. This is private property. You have absolutely no right —'

He broke off as the figure beneath the sheet emerged. She had an aerosol can in one hand and a small glass phial in the other. As she made herself comfortable in a pose both detectives recognised from the DVD, Winter became aware of her body splintered in the jigsaw of mirrors at the head of the bed. She had big breasts for such an angular frame, and her legs seemed even longer in real life. When Winter repeated his invitation to get dressed, she laughed softly, then ringed her nipples with cream from the aerosol before slipping her hands behind the head beneath her and offering him a taste. He lapped at her, first one breast then the other, before wiping his mouth on the back of his hand and settling back on the pillow.

'Low-fat Chantilly.' He looked up at Winter, then yawned. 'You can get it from Waitrose.'

'Did you hear what I said, sir?'

'Of course I did. Now fuck off. Both of you. Maddox?' He smiled up at her with his pale, dead, hooded eyes. 'I think our new friends are going. Manners are everything. We should say goodbye.'

The girl tipped her head back, the fall of black hair halfway down her spine. Then she muttered something Winter didn't catch before slipping off the bed. Dropping the aerosol and the glass phial on the carpet, she disappeared into the en suite bathroom without a backward glance.

Suttle, for one, was impressed. Back in the hall, with the bedroom door closed, he drifted across to one of the photos while they waited for the search team. Winter was on the mobile to Cathy Lamb, as gleeful as ever. The intelligence had proved spot on. These guys were doing serious gear. Plus he'd busted the classiest fuck-palace Pompey was ever likely to see. *Plover*, in short, was on a roll and the best news of all was Mr Scumbag Singer's name in the frame. The conversation over, he sauntered back across the hall. Suttle saw him coming, the familiar portly image reflected in the glass.

'Result or what?'

'Definitely.' Suttle sounded wistful. 'You think she's ever heard of police discount?'

'She's a tom, son.' Winter slipped his bulk between Suttle and the photo. 'Who wants a slice off a cut loaf?'

Alone in the Bargemaster's House, Faraday treated himself to another helping of Mahler. He'd got back from the island in time to catch Willard before he left the office. Although he'd never admit it, the Detective Superintendent had been pleased with the news about Aaron Tolly. More and more often Major Crimes were picking up rubbish jobs from division – half-baked might-be crimes that swallowed precious resources for absolutely no measurable benefit – and Willard for one wasn't having it. The quicker DIs like Colin Irving realised that Major Crimes weren't in the waste disposal business, the quicker the message would spread around the other divisions.

At the same time, rather unnervingly, there was a definite lull in the ongoing war against serious villainy. For whatever reason, folk had suddenly stopped doing serious damage to each other and the last couple of weeks Willard had begun to think hard about reopening that treasured collection of unsolved crimes that he'd tucked away for exactly this contingency. Hence, perhaps, his preparedness to listen to Faraday's musings about Webster's headless body.

Faraday had spent nearly two hours on Tennyson

Down. Without the benefit of the file he'd only the vaguest idea where the body might first have been spotted but he'd done his best to put himself in the head of the birdwatcher, and his knowledge of site-faithful peregrine falcons took him to a stretch of cliff within sight of the brooding Celtic cross that marked the Tennyson Memorial. The cliffs were high here, three hundred feet plus, and it had taken all of Faraday's nerve to get down on the damp turf, crawl to the edge and peer over. The dizzying sight of the jumble of chalk boulders beneath, washed by the surging aftermath of the morning's gale, had been quite enough to set the scene, and it was only afterwards, talking to Webster again in the car, that he'd properly been able to order his thoughts.

With every new situation like this the key priority was establishing an ID, a name to attach to the chilled remains in the hospital mortuary in Newport. In this respect, by his own account Webster had put all the right ticks in all the right boxes. The post-mortem had been in the hands of one of the duty pathologists at St Mary's and she'd estimated an immersion time of at least four months. The head had been severed at the sixth cervical vertebra and she'd found substantial swelling of the subcutaneous tissues due to decomposition of the internal organs. Fish and crabs had eaten into the flesh on the fingers and toes, and there was further damage to the genital and neck areas where soft tissue had been stripped back. The fact that most of the major bones – legs, arms, pelvis, shoulder blades, ribs – were intact argued against a fall from the cliff, and DNA had been extracted from bone marrow ready for matching against printouts in the national data bank. In terms of age, on the evidence of bone analysis the pathologist was suggesting a white male of between thirty and forty. With a head on his body she thought he'd measure an inch or so under six feet.

The probable elimination of a cliff fall had aroused Faraday's interest. It was by no means unusual for suicides to plunge naked to their deaths – he knew a couple of instances when a pile of neatly folded clothes had marked the deceased's final point of departure – but four months was a long time for an individual to go AWOL, and the fact that Webster's inquiries at the national Missing Persons' Register had so far drawn a blank simply deepened the mystery. No one had done a runner from local psychiatric institutions. No one had been reported overboard from either UK commercial or naval shipping. And local media appeals through TV, radio and the island press had failed to attach a name to the headless corpse.

Darren Webster, naturally keen to break the case, had begun to explore more exotic lines of inquiry, but these too had so far come to nothing. The International Maritime Organisation had promised to circulate details amongst commercial operators and fishermen using the shipping lanes on the other side of the English Channel but a precautionary call to an expert in tidal currents at Southampton University's Oceanography Centre suggested that this would be a very long shot indeed. The designated shipping lanes were way south of the Isle of Wight and any corpse floating around in this area was liable, he said, to end up on a French beach. Likewise, Webster's brief interest in burials at sea had come to nothing. The area reserved for these ceremonial farewells lay to the west of the Needles, but the coastguard thought it highly unlikely that a body would escape the weighted, tightly stitched canvas shroud, somehow lose its head and finally wash ashore at the foot of Tennyson Down. No, there had to be another explanation.

Listening to Faraday's account of Webster's inquiries, Willard had made the sensible point that these were early days. Although the mystery corpse had obviously been dead for a while, it might yet be weeks before Webster's patient phone calls triggered a memory or two. In the meantime Willard was more interested in why Webster had made such an impression on Faraday.

'Do you see yourself in him, Joe?' he'd enquired, reaching for his jacket and his car keys, 'Young island boy, keen to make a name for himself?'

At the time Faraday had dismissed the comment as a joke, the kind of parting shot Willard favoured on a quiet Friday afternoon, but now – stretched full-length on his sofa in the Bargemaster's House – he wasn't so sure. It hadn't taken much to bridge the gap back to his days in Freshwater Bay, and that afternoon, standing in the fitful sunshine at the foot of the Tennyson Memorial, he remembered only too well the strange feeling of being banged up on an island he'd only ever seen from the beach of his native Bournemouth.

At first, after eighteen months in the USA, the place had felt impossibly small. With a pregnant American wife and absolutely no money Faraday had managed to find himself a driving job, delivering fancy goods and other summer knick-knacks to a long list of cafés, caravan camps, souvenir shops and amusement parks. His father, tormented by the prospect of another stroke and bewildered by the abruptness of his son's marriage, had made his new daughter-in-law far from welcome, but his mum – an ex-theatre nurse with a hard, practical intelligence – had taken to Janna at once.

With Faraday careering around West Wight at the wheel of an ancient Bedford van, the two women had spent a great deal of time together. Janna helped out with the Freshwater B. and B., full to bursting in high summer, and it was at Alice Faraday's insistence that Janna had accepted payment for her labours. With two incomes, plus a temporary loan, Faraday and Janna had managed to scrape enough together for a deposit plus three months' rent on a draughty bungalow half a mile from the parental home. They'd moved in on a blustery still-warm day in late September, Janna splashing out on a supper of clam chowder and Maryland crab cakes as a thank you for two months' precious rent-free hospitality, and Faraday remembered their first night together under the new roof, the wind howling through the loose tiles, the itchy scrabble of field mice behind the wainscoting, the warm bulk of Janna beside him beneath the borrowed blankets. At the time this new life of theirs had seemed close to perfect but several days later, in a deeply private conversation, Faraday's mother – ever observant – warned him that all was not well. Your wife is sick, she told him. You need to get her to a doctor.

Faraday lay back, his eyes closed, letting the music flood over him. Gustav Mahler was a recent discovery, a supplement to the Berlioz CDs that had underscored the last couple of years, and the third symphony – with its haunting brass motifs – was eerily apt for moments like these. Older now, and wiser, he realised why Janna had shielded him from the knowledge of her previous tussle with breast cancer. She was in remission. The drugs had worked. And if three gruelling months of chemo owed her anything then it was surely the chance to start again: a new relationship, a new country even, absolutely nothing shadowed by the possibility of another round or two with the Grim Reaper. Her pregnancy had come as a surprise and it was a testament to the strength of his feelings that Faraday had begun at once to plan for the years ahead. Hence his decision to take Janna home. And hence – after a summer at the wheel – his abrupt appearance at Freshwater's tiny police station. I'd like to be a cop, he'd told the startled desk sergeant. How do I go about applying?

In the event it had been harder than Faraday had ever expected. Not because he hadn't got the brains or aptitude for the job but because the selection interviews, and everything that followed, had collided with a catastrophe so enormous it had taken him years to properly come to grips with.

The cancer had returned, more aggressive than ever. Within months of J-J's birth Janna was dead. Faraday had nursed her till the end, turning a deaf ear to offers of a bed in the old hospital over in Newport. His mother, bless her, had helped, first day by day, then hour by hour, respecting every moment of their time together. By the time Janna slipped away, a cold bright morning in December with two electric fires on the go, Faraday was helpless with grief. Only John-Junior kept him going, with his gummy eyes and incessant hunger, a debt Faraday spent the next twenty years trying to repay.

Was this why he'd spent an hour or two listening to an ambitious young island detective hungry for battle honours? Was this why he'd passed the message back to Willard, salted the facts with a thought or two of his own, tried to pave the way for a possible referral to Major Crimes? Had this been, in one of the ironies that increasingly seemed to shape Faraday's life, the real thrust of his little expedition over the water? To knock one job on the head and then – thanks to Webster – draw a steadier bead on another? He didn't know, and just now he didn't much care. He plumped the cushion behind his head and settled back. If the sleeve notes were right and Mahler really was in the business of challenge and resolution, then the next couple of movements would be the test.

An hour later Faraday awoke. Apart from the chuckle of a lone turnstone out on the harbour, he could hear nothing. Then it came again, the *beep-beep* from his laptop that signalled a priority incoming message. He struggled to his feet and climbed the stairs to his study. In the spill of light from the hall he could see the email highlighted at the top of the day's missives. He settled at the desk, reached for the touchpad. Eadie, he thought.

She'd made it to Melbourne, taking the morning seaplane shuttle from Vanuatu to Sydney and then a domestic flight out of Kingston Smith to Tullamarine. Her description of the take-off – the colours, the spray, the sudden feeling of release as the little floatplane hopped into the air – occupied two paragraphs. The pilot's father, she wrote, had once been a pupil of her dad's and so he'd spoiled her with a twirl or two around the island before setting course for Oz. The sight of her family house from the air had been weird – so fucking small – and she'd found herself laughing at how close the beach had once seemed to the gate in the white picket fence that marked the front of the property. As a kid the walk to the ocean had been a big deal, a major expedition. Yet thirty years away had shrunk it to a mere spit. Was this what growing up did to a girl? Could a good lawyer make a case and get her fantasies back?

Faraday smiled at the traffic jam of questions. Eadie Sykes tore into life with a zest and an appetite that had always left him slightly awed. Professionally, he was sure that it had helped her no end when it came to putting other people's stories onto film. She blew into their lives with the force of a gale and her very candour, her cheerful bluntness, always seemed to do the trick. Even Faraday himself had opened up, and here on the laptop was yet more proof that she could still reach out and touch him.

At the same time, when he was honest with himself, he knew that he didn't really miss her. They'd had great moments together, probably still would, but every conversation – even at this distance – was proof that Eadie Sykes would always go her own way. She'd flown thirteen thousand miles to explore the landscapes of her youth. She'd be staying on the other side of the world until her money ran out. That might be a couple of months, might be longer. Whatever happened, she'd keep him posted.

Faraday scanned the rest of the email, then sat back in his chair, gazing out at the blackness of the harbour. The more he thought about it, the more he realised that twenty-six years in the job had changed him. For better or worse he was in the evidence business and deep down he'd finally admitted to himself that she didn't need him. Not now. And very probably not ever.

He reached for the touchpad a moment, thought about tapping out a reply, then changed his mind and swivelled the chair away. He could see the shape of his upper body in the window, silhouetted against the oblong of light through the open door. His fingers found the thick growth of greying stubble on his chin and he wondered again whether it was really such a good idea to be growing a beard. Might this be some kind of defiant proclamation about his age? Or was it simply another way of curtaining himself off from a world to which he increasingly appeared to have only visiting rights?

He began to swivel the chair again, describing a slow, lazy half circle before stilling the motion with his foot. Something had been bothering him about Webster's headless corpse, and he suddenly realised what it was.

Two

Saturday, 21 February 2004

Winter was halfway through a *Good Housekeeping* recipe for Chicken Supreme when his number began to blink on the waiting-room wall. He picked his way between the blank-faced grannies and the squalling kids, pausing to step over a family of stuffed animals on the carpet beside the door. Any more cuddly bears, he thought, and this place would start feeling like the PDSA.

Winter's GP, Dr Jessop, looked younger than he probably was, a thin, alert, bespectacled northerner with the kind of complexion that went with ten-mile runs and sensible drinking. Over the last couple of months, much to his alarm, Winter had got to know him well.

'How's it going?' Jessop was catching up with Winter's notes. 'Still getting the headaches?'

'Yeah.' Winter nodded.

'Any better?'

'Worse.' Winter's fingers tracked a path across the tops of his eyebrows. 'Here to here. A couple of times last week I thought I was going blind.'

'*Blind?*' Jessop at last looked up. 'What do we mean by blind?'

His use of the word 'we' irritated Winter intensely. It was bad enough explaining his troubles to someone half his age, worse when this eager young puppy treated him like a retard. He began to describe the last episode. He'd surfaced at seven with a pounding head, thrown up most of his breakfast within minutes, and spent most of a difficult morning trying to keep the rest down. Chasing teenage hooligans round the wastelands of Somerstown was challenging on a normal day. Trying to nail them through a rising curtain of brightly coloured bubbles was close to hallucinogenic.

He did his best to describe the sensation. Jessop looked blank.

'Bubbles? I'm not with you.'

'Round jobs. You look hard at something – the pavement, the road, whatever – and all you get are these bubbles. They're everywhere. They float up. Ever watched a goldfish in a tank? That's me.'

'And pain, you say?'

'Yeah. Above the eyes, behind the eyes, all over.'

'Can we be more specific?'

'I just was. I take the tablets. I don't cane the Scotch any more. I've even eased up on the telly. But it just gets worse.' He leaned forward in the chair. 'There's another thing, too. I've got a memory problem. I keep forgetting things, the simplest things. In my game that can be tricky, believe me. You think it might be early Alzheimer's?'

'How old are you?' Jessop's eyes returned to the notes.

'Forty-five.'

'Then I very much doubt it.' Jessop uncapped a fountain pen and scribbled himself a note. Then he reached for the PC keyboard and began to scroll through a list of names. Just the effort of concentration was enough to trigger the familiar drumbeat behind Winter's eyes but he did his best to keep track. Jessop double-clicked on a Mr Frazer. A new window appeared. Frazer was a neurological consultant.

'You'll have to join a queue, I'm afraid. How much notice do you need for an appointment?'

Winter thought of the logjam of jobs awaiting him back at the squad office. Lately, one or two of Cathy Lamb's more ambitious operations had flushed out some of the city's hard-core lunatics, especially in the drugs biz. Each of these stake-outs generated hours and hours of paperwork, and getting time off under this kind of pressure wouldn't be easy, but the thought of what might lie beyond the bubbles was beginning to frighten him. Better to risk the wrath of his DI, he thought, than end up on the wrong end of a Labrador and a stick.

'Couple of days,' Winter grunted. 'Just give me a bell.'

Back outside the surgery, armed with a new prescription, Winter popped the last of his painkillers and crossed the road to his Subaru. At half eleven he'd agreed to meet Suttle at the Bridewell. They needed an hour or so with each of the young slappers from last night's bust, formal interviews that could normally wait until Monday, but one of them was off skiing on Sunday night and had volunteered to come in early. He'd told Suttle on the phone that there was no need for him to attend – neither girl would be facing charges – but Suttle wasn't having it. After the bust at Camber Court he'd suddenly developed a powerful interest in Operation *Plover*. Copping out of the interviews, he'd insisted, just wasn't an option.

Driving back into the city, Winter felt the tablets beginning to ease the pressure behind his eyes. The girl they'd be meeting this morning was the girl in the photos. Just the mention of her name – Maddox – had been enough to get the young detective out of bed, and Winter began to guess what colour shirt he'd be wearing by the time he made it down to the Bridewell. Suttle by name, he thought. Suttle by nature.

At the Bridewell Winter checked in with the Duty Sergeant and retired to one of the empty interview rooms with a cup of coffee. By the time Jimmy Suttle appeared, he was deep in the first of the statements they'd taken last night.

Singer, one of the city's higher-profile solicitors, had been winding up the likes of Willard and Cathy Lamb for years. He specialised in representing the city's more successful criminals and had made a small fortune from a series of cleverly argued acquittals. It was common knowledge that he cut every judicial corner in the book to return his clients to a life of crime and with his success had come a belief that he was somehow immune from the attentions of the detectives he openly mocked in – and out of – court. Last night, to Winter's deep satisfaction, that immunity had come to an end – and what made Singer's arrest even sweeter was the prospect of celebrating this trophy pull with Cathy Lamb.

Like most DIs she'd seen absolutely no sense in wasting precious time and effort in pursuit of the errant middle classes. These were people who had plenty of money and would never dream of house-breaking or thieving from vehicles to fund their recreational foibles. In that sense their drug use – though obviously illegal – was close to a victimless crime and at first she'd flatly refused to sanction Winter's plans for the Old Portsmouth stake-out. Winter, though, had already acquired a client list from the Portsea girl who did Richardson's cleaning, and mention of Singer's name had won Cathy's grudging approval of last night's bust. News of the solicitor's appearance before the Bridewell Custody Sergeant, to Winter's certain knowledge, would be round the force in hours.

Not that Singer was going down without a fight. In last night's interview he'd admitted the possession of a couple of wraps of cocaine but denied using sexual services offered by Richardson at Flat 10, Camber Court. The latter, he'd pointed out, was not indictable under the Sexual Offences Act and in any case the visit he'd paid to Old Portsmouth had been purely social. Steve Richardson was an old friend and – as it happened – a bloody good cook. They'd enjoyed a meal together, had a drink or two, then he'd pushed off home.

Asked to explain the cocaine, he said he'd bought it from a dealer whom he wasn't prepared to name, but denied it was Richardson. Challenged with the credit card slip for eight hundred pounds retrieved from the stash Richardson kept on a hook in the kitchen, Singer said it was a personal debt. Richardson had bought a painting on his behalf and he was simply paying him back. As Suttle had pointed out last night, this fiction was strictly for the sake of his missus. A coke head in the marital bed she could probably deal with. Her husband blowing the housekeeping on some bint half her age, she probably couldn't.

Suttle had settled himself across the table in the interview room. The shirt, to Winter's amusement, was salmon pink.

'What about the other guy. The one in bed with Maddox. Monster, wasn't he?'

Winter could only agree. The punter's name was

Maurice Wishart. Last night he'd given a Port Solent address, a third-floor apartment with marina views, and said he headed up a rapidly expanding company in the defence business. Visibly irritated by what had happened to his evening, he'd consented to a personal search. When nothing had surfaced in the way of narcotics, he'd laughed in Winter's face and then tossed him his car keys and told him to help himself.

His blue Jaguar had been parked in the courtyard below. Again, nothing. Back upstairs, Winter had found him on the sofa in the huge expanse of living room, locked into a lengthy call on his mobile. Winter had tried to bring the conversation to an end but Wishart had simply waved him away. He was talking to a client in San Diego. The rest of this pantomime could wait.

In the end it was Suttle who had presented Wishart with his bill for the evening, another credit card slip, again for eight hundred. Wishart had looked at it and shrugged.

'So?'

'We're suggesting some of that money paid for cocaine.'

'On the contrary. All of it goes to Maddox.'

'So why pay Richardson, Mr Wishart?'

'Because that's the way I choose to do it. It's very collegiate here. I pay Stephen. Stephen pays Maddox. We meet regularly. We enjoy ourselves. Stephen takes a modest sum for food and drink and Maddox gets the rest.'

'Richardson is running a brothel, Mr Wishart. He's living off immoral earnings. That's an offence.'

'Wrong. Stephen is an extraordinarily generous host. He introduced me to Maddox and for that I'm deeply grateful. If I choose to give Maddox money, that is entirely my prerogative. Unless, that is, there's a law against screwing. Have we finished? Or must I phone my solicitor?'

Winter had dearly wanted to arrest Wishart, drive him down to the Bridewell and bang him up for the night, but both men knew he had no grounds. Wishart was right. Screwing Maddox and paying the going rate wasn't an offence. Only a drugs charge, properly evidenced, could possibly stick.

Now Winter looked glumly at his watch. The girl Maddox was late. Across the table Suttle was toying with his coffee.

'How many other blokes do we think she's shagging?'

'Half a dozen, at least.'

Winter had retrieved an appointments book from the Camber Court flat, the passing weeks littered with Richardson's neat entries. The code had been elementary. M stood for Maddox, C for the other girl, Cécile. Punters had likewise been reduced to a single capital letter, but by matching the entries to the credit card slips Winter had quickly been able to confirm the information he'd acquired from the Portsea cleaner. These were well-known names from the Portsmouth social register: a Persian restaurateur, a successful young accountant, a local property developer, two Premiership footballers and a Southampton-based sports agent had fallen for Maddox's charms, and none of them had paid less than eight hundred pounds. Working an average of three nights a week, Winter estimated she was turning over nearly ten grand a month.

Suttle was doing the sums.

'That's three hundred quid an hour. Give or take.'

'Yeah? But can you imagine screwing a tosser like Wishart? There wouldn't be a cheque big enough.'

Winter got to his feet. He needed to touch base with Cathy Lamb again and he wanted to do it in the privacy of the corridor. She'd been on first thing, before he'd set off for the surgery, and while she was delighted at Singer's arrest she was demanding yet more scalps from *Plover*. In the year since Bazza Mackenzie's effective retirement the local market for good-quality charlie had been wide open to every passing scrot and Cathy was determined to keep the supply chain well and truly disrupted. So where did Richardson source his goodies? And which doors should the squad be kicking in next?

In the corridor, on the point of phoning Cathy Lamb on his mobile, Winter spotted Maddox. She was standing beside the water cooler, chatting to one of the uniformed PCs. Catching sight of Winter, she gave him a smile. She was wearing a long suede coat, beautifully cut, and a pair of black leather ankle boots. Folds of blue and white were tucked around her neck and it took a moment or two for Winter to realise he was looking at a Pompey scarf.

She stepped towards him, extending a hand. Black gloves, the softest touch of leather.

'Newcastle at home.' She was unpeeling the scarf. 'Three o'clock kick-off.'

'You're not serious.'

'Of course I am. I have a season ticket. I even go to the away games when it's somewhere interesting.'

Winter caught the PC's eye. Like Suttle, his brain seemed to have disengaged.

'This way, love.' Winter shepherded her towards the corridor that led to the interview suite. The scent of her perfume took him back to last night. He fought briefly against the tide of images, and lost. Wishart, he thought grimly. Lucky bastard.

Suttle was already on his feet when Maddox stepped into the bareness of the interview room. He'd obviously decided to play the tough cop.

'Take a seat.' He nodded briskly at the empty chair across the table from his own. 'This shouldn't take long.'

Maddox hung the Pompey scarf on the back of the chair and unbelted the coat. The white T-shirt beneath was tucked loosely into a pair of deep burgundy corduroy trousers, and Winter was impressed by the fact that she hadn't dressed to accentuate her figure. Given what he'd seen last night, every other slapper in this city would have gone for the tightest of tops. A truly class act, he thought.

Maddox settled herself in the chair while Suttle clarified the legal situation. She wasn't under caution and she was free to leave whenever she chose. At the same time, with her permission, he'd like to record the interview in case there was any need to refer to it later.

'Of course.' She shrugged. 'Why not?'

Winter was still looking at the T-shirt. It carried the image of a young man's face, a mop of dark hair over the vaguest of gazes.

'Who's that then?' Winter nodded at her chest.

Maddox had peeled off her gloves. A black-lacquered nail touched the front of her T-shirt.

'You mean this guy?'

'Yes.'

'Arthur Rimbaud.'

'Who?'

'He's a poet. Or was.'

'You buy it off the shelf?'

'Yes.'

48

'Pompey?'

'Paris.' She settled herself back in the chair. 'Do you know anything about French literature? Only Rimbaud was a bit of a legend. Wild child, really. Decamped to Africa and swapped poetry for gun-running.'

Winter nodded, out of his depth. Suttle pressed the RECORD button on the audio stack and Maddox's eyes flicked to the four cassettes as he invited her to account for what they'd found at Camber Court. It was a leading question, and she knew it.

'Found, how exactly?'

'You in bed with Mr Wishart. The state of the other bedroom. Cocaine everywhere. Visa slips. Sex toys. Pornography. It's a knocking shop, isn't it?'

'Of course.'

'You're not denying it?'

'No. Why should I?'

'Because it's illegal.'

'Not from my point of view it isn't.'

'That's as may be but we're talking offences here.'

'Like what?'

'Like living off immoral earnings. You're telling me Mr Richardson isn't pimping?'

'*Pimping*? Stephen?' She laughed. 'Sweet thought.'

'He doesn't take a cut? Make a living?'

'He takes enough to keep us in champagne and something half decent to eat. He pays the rates and the electric and puts a bit aside for the odd night out. Just like every working girl.'

'I find that hard to believe.'

'I'm sure you do but that's the way it is. He's a fun guy. He's like the rest of us. He's out for a good time and more to the point he's got a bit of taste. The way

Stephen sees it, it's a vocation, not a scam. He wants to please people. And believe me, he does.'

'For a price.'

'Of course. We're dealing with wealthy people here. It's a market. We strike a deal. No one loses.'

'How much do you take? For each trick?'

'Eighty per cent.'

'That's high.'

'It's what we agreed. We've never quarrelled over money. That would be sordid.'

'*Sordid?*' It was Suttle's turn to laugh. 'You don't think . . .?' He began to shake his head.

'What? What don't I think?' Maddox was leaning forward now, interested, engaged.

'You don't think . . . fat middle-aged guys . . . people with money to burn . . . You don't think any of that's pretty gross . . . selling yourself . . . doing their bidding?'

'Not in the least. And even if it was, so what? Gross is everywhere. Since when has it been an offence?'

The question stopped Suttle in his tracks. Winter was beginning to enjoy this. Not just a class act, he thought, but bright as well. No wonder she was coining it.

'Tell me about the drugs,' he said.

Maddox was still looking at Suttle. At Winter's question she began to withdraw.

'I know nothing about the drugs.'

'You knew Richardson keeps cocaine on the premises?'

'Of course. We all have our weaknesses.'

'You don't use the stuff yourself?'

'Never.'

'Have you ever offered it to punters?'

'Absolutely not.'

'Not even if they've asked for it?'

'No. I'll do anything I can for them physically, anything they want within reason, but the rest of it . . .' She shook her head, emphatic. 'No.'

'You're telling me Richardson supplies other substances?'

'I'm telling you I don't get involved in that side of it.'

'*Does* he offer other gear?'

'I've no idea. He has exquisite taste in wine. His cooking is inspired. Our clients get plenty of attention afterwards. I can't believe they'd ever need anything else.'

Winter sat back a moment, mentally tallying the fruits of last night's search.

'All that stuff in the wardrobe in the big bedroom. Is it yours?'

'Yes.'

'You dress up for the punters?'

'When they make a request, yes.' She looked at him a moment, then warmed the space between them with a sudden grin. 'Forties French gear is the biggest turn-on. You've no idea how many men like to fuck Resistance heroines.'

'You play the role?'

'Of course. The gear. The walk. The come-ons. The make-up. *Tout ça.*'

'You speak French?'

'Yes.'

'You fuck the punters in French?'

'*Bien sûr.*' She began to laugh again. '*Si tu veux.*'

Winter exchanged glances with Suttle, knowing she'd got the best of both of them. Nothing usable was going to come of this interview and if Cathy Lamb ever got hold of the tapes she'd have a fit. This wasn't evidence gathering. This was a floor show.

Winter reached out, pressed the STOP button. Then he sat back, looking Maddox in the eye.

'You know what really interests me?'

'Of course I do.'

'What is it?'

'You want to know why I do it.' She smiled at him. 'Is it the money? Is that why I do it?'

She let the question hang between them. Very slowly Winter shook his head. For the first time in weeks he'd stopped worrying about the pain behind his eyes.

'No,' he said. 'It's not the money.'

'So what is it then?'

'I've no idea.'

'You're lying. You're like every other man. You just don't want to admit it.'

'Admit what?'

'That I might enjoy it.' She reached for her gloves. 'Does that help your enquiries?'

Faraday was in Eadie's apartment on the seafront when he got the call. J-J was busy in the kitchen preparing a late lunch, a mountain of chopped onions browning in the pan. Faraday fumbled for his mobile and walked across to the big picture window at the other end of the room. Fitful sunshine puddled the Solent.

'Mr Faraday?'

'Yes.'

'It's Darren Webster, sir, from Newport. We met yesterday. Hope you don't mind me calling.'

'Of course not. What's the problem?'

'It's not something I can discuss on the phone, sir. I'm in Pompey this afternoon, over for the football. I was just wondering . . .'

'You want a meet?'

'Yes, sir. If it's not too much trouble.'

Faraday was watching a pilot launch ploughing out through the churning tide, trying to weigh the implications of this sudden development. He'd spent most of the morning reviewing what little anyone seemed to know about Webster's headless body, and the more he thought about the implications, the more interested he became.

'Is this to do with Tennyson Down?'

'Yes, sir.'

'Does your DI know you're making this call?'

There was a pause. The pilot launch had changed course, heading for the distant bulk of an incoming container ship. Finally Webster was back on the line.

'No, sir.'

'Then tell him. As long as you do that, no problem. You know Fratton nick? Half five. Ask for Major Crimes.'

Faraday pocketed the mobile and lingered at the window a moment longer before turning back into the room. J-J was watching him from the other side of the breakfast bar. Deaf since birth, he communicated with the outside world in a flurry of hand signs, a private vocabulary that had always amazed onlookers by its sheer range of expression. One of the lessons J-J had learned about his father's life was its unpredictability. Mobile calls were often a cue for an abrupt departure.

'You still want to eat?' he signed.

'Of course.'

'You want a lager first?'

'Silly question.'

Faraday watched his son as he opened the fridge and produced a couple of cans. San Miguel had been Faraday's favourite for years, ever since he'd started going to Spain on birding expeditions, and it warmed him to think that this boy of his had taken the trouble to lay in supplies.

J-J poured the lager, then returned to the pan. Faraday had caught the scent of garlic and cumin seed, another reminder of the long years they'd spent together in the Bargemaster's House.

'Heard from Eadie?' Faraday signed.

J-J nodded, and gave the onions a final stir before wiping his hands on a dishcloth. Eadie, he signed, had emailed him twice in the last twenty-four hours. He thought she'd had enough of tropical islands.

'What makes you think that?'

'She's been in touch with those people in the council. They've said yes to the project.'

'What project's that?'

'The video for next year. I told you last week.'

'You did?'

J-J shot his father a despairing look and turned to rummage in a cupboard beside the fridge. Eadie Sykes ran a video production company from a modest suite of offices in Hampshire Terrace. She specialised in documentary work – ruthlessly edited studies with a radical bite – and a recent production had sparked a great deal of controversy. J-J's reward for helping her on this project had been a full-time job, an offer that had finally won him the independence he'd craved. Just now he was flat-sitting for his boss but when she returned he'd find himself a place of his own.

'Remind me.' Faraday swallowed a mouthful of San Miguel. 'This new video.'

'Next year's the biggie.' J-J's bony hands shaped an ever-expanding space. 'The city wants something special to pull people in.'

'That's not documentary. That's marketing.'

'That's what I said.'

'And Eadie?'

'She thinks she can do it her way.'

'Surprise, surprise.'

'Yeah, but she's got loads of ideas.' J-J nodded at the laptop on the low table in front of the sofa.

Faraday abandoned the stool at the breakfast bar. Next year, 2005, marked the two-hundredth anniversary of the Battle of Trafalgar, a peg on which the city fathers were going to hang Pompey's battered hat. Even a year away there were detailed plans for a Royal Fleet Review, an International Festival of the Sea, plus countless other crowd-pulling events which might finally make Portsmouth the must-visit heritage destination.

Eadie's latest email showed on the laptop's screen, and a quick scan brought a smile to Faraday's face. In certain moods this woman with whom he'd shared the last couple of years was irresistible. She wrote like she talked, and each new paragraph was a fresh insight into the fertile anarchy of her imagination. She had total faith in herself, a self-confidence unchallenged by a moment's self-doubt, and Faraday loved that.

Her video was to begin with a montage of comments from the Pompey diaspora, a message or two from those thousands of folk who'd bailed out of the city and sought a better life overseas. On the face of it this was a bizarre proposition – why waste precious screen time on turncoats who'd opted to leave? – but the more Faraday read, the more he found himself nodding in agreement. Portsmouth, after all, had always been in the export business, if not violence then people, and what trademarked the quotes that Eadie produced in evidence was a collective agreement that Pompey wasn't simply special but unique.

A Tipner-born boatbuilder she must have met in the

New Hebrides talked wistfully of his apprenticeship in the naval dockyard. A retired nurse, on vacation from Adelaide, remembered playing amongst the buddleia on the post-war Southsea bomb sites. A young globe-trotting music promoter she'd sat next to on the flight from Singapore, ex-Portsmouth University, had ring-fenced his first million to build himself a mansion on Portsdown Hill. These were people, Faraday thought, that Eadie had either bumped into or invented, but real or unreal their message was the same, a distant echo of the roar that rose from the terraces at Fratton Park. We are all the prisoners of our birthright. Pompey Till I Die.

Faraday caught J-J's eye.

'And the council's said yes to all this?'

J-J nodded, then peered briefly at the pan.

'You think four chillies will be enough?' he signed.

Winter's phone was ringing when he finally made it back home. He and Jimmy Suttle had found time for a drink after Maddox's departure from the Bridewell, sharing a city centre pub with a trainload of Newcastle supporters busy fortifying themselves for the ten-minute sprint to Fratton Park. The ones who were drinking fastest had resigned themselves to the rumoured ambush. The ones who weren't couldn't wait to get stuck in.

Now, Winter lifted the phone wondering why the caller hadn't tried his mobile. Seconds later he found himself listening to Willard's gruff tones. The Detective Superintendent had been talking to Terry Alcott at headquarters. Alcott was the Assistant Chief Constable in charge of CID and Special Operations and had taken an early morning call from a Maurice Wishart. He'd bumped into Wishart at some pre-Xmas drinks party, and now Wishart was using this brief social encounter to register his outrage over an incident that was alleged to have taken place last night in Old Portsmouth. Alcott hadn't got a clue about the details but Wishart was claiming harassment and threatening to go to the press.

'Sir—?' Winter tried to interrupt. Willard told him to listen.

'Alcott doesn't care a stuff about Wishart. He says the guy can talk to whoever he likes. But I'm telling you to ignore any calls from the *News*. If those bastards phone you, refer them to me. Understood?'

'Yes, sir.'

'Good. And well done for Singer.'

The line went dead. Winter held on to the phone for a moment, feeling the warmth flood through his body. He was still looking for the bottle of Scotch he kept on the go when he remembered Suttle. A call to his mobile found him in the crowd at Fratton Park.

'About last night. Has anyone rung you from the *News*?'

'The what?'

'The *News*.'

'Yeah.' Suttle was shouting. 'Woman called Kerry. She wanted to know what we were up to. Address. Names. Details. The lot. Wouldn't say where she got the whisper but my money's on someone from the Bridewell.'

Winter tried to focus on the familiar view from his sitting room. Instead of the sodden midwinter greens and browns of the long back garden, all he could see were bubbles.

'So what did you say?' he managed.

'Fuck all. When she started to try it on I told her to get a life, phoning a bloke on his day off. Shit—'

'What's the matter?'

The crowd in the background had gone very quiet. Finally, Suttle was back on the line.

'Unbelievable.' He sounded choked. 'Newcastle just bloody scored.'

Darren Webster was already at Kingston Crescent police station by the time Faraday had fought his way through the traffic and climbed the stairs to the Major Crimes suite on the second floor. A young DC tackling a backlog of paperwork had rescued Webster from the front desk and made him a coffee. Now, seated in the big office that served as the major incident room, he seemed perfectly at home.

Faraday gestured him down the long central corridor.

'How was the match?'

'I didn't go in the end, sir. A mate of mine called up to check out a new launch site on Boniface Down. Crap unless you've got a death wish.'

'So you've come over specially?'

'Yes.'

'And told DI Irving?'

'Yes, sir.'

'OK.' Faraday paused outside his office, unlocked the door, and then waved Webster into an empty chair. 'So what have you got for me?'

The young detective's eyes had gone immediately to the display of bird shots pinned to Faraday's wall board.

'Cool,' he said. 'Did you take those?'

'My son, most of them.' Faraday sank into the chair at the desk. 'Tell me what's brought you here.'

Webster took a final look at the photos, then leaned forward, almost conspiratorial, and told Faraday about a call he'd taken late yesterday afternoon. The CID intelligence cell for the island was housed in Shanklin but all IoW informants were managed by the divisional handling unit under the stewardship of a mainland-based DS. One of the thoroughbreds in his stable was a 23-year-old small-time thief and occasional drug dealer. Gary Morgan was local to the island, lived in a basement flat behind Sandown station, and had a story to tell.

'What was he offering?'

'Information on a bloke called Pelly. Rob Pelly. He runs a residential home for oldies in Shanklin. Been known to us for a while.'

'Form?'

'No convictions, nothing to speak of, anyway. But plenty of other stuff.'

'Like?'

'Like rumours about people smuggling, bringing asylos in, maybe gear too. He goes abroad a lot; owns far too many properties for someone legit – loads of DSS places in Shanklin and Ventnor. According to people in the know he has a bit of an attitude problem, likes a drink, throws his weight around, doesn't care who he pisses off. You can imagine how that goes down, place like the island.'

'So what did Morgan say?'

'He said that this Pelly character had a huge run-in with another lad, back end of last year, something to do with one of the old dears at the home. Apparently the lad's her grandson. He comes across a lot and often pays her a visit.'

'Comes over from where?'

'Here. Pompey.'

Faraday pulled a pad from a drawer. Every inquiry

worth pursuing began with a blizzard of names. Best to get them sorted.

'Pelly runs the old folks' home. Morgan's the grass. This other guy . . . ?'

'Chris Unwin. Apparently he drives a van for a living, delivers all kinds of stuff: Pompey, the island, London, the Midlands – you name it.'

'And this row in the home? Where did Morgan get that from?'

'He wouldn't say.'

'Was he there?'

'The DS says not. Morgan must have a source in the home.'

'So what happened?'

'They were in Pelly's office, the two of them. The door was half closed. After lunch Pelly's often legless. This was late afternoon.'

Faraday was still waiting for the real thrust of the story, the reason that Webster had bought himself a hovercraft ticket.

'So what happened?' he asked again.

'The two of them were screaming and shouting at each other. Then Pelly threatened to do him, sort him out, said he was a waste of space, deserved everything that was coming to him. At that point, someone intervened.'

'Who?'

'Morgan wouldn't give a name.'

'Do we believe him?'

'I've no idea, sir. I haven't met him yet.'

'But you're going to?'

'Of course.' He glanced at his watch. 'Half eight. Pub in Shanklin High Street.' He paused, enjoying himself now, waiting for Faraday to put the obvious question. Faraday obliged.

60

'So where's Unwin now?'

'Pass. No one's seen him since October. Before that, like I say, he was in and out of the home a couple of times a month. Christmas was always extra special. His nan's apparently off the planet but he'd bring her presents, plus flowers and booze for the staff. Never failed.'

'And this Christmas?'

'He never showed. Not a peep, not a phone call, card, nothing.'

Faraday sat back in his chair, struck again by what the inexplicably headless body should have told him from the start.

'The pathologist's report,' he began. 'She definitely found no injury marks?'

'Nothing for sure. The bloke was blue all over, swollen – you know what they're like. There was damage, obviously, but nothing that would hundred-per-cent put him in a crime scene.'

'The head might have done that.'

'Of course, sir.'

Faraday began to doodle a series of circles on the pad. Webster was looking at the bird shots again.

'And Unwin's age?' Faraday enquired at last.

'Late twenties, sir.'

'Height?'

'Around six feet.' There was a moment's silence, broken by Webster. 'You'll be wondering why I'm bothering you with all this. Only it occurs to me that my DI might be calling you lot in. Major Crimes. It's a resource thing, I know it is.'

'And?'

'I was just thinking . . .' He shrugged, embarrassed now. '. . . There might be times you'll need local knowledge, someone who reads the island really well, lived there all his life, knows the players, listens to the crack, all of that . . .' He let the sentence trail off into silence.

Faraday stirred, giving nothing away.

'And that someone . . . ?'

'Is me –' Webster smiled at Faraday '– sir.'

Three

Faraday happened on the invitation entirely by chance. Half past eight on a leaden Sunday morning, it was beginning to rain again. Consulting the BBC weather map on his laptop, he gazed at the long curl of an incoming front. By lunchtime, without a great deal of enthusiasm, he planned to be walking south on the coastal path that skirted the Purbeck Hills. Given the depth of the ugly, grey swirl of cloud, he'd be lucky to have dried out by dusk.

Abandoning the laptop, he was wondering whether he might tempt J-J to the movies when he noticed the unopened envelope poking out of the nest of mail in the shoebox beside his desk. Pompey postmark. Awkward, backward-sloping handwriting. His name misspelled, one too many 'r's. The letter had been addressed to the Highland Road police station and one of the reasons it had taken a while to make its way through the system was the lack of rank on the envelope. 'Mr Farraday', it read, 'Detective'.

Inside the envelope, he found a single sheet of blue-lined paper. His eye went at once to the foot of the page: Gwen Corey, a name he didn't recognise. Returning downstairs, he plugged in the kettle for another pot of tea. Then he read the letter.

The tone was apologetic. Gwen Corey was sorry to be writing to him out of the blue like this. She hoped he didn't mind the intrusion but her mum's best friend had recently passed away and Gwen had been put in charge of a party to mark her going. The party was today. The deceased's name was Grace Randall and she'd evidently left a list of invitations she wanted sent. One of these invitations had Mr Farraday's name on it. Not only that but a little note beside it had instructed Gwen to make sure he came. 'You'll like him,' Grace Randall had written. 'How often do you meet a gentleman these days?'

Grace Randall? Faraday circled the kitchen, trying to sort through the ever-lengthening list of names thrown up by the drumbeat of recent inquiries. It had to be a job he'd done, had to be. A woman in her seventies, or older. Someone on whom Faraday had evidently left a bit of an impression. He tried to visualise the files in the bottom drawer of his desk at work: inquiries that had made it to court, jobs that the CPS had thrown out, still-open cases that awaited further attention. Then, for no reason at all, he had it. Grace Randall. 131 Chuzzlewit House.

Faraday had met her on day one of an inquiry that had very nearly killed him. A young teenage girl had thrown herself off the top of Grace Randall's block of council flats and Grace herself had unwittingly provided one of the keys that had finally unlocked the case. Faraday could see her now, a thin, game, wheezy figure bent over a Zimmer frame, embroidered night-dress, pink slippers, little silver bells on the toes. She seemed to exist on a diet of ham sandwiches and Asda sherry. A big gas cylinder she hauled round the flat on a trolley forced oxygen into her heaving lungs, and her proudest possession – in a living room crowded with souvenirs – was the view from the window.

Up on the twenty-third floor, the view was sensational: the muddle of houses around the ancient bulk of the cathedral in Old Portsmouth, the dull green spaces of the Common, the sturdy sentry box of Southsea Castle, the tiny bathtub ships out on the tideway. Grace, it turned out, had spent her twenties and thirties as a singer on the big transatlantic liners out of neighbouring Southampton and had a treasured display of black and white photos on her drinks cabinet to prove it. That first time they'd met, Grace Randall been playing Puccini. 'Come here, young man,' she'd gasped, beckoning him towards the view, bent on explaining how the grand old Cunarders had slipped away to America, hogging the deep water over by Ryde Pier.

Faraday had returned to the flat a number of times, slowly piecing together the jigsaw to which Grace Randall held some of the parts, but until now it had never occurred to him that he'd been anything but a passing irritation in her life. Gentleman? He was intrigued, as well as flattered.

A little later, mid-morning, an email arrived from J-J. He'd got two complimentary tickets for a photographic exhibition in Chichester. His mate had called off and he could use a lift. How did Faraday fancy a couple of hours with some amazingly cool black and whites? Faraday, by now deep in the Sunday papers, declined. 'Previous engagement,' he tapped back. 'Sorry.'

The Church of the Holy Spirit's hall lay in the heart of Southsea, an area of terraced streets, second-hand furniture shops, Chinese takeaways and smoky street-corner pubs. Faraday at last found a parking space and did his best to avoid the worst of the rain. By the time he pushed into the hall through the big double doors, it was already late afternoon and he was soaking wet.

The music engulfed him at once, a soupy wave of nostalgia. At the far end of the hall, up on the stage, a nine-piece band was belting out Glenn Miller numbers in front of a huge poster of the *Queen Mary*. Balloons hung in nets from the ceiling and pinboards on each side of the band featured more shots of the great Cunarder. Long rows of tables piled with food and drink lined each side of the hall and the space in between was a slow blur of couples dancing.

Faraday watched them from the doorway, aware of his anorak dripping onto the scuffed parquet floor. Gwen's invitation hadn't mentioned anything about fancy dress. How come he'd stepped into a 1940s time warp?

A woman in a striking green dress made her way towards him through the sway of dancing couples. A mass of frizzy grey curls framed a wide smile.

'Mr Faraday?' She had a broad Pompey accent.

'How did you know?'

'I've lived here all my life. Spot a copper a mile off.' She extended a hand. 'Gwen Corey. It's nice of you to come.'

'Joe.' Faraday was looking for somewhere to hang his coat. 'I'm afraid I'm underdressed.'

'No problem. You need a drink. Come with me.'

She led him by the hand, back across the dance floor, acknowledging a series of fluttery waves. Most of the guests were in their sixties, some of them older, and they were plainly having the time of their lives. A makeshift bar beside the stage offered everything from spirits to a wooden barrel of real ale.

'Or we've got cocktails if you'd prefer it.' Gwen beckoned the elderly barman. 'Charlie was in the First

Class lounge on the *Elizabeth*. The real thing. And a great friend of Grace's.'

Charlie capped the introduction with a shy little nod. His velvet waistcoat had definitely seen better days but Faraday guessed it was probably original. He settled for a pint from the barrel, much to Charlie's disappointment.

'You sure I can't fix you something stronger, sir?'

''Fraid not. Beer's fine.'

The end of *American Patrol* sparked a cheer from the dance floor. Faraday, glass in hand, followed Gwen to a nearby table. She might have known him for years, a warmth all the more welcome for being so natural.

'This is my mum.' Gwen was bent over a frail-looking woman forking her way through a tiny helping of cocktail sausages and Russian salad. 'Her name's Madge.'

Faraday extended a hand.

'Madge . . . I'm Joe.'

The woman peered up at him and smiled. The eyes were milky with cataracts but she had the complexion of someone half her age. Faraday began to say something inconsequential about the music and the fancy dress then became aware of a voice in his ear.

'My mum's been dying to meet you. She's the one who knows all about you and Grace.'

Faraday looked round, but Gwen was already stepping back onto the dance floor as the band picked up a new beat. She gave him a little wave, then began to jitterbug with a man in white trousers and a striped blazer.

Faraday sank into an empty chair, Madge beside him. He felt like a stranger inexplicably made welcome at someone else's hearth. There had to be a subplot

67

here, an explanation for these open arms, but he hadn't a clue what it might be. He reached for his glass and took a long pull at the beer. Then came the gentlest of pressures on his other hand. It was Madge. She beckoned him closer.

'Gracie thought the world of you.' She was beaming now. 'She used to phone me up after you'd gone. Just think what an impression you made.'

She nodded, part encouragement, part applause, the way you might be proud of a favourite son, and over the next hour or so, whenever the music permitted, Faraday began to tease out Madge's story.

She and Grace had been childhood friends – same school, same church. Before the war, for a couple of summer seasons, Grace had gone to sea with the Cunard line. She'd been a skivvy first, then a waitress, and had finally caught the purser's eye. She had a good voice, lovely figure, nice temperament, and one evening at an American family's insistence she'd been given her chance onstage in one of the cocktail bars.

Then came the war and she was back in Southsea just like everyone else, scared out of her wits one moment, bored stiff the next. After the worst of the Blitz, the news had got slowly better. Soon you got to see Canadians and Yanks in the streets. Grace had found herself a GI from West Virginia, nicest manners, generous to a fault, but he went off to the west somewhere, Dorset, Devon, and that was the last anyone ever saw of him. Then the invasion happened, all those thousands of boats, and before you knew it Gracie was back on the liners, the *Queen Mary* this time, singing for her supper.

'And you?' Faraday, on his third pint, was beginning to enjoy himself.

'Me, dear?' Madge looked blank.

'Your war? Did you find yourself a Yank?'

Madge looked at him a moment, the eyes clouding again, then shook her head. The band had stopped for good this time and the dance floor was rapidly emptying.

'I didn't need to,' she whispered. 'Not a Yank.'

'You had someone else?'

'Yes.' She nodded, watching her daughter carrying a tray of drinks around the band.

'Do you mind me asking who?'

'Not at all.' Madge's gaze returned to Faraday. 'In fact you should. Gracie was right. Harry would have looked just like you. Especially with this . . .' Her thin hand reached out and touched the side of his jaw where the growth of stubble was beginning to sprout into a decent beard. 'Soon you'll be looking just like my Harry. Trust Gracie. Always the first to spot it.'

Gwen had returned from the stage. She wanted to know whether her mum was comfy. Faraday found himself answering on her behalf.

'We're fine,' he said. 'Just fine.'

'What's she been telling you?'

'Family secrets.' Faraday looked up at her. 'Who's Harry?'

Gwen smiled but said nothing. Then, from nowhere, there was suddenly another woman beside her – early forties, same eyes, same build, dressed as a cabin boy. She had a quizzical smile and snapped a salute as Gwen did the introductions.

'This is Karen, my eldest. Karen . . . Joe.'

Faraday got to his feet. This family was unrolling before him, a seemingly endless carpet of Pompey generations. Karen was looking from Faraday to her nan, trying to work out the connection. Then she got it.

'You're the policeman, right?'

'That's right.'

'OK.' The smile was warmer. 'Nice to meet you.'

Madge was going through the contents of her purse. Gwen whispered something in her daughter's ear, then she was gone again. Karen bent over her nan, trying to help. Faraday watched her a moment, saw the way the old woman leaned into her, total reliance, total trust. Then the thin, pale fingers found the photograph she'd been looking for. She held it out to Faraday, insisted he look at it.

The photo was black and white, curled at the corners, with a watermark down one side that was beginning to lift the emulsion. It showed a smiling young man in his prime with a broad, weather-roughened face and a full beard, carefully trimmed. He was wearing a white roll-necked sweater, heavy-duty wool, service issue. His hair was swept back, no parting, and his eyes were narrowed against strong sunlight. In the background Faraday could see a canoe pulled up on a pebble beach, but it was the face that held you. It was a face full of resolve. This was someone, Faraday thought, whom you'd be wise never to underestimate. Whatever he'd just said, whatever he was thinking, this man meant it.

'My Harry.' Madge retrieved the photo and then reached for a paper napkin and dabbed at her mouth.

Faraday, looking down at the face in her hand, didn't quite know where to take the conversation next. Is this really what I look like, he wondered. Was this why Madge's daughter had trekked up Highland Road and handed her envelope to the desk clerk? He glanced round. Most of the couples from the dance floor had found seats, helping themselves to platefuls of cold chicken and potato salad, and for the first time

70

Faraday became aware of the presents stacked on a trestle table in the far corner of the hall.

'I thought this was a wake?'

Karen looked back at him and grinned.

'It is,' she said. 'But it's also my mum's sixtieth.'

'You mean Gwen?' Faraday was looking for the green dress.

'That's right.' Karen laughed. 'Two old birds. One big stone.'

'And the décor? The band?'

'My idea.' Karen took a little bow. 'I know it's obvious but the oldies love all the dressing up; makes them feel young again. What do you think, then?' She did a twirl in her cabin boy's outfit, struck a stagy pose. 'Twenty-quid hire from a shop in Albert Road. Another tenner and it's mine for life. Don't laugh. Next time I have trouble with the mortgage, I'm off to sea.'

She sat down again and drew her chair closer to Faraday's. Then she reached for Madge's hand and gave it a squeeze.

'Nan misses Gracie, don't you, Nan? We used to take them both to bingo, Wednesday nights, me and Mum. On a good night we'd blow the winnings in the pub afterwards. You know the George?'

Faraday nodded. The George was a genuine relic, a timbered alehouse deep in Portsea, a stone's throw from the dockyard walls. With its yellowing photos of long-ago warships and ageing clientele, it had so far resisted canned music and the blessings of Sky Sports.

'You still go there?'

'No. Madge doesn't get out much these days, do you, darling?'

Madge was returning the photo to her purse. Karen leaned across to help her.

'So what happened to Harry?' Faraday said at last.

'He was in some kind of top-secret outfit during the war. Amazing stuff they did. Mum's got all the details.'

'And?'

'Something happened. It was way before D-Day, winter time, but I don't know what except that Harry didn't make it.'

Faraday was looking at Madge. She was erect in her chair, her eyes closed. A handful of the musicians had returned to the stage and her head was nodding for the opening bars of 'Night Train'. Faraday gazed at her a moment longer, unaccountably moved, and then returned to Karen. He wanted the whole story.

'Harry died?'

'Yes. My nan never got over it, never married, never looked at another man. Never wanted any of that.'

'And your mum? Gwen?'

'She was Harry's. Mum was two months old when he died. Mum was all Nan had left.'

Faraday reached for his glass and raised it in a silent toast. It seemed worlds away, this story, yet here was the living evidence, dressed as a page boy, that a precious bit of Harry lived on. He could see it in the eyes, in the tilt of the chin, in the readiness of the smile.

Karen was asking him whether he fancied a dance. Faraday eyed the empty floor, then reached for his glass.

'What about your mum? And you?'

'What d'you mean?'

'You've got husbands? Families of your own?'

'Kids, yes. Husbands, no. Mum's divorced, so am I. Nan's the only one with a clean conscience.' She grinned, extending a hand. 'But I suppose you can blame the war for that.'

*

In the brief truce his body had declared between a hangover and the next blinding headache, Winter brooded. Sunday nights, he'd long concluded, were the worst. Fuck all on the telly, a mini-roast for one still cooling in the oven, and the newspaper full of cheating footballers and so-called lifestyle articles. He was gazing at one now. He'd spent most of his adult life peering under other people's stones and knew the kind of sludge you could find there but was he seriously interested in the memoirs of a practising vampire?

Abandoning the *News of the World*, he got up to pull the curtains. It was dark outside now and for that he was glad. In moods like this nothing depressed him more than to look out on Joannie's precious garden. Even in winter, when nothing grew, the prospect of untended borders and unweeded flower beds served as a wagging finger from beyond the grave. Spring would reveal the sheer depth of his neglect – anarchy amongst the daffodils – and then would come the moment when he'd have to bother the rug of a lawn with the rusting mower he kept at the back of the garage. He hated gardening. Only the thought of having to pay some dosser to do the work on his behalf was worse.

Joannie had been gone for nearly four years now, a period of time that seemed – if anything – to shrink with every passing Christmas. With a stoic good grace and a kind word for more or less everybody, his wife had succumbed to pancreatic cancer. At first, to Winter's immense pride, she'd put up a real struggle and Winter liked to think he'd been a comfort to her through those endless days of tests and consultations, the terrifying truth dressed up in words he couldn't even spell. Then, quite suddenly, she'd seemed to conclude that all this trouble, all this fuss, simply wasn't worth it, and it was only later, after she'd gone, that he realised her rapid collapse those last few weeks had partly been Winter's fault. She simply couldn't bear another scene. One more bedside ruck, with her husband accusing the oncologist of negligence, and she'd be pleading for a still-heftier dose of morphine. Had he embarrassed his wife to death? Winter simply didn't know. But Joannie had always been there for him, eternally forgiving, and the sheer depth of the hole she'd left behind had begun to unnerve him.

At first, those early months alone in the bungalow, he'd relied on the job for light relief. As ever Pompey had obliged and on division, working out of the sunny first-floor office at Highland Road, he'd been able to keep his grief at arm's length. With even more zest than usual, he'd plotted elegant traps for shoplifters, skag heads, and other assorted lowlife. A decent number of these vermin he'd put away – more, certainly, than any other DC – and his strike rate didn't end with successful convictions. Evidence that wouldn't guarantee a result in court he used in other ways, spending immensely productive hours with overnight prisoners in the holding cells, listening to the usual rubbish about debts and domestic crises before recruiting these apprentice lags for his city-wide army of informants.

The memory of those days brought a smile to his face. Winter, it was generally acknowledged, was something of an artist when the cell door closed and it all boiled down to conversation. With his matey smile and cheerful bulk he could clamber into any man's head and make himself thoroughly at home. He'd share gossip, hint at money down the line, invite confidences, sympathise with a pat on the shoulder and a tear or two in his own eye. His colleagues had always regarded him as a loner, reckless and dangerous, a man without a shred of honesty or compassion, but the truly bizarre thing was that the people he arrested – like the countless women he took to bed – rarely had a bad word to say about him. They all opened up to Paul Winter. They all believed every word he said. And even a couple of weeks later, when these new friends of his recognised how cleverly they'd been screwed, they still managed a wry smile at the mention of his name. Seasoned detectives at Highland Road shook their heads at this display of human folly but one or two others, more perceptive, likened Winter to an American evangelist. These people *like* Winter, they pointed out. And more than that, they need him.

Winter, of course, relished comments like these. To him they came close to the truth of what he did. He was in the ambush business. He was there to lay false trails, to bait traps, to snare his quarries and then bring them face to face with their own frustrations, their own fears, and finally their own fatal dependence on Winter's goodwill and support. This was how he could tempt a man into grassing up his mates. The odd phone call. A name. Premises about to be screwed. Even, on occasions, the make and number of the motor involved. Information like this, largely kosher, saved thousands on the surveillance budget, and if there was a bill to be paid at the end then it certainly wasn't Winter who wrote the cheque.

On several occasions his snouts had been badly hurt. One, a small-time drug dealer, had been beaten to death by a bunch of feral adolescents on a Somerstown street. But in every case Winter had simply shrugged. No flowers. No regrets. None of that sentimental old bollocks about good intentions and hearts of gold. No, the point about snouts was simple. They were trash, scum, good for nothing except the next whisper. End of story.

Winter sighed. Transferred off division, he'd spent the last year and a half on the Portsmouth Crime Squad. In theory, mountains of intelligence were supposed to turn Cathy Lamb's troops into ace proactive thief-takers, ten steps ahead of the game. In practice, though, thanks to the classier villains in the Pompey underworld, it was rarely that simple. These were the once-young headcases that had livened up the eighties with their all-night Ecstasy raves and heroic pillaging expeditions to France and Switzerland. They'd later made a fortune in cocaine and property development and now, in their comfortable middle age, they viewed decent crime as a strictly recreational option, a bit of extra excitement between horse racing in Dubai and a week or two floating around on some mobster's yacht off Marbella.

These people weren't stupid. They weren't on the same page as the young scrots who littered the Bridewell cells on a Monday morning. And, more to the point, they'd had a couple of decades skirmishing with the likes of Paul Winter and knew exactly what to expect. They viewed him, if anything, with affection: spared him a wave when they swept past in their gleaming 4 × 4s, bought him a drink at Goodwood or Fontwell, even offered a derisive bung if he'd promise to get himself a new car coat. The fact that people like these maintained control of the Pompey drug scene was neither here nor there. Sure, they were making huge profits. Sure, half the city knew they were at it. But serious money had its uses and one of the things it very definitely bought you was immunity from maggots like Winter.

Maggots. Winter shook his head. For once they'd

found a word that truly hurt him. He'd heard it first at a Gunwharf bar, one Friday night. One of Bazza Mackenzie's mates was standing an enormous round and tacked Winter's name on the end of it: *Double Bell's for the maggot in the suede coat over there. A treble if he'll fuck off out of it.* The dig had brought the house down – big sweaty faces, an ocean of shaved heads, wall-to-wall CK T-shirts – and if Winter had weathered this particular storm then it was thanks to years of otherwise untroubled repartee. When the glass of Scotch had finally appeared at his elbow, he'd raised it with a flourish. 'Old times.' He'd beamed down the bar. 'And God help all those poor fuckers who ever thought you lot were class.'

Winter, like any detective, had his pride. He'd always made a point of sailing extremely close to the wind, bending procedural rules to shorten the odds on a particular result, but lately he'd begun to suspect that the sheer force of the tide was against him. Barely a week went past without a new piece of legislation appearing on the Hantspol intranet. Ambitious young superintendents, frequently with degrees, appeared to believe all the guff about sectorisation and problem-orientated policing. The cold-eyed ninjas from Professional Standards seemed to be lurking in every canteen. Even the pre-Christmas piss-up had developed into a glum ruck over pension rights. Feeling older by the day, and dizzied by pains in his head, Winter had finally come across a discussion paper from the Health and Safety people at HQ. It dealt with the gleaming new mountain bikes imported for bobbies on the beat. Mounted PCs should be aware of the scrotal implications of poor saddle posture. In circumstances where an arrest appeared likely, it was advisable to dismount. Winter had circulated this document with a derisive note of his own but the fact that no one appeared to be remotely surprised was probably more depressing than the thing itself. Was this what the job now boiled down to? A risk assessment on *mountain bikes*?

Drifting into the kitchen, Winter eyed the clock on the wall. Five past nine was hopelessly early for bed but he could think of no good reason not to put the blanket on. Then he began to wonder about tomorrow, about the pimp Richardson and about the pleasures of plotting Singer's downfall.

Richardson, released on police bail and due back at the Bridewell tomorrow morning, would know a great deal about his clientele's darker commercial secrets, and the prospect of a prison sentence often loosened tongues. With a bit of effort in the interview room the other girl – Cecile – might also come across. Both interviews, artfully handled, could yield enough evidence for a further round of headline arrests.

Singer, meanwhile, was in deep shit. Forensic chemical analysis might well tie Singer's personal wraps of charlie with the stash seized in Camber Court, giving the lie to the solicitor's claim that he'd acquired the stuff elsewhere. Better still, there might even be incriminating footage of Singer enjoying a toot or two amongst the small mountain of Richardson's home movie DVDs now awaiting Suttle's attention in the Crime Squad office. Either line of enquiry would offer rich pickings in court, a long-delayed revenge for years of aggravation. Of all the scalps Winter had ever taken, and there were many, Singer's might prove to be the sweetest.

Winter grinned and turned his back on the clock, feeling immeasurably better.

It was Karen, the youngest of the Coreys, who drove

Faraday home. The party in the church hall had broken up around nine in the evening and Faraday had been on the point of phoning for a taxi when Karen intercepted him.

'You're not driving, are you?'

'Hardly.'

'I'll give you a lift, then. Mum insists.'

There was no room for argument. She had a small Renault. Inside, it smelled doggy.

'Staffordshire bull terrier,' she explained. 'World's ugliest pooch. It used to belong to my partner but he left it behind.' She laughed. 'Sweetest thing.'

'Your partner?'

'The dog.'

She drove east across the city, picking her way nimbly through the maze of terraced streets. She'd grown up here; knew it backwards. After they'd passed the house where her best friend used to live and the Co-op where her mum still worked Faraday asked her what she did for a living.

'I'm a teacher.'

'Whereabouts?'

'George Meredith.' George Meredith was a big comprehensive on the fault line between Portsmouth and Southsea.

'You enjoy it?'

'Most of the time, yes. It was mum's idea I went off to teacher training. She'd left school as soon as she could and didn't want me behind the checkout all my life.'

She said she taught geography. The subject had always fascinated her and recently she'd got into the habit of regarding holidays as preparation for next term. Her daughter was now nineteen, well able to look after herself, and so Karen took every opportunity to remortgage herself to the hilt and follow her nose until the money ran out.

'So where have you been?'

'Europe mainly. Scandinavia was great but pricey. Eastern Europe brilliant. France so-so. Spain was lovely away from the coast. Next on the list is Italy and then the Balkans.'

'And you do these trips alone?'

'Mainly. When I went to Andalusia, Kelly came too. She fancied Siena as well but fell in love the week I had to book. Nazrul. Nice lad. Asian.'

'Kelly's your daughter?'

'Yes.'

They were closing on the Bargemaster's House now. Faraday pointed out the cul-de-sac that led down by the water, wondering what he could muster in the way of a nightcap.

'Last house on the right.' He could see the light at the end of the street. 'I've got some decent Rioja if you fancy it.'

The Renault coasted to a halt. Karen looked across at the shadowed trellis in the garden, the white timber cladding on the first floor, the big glassed-in study on the harbourside corner that Faraday used as his private perch. It was a sturdy, mid-Victorian house on the very edge of the island, and Karen seemed to be having difficulty associating a place like this with the man sitting beside her.

'How long have you lived here?'

'Twenty years, give or take.'

'You've got a family?'

'A son. He fled the nest a while back.'

'So you live here alone?'

'Yes.'

She nodded, taking in this little clue, then pointed at the darkness beyond the house.

'And what's over there?'

'Langstone Harbour. Wake up on a morning with no clouds and there's more sunshine than you can cope with.'

'That's impossible.'

'Bet?'

Faraday smiled at her, happy to offer a glimpse or two of his solitary life. To his considerable surprise, back in the hall she'd got him dancing. She'd found a space amongst the older couples and bribed the band to up the beat. No one else was jiving but it hadn't seemed to matter.

'I ought to get home,' she said at last. 'It was great that you came. You made my nan's day, probably Mum's too. We don't meet too many detectives.'

'Lucky you.'

'Yeah?' She looked at him, suddenly uncertain, then frowned. 'There's something Mum asked me to mention. I'm not sure . . .'

'What is it?'

'You really want to know?'

'Try me.'

'It's about Harry, mum's dad, the one in the photo . . .' She trailed off again.

'And?'

'This is going to sound mad.' She bit her lip.

'Why?'

'Well . . . to be honest, I think he's become a bit of an obsession. Not just Nan but Mum too. It might be a hero thing, I don't know, but we haven't been too clever with men in our family so maybe Harry's all they've got left.'

'And you?'

'I'm too young. I've seen all the photos, listened to Nan talking about him, but it's all a bit remote. Men have never been an issue with me. Not like Mum and Nan.'

'Meaning?'

'Meaning that . . .' She frowned again, annoyed to be in this position, tongue-tied in front of a virtual stranger. She stole another glance at the house and then turned off the engine.

'A quick coffee,' she said, 'would be fine.'

Faraday brewed up in the kitchen while she toured the downstairs lounge. The click of a lock and the rumble of the big French doors told Faraday she'd stepped out into the garden. After a moment he could feel the cold breath of the harbour through the open kitchen door. Low tide was an hour after midnight and the mudflats would be busy with waders poking about amongst the bladderwrack for a late supper. By the time he carried in the cafetière and coffee cups, she'd just returned, closing the doors and pulling the curtain behind her. Sharing his lounge with a cabin boy was something of a novelty.

'Checking the view?'

'It's lovely . . .' She nodded. 'So peaceful. Round my way it can be mad at weekends.' She sat down on the sofa, studied her hands for a moment. 'Mum's a spiritualist,' she said at last. 'You ought to know that. She goes regularly to the temple in Victoria Road. Gets in touch with the dead. Has conversations. Really believes in it all.'

'Milk? Sugar?' Faraday glanced up, cafetière in hand.

'No, thanks.' She reached forward for the proffered cup. 'Do you mind me talking about all this?'

'Not at all.'

'OK.' She sat back, the coffee cup balanced on her knee. In the slant of light from the spots on the wall she looked more boyish than ever. Her hair was blonde, cut short and shaggy, and she had a snub button of a nose that gave her face an air of mischief. Kids would listen to someone like this, Faraday thought.

She was talking about her mum again. Gwen went to the temple every Sunday, never failed. The services could last a couple of hours. Karen had gone along a couple of years ago as moral support when her mum was feeling a bit low but once was enough.

'You're not a believer?'

'No. To be honest, it embarrasses me.' She sipped at her coffee, then looked up again. 'The last couple of weeks since Christmas Mum has been taking Nan. Mum says they got in touch with Harry again.'

'Again?'

'Mum's talked to him before. I know it sounds daft but it became quite a regular thing. This last time, though, Harry apparently mentioned you.'

'*Me?*' Faraday began to check his bearings. He hadn't seen her take a drink all evening. The last thing he could blame was alcohol.

'You want to know what Harry said?'

'Yes, please.'

'He said that Mum would meet a younger man with a beard, a detective, someone who'd known Gracie. He asked her to make this man feel at home, make a proper fuss of him.'

'Why? Why would he want that?'

'Mum didn't know but Nan was there too, and when they got back to Nan's place she showed Mum Grace's invitation list, the people she wanted to come

83

to the party. Your name was on it though no one had a clue who you were.' She suddenly grinned. 'Spooky or what?'

Faraday was thinking of the envelope that had arrived for him at Highland Road. 'Mr Farraday Detective'.

'What else did Harry say?'

'He told Mum to get Nan to show you his letters.'

'What letters?'

'The letters he wrote to Nan during the war. I've never seen them. She never lets them out of her sight.' She gazed down at her empty cup. 'I'm right, aren't I? It's crazy.'

Faraday, for once, was lost for an answer. Gwen's invitation had come as a surprise. A bigger surprise awaited him at the hall – the warmth of the welcome, the glad company of strangers. Now this.

'I'm flattered,' he said at last. 'But what would you want me to do with these letters?'

'Just read them, Mum says.'

'Why didn't she ask me herself?'

'I don't know . . .' Her voice began to falter again. 'I can't think why but maybe she felt this kind of stuff might come better from me.'

'Because you don't believe it?'

'Because I'm more your age.'

Faraday was toying with the cafetière. He liked this woman. He liked her directness and her cheerful candour. He hadn't jived for years, not since a memorable Christmas long past when he'd tried to teach his flailing son, but it had felt fine with her back in the church hall. She knew the moves. She made him look good. At the same time, occupational hazard, he was wary about this sudden turn in the conversation.

In his job there were lines you shouldn't cross and something told him he was close to one of them.

At length he got to his feet. Karen had said no to more coffee.

'Tell your mum I'll be in touch,' he said. 'Tell her I promise.'

'You've got the number?'

'It's on her letter.' He smiled at her. 'And thanks for this afternoon. I enjoyed it.'

'Including this?'

'Including this.'

Karen looked at his outstretched hand, then took a tiny step forward and kissed him on the cheek.

'Pleasure,' she said. 'Gracie was right about the gentleman.'

Four

Monday, 23 February 2004

Faraday awoke to the trilling of his mobile. It was Nick Hayder, his fellow DI on Major Crimes whom he'd followed to the Isle of Wight. Faraday was peering at his watch. 07.06. Something was pricking at his conscience.

'Is this to do with Aaron Tolly?'

'Not at all.' Hayder sounded tense. 'Tolly's dead and buried. Just like you recommended.'

Faraday nodded, relieved, and then swung his legs out of bed and padded across to the window. Dawn had come late, a thin grey mist that shrouded the distant stripe of Hayling Island. On the foreshore below the house a muddy-looking Labrador was nosing around amongst the debris on the tideline. Naked at the window, Faraday shivered as the dog plunged into the water, chasing a stately line of mallard.

Hayder was brief. He'd just been assigned a double homicide in a cottage in the New Forest. A couple of hours ago the milkman had found the door open and the lights on in the downstairs sitting room. One body, a woman, on the carpet. Another, evidently her husband, at the foot of the stairs. Multiple injuries to both. Blood everywhere.

'Willard's blitzing it,' Hayder was saying. 'Himself as SIO, me as Deputy, plus all the troops he can lay his hands on. The bloke's some kind of hotshot TV producer. *Loads* of publicity.'

According to Hayder, the dead man had been the brains behind a new reality show that was notching up huge ratings. In his spare time, to keep himself sane, he did a bit of birdwatching. Hayder, who knew about Faraday's birding expeditions to the New Forest, wanted a steer on who he might talk to.

'Do they have wardens in the forest? Rangers? Organisations for twitchers? People who might know him? We've got to build a profile of this guy. Willard wants the full SP by lunchtime.'

'Try his production team.'

'They're on the list. I'm trying to think outside the box. Local contacts, not telly.'

'Where does he live?'

'Newbridge.'

Newbridge was a straggle of houses on the eastern fringes of the forest, with easy access to nearby Southampton but hardly great for birdwatching. Faraday couldn't think of anything productive to suggest. He was still watching the Labrador.

'No names?' Hayder was running out of time.

'Afraid not. You could try a couple of birding websites, though. There's a good one called HOSLIST. Hang on a moment—'

Hayder told him to forget it. Willard was already screaming for a brief meet prior to hitting the road west. The cars were waiting downstairs. In a couple of minutes they'd be off.

'One other thing.' Hayder was on the move, more voices in the background. 'Willard wants you on parade sharpish. Nine o'clock in his office. Thanks for all the help, Joe. Back to bye-byes, eh?'

The phone went dead and Faraday found himself

wondering why he, rather than Hayder, wasn't heading for the M27 with a multiple murder to sort out. Nick was right. He knew the forest well and if the victim happened to be a part-time birder, then there were two good reasons for putting him on the team. He felt a brief pang of regret, denied the glorious jolt of adrenalin that trademarked a high-profile inquiry like this, but knew it was pointless to second-guess Willard's decisions. Hayder was a good detective, one of the best, and after a lengthy convalescence he was desperate to get back in the action. A week or two in leafy Hampshire, at the very least, would be a nice change from homicidal Scouse drug dealers who ran you over not once, but twice.

Faraday checked his watch again, reached for his dressing gown and headed downstairs. A man who's given up shaving, he thought, has plenty of time for a decent breakfast.

Hayder was right about Willard. The Detective Superintendent was at battle stations, his office door open, his printer spewing page after page into a wire basket that was already brimful. This was as close as Willard came to a state of some excitement and Faraday, like every other detective on the team, could recognise the symptoms: the jacket off, the sleeves rolled up, the coffee at his elbow untouched.

Willard nodded at the row of seats at the nearby conference table. He had the phone pressed to his ear and was giving some luckless bean counter an extremely hard time about Major Crimes' forensic budget.

'I don't care a fuck about that kind of overspend,' he was saying. 'If you're sitting where I sit there are times when operational need overrides everything. That happened to be one of them. OK?'

Willard was a big man but surprisingly light on his feet. He pushed the chair away from the desk and got up, peering at an incoming email. At length, he sealed the phone conversation with a grunt, scribbled himself a note, and joined Faraday at the conference table.

'Pillocks,' he muttered. 'This job used to be fun once.'

Faraday knew better than to turn this into a conversation. In these moods Willard was talking to himself.

'Newbridge,' he said instead. 'Nick phoned.'

'Good.' Willard brightened at once. 'Tasty job. Fifteen bodies should do for starters. Thank God we're not stretched at the moment.'

He began to muse about the press conference already scheduled for eleven o'clock. The media boss at HQ had hinted at interest from the London broadcast networks and although he'd have very little to say, Willard wasn't a man to underestimate the career benefits of a couple of minutes exposure on the lunchtime news. Listening to him plot his opening remarks – a savage double killing, no obvious lines of enquiry, the need for teamwork and unceasing effort – Faraday began to suspect that the canteen rumours about Willard were true. He really had drawn a bead on the Head of CID's job. The current incumbent was retiring, and Willard obviously fancied his chances.

His phone was ringing again but Willard ignored it. Time was moving on and he needed to talk to Faraday about the Isle of Wight.

'Colin Irving was on to me yesterday,' he said briskly. 'Seems that young DC of yours might have turned something up.'

'Webster?'

'Yes. The lad got a shout from intelligence, followed it up; says he's on to a really strong lead. Irving thinks he might be a bit hasty but needs a second opinion. Irving's cuffing it again of course, obsessed by his bloody PIs – doesn't want Webster off the leash – but this time he might have a point. I said we'd take a look at it, strictly exploratory, no commitment, especially now with this lot kicking off . . .' He waved a hand towards his laptop, already black with unread emails.

'You want me to go over there again?'

'Yes. You and young Tracy.'

'Who?'

'Tracy Barber. She booked in this morning, subbing for Mel Fairweather. You'll love her.' Faraday detected the hint of a grin. 'She's ex-SB.'

SB was police-speak for Special Branch. Willard checked his watch and got up. When the phone began to ring again he returned to the desk, then paused.

'Barber's booked you both on the car ferry. She's probably back in your office by now. And keep tabs on Irving, eh? That man's too ambitious for his own good.'

Faraday's office was empty. He flicked through the morning's mail, understanding at last why he wasn't over at Newbridge kicking the Major Crimes' investigative machine into action. Darren Webster had obviously struck lucky with his meet in Shanklin and now his divisional boss was counting the cost of what might lie in wait down the road. The problem with homicide inquiries was the quality of the evidence you had to gather. With the prospect of a lengthy court case, you'd be mad to skimp on resources. Hence Irving's call to the specialists.

'DI Faraday? I'm the new Mel.'

Faraday looked round to find himself looking at a tall, well-built woman in her late thirties. She had a big square face and a nicely cut two-piece suit that showcased a fine pair of legs. Special Branch often turned into a life sentence for malicious sociopaths with the worst possible take on human nature. Tracy Barber, by contrast, looked positively cheerful.

'Let you out, have they?'

'I'm on parole. For good behaviour I get to stay here a while. Otherwise, it's back in my box.' She shook Faraday's outstretched hand. 'There's a rumour we're off to the island. I've booked for eleven o'clock. That OK with you, boss?'

They had coffee aboard the car ferry that churned across the Solent to Fishbourne. Barber, it turned out, had known Mel Fairweather since they'd been DCs together in Southampton. Mel was currently away on compassionate leave following a traffic accident that had nearly killed his wife, and Tracy Barber had been glad of the opportunity to sample life on Major Crimes. SB, she readily admitted, had its attractions but lately she'd spent far too much time trying to penetrate the Animal Liberation Front, and months of pretending she was a lifelong vegan were driving her barmy.

'I made the mistake of wearing a leather jacket to the first meet.' She shook her head. 'I thought the woman was going into cardiac arrest.'

'What happened?' Faraday was smiling.

'Nothing. I told her I was a dyke, got in a muddle sometimes, and after that it was fine. Takes one to know one. Best buddies ever since.' She paused, looking Faraday in the eye. 'But that's good tradecraft, isn't it? Making the best of your funny little ways?'

'You mean a meat diet?'

'Hardly.' She tipped her head back and laughed. 'This Darren Webster. What do you think, then?'

'Difficult to say. He's bright, ambitious, impatient.'

'Hanging offences?'

'Not at all. But sometimes you get a feeling about people, don't you? He wants a ticket out and something tells me he's just found one. That's enough to warp anyone's judgement, believe me.' Faraday nodded at the approaching channel into Wootton Creek. 'There's a Pompey boy called Unwin we ought to talk about.'

Colin Irving was waiting for them in the DI's office at Newport. Darren Webster was hanging on a phone call at his desk down the corridor but first Irving wanted a confidential word.

'I understand DC Webster came to see you on Saturday.' He was looking directly at Faraday and he didn't bother to hide his anger.

'Yes. But only after he'd told you first.'

'Really? Is that what he said?'

'Yes. In fact I made a point of it. Happy to talk to you but make sure your boss is in the loop.' Faraday raised an eyebrow. 'You're telling me that never happened?'

Irving didn't answer but his body language suggested that some time soon Webster was in for a spot of blunt career advice. In the meantime the lad would update them all on developments.

Irving lifted the phone.

'Webster?' His voice was icy. 'When you're ready.'

The young DC was in the office within seconds.

Faraday introduced Tracy Barber. Already, it felt like some kind of audition.

'You met the man Morgan . . .' Irving was brisk. He'd obviously been through all this already. 'Tell DI Faraday what happened.'

'I caught up with him on Saturday night, pub in Shanklin. We knew Pelly was a naughty boy but Morgan fleshed it out. Number one, the man's supposed to be running asylum seekers into the country, mostly by boat, mostly out of Cherbourg.'

'Cherbourg's a major port,' Faraday pointed out. 'French Immigration, CRS, Gendarmerie, the lot. Every other man you see's in uniform.'

'Doesn't matter, sir. Pelly pays French fishermen for the Channel crossing. The people over there turn a blind eye.'

'It's true.' It was Barber. 'When it comes to refugees, the French can't wait to get rid of them. It's the same across Europe. If you can move the problem on, that's exactly what you do. There's the border, boys. Go for it.'

'OK.' Faraday conceded the point. 'So what happens this side? You're telling me the fishermen come inshore?'

'Not at all, sir.' Webster shook his head. 'Pelly's got a fishing boat of his own, proper seagoing launch. He meets them off the back of the Wight, miles out. They transfer, then he brings them back. He's got a mooring in Bembridge Harbour. I've checked it out. Piece of cake.'

'And the cargo? The refugees?'

'He's got properties all over Shanklin, Sandown, Ventnor. He sticks them away, ten to a bed, and finds them work through an agency he runs. That way he can help himself to most of what they earn. The work's mostly seasonal – nurseries, holiday camps, hotels, fruit picking. This time of year can be tricky. Which is where Unwin comes in.'

'Unwin's the bloke who's allegedly gone missing.' Faraday was looking at Tracy Barber. 'Pompey lad. The one mentioned on the ferry.'

'That's him.' Webster nodded. 'Round October time the jobs on the island dry up so Unwin's the man with the van. Drives them over to the mainland, ferries them wherever. Brum, Manchester, Leeds – you name it. Some of them have relatives up there. Whatever happens, you can bet Pelly takes a slice.'

Faraday was following this chain of events in his head. It sounded all too plausible.

'Evidence?' he queried.

'Gary Morgan.'

'Just him?'

'So far, yes, but it all stacks up, believe me.'

'Did Morgan give you addresses for these properties?'

'Yes, and I knocked on the odd door yesterday, mainly neighbours in Ventnor. Just the sight of the warrant card and they were all over me. What these people get up to. The way they live. The noise, the music, the cooking, the smells. One old girl's been trying to sell up for a year, not a prayer.' He leaned forward in the chair, keen to make the point. 'I'm not wasting your time here. Morgan's kosher.'

'But why? What's in it for him?'

'He hates Pelly. Can't stand the man.'

'And why's that?'

'He wouldn't tell me.'

'And you've not talked to anyone else?'

'No.' Webster glanced briefly towards Irving. 'It's a

bit hectic just now; stacks of stuff I haven't even looked at.'

'But what about this man Pelly?' It was Barber again. 'Did you try for an interview?'

'Of course. I went up there yesterday. He runs an old folks home in Shanklin but he was away all day, back late last night.'

'What was the place like?'

'OK. Bit shabby maybe but nothing horrendous.'

'Any refugees working there?'

'None that I could see.' Webster returned his attention to Faraday. 'What I really wanted, sir, was a steer on Unwin. If his granny's really up there at the home then there'll be a record of next of kin. Might be a daughter, son, whatever. That would take me to Unwin, give me an address at least.'

'And what happened?'

'The records are all in a filing cabinet in Pelly's office. No one seemed to have a key.'

'Has he got a wife up there? Someone else in charge?'

'Hard to tell, sir. The girl I talked to was local, can't have been more than eighteen. That kind of detail needs proper investigation.'

Faraday glanced at Irving. The DI hadn't taken his eyes off Webster. Odds on, Newport's star DC was in for the bollocking of the year.

'So what's your theory?' Faraday had returned to Webster. 'About the lad Unwin?'

'You mean motive, sir?'

'I mean what may have happened.'

'Well, sir, from where I'm sitting it's one of two things. Either he and Pelly had a monster ruck about Unwin's granny and that was enough. Or Unwin and

Pelly have been in some kind of partnership and fell out.'

'Enough for what?' Tracy Barber was picking a hair off her skirt.

'Enough for Pelly to do him.'

'You mean kill him?'

'Yes.'

There was a moment or two of silence, broken by the hiss of air brakes from a bus outside. At length Irving stirred.

'That's a big step to make.' He was looking at Webster.

'I know, sir. But that's what we're paid for, isn't it? Putting two and two together?'

'You're paid to gather evidence, son. All we've got here is allegation –' he sniffed '– and gossip.'

'I know, sir. And that's why I need more time.'

Faraday was back on the cliff at Tennyson Down, peering over at the giddying drop.

'What about the head?' he said quietly.

'I've no idea, sir. Pelly might have done it himself, sawn it off, whatever. Makes ID a real problem. Happens all the time.'

'You think he's capable of that?'

'Definitely. The way Morgan tells it, this guy's aggression on legs. Shortest fuse on the island. Famous for it. I know that doesn't make him a murderer but the way I see it, it certainly puts him in the frame.' He paused to check his trilling mobile, then looked up again. 'And I haven't mentioned the gear. Apparently he's knocking out sizeable amounts of smack. Most of it comes in from Spain. Gets him in trouble with the local Scousers.'

'We still have an issue with our friends from Liverpool.' Irving ignored the smile on Faraday's face.

'We thought we'd cracked it but it turns out we were wrong. These animals are like bindweed. Put a dozen away and the next lot turn up. You just have to keep at them.'

'And Pelly?' Faraday turned his attention to Webster.

'He doesn't give them the time of day, sir. Morgan says they tried to stitch him up, grassed him to the Drugs Squad back in Liverpool, but nothing ever happened. Then they tried to sort him out themselves, waited for him outside a pub one night and went at him with Stanley knives. Pelly put one of them in hospital.'

'How?' Barber was intrigued.

'Ran him over. The kid was so angry he nearly pressed charges.'

'Says?'

'Morgan.'

Another silence, this time broken by Faraday.

'Right then.' He glanced at Irving. 'All this is on file? Addresses? Contact numbers? Pelly? Morgan?'

'Of course, Joe.'

'Good. We'll go through the stuff you've got, then make some decisions. That OK with you?'

'No problem.'

Faraday began to get to his feet. Webster, not believing his ears, could only look from one face to another. Eventually, his gaze settled on his boss.

'And me, sir?'

'You can stay behind, son.' Irving had the coldest smile. 'One or two things we ought to discuss.'

DC Paul Winter knew at once that he'd picked his moment. DI Cathy Lamb had just had a lengthy phone conversation with one of the Assistant Chief Constables and was much heartened by what he'd told her.

The ACC in question, she said, was Terry Alcott, in charge of CID and Special Operations. He'd confirmed to Lamb that he'd taken a call on Saturday morning from Maurice Wishart. Far from being a mate of his, said Alcott, Wishart was simply a businessman he'd bumped into at a social function. He was well connected in defence circles and like many successful men he seemed to have finessed passing acquaintance into something altogether weightier.

The allegations of harassment he'd levelled against DC Winter had certainly intrigued the ACC and he'd moved swiftly to make sure that nothing silly got into the hands of the press. Hence, Lamb assumed, the call that Winter had taken on Saturday afternoon from Willard. But what intrigued Alcott more than Wishart's crude attempt at pressure were the nuts and bolts of the operation that Winter had put together on DI Lamb's behalf.

Cathy had filled the ACC in on *Plover* – the alleged existence of the brothel, the modest investment she'd made in surveillance, the rumoured nature of the clientele, the likely presence of Class A narcotics on the premises – and had been delighted by Alcott's reaction.

Given last year's abrupt collapse of Operation *Tumbril*, a cripplingly expensive bid to snare both Bazza Mackenzie and the small army of accountants, lawyers and assorted professionals who'd helped construct his multimillion-pound drugs empire, Alcott felt – quote – 'somewhat aggrieved'. These bastards were giving the forces of law and order the runaround and that wasn't good for morale. What they needed, what the city needed, was a bit of restorative justice and in the shape of the Camber Court bust Cathy Lamb's squad appeared to be supplying exactly that. Both she and Winter had Alcott's full support. He was delighted by Friday night's developments, and especially pleased by the first of the arrests. It was bloody time, he muttered on the phone, that a disgrace like Singer reacquainted himself with the word justice. Alcott wanted to be kept abreast of events as they developed and would be pleased to make good any token damage to the squad's overtime budget. Operation *Plover*, as far as he was concerned, was a definite runner.

Now, DI Lamb was impatient for the latest developments.

'So what's happened with Richardson? You've interviewed him?'

'This morning. He got a brief down from London to represent him, a woman called Hersch. The Old Portsmouth flat's owned by a Lebanese guy, Hakim, and I get the impression Hersch is on the payroll.'

'How did it go?'

'It didn't. Richardson went no comment, wouldn't give us anything. Friday night he copped for the lot – the cocaine, the girlies, even showed us a recording of Wishart doing the business. This morning? Fuck all.'

'You got a statement Friday night?'

'Of course. We didn't charge him, though, because I was convinced there was more to come. He knew he was looking at a possible seven and he had the whole weekend to get himself in the mood for a sensible conversation. It was all there, Cath, I know it was. In return for a deal, he might even have coughed a name or two on the cocaine.'

Winter sensed that Cathy's new-found confidence in *Plover* was already beginning to ebb. She was a big, sturdy woman who believed in rewarding loyalty and hard work with unswerving support, and her pre-paredness to risk anything for her troops even extended to Winter. They went back more years than either of them cared to remember. They'd had endless head-to-heads over Winter's wilder initiatives but she was realistic enough to accept that he usually delivered, even if she wasn't quite sure how.

Now, she was trying hard not to show her disap-pointment. Winter, she told herself, was right. A weekend thinking about seven years banged up in Belmarsh or the Scrubs would concentrate any man's mind.

'So how did you play it this morning?'

'I told him what to expect. Painted a picture. The food, the company, the animals he'd meet along the way. Richardson's gay, Cath. He's got poof written all over him and he's used to fancy cuisine. How's a guy like that going to cope with rissole stew on sliced white with half the wing up his arse?'

'And his answer?'

'No comment. His brief said we were trying to put the fear of God up him and she's right; of course we were. And it worked too. He was bricking it. Half an hour alone with the guy and he'd have sold me his mother.' Winter frowned, denied his just deserts. 'The brief was a pain. We had a private conversation, just her and me, before we charged him. I tried to point out that she wasn't serving Mr Hakim's best interests by putting Richardson away but she wasn't having it. In fact she accused me of undue pressure on Friday night – oppressive questions, self-incrimination, all that bollocks. These London people just aren't on the same planet, you ever notice that? Offer them a deal and anyone'd think you just stepped on a turd. Absolutely clueless.'

'So how did you leave it?'

'I said I'd see her in court.'

'And Richardson?'

'We charged him with living off immoral earnings. He looked kippered. He knows exactly what's coming his way and I just hope Mr Hakim makes it worth his while.'

Cathy Lamb was looking glum now. A formal charge brought the interview process to an end. Whoever asked Richardson the next set of questions, it wouldn't be a detective.

'That's a shame,' she said at last. 'Mr Alcott's got the highest hopes.'

'Good.' Optimism and Paul Winter had always been the best of friends. 'There's still Cécile, one of the girlies. She's in this afternoon.'

'And the other one?'

'Maddox. We talked to her on Saturday. Hopeless. She left us for dead. I'd blame it on my age, Cath, but Jimmy was there as well and he did even worse.'

'But she's broken no law. What did you expect?'

'I dunno.' He shrugged. 'A bit of cooperation would have been nice. Jesus, we could have been punters the way she treated us.'

'Serves you right.' Cathy's laughter had a hollow ring. 'Where is she now, this Maddox?'

'Skiing.' Winter frowned, hunting for the name of the resort. 'Courchevel?'

Cathy wasn't interested. She was still looking for ways of squeezing the best out of *Plover*.

'So where are we with Singer?'

'He's put his hands up to the cocaine. Says it was just personal. Wouldn't dream of supplying.'

'Where did it come from?'

'He won't tell us but he swears blind it had nothing

to do with Richardson. That's probably bollocks and when the forensic comes back we'll prove it.'

Winter went on to tell her about the DVDs seized from Camber Court. DC Suttle had spent most of the morning going through the discs and so far there were no pictures of Singer getting the white powder up his nose, but like Wishart the solicitor had recorded some souvenir bedroom footage. Much of it was extremely graphic and if his wife had any kind of hang-ups about anal sex then she was in for a bit of a shock.

'He's in enough shit already.' Winter laughed. 'Turns out his missus runs the local branch of Relate; spends her life telling other people how to sort out their relationships. Can you imagine her watching this kind of stuff? The marital dick up some tom's arse?'

'Does Singer know we've got the DVDs?'

'No, but he will. And there's something else, too. Jimmy Suttle picked it up the tenth time he went through the blow-job sequence. The girl Cécile's on the job while Singer's telling her office secrets.'

'Like what?'

'Like the kind of strokes he pulls for his dodgier clientele. The recording isn't brilliant but if you listen hard you can get the drift and Singer's definitely pissed enough to be showing off. How he cooks up alibis for his heavy friends. How he coaches these animals to lie their arse off in the dock. How everything's possible if the price is right.'

'You're serious?'

'Yeah. And under the rules of disclosure, guess who gets to see it?'

'His defence lawyer.'

'Precisely. They know what we've got so there's no place for Singer to hide. One call to the Law Society and the man's fucking history. Sweet or what?'

Winter mentioned a couple of Singer's clients. The names put the smile back on Cathy's face. Then came a knock at the door. She looked up to find the squad DS looking for Winter. He'd just taken a call. It sounded urgent. The woman was still on the line.

'Who is she?' Winter was eyeing him with interest. The DS consulted a scrap of paper.

'Maddox?' he queried.

Tracy Barber and Faraday were killing time in a café in Shanklin. They'd been up to the nursing home to talk to Rob Pelly but he was out on an errand and wouldn't be back until half past two.

Barber wanted to know where Darren Webster had acquired his tan.

'Hang-gliding.' Faraday glanced up from the paper. 'The boy's mad about it. Can't keep him off the clifftops.'

'Are you kidding? Hang-gliding's for losers. I had a girlfriend once who was silly enough to have a go. One of those sampler weekends, somewhere in mid-Wales. Broke both legs; put her in hospital for six weeks. Poor, sweet girl. Does absolutely nothing for your sex life, an accident like that.'

Tracy Barber snorted at the memory, tidying the remains of her all-day breakfast onto a corner of fried bread. Then she looked up.

'What's your situation then, boss? You mind me asking?'

Faraday shook his head, and folded the paper. Coming from someone his own age the question was oddly inoffensive, simply two strangers comparing notes.

Faraday gave her the bare bones. Married young. A

widower months later. One son. No replacement spouse.

'Has that been tough?'

'Not after a while, no. My son was a handful. The boy was born deaf. That gives you plenty to be going on with, believe me.'

'How did you ever get through to him?'

'Sign. Games. Adventures. I suppose we grew up together, in a way. Then there were the birds.'

'*Birds?*'

'Yep. I was at my wits' end. The boy was four coming on five, and we just weren't coping, either of us. Then I bumped into a friend of mine; hadn't seen her for years. Turned out she'd pretty much been through the same thing. The way she coped was through birdwatching. She knew nothing about it, absolutely nothing, but her daughter didn't either, and she was deaf too. So there was the start to it.'

Faraday smiled, remembering those first trips to the city's Central Library, walking J-J back home with an armful of bird books. They'd planned it like an expedition, one page after another. First the birds they could see from the Bargemaster's House, shelduck, mergansers and godwits, then a night with the moorhens and coots that sculled around on the nearby freshwater ponds. After that came the dazzling little egrets that strayed over from Thorney Island, and finally Faraday had discovered the more exotic raptors – merlins and harriers – that put in an occasional appearance over the marshy RSPB reserve at the top of the harbour.

One evening when J-J was still barely seven they'd come across a saker up at Farlington, dive-bombing a flock of terrified seagulls. According to the handbook Faraday carried everywhere the hawk was a stranger to

Britain so it must have escaped from a private falconer. They'd watched it together, standing stock-still on top of the seawall that circled the reserve. Back home that night, after his bath, J-J had spent hours pretending to be the saker, dashing round the living room with his arms stuck out, making the strange tuneless cackle that was all he ever managed.

At the time it hadn't seemed the least bizarre and Faraday remembered the expression on his infant son's face as he drifted off to sleep. He'd become something else, an escapee from the confines of his silent world, and the magician who'd conjured this miracle was none other than his dad. Some days later, by chance, Faraday had happened across the friend who'd first suggested birding and he'd bought her a thank-you drink in a nearby pub. Fumbling for a phrase that did justice to this transformation, he'd finally settled for what sounded like a hopeless cliché. 'We've found the lock on the door,' he'd told her. 'And we've both got a key.'

Real-life expeditions followed as J-J got older. To Titchfield Haven for grey herons. To the New Forest for nightjars, spoonbills, cattle egret, Cetti's warblers – a taste of Europe on the fringe of England. And one unforgettable weekend, to Bempton cliffs up in Yorkshire, for a sky full of gannets plunging into the boiling waves. This was the weekend that introduced J-J, by now fourteen, to the stills camera, an ancient Nikon that had once belonged to his mother. In a heaving boat Faraday's ever-eager son had got lucky with the focus ring on the big zoom lens and the resulting shot – perfectly composed – was still pinned to the wall board in Faraday's office: the diving gannet inches from the water, wings tucked in, a feathered arrow in the ceaseless battle for survival.

Barber, the remains of her breakfast long forgotten, was transfixed. She'd heard rumours about the Pompey-based DI with the deaf son but she'd no idea about the kind of relationship they'd managed to build.

'You did all that? You and your boy?'

'And more. But we're talking years here, years and years. It wasn't all sweetness and light, believe me.'

'And now? This J-J of yours?'

'Gone . . .' Faraday looked suddenly wistful. 'He's twenty-four years old, his own man, stubborn as you like, never wrong, great cook, total nightmare with the washing-up . . . But, yeah . . .' He nodded. 'Gone.'

'Do you miss him?'

'I did to begin with. Not any more.'

'You still see him?'

'Of course. He lives in Pompey so most weeks we bump into each other, catch up, drive each other nuts, father and son. Old story.'

'He sounds lucky to me. Most dads . . .' She shrugged. 'Not that I'd know.'

'That's kind of you but it's not that simple. Never was, as a matter of fact.' Faraday got up and glanced at his watch, trying to mask the sudden flood of emotion. 'Twenty past,' he said briskly. 'We ought to be off.'

Five

The Boniface Nursing Home lay in a quiet cul-de-sac a mile or so inland from the sea. This was where Shanklin began to peter out, the muddle of streets and houses giving away to a mosaic of scruffy fields and meadowland before the long green swell of St Boniface Down.

Faraday parked the Mondeo and accompanied Barber up the steep gravel path to the front door. The house seemed to sprawl in all directions. At its heart lay a sturdy red-brick villa, neatly proportioned, with big sash windows on the ground floor and a white-painted wooden balcony running the width of the floor above, but various additions had given the place an air of over-hasty ambition. To Faraday's eye it looked like the kind of structure a bored child might put together on the sitting-room carpet, paying little attention to whether the various bits really fitted.

On the square of paved patio beside the door an elderly woman sat huddled in a wheelchair in the chill sunshine. She answered Barber's smile with a blank stare, her hands stirring beneath the thick folds of plaid blanket. Faraday rang the doorbell. They had no appointment with Pelly, just the earlier assurance that he'd probably be in.

After a while the door opened. It was a young girl,

pretty, no more than eleven. She was wearing jeans and a Busted T-shirt. Her feet were bare.

She peered out at them.

'Yeah?'

'Mr Pelly in?'

'Yeah.'

The girl turned away, leaving them trying to make conversation with the woman in the wheelchair. Tracy was still talking about the weather when a man rounded the corner of the house and strode towards them. He was tall, thin-faced, fit-looking, with a mop of greying hair gathered into a longish pony tail. The paint-splashed jogging bottoms had seen better days and the rest of his wardrobe seemed to have come from an army surplus store, but he had a very definite sense of presence. This wasn't the bloated lush Faraday had been led to expect. Far from it.

'Mr Pelly?'

'That's me.'

'DI Faraday. This is DC Barber. We'd appreciate a word if we may.'

Pelly had stationed himself between Faraday and the front door. He ignored the proffered warrant card.

'Why?' he queried. 'What's this about?'

'I'd prefer to explain inside if you don't mind.' Faraday nodded towards the bent old figure in the wheelchair. 'Somewhere a bit more private.'

'This one? She's lost it.' Pelly stepped towards the wheelchair and gave the woman's thin shoulder an affectionate squeeze. 'Sweet old thing but mad as a coot. Tell her the time of day and she'll ask you for two sugars. Won't you, dear?' He looked down at the face in the wheelchair a moment longer, then turned back to Faraday and shrugged. 'OK, then. Better be quick, mind. Time's money.'

Faraday followed Pelly into the house. Even with the lights on, the hall was gloomy. Handrails and other aids had robbed the interior of whatever style it might once have possessed, and as they picked their way through the maze of corridors the smells got ever stronger: rancid cooking oil with a thin top dressing of urine and bleach.

Pelly's office lay at the back of the house. Invoices and other paperwork spilled from a wire basket on the cluttered desk and a big marker board occupied most of the wall. The board was sectioned into days of the week, each day subdivided into shifts, and a scribbled list of names occupied each of the squares. Judging by the crossings-out, Pelly had a big problem with absentees.

'So?' Pelly had made himself comfortable behind the desk. His eyes, more grey than blue, never left Faraday's face.

Faraday began to sketch out the reason for their visit. He had grounds to believe that Pelly knew a young van driver from Portsmouth, Chris Unwin, who came over to the island from time to time to see his aged gran. True or false?

For a long moment Pelly didn't answer. Faraday had noticed the blue tattoo on his forearm, a tiny winged dagger. SAS, he thought. No wonder he keeps himself together.

'Who told you that?' Pelly muttered at last.

'Can't say, I'm afraid.'

Pelly watched him for a moment longer, then leaned forward over the desk. The colour seemed to have drained from his face.

'Gary, wasn't it? Little tosser. Go on, deny it. Gary fucking Morgan.'

Faraday refused to rise to the bait. Through the

window behind Pelly he could see a child's swing at the end of a length of threadbare lawn. Beside the swing was some kind of hole that might once have been a sandpit. Beyond, in a carefully dug flower garden, the first daffodils of spring.

'Shall I tell you something about Mr Morgan?' It was Pelly again. 'Put yourself around a bit, and you get to realise there are people in this world you don't cross. I happen to be one of them. Did twatface take the least bit of notice? Of course he didn't. So what do you think that made him? Apart from stupid?'

'You're telling me you and Morgan had a run-in?'

'A tiff, yes.' Pelly barked with laughter. 'Run-in's a bit strong.'

'What happened?'

'That's my business. But next time you see Mr Morgan just pass him a message, eh? Tell him he was fucking lucky. Tell him next time round I might mean it. Now, if that's all you've come about, I'll say goodbye. In this game there's never an end to it.'

'An end to what, Mr Pelly?'

'Work.' He nodded towards the open door. 'Painting, maintenance, fire equipment, escape routes, seagull shit all over the patio – you name it. I wake up every morning with a list of jobs you wouldn't believe – and you know why? Because we get inspected to death. They come knocking at my door, these clowns. They've got their little clipboards and their fancy IDs, and I bet none of them have done an honest day's work in their lives.' He shook his head at the injustice of it all. 'You know what the last one told me? He'd gone around and done a headcount, got to eighteen bodies, refused to believe I could make a place like this pay on those kinds of numbers. So you know what he said? He said you've got a couple stuffed away somewhere, haven't you? Couple of old biddies you never declared. Not to the taxman. Not to the VAT. Just readies, cash in hand, ghost income. Christ, I just wish it was that simple. You know what I did? I gave him a wrecking bar and a hammer, told him to lift a floorboard or two, *any* fucking floorboard, check the place out properly. Phantom grannies . . .' He turned to stare out of the window. 'My arse . . .'

'This lad Unwin . . .' Faraday began. 'Do you know anyone of that name?'

'Unwin . . .' Pelly put his head back and closed his eyes, muttering the name to himself. Faraday noticed a scar that ran from the hinge of his jaw to the point of his chin, a tiny raised line of tissue. 'Young Mary.' Pelly turned back towards Faraday. 'She's an Unwin.'

'She lives here?'

'Has done for years. Eighty-seven last birthday. Grand old dame. Ideas above her station but I suppose you can blame that on her condition. It's people like her take the edge off Alzheimer's. Catch her on the right day and she's almost sane.'

'Does she have next of kin?'

'Everyone has next of kin.'

'Do you have her records?'

'Of course I do. I'm in charge of her. I'm her keeper.'

'May I see them?'

Pelly didn't answer, not at once. Then he threw back his head and laughed again, a deeply private joke that was lost on Faraday.

'You people kill me.' A wave of his hand encompassed them both. 'You come in here, put your little questions, lots of pleases and thank yous, very polite, bit of respect, and yet you and I know it's all a game, don't we? Of course I've got fucking records. But just say I refuse to part with them. Just say I cop a moody because all that stuff's confidential and tell you to get the fuck out of here. You'd be back, wouldn't you? You'd be back with your search warrant and your mates and you'd probably tear the fucking place apart.'

'Why would we want to do that?' It was Barber.

'Because that's the way you are, love. Because that's the way it works in this khazi of a country. On the surface, sweet reason. Underneath, all kinds of vileness.' He switched his attention to Faraday. 'Listen, my friend. I could take you to places in this world that are truly horrible, places not two hours in a plane from here, but you know something? You get to know these shitholes and one thing hits you in the face. No one's pretending it's anything but evil. They all own up. Here? Us? We want it both ways. You believe all that Merrie England crap? Merrie England, my arse.'

He got to his feet and bent to an ancient filing cabinet. A couple of seconds in the middle drawer and he'd located the folder he wanted. He tossed it across the desk. Mrs Mary Belinda Unwin.

Faraday reached for his pocketbook. Webster, after all, hadn't got it wrong. This man was a ticking bomb, primed to explode at the least hint of offence. Faraday opened the folder, aware of Pelly watching him.

'You want a pen?' He opened a drawer and slid a biro across the desk, a giveaway from Dinosaurland.

Faraday produced a pen of his own. Mary Unwin's last address was in south-east London. Her next of kin also lived at 14 Havelock Road.

'Is Ellie Unwin Mary's daughter?'

'Haven't a clue. Could be.'

Faraday wrote down the address and phone number. Then he looked up.

'And Chris Unwin? Would he be Ellie's son?'

Pelly shrugged; didn't bother to answer. From nowhere he'd produced a string of worry beads, and now he began to slip them between his fingers, first one way, then the other.

'Where's all this going?' he asked at last. 'Why the interest in Unwin?'

'Because we need to talk to him.'

'But why? What's he done?'

'Is that anything to do with you?'

'Yes, if it brings you here.'

It was a fair point. Tracy Barber edged Pelly back on track.

'How well do you know this Chris Unwin?' she asked.

'Who's saying I know him? You?'

'OK.' Barber rephrased the question. '*Do* you know Chris Unwin?'

'As it happens, yes.'

'So how well do you know him?'

'So-so. He comes here sometimes, visits his gran.'

'And what does he do for a living, Unwin?'

'He drives a van.'

'He owns the van?'

'Haven't a clue.'

'What does he do with the van?'

'Fuck knows. Deliveries? House clearances? Removals? Weddings and funerals? How am I supposed to know? What it boils down to is this, love. The guy drops by. His granny asks us who he is. They have a cup of tea together. He gives her a kiss, tells her he loves her, and fucks off back to the ferry. That's how families work in this country – and I'm the one to know because it's people like me who look after the cast-offs. These old dears are scrap, they're gash, they're surplus to requirements. One day we'll put them in bins on the seafront. For the time being they still come to us.'

'Does that upset you?'

'Not me, love, not me personally. It's a living; it's what I do. But on their behalf? Of course it fucking does. I love 'em to death, the old dears, anyone half decent would.' Pelly shifted in his chair. 'You know what I think about Alzheimer's, *really* think? I think it's self-inflicted. My old ladies have seen what people are really like, their own bloody kith and kin for God's sake, and they've decided to pull the blanket over their head. Alzheimer's is a way out. It wipes the slate clean. And from their point of view, not before bloody time.'

'You're telling me Chris Unwin comes regularly?'

'Came. He's stopped lately.'

'Why's that?' It was Faraday.

'God knows. Maybe he's got better things to do. Maybe Pompey in the Premiership has gone to his head. Maybe he's fallen in love, got a puncture, signed up with Al-Qaeda – how am I supposed to know?'

Faraday was gazing at a snap Blu-tacked to a corner of the marker board, waiting for Pelly to calm down. The photo showed a sleek-looking motor launch, bright yellow, tied to a buoy. Some kind of cabin up front, a big expanse of open deck at the back.

Pelly followed his eyeline.

'You into fishing at all?' he enquired. 'Only I can do you a deal. Couple of hundred quid and I can take you to sea the whole day. That's cheap, believe me. Bait and rods supplied. Bring half a dozen mates and you'll have a ball. This time of year, I can guarantee cod, maybe even a knackered old bass. You know how many fish the last lot came home with?'

Faraday ignored the question. Barber asked Pelly where he kept the boat.

'Bembridge,' he said. 'It's on a mooring. Costs an arm and a leg. That's why I do the charters. Best to make your hobbies pay, eh?'

Barber scribbled herself a note. Pelly turned back to Faraday.

'You want to know about Unwin? I'll tell you. The bloke's a waste of space. He's an idiot. He's one of those people you know right off he's got a screw loose. But fair play to the lad, he's been over here to see his old granny, and there aren't many people who do that, believe me.'

'I thought you just told me no one cares?'

'They don't, by and large, but at least Unwin had a stab at it; went through the motions.'

'So when did you last see him?'

'Can't remember.' Pelly was back with the worry beads. 'Where are we now? February? Must have been way before Christmas, maybe October, maybe earlier. That's the thing about this game. Close your eyes, count to ten, and there's another year gone.'

'Did you ever have a row with the man?'

'A row? About what?'

'I don't know.' Faraday paused, choosing his words carefully. 'Was there ever a time when you were together in here? Having a bit of a shout?'

'Who says?'

'That doesn't matter.'

'It does to me, my friend. And you know why? Because it's not true.' He paused a moment, staring at Faraday. 'Is that why you've come? To check out some piece of gossip about Unwin? Me and him having a ding-dong? Is that it?'

Faraday held Pelly's gaze. Under different circumstances, he thought, this man could be truly scary.

'Do you have an address for Unwin?' he asked at last.

'No.'

'And you're absolutely certain nothing ever –' he gestured at the space between them '– happened between you?'

'Absolutely one hundred per cent fucking certain. And you want to know why? Because getting involved with inbreds like Unwin isn't what I do. Listen, I'm a busy man. I run a couple of businesses. This is one of them. I don't have the time to fuck around with conversation, and if you want the truth it isn't something I miss. So, if you'll excuse me—'

Barber headed him off.

'Two businesses, Mr Pelly?'

'Yeah.'

'So what's the other one?' She nodded at the boat on the board. 'Fishing?'

'Fishing, my arse. Fishing's a hobby, like I say, an excuse to get away. But what's it to you what else I do?' He stared at her, daring her to come up with an answer, then he looped the worry beads round one finger, pushed the chair back and propped his feet on the edge of the desk. 'Listen, love, this is for once and once only, OK? One of my companies runs this place. The other is an employment agency. Both are privately owned. We have books, an accountant, two VAT numbers, and we pay a small fortune in taxes. Talk to the Revenue. Talk to the people at the town hall. Talk to whoever you fucking like. I don't owe anyone a penny. I'm fully paid up. In fact I probably keep half the country going, the amount they take off me.'

'Employment agency?' The question came from Faraday.

'Sure. Casual labour. Blow-ins. Overners. People who come looking for sunshine and a job.'

'English people?'

'Not necessarily. I take anyone, doesn't matter what their colour is, where they've come from. As long as they're honest – fair day's work, fair day's pay – I'm happy to oblige. People on this island are crying out for labour and you know why? Because the locals can't be arsed to get out of fucking bed in the morning. It's the blow-ins who need the money and I'm the bloke in the middle who makes it all happen. Capitalism in action. Sweet, eh?'

'The foreigners have paperwork? They're legal?'

'Of course they fucking are. You think I'm stupid?' He stared at Faraday for a long moment. 'That's Morgan again, isn't it? I can hear the little tosser marking your card. Did you pay him, or what? Only if you did I only hope for his sake that you made it worth his while.' He leaned forward, swung his legs off the desk, white with anger. Then, quite suddenly, he seemed to relax. Even managed a smile.

'You know what Morgan did?'

Faraday shook his head.

'Tell me.'

'He came sniffing round my wife. He was clever. He dressed it all up, pretended they had mutual friends, made it look the most natural thing in the world for her to pop down the pub and have him buy her a drink or two. And you know what I told him when I found out? I said you lay a finger on my wife, one finger, a glance even, and you'll be avoiding mirrors for a very long time.' He gazed at Faraday, the smile broader. 'You didn't notice when you met him? Or was it so dark you couldn't see the little twat?'

*

Winter had been waiting for nearly an hour before Maddox finally arrived. The Lime Tree Café occupied a sunny corner of Albert Road, a mile or so of antique shops, hippy outlets, record stores and cheap ethnic restaurants that reminded older residents of the glories of the Fulham Road before the big money arrived. Winter, who was clueless when it came to London chic, had an altogether earthier take on the area. Albert Road figured in most of the volume crime he'd tackled as a DC on division and nothing much had happened since to change his opinion. Whether it was fenced gear, dodgy meat or a vanload of contraband fags off the ferry, this was where you sold it.

Maddox was wearing an ankle-length black leather coat, lace gloves and a huge pair of dark glasses that seemed to hide half her face. She might have stepped out of the pages of *Hello* magazine the morning after a particularly savage party.

'You're meant to be skiing.' Winter was on his feet.

'I blew it out.'

'Why?'

'It's a long story.'

'Do I get to hear it? Only I've been here a while.'

'My fault.' She slipped off the gloves and put her hand over his. Her flesh was ice cold and the moment he looked harder he knew that something was badly wrong. There were cuts on the back of her hand. A couple of nails had been torn.

Maddox watched him inspecting the other hand, then she took off the glasses. A couple at a nearby table caught her image in the mirror behind the tiny counter and swapped glances. One of her eyes was nearly closed, the cheekbone beneath purpled with bruising. The other eye, less swollen, seeped a thin straw-coloured liquid. Maddox produced a tissue and gave it to Winter.

'Do you mind? I keep missing.'

Winter dabbed at the eye. You had to get into something serious to end up looking like this.

'You want to tell me what happened?'

'Not really, if you want the truth.'

'So why phone?'

'Good question.'

For a long moment Winter thought she wasn't going to come across. He'd been wrestling with a truly brutal headache since lunchtime, a particularly vicious pain that jellied his stomach, and the last thing he needed just now was this.

He gestured her closer, whispered in her ear.

'I'm going to count to ten,' he murmured. 'Either you tell me what happened or I'm off. One other thing.'

'What?' She was staring at him. She looked terrible.

'I get to keep these.'

She almost laughed. Winter slipped the glasses back over the wreckage of her face, then reached for his car keys.

'Somewhere quieter.' He'd taken control. 'Your place?'

She lived in an imposing block of 1960s flats on the seafront. Winter hadn't been to Rose Tower since he'd arrested a retired scrap dealer for funding a race-fixing scam at the city's greyhound stadium. From the tenth floor the view was sensational.

Maddox dropped the blinds. The low winter slant of the sun hurt the one eye that still worked.

'You don't mind an early dusk?' She dumped her

coat on the zebra-skin sofa, a blurred figure in the half-light, and stooped to a lamp on the nearby table.

'Not in the least.' Winter rubbed his own eyes and wondered whether to ask her for half a dozen aspirin but decided against it. 'Where did you get those?'

He was looking at a series of framed sepia prints, stepped across one wall. The photos showed scenes from a sand-blown treeless township in the middle of nowhere. It looked like desert country, maybe Africa. In one shot, a native in a turban was posing between two camels. In another a hollow-eyed white man in the rags of a shirt peered out of a gloomy interior. The table at which he sat appeared to be the only furniture in the room.

Maddox followed his pointing finger. She'd uncapped a bottle of Armagnac but seemed to be having trouble finding the right glasses.

'Remember you asked me about the face on the T-shirt the other day?' She nodded at the figure seated at the table. 'That's Rimbaud. He was a poet. Packed it all in and went off to Abyssinia. Lord of all he surveyed. Sort of.'

'But why's he on your wall?'

'I'm doing a PhD on him. At the university.'

'You're telling me you're a *student*?' The very idea made Winter take the weight off his feet. He found a chair by the window, some kind of antique, immensely uncomfortable.

'Mature student.' Maddox had settled for cut-glass tumblers. 'I got a BA years ago.'

'Here?'

'Bristol.' She poured a hefty measure of brandy and passed him the glass. 'This is to say sorry for keeping you waiting. If you want the truth, I nearly had second thoughts.'

'About talking to me?'

'About going out. Every girl has her pride. Even me.'

There was a hint of self-pity in her voice that didn't sit comfortably with a grand's worth of leather coat and a flat that gave you a seat in Southsea's dress circle. Actress, Winter thought, tucking the proposition away for later.

He tipped his glass to her in a silent toast and then swallowed a mouthful of Armagnac, relishing the way it torched a path down to his belly. Almost at once he began to feel better.

'You gave someone a smacking,' he suggested peaceably. 'And then they smacked you back.'

Maddox was in the kitchen now. He could see her through the half-open door. She was looking for something in the fridge. She seemed to have an obsession with making people feel good.

'You like hummus?' Her battered face appeared at the open door.

Winter hadn't a clue what she was talking about.

'Love it,' he said.

A plate arrived within seconds, a moist little hillock of beigy paste on a crescent of pitta bread. Another followed, a hastily chopped salad, garnished with parsley and pine nuts.

'Apologies for the tomatoes.' The scowl made her face even more lopsided. 'This time of year they're like bullets.'

'You still haven't told me.'

'I know. I'm getting there. Think opera.' She nodded down at the plate. 'This is the overture.'

She left the room. When she came back she was wearing baggy jeans and an oversize pullover. Winter's second mouthful of Armagnac had slipped effortlessly down but about the hummus he was less certain.

'You know something?' Maddox curled up on the sofa, unpeeling a banana.

'What?'

'You make me very nervous.'

'Why would I do that?'

'I don't know. It's not nervous like you might think. You don't exactly make *me* nervous. It's a holistic thing – something not quite right. Not with me, but you. Am I making any sense?'

'None. You gave me a bell, begged for a meet, and here we are. Is that a problem?'

'Not at all. But you're angry, I can tell. Either that or you're hurting. Am I right?'

In spite of himself Winter had to smile. She was more right than she could possibly know, though the last thing he planned to do right now was own up.

'Listen,' he said. 'This is a freebie, totally off the record. I know what you do for a living and there's nothing there that's going to put you in the shit. On the other hand I'm talking bollocks, aren't I?' He nodded at her face. 'Because you obviously *are* in the shit.'

Maddox eased her head back against the plumpness of a cushion.

'You're right. But in my defence I'd no idea.'

'About what?'

'That it would come to this.' Her hand briefly fluttered under one eye. 'You think you know someone, read them well, understand them. Then, wallop, it all kicks off . . .'

She turned her head towards the window, abandoning the banana and reaching for a box of tissues. Winter watched her, dimly beginning to understand.

'Who are we talking about?'

'Who do you think?'

'Wishart.'

'You're right.' She sniffed. 'Very perceptive, Mr Winter. The lovely Maurice. He of the Centurion Amex card and pigskin upholstery. Who'd have thought, eh? A man of his many talents.'

'Arsehole.' Winter reached down for his glass, surprised by the numbness in his fingertips. 'He really thumped you?'

'Last night. In this very room.'

'Why?'

'Because . . . ?' She frowned, turning the word into a question. 'I don't know, I just haven't a clue. Truthfully. It's a mystery to me. One minute we were talking about some gallery he wanted to take me to. The next I'm flat out on the carpet down there wondering what the fuck's going on. This wasn't playtime. He wasn't kidding. He meant it.'

'Did he say anything? Had anything kicked off earlier? A row maybe?'

'We don't row. It's not in the contract.'

'Was he pissed off, then?'

'About Friday night, definitely. That's why he came round. He thought it was gross, what happened at Steve's place. An outrage.'

'*He* thought it was gross.' Winter began to laugh.

'No, seriously, that's what he called it, an outrage. He said he had contacts. He said he'd be screwing you for trespass, or harassment, I forget exactly what. In any case that wasn't really it. Shit, I don't know. You do your best for a guy – try and please him, give him what he wants – but it's just never enough, you know what I mean?'

'Not really. What does he want?'

She gave the question some thought, then reached for another tissue.

'Me, all of me, all the time. He wants to lock me away.' She dabbed at her eye, then balled the tissue tightly in her fist. 'Take this place. He wants to pick up the rent, buy the lease, wrap it up in fancy paper, give it to me as a present with his name all over it.'

'And you?'

'I don't want any of that, don't need it. He buys three hours of my time twice a week and pays what I charge him. Beyond that, he hasn't got the right to a single second of my life. He knows that. He's a grown-up man. I'm selling a service. It's like I was a physiotherapist or a piano tuner or something. It's just a transaction. It's just business. And Christ, he seems to know enough about that.'

Winter listened to her, then ducked his head. There was a flaw in her argument, a bloody great hole, and he knew at once what it was.

'You've got it wrong about men, love. They never grow up.'

'Yeah? Maybe you're right. Doesn't help, though, does it? Wishart's a nightmare. He doesn't understand the word "no". He thinks there's nothing he can't buy, nothing he can't walk away with. Believe me, control freak doesn't begin to cover it.'

Winter nodded, mellow now. Time for some gentle research.

'What does he do for a living, then? How come all the dosh?'

'You really want to know?'

'Yes.'

'Why?'

'Because that's what I do.'

'Well . . .' She lay back, nursing her glass. 'He's got a company of his own, maybe more than one. He's forever giving me stuff. Hang on—'

She stored the glass carefully beside the sofa and slipped out of the room. Moments later she was back with a glossy-looking presentation pack. On the cover, expensively embossed against a montage of heavy weaponry, was the company name. 'Simulcra', it read, 'Tomorrow, Today'. Winter studied it, amused.

'What's in here, then? Bedtime reading?'

'It's a boast, a trophy. You're right, men are kids like that; they have to show off.'

Winter flicked through the material inside the pack. Simulcra appeared to offer state-of-the-art presentational services to military and aerospace people in the know. One brochure talked of three-day brainstorming sessions with an unlimited event horizon. Another listed the names retained by the company for high-profile roles within specially designed threat scenarios. Winter recognised some of these faces, people he'd last seen behind a desk on ITN news.

'I don't get any of this.' He tossed the pack back to her. 'What does he actually *do*?'

'It's hard to say. He started in the navy; high-flyer, got out early. Then he seems to have joined some chums over in Hamble. They were building motor cruisers, those big fuck-off boats you see in Antibes, and Maurice persuaded them to get into military stuff. I don't know the details. He's told me a million times but I never really listened. I know he was flying out to Africa a lot. Does that make sense?'

'No idea.' Winter nodded at the pack in her lap. 'How come he's buying all these names off the telly?'

'He says it's packaging. Glitz. What the client wants. He runs these conferences. They all get together in some huge RAF hangar in the middle of nowhere and he spends a fortune decking the place out, sets, video gear, special lighting, nice eats and drinks and then the celebs turn up to front the whole thing and the punters sit around for a day or two and basically get stuck into a huge video game. As far as I can gather, it's always about the end of the world. Maurice gets scriptwriters to plot out all this stuff, set little traps, and then the punters have to work out what to do, but it's Maurice who's pulling the strings. That's him in his element. He gets to play God for two whole days.'

'And there's money in it?'

'Shedloads. He's taking the whole thing public, going for a market listing, the whole PLC number. If I remembered the figures I could put you in a coma in seconds. He's obsessed with it.'

'And you understand all this bollocks? PLC? Public listing?'

'I'm afraid so. My brother's in the City, talks the same language. He and Maurice are made for each other.'

Winter fell silent, toying with his empty glass. It was difficult to be in this woman's company and not remember the wilder images from Friday night. For a moment, watching her stretch out on the sofa, he was overwhelmed with the thought of Chantilly cream. Then he pulled himself together. No wonder Wishart had got himself into a bit of a state.

'Is there a Mrs Wishart?'

'Of course there is. They're all married, every one of them.'

'Where does she live?'

'Wimbledon. Three kids, one still at school, two at Oxford. Summer hols on some fat cat's yacht. Christmas in Cape Town. The very best of everything.' She began to mimic Wishart's drawl. 'Alicia does it for me, Maddox. Best mother on the planet. Thinks in three languages. Cooks like an angel. Fucks like a bunny. Worships every bone in my feeble body.'

Winter laughed again. He was right about the actress. She loved performance, the chance to try a new role, and she was bloody good at it.

'So how did that make you feel?'

'Relieved, to be honest. It's all bullshit, of course. He makes it up to salve whatever conscience he has left but at least he still remembers her name.'

'And you think she knows about you? Camber Court? Eight-hundred-quid holes in the housekeeping?'

'Haven't a clue. Probably not, not in any detail, but she'd be stupid not to make the odd assumption, wouldn't she? People like Wishart are like dogs. They can't pass a lamp post without wanting to piss on it. It's all smell, scent, territory. Take the world by the throat, never let go. We understand that, us girlies, and some of us have the wit to turn it into a decent living. But that's not what he wants now, not any longer. So far I've been a decent entrée in his life. Now he wants the whole fucking menu.'

'Yeah.' Winter nodded. 'And the cook.'

'Exactly. But there's a problem, *n'est-ce pas?* Because the cook ain't for sale.' She stared at him. 'What's the matter?'

Winter had got to his feet. With a terrible certainty, he knew he was going to throw up. He made it as far as the bathroom. Maddox found him hugging the bidet.

'Hummus.' She was looking down at the bowl. 'My fault.'

Winter groped blindly for a towel. She knelt beside him with a damp flannel, mopped his mouth, cradled his bursting head.

'I think I'm going to die,' Winter gasped.

Maddox said nothing, just held him. Then, very softly, she began to sing. It was a song he'd never heard before, a lullaby, something French. Another part to play, he thought dimly. Another role in some passing stranger's life. Would she be charging him for the last couple of hours? Handing him a bill at the door? The thunder in his head grew and grew. Desperate now, he reached for the bidet again. More hummus. What a state to get into.

At length his stomach was empty. He struggled uncertainly to his feet, felt for the edge of the handbasin, refused to look at the face in the mirror. He could sense, rather than feel, her presence behind him. Then came the lightest of embraces, her arms around him, her head nestled on his shoulder.

'I was right, wasn't I?' she murmured. 'There's something very wrong with you.'

Six

Monday, 23 February 2004

A four-hour search for Gary Morgan ended at ten to eight, in Sandown. He was watching football with a noisy crowd of locals in a pub called the Smugglers, a couple of streets back from the seafront. Five minutes into the first half, Arsenal were winning 1–0.

Faraday slipped into the empty seat beside him. In this company the last thing Morgan wanted on public display was a warrant card.

'The name's Joe.' Faraday patted him on the arm. 'Friend of Darren Webster.'

Morgan shot him a look. He was on the small side, paunchy, with thinning hair and a small gold cross hanging from one ear lobe. The bruises around his eyes and cheekbones had yellowed but the damage was unmistakable.

He reached for his drink, visibly alarmed.

'Workmates, are you?'

'That's right.' Faraday smiled. 'Shall we do this outside?'

Tracy Barber was waiting in the back of the car, fifty metres up the street. She'd cracked the final clue to Morgan's whereabouts, returning to his basement flat and managing to make contact with the neighbour upstairs. No friend of Morgan, she'd advised Barber to try the Smugglers. Little creep spent most evenings there. God knows where he got the money.

Faraday held the rear door open while Morgan slipped into the back. He'd zipped up his leather jacket against the chill of the evening and he grunted something Faraday didn't catch as Barber patted the empty seat beside her.

Faraday got behind the wheel.

'Where to?' He caught Morgan's eye in the rear-view mirror. 'Your shout.'

Morgan told him to take a left at the end of the street, then follow the main road north towards Brading. Once they'd left the clutter of Sandown, he warned of a side road off to the right.

'It's just before the next bend,' Morgan muttered. 'Easy to miss.'

Slowing for the turn, Faraday wondered just how many times Morgan had made this journey before. The side road was narrow and began to steepen at once, tall hedgerows on either side, gaunt, leafless trees looming briefly out of the darkness in the glare of the headlights. At the top of the hill Faraday spotted an open farm gate and an apron of churned-up mud, compacted with ashes.

'Here's fine. Just park up behind the hedge. Kids use the field for scrambling. This time of night nobody bothers you.'

Faraday took his word for it. It was important that Morgan felt at ease. Better this, he thought, than the over-lit menace of an interview room at Shanklin nick.

Faraday killed the engine. Barber was to take the lead.

'We talked to your mate Pelly this afternoon,' she said.

'*Mate?* You have to be joking. He's a psycho, that man. Americans make films about nutters like him.'

He began to tally the number of locals Pelly had

nearly put in hospital. A plumber who'd had one too many moans about late payment on an invoice. A learner driver off an estate in Lake who'd got in Pelly's way in the big Tesco car park over towards Ryde. The postman on Pelly's round who'd left the gate open three mornings running. Listening to this catalogue of alleged assaults, Faraday wasn't altogether convinced. Neither was Barber.

'He beat them *all* up? Every single one?'

'As good as.'

'And no one complained?'

'You wouldn't. You don't. Not with a bloke like him. He's scary. Paranoid as fuck.'

'What about you?'

'Yeah, exactly. You think I got this lot by walking into a door or something? Falling downstairs?'

Barber's soft laugh died away. Faraday could hear wind in the trees and, very faintly, the call of a lapwing.

'If he's that bad, why did you cross him?' he asked.

'Me? Cross him?' Morgan leaned forward, outraged. 'What did he tell you, then?'

'He said you were after his missus.'

'That's bollocks.'

'He said you fancied her and invited her down the pub for a drink. The pub bit's right, at least. We checked up this afternoon. Friday before Christmas, wasn't it? Happened outside in the street. Landlord had to call an ambulance.'

'Yeah, dead right. Imagine what kind of Christmas I fucking had. You could have strung my head up with the balloons. I looked like the Elephant Man.'

'And was his wife in the pub with you?'

Morgan hesitated a moment, sat back again.

'Yeah . . .' he admitted.

131

'What's she like, then?'

'Lovely.'

'What does that mean?'

'Just lovely. Young, pretty, sweet – ask anyone. They're not married, though. Not really.'

'That's not what Mr Pelly says.'

'Of course he doesn't and he ain't about to either, is he?' He lapsed briefly into silence, picking at a scab on his chin. 'The woman he shags is Brenda Atley. Everyone knows that.'

'So what about this wife of his?'

Another silence. Miles away, back on the main road, the growl of a heavy truck grinding up a hill.

'Her name's Lajla,' Morgan said at last. 'She's Bosnian; grew up there. Must have put up with all sorts.'

'The war, you mean?'

'Yeah, that and now Pelly. Fuck knows what she's doing with him.'

'She definitely lives there? In the home?'

'Too right. She's got a little girl, a daughter, Fida.'

'What sort of age?'

'Eleven last birthday. I bought her a Walkman. Thrilled to bits she was.'

'Is Fida blonde? Pretty?'

'That's her.'

Faraday nodded to himself. Fida must have been the girl who opened the door to them this afternoon, up at the home.

Morgan was opening up now, warmed by their interest.

'Lajla and the little girl have got a flat at the back of the old folks' home. They've been there forever as far as I know.'

'But the girl's not Pelly's?'

'No way.'

'How do you know?'

'I asked Lajla. She said she brought her daughter with her when she left Bosnia.'

'What else did she say?'

'Nothing. She won't talk about that side of it at all. But you get her by herself, right mood, and like I say, she's lovely.'

'Fine.' Barber's voice was edged with impatience. 'But I still don't get it about the marriage. She and Pelly, are they married or not?'

'Pelly says so.'

'But he'd know, wouldn't he? You get one of those nice certificates. Have a party.'

'Pelly doesn't do parties. He's that tight . . . miserable bastard.'

'What about the certificate?'

'She's certainly got one of them . . . But then she'd have to, wouldn't she?'

'Why?'

'To stay in the country. I know the rest of Pelly's foreign friends are illegals but they're not on the premises like Lajla. She's a bit close to home. You'd be asking for trouble.'

'You're saying he married her to make her legit?'

'I'm telling you they don't screw. If you don't believe me, go and take a look at Brenda Atley. She works as a receptionist at the VW garage in town, gets Pelly deals on his servicing. Built like a brick shit house. Just right for an animal like Pelly.'

'And Lajla?'

'Brenda would piss all over her. I swear it, God's honour, there's nothing between them.'

'So why did he beat you up?' Faraday asked.

133

'Good fucking question.' Morgan sounded genuinely aggrieved. 'You think I'd go messing with Lajla if I really thought they kipped together? If I fancied suicide, I'd find myself a cliff. Plenty round here, I tell you, and a fuck sight less painful.'

Faraday stared into the darkness, thinking of Tennyson Down. Maybe Morgan was luckier than he knew.

'So why did he thump you?' Faraday repeated. 'If it wasn't over Lajla?'

Morgan didn't have an answer. At length he mumbled something about Pelly being a sadist, about decking blokes for the pleasure of it, but it didn't take Faraday any closer to the truth.

Barber stirred in the back.

'You told DC Webster that Pelly brings in asylum seekers.'

'He does. Half the island would tell you that.'

'Can you prove it?'

'No, and I'm not doing any statements or anything, but Darren's got a list of addresses I gave him, doss places here and down in Ventnor, and I'm telling you they're no go for white guys. Say you're from up north somewhere, English born and bred, got a passport, driving licence, down for the summer jobs, you wouldn't have a prayer if you wanted a room in one of Pelly's places. It's wall-to-wall asylos and I bet they haven't got a passport between them. So how come no one's asking questions? How come he gets away with it the way he does?'

It was a good question and just now Faraday didn't have an answer.

'He brings drugs in as well?' he queried.

For the first time Morgan was less eager to blacken Pelly's name. There were some heavy people out there, he muttered. Ryde on a Monday lunchtime was full of

Scousers making delivery runs, hot over from Pompey. They'd sewn up the local market for smack and crack cocaine and Pelly, oddly enough, had been the only one to take them on.

'Brave fucking move,' Morgan conceded. 'Must prove he's a nutter.'

'But you're saying he's in the same business? Ships heroin in from abroad?'

'That's the word.'

'And you believe it?'

'I . . . I don't know. If there's money to be made – and there is – he probably couldn't resist it. But hand on heart? Pass.'

Faraday was spooling backwards through this afternoon's exchanges with Pelly, trying to remember what else he needed to check out before he got to the meat of this interview. Barber cut in.

'Chris Unwin . . .' She was looking at Morgan. 'You told DC Webster there was some kind of row at the home, back in October.'

'There was.'

'How do you know?'

'Lajla told me. She was the one who overheard what was going down. He's got some kind of office in there. The door was open. The two of them were yelling at each other. She caught Unwin's gran's name, assumed it was all about her.'

'And threats?'

'Pelly promised to do him. That's not a threat, not coming from Pelly it isn't.'

'Do him?'

'Kill him.'

'Over Unwin's *granny*? Are you serious?'

'Doesn't have to be just her.' Morgan was on the defensive now. 'Maybe there's other stuff between

135

them, stuff we don't know about. Unwin's not from round here. He's a Pompey boy. Could be up to anything.'

'Like what?'

'No idea. But there's got to be someone to ship all those blokes over to the mainland when the work dries up, hasn't there?'

'That's a supposition, Mr Morgan,' Faraday pointed out. 'Pelly says this row never happened. No confrontation. No shouting. No threats. Nothing.'

'Well he would, wouldn't he? Why don't you talk to Lajla? She's the one who knows.'

'We will.'

Faraday eyed Morgan in the rear-view mirror. There was something about the timeline here that disturbed him. At length, he put it into words.

'You got in touch with the Intelligence DS at Shanklin on Friday. Is that right?'

'Yeah. There or thereabouts.'

'And a couple of days earlier the media carried details of a headless body under the cliffs on Tennyson Down. White male. Maybe Unwin's age. It was on TV on Tuesday night.'

'That's right. That's where I saw it.'

'Which is why you made the call in the first place. Putting two and two together . . .'

'Exactly.' Morgan sounded pleased with himself, the good citizen doing his bit for law and order.

There was a long silence. Barber had her head back on the seat, her eyes closed, a smile on her face. Finally Faraday shifted his weight in the front, peered round at Morgan. He was choosing his words carefully.

'Would it be silly of me to wonder why it took you three days to pick up the phone?'

'I was busy,' Morgan said at once. 'It never occurred to me.'

'Never occurred to you to do what?'

'To associate Unwin with this body they were going on about.'

'It didn't? You hadn't been looking in the mirror, every day since Pelly roughed you up? Hadn't been wondering how you could –' Faraday shrugged '– repay the favour?'

'I'm not with you.'

'Yes, you are. It may not explain everything, it may not even be relevant, but I'm just wondering how many birds you knocked down with that one call. Get Pelly off the plot, maybe scare him off the island, and it's suddenly looking good, isn't it? You and the lovely Lajla? No one to worry about when you walk her home?' Faraday reached for the ignition key and stirred the engine into life. 'Just a thought, my friend, that's all.'

Winter awoke in darkness. For a second or two he hadn't a clue where he was. There was a sharp scent of lemons, underscored with something muskier. A strip of light on the wall opposite suggested a window and he could hear the soft nudge of blinds against the frame. He rolled over, mystified, and reached out. Nothing. Except four green digits on a bedside clock. 19.17. Impossible.

'What happened to the rest of the day?'

He'd walked into Maddox's lounge. She was sprawled on the floor, still in her jeans and pullover, absorbed in a movie. Winter watched it for a moment or two. *The Bridges of Madison County*. He'd seen it four times.

He rubbed his eyes. His headache, by some miracle,

had gone. He could even read the label on the leather coat she'd left draped over the back of the sofa. Monsoon.

'So what happened?'

'You don't remember?' Maddox was looking up at him. Her face, if anything, looked worse, the blacks and blues beginning to acquire a faint tint of yellow.

'Nothing. I threw up in that nice bathroom of yours, made a real mess of it, then . . .' Winter shrugged. 'Nothing.'

'That's a good sign. I did some reiki.'

'Some what?'

'Reiki. It's energy healing. You were out of it really, flat on your back in the spare bedroom.'

'You mean unconscious?'

'That's what it looked like.'

'You didn't think –' Winter was trying to visualise the scene '– to call an ambulance? Get a doctor?'

'No, reiki's better. You also came to at one point and asked for tablets. I happened to have some arnica. Double-dosed you.'

'Really?' She might have been describing a week or two in some foreign country, a remote Spanish village he'd never heard of. 'Arnica?'

'It's homeopathic. You feel any better?'

'Heaps.'

'Well then . . . ' She pulled down a couple of extra cushions from the sofa and made room for him on the carpet. 'This bit's where they get it on in the kitchen. Meryl Streep's unbelievable.'

The movie over, she made him some scrambled eggs. Given the prospect of what awaited him at home in the bungalow at Bedhampton – an empty fridge, the ticking of the kitchen clock – Winter was only too happy to prop himself against the sofa, balance the plate on his knees and settle in for the evening. He hadn't the first idea what Maddox wanted but if it boiled down to company then it very definitely suited his immediate plans. Already, she seemed to be viewing him like some kind of elder brother. Being with her felt the easiest thing in the world.

'What will you do with all those punters of yours?' The eggs were delicious. 'Now that Camber Court's off the plot?'

She said she didn't know, and what's more she didn't care. After last night nothing mattered except putting Maurice Wishart back in his box. She never wanted to see him again and if that drew a line under her career as a call girl, then so be it.

'Eight hundred quid a trick?' Winter couldn't believe it. 'Where else are you going to find that kind of money?'

'You think I should just pick up somewhere else?'

'Of course. Otherwise you'll end up in some bar or other. Four fifty an hour serving infant drunks all night. No contest, is it?'

'You're right . . .' She mopped her plate with a crust of bread. 'But it's not that simple. If it was just the sex I could hire a room somewhere, go to a decent hotel, but Camber Court was about all kinds of stuff. Classy food, the right wines, nice civilised vibe, good conversation. The guys used it like a kind of gentlemen's club and that worked for me, too. So whatever happened, I'd still need a Steve Richardson.' She glanced sideways at him. 'Are you offering?'

'I'm a crap cook. Plus I'm not gay.'

'Would that matter?'

'It might. Got any more of this?'

She fetched the saucepan from the kitchen and

spooned the remains onto Winter's plate. She'd put something extra in it, a smokiness he couldn't explain.

'Nam pla.' She licked a finger. 'Thai fish sauce.'

She got to her feet and began to sort through a box of DVDs. She wanted to show him a French movie she'd just bought.

'Has it got subtitles?'

'If you need them.'

'I need them.'

'Why don't I translate for you? Might be more fun.'

'OK.' Winter shrugged. 'Whatever.'

She found the DVD, then hunted for the remote control. The TV was brand new, a monster Panasonic with surround sound, and Winter caught himself working out how many hours she'd have to spend hosing down her clients with Chantilly cream to afford it. Maybe she was right. Maybe she was just like every other lifestyle professional, an expensive physio with no hang-ups about turning other people's fantasies into the real thing.

The movie began. Two scruffy French kids were walking down a country road, having a laugh.

'Do you enjoy it? Seriously?'

Maddox was trying to keep pace with the dialogue. She broke off in mid-sentence.

'Enjoy what?'

'The sex. Getting it on with punters like Wishart?'

'Yes, I do. It helps not to think too hard . . . but yes. The answer's yes.'

'But he's horrible.'

'No, he's not. Not until last night, anyway. He's just a guy I shag. I please him. He gives me money. He makes a fool of himself. He thinks he's in control. That makes me laugh sometimes, the expression on these guys' faces. It's not just Maurice, it's all of them. They're all naked in ways they'll never understand.'

'You've got a favourite?'

'Yes. But I'm not telling.'

'What makes him a favourite?'

'Not what you think.'

'What, then?'

'You really want to know?' Winter nodded. 'It's his sense of humour. He sees through it all. Inherited money. Makes all the difference.'

'You're serious?'

'Absolutely. The problem with people like Wishart is they've come from nowhere, or nowhere very special. They've had to fight for what they've got. They have to believe in themselves, be aware of themselves, and that can limit conversation, take my word for it. These people have no sense of perspective, no hinterland. They're forever banged up with their own bloody self-importance. Me, me, me. And another thing –' she'd abandoned the film completely '– they know the price of everything and the value of nothing. It's all numbers to them. Let a guy like Maurice screw you three times in a session and he's very, very happy.'

'And this other bloke, whoever he is?'

'He thinks it's all a huge joke. He's not an idiot, far from it; in fact he's exceptionally bright. With him I learn things and one of the reasons I learn things is that he makes it easy for me to listen. Often we don't make love at all, not properly.'

'Really?' Winter tried to visualise eight hundred quid's worth of quality conversation but couldn't. The two urchins on screen were in a wood now. Cutaways to a truckload of German troops suggested something nasty in the offing. Winter turned back to Maddox, still wanting answers.

'So how come you're so bloody sure of yourself?'

'What do you mean?'

'All this stuff about self-made men. I'm not saying you're wrong. I just want to know how you've sussed these people.'

'My family have a huge estate in Wiltshire.' She tried to soften the news with a lopsided smile. 'Inherited money, I'm afraid. So maybe that makes me an expert.'

Winter was vague about the ways of the aristocracy. Titled families were thin on the ground in Pompey but the thought of Maddox as a duchess brought an added sparkle to the evening. He put his empty plate to one side.

'Do they know what you're up to? Mummy and Daddy?'

'Christ no, but I'm not sure they'd care, even if they did. The last time I saw my mother was six years ago. She met me off the train at Templecombe station. She was so pissed I had to try all the cars in the car park until one fitted her key. Turned out to be a Metro she'd borrowed from one of the gardeners. There's a little glove pocket on the driver's side that's perfect for those quarter-litre bottles of vodka. Getting home was a problem, too. It was dark and she couldn't remember the way. Ever ended up in Gillingham? Don't bother . . .'

Winter fought the impulse to applaud. Not only had she cured his headache. She also made him laugh.

'So where's Daddy in all this?'

'He lives in Paris with a Russian princess, a descendant of the Romanovs. They've got this huge apartment near the Bois de Boulogne. That's where I learned my French.'

'You still see him?'

'Once in a while. He's a gorgeous man but he was the one who disinherited me so it can get quite tricky.'

'We're talking serious money?'

'More than a million.'

'Shit. How did you upset him?'

'By coming here.'

'Pompey cost you a million quid?' Winter thought that sounded harsh.

'It wasn't the city, it was the company I was keeping. Daddy had a friend. This guy had been a para colonel in Algeria during the emergency and he joined the plot against de Gaulle. Daddy thought that was shameful and told Philippe so, warned him he'd be opening the door to the communists. They had a gigantic falling-out, which was a shame because a couple of years ago I came along and fell in love with the man. He's more than twice my age, quite a lot more, but he's an angel in every way. Men are like furniture. You shouldn't look at anything less than sixty years old.'

Winter did the sums. Fifteen years to go, he thought.

'You brought this guy here?'

'I did. I'd just started the PhD and I wanted to find out about the place. We had a little flat off Albert Road. *Mon père* had cut me out by then so I was teaching a bit of French at the university to help out with the groceries. I'm afraid Philippe didn't survive Portsmouth. Or maybe it was me he couldn't stand. Either way, he was back in Paris by Christmas, ringing my dad up and telling him what a mess I was making of my life, so I expect they're best buddies again now.'

'And the money?'

'The Russian princess has been doing her best, she's a sweet old thing, but my pa is one of those people who dig themselves in. Point of honour. Never change

143

your mind. Sad really, isn't it? *Desheritée. Définitivement pour toujours.*' She rolled over, her face inches from Winter's. 'So what's your secret?' she whispered. 'How come you passed out in my bathroom?'

Winter said he didn't know. He'd been getting pains. He saw bubbles everywhere. Sometimes he spewed.

'Have you seen anyone about it?'

'The doctor. I'm on some kind of list. One day they'll put me in front of a consultant. Then they'll cart me off to the knacker's yard.'

He told her briefly about Joannie, his wife. Afloat on an ocean of morphine, she'd sailed off to God knows where. To be honest, he said, he thought he was heading the same way. Worse still, the thought was beginning to frighten him.

Maddox chuckled. One finger was tracing patterns across his face.

'There's always an alternative,' she murmured. 'Believe me.'

'No chance. They wrote her off the moment they saw her.'

'I meant you.'

'Oh yeah . . . ? He looked at her. 'Like what, exactly?'

'Like we do a deal.'

'A what?'

'A deal. You sort out Mr Wishart and I mend your head.'

'How?'

'Trust me.' She propped herself on one elbow. 'No queues. No waiting lists. No angst about the men in the white coats.'

'Are we talking sex here?'

'No.'

144

'Shame.' Winter gazed at her a moment. 'What is it, then? What's in it for me?'

'You get your head back. And maybe other bits of you, depends on how good a subject you are. And if you're *really* lucky—'

Winter's mobile began to ring. He fetched it from his jacket pocket, checked the number. Jimmy Suttle.

'So where were you?' Suttle demanded.

'When?'

'This afternoon. At the Bridewell. I waited the best part of an hour.'

It dawned on Winter that they'd agreed a session in the interview suite with the girl, Cécile.

'I thought I'd leave it to you,' Winter said at once. 'How did it go?'

'It didn't. She never showed. Thanks for the support, though. Appreciate it.' Winter heard an explosion of laughter in the background. Pub, he thought. Then Suttle was back on the phone, more acid than ever. 'So where do we go next, then? Blag a couple of Easyjets off Cathy Lamb? Fly down to Courchevel? Take our ski gear? Try our luck with Maddox again?'

'No need.' Winter began to chuckle. 'I'm looking at her now.'

'You're *what*?'

'Forget it, son. Bell you later.' About to end the call, he put the mobile to his ear again, still laughing. 'Ever had hummus?'

Seven

Tuesday, 24 February 2004

The Major Crimes Suite at Kingston Crescent was virtually empty when Faraday arrived the following morning. He paused outside the office shared by the two Management Assistants. Their door was open.

'Where is everyone?'

'Newbridge. Nick turned up a really tasty lead and Mr Willard's gone for broke, thrown everyone at it.'

'Tasty how?'

'Nick thinks it may be some kind of media tiff, maybe a revenge killing. We don't know the details but Nick says we're talking household names. The press and telly are all over it. The boss thinks it's Christmas.'

Faraday was trying to imagine a professional falling-out serious enough to warrant a double homicide. On the face of it a line of inquiry like this would seem far-fetched but the more he'd seen of TV recently, the more he'd begun to wonder about the blurring of the line between fact and fiction. People thrived on the bizarre. They'd do anything to get noticed. So maybe Nick Hayder was right. Two bodies would certainly compel attention.

'He's on the mobile? Willard?'

'Was ten minutes ago.'

Faraday walked down the corridor to his office. Tracy Barber appeared from the tiny kitchen at the

146

end. She was carrying two cups of coffee and had a packet of Jammie Dodgers tucked under one arm.

They settled in Faraday's office. Barber broke out the biscuits while Faraday talked on the phone to Willard. The Detective Superintendent, it appeared, had made himself at home in the Control Room Support Vehicle. This mobile unit carried an awesome range of kit and was a prized force resource. If you were looking for evidence that Willard had struck career gold, then this was surely it.

'The Isle of Wight, sir,' Faraday reminded him. 'Bloke with no head.'

Willard, in the excitement of the last twenty-four hours, seemed to have forgotten about Tennyson Down. Faraday updated him on yesterday's developments. This morning he was proposing to drive up to London and talk to Chris Unwin's mother. DC Barber had already made contact and Mrs Unwin would be available at noon.

'Do it.' Willard was juggling this conversation with at least two others. 'What about Colin Irving's lad?'

'Webster? He's still on division, sir. And that's probably where he belongs.'

'You don't need help?'

'Not so far.'

'Good. Keep me briefed.'

The line went dead. Barber was looking troubled. She and Faraday had talked about Darren Webster on the ferry back last night and she'd done her best to defend the young DC. Now it was all too obvious that she'd wasted her breath.

'You don't think you're being a bit harsh on the lad? Ambition's not a crime.'

'Never said it was, Tracy, but the boy lied. Thought he'd get away with it and didn't. That makes him arrogant as well as stupid.' He tucked an *A–Z* into his briefcase. 'Twenty years ago he'd have been back in uniform for a stunt like that.' Faraday glanced at his watch. 'We off then?'

After making contact on the phone, Tracy Barber had arranged to meet Ellie Unwin at the family health centre where she worked as a practice nurse. The centre was a low, modern-looking complex tucked away behind a shopping mall in the middle of Lewisham. The tiny car park was full and Faraday had to drive around the neighbourhood for a while before he spotted a space. Back at the health centre one of the receptionists showed them into a small, bare office which evidently served as a crash pad for the stroppier clientele. Apart from a table, three chairs and a handbasin, Faraday could see nothing breakable.

'The mid-afternoon drunks are the worst,' the receptionist said cheerfully. 'You lot won't turn out any more for harassment so we stick them in here with a pile of comics and keep our fingers crossed.'

Ellie Unwin joined them minutes later. She was a tall, attractive woman in her late forties who seemed strangely suited to the uniform. She had full lips and a slightly nervous smile. Tracy Barber eyed her with interest.

Faraday explained briefly that they were trying to trace her son. They'd be grateful for his full name and date of birth.

'Chrissie? Why?'

'At this stage, Mrs Unwin, I'm afraid I can't say.'

'Is he in trouble?'

'We hope not.' He smiled at her, then asked again for a date of birth.

'Twenty-first of October 1976.'

'Full name?'

'Christopher Dudley Unwin.'

'And when were you last in contact?'

She looked at Faraday a moment, then found a perch on the table and frowned. DC Barber was making notes.

'A while back,' she said finally. 'In fact last summer. July? August? He was up here for some concert or other. Dropped in to see Julie's new baby.'

Julie was her daughter. She had two young kids of her own and still shared the house with her mother. One day, said Mrs Unwin, she might get the place to herself but she wasn't counting on it. With kids these days, babies seemed to be a lifestyle option.

'Have you been in touch with your son since August? Talked on the phone at all? Got a letter? Postcard?'

'No.' She shook her head. 'And he's my stepson, not my natural son. Not that that should make a difference, of course.'

Faraday and Barber exchanged glances. DNA from Mrs Unwin might have been a useful match for the body in the fridge.

'What about his father?' It was Barber.

'We divorced ten years ago.'

'Are you still in touch?'

'No.'

'His natural mother?'

'She died years ago. Fell off a mountain in Scotland.'

Faraday, making notes, looked up. Helpful DNA simply wasn't available.

'So you haven't seen Chris since last summer. Is that normal? Not being in touch for so long?'

'Oh yes, yes, perfectly normal. Chrissie goes months and months and no one hears a peep.'

'Don't you wonder where he is? What he's up to?'

'Of course I do, always have done, but it makes no difference. He's twenty-eight now but even when he was younger he just upped sticks and did his own thing. Free spirit, Chrissie. Can't ever pin him down.'

'Do you have an address for him, Mrs Unwin?' It was Barber again.

Ellie Unwin nodded. The address was in her book at home. She could phone through and ask Julie to look. She went back to the treatment room to make the call. When she returned, she handed Tracy Barber a slip of paper.

'Sorry about the writing,' she said.

Barber peered at the address, then handed it to Faraday. Number 267 Bath Road, Southsea. Faraday tried to visualise the street, one of a number that straddled the border between Southsea and Portsmouth. Terraced houses, he thought. Nightmare parking and far too many students.

'Has he lived there long?'

'Quite a while, I think. Couple of years maybe.'

'Does he live alone?'

'Depends. Sometimes he gets lucky but nothing seems to last.'

'You mean relationships?'

'Yes.' She looked from one face to the other, apologetic. 'To be honest I'm a bit out of my depth here. Chrissie and us . . . we're not really that close. It's not like me and Julie . . .'

'So he may have moved on?'

'Yes.'

'Without you knowing?'

'Yes.'

Faraday nodded, wondering if something similar would ever happen to himself and J-J. Just now it seemed inconceivable but more and more families appeared to be coming apart at the seams.

'What about Chrissie's grandmother? We understand—'

'Loves her to bits,' Ellie Unwin said at once. 'She's not a real granny, not a blood granny, but he worships her. Always has.'

She began to talk about the home on the Isle of Wight, how her son made the time and effort to keep in touch, dropping in whenever he could. When he was in his teens and his gran was living by herself in the big family house in Haslemere, he'd often take the train up there and stay for a couple of days. To be frank, she often thought that he preferred Granny's company to her own.

'Funny, really,' she concluded. 'These days Mum hasn't got a clue who Chrissie is most of the time yet it doesn't seem to make the slightest bit of difference. When I phone up the home sometimes, just to find out how Mum is, they'll tell me Chrissie's been over again. Apparently he'll sit with her for hours, just nattering away to her. Maybe that's the secret. Maybe we got a bit much for him. Maybe he prefers talking to a virtual stranger.'

Barber asked her whether she had any photos of her son. She thought about the question.

'You mean something recent?'

'Yes.'

'Afraid not. The last one I can think of at the moment is when he was at school. That's years ago.'

'No holiday snaps? Nothing from a family get-together? Someone's wedding, maybe?'

'No.' She shook her head. 'Chrissie was never interested in that kind of do.'

'How about Christmas? Did you hear from him then at all? Card, maybe? Text message?'

'No.' She was thinking hard. 'Definitely not.' She held her hands wide, embarrassed now. 'I know it might sound odd but that's the way it is. Chrissie's fine. He'll always be fine. I'm sure he gets into the odd scrape but that boy could charm his way out of a paper bag.' The smile again, ever more anxious. 'Know what I mean?'

The Eldon lies on the western edges of Somerstown, a pub favoured by a clientele that changes by the hour. Lunchtimes, it attracts barristers and the odd journalist from the nearby Crown Court. Sitting at a table in the window, Winter could hear the bells of the Guildhall clock as he tucked into a plateful of steak and kidney pie. Noon, he thought, reaching for the brown sauce.

He'd spent the morning with a solicitor from the CPS, tidying up details on a drugs case due in court early next week. Jimmy Suttle, fresh from a morning at his desk in the squad room at Kingston Crescent, would be joining him any minute. For the time being, though, Winter relished the chance to review the last twenty-four hours.

He'd been in the job since he'd left school. The transfer to CID had come relatively early, and twenty years as a detective had given him a profoundly cynical take on human nature. He'd met men who raped and tortured because they felt in the mood. He'd spent profitable hours befriending junkies who'd sell their kids for the price of the next fix. He'd stalked bent traders through jungles of paperwork to discover scams so elegant that they deserved a quiet round of applause. Yet never had he come across anyone quite like Maddox.

Even the name was a challenge. Was Maddox her Christian name? Was it the name of the dynasty that stretched back over generations of Wiltshire land-owners? Did it appear in her passport and driving licence? Her bank statements and birth certificate? Or was Maddox a label she'd discovered under some stone or other, taken a fancy to, and now adopted for any purpose it might serve? Back last Friday at Camber Court, with Richardson's flat being ripped apart by the search team, she'd identified herself as simply Maddox and refused to qualify it in any way. Four days later, as both detective and perhaps friend, Winter was no closer to pinning her down.

It was this elusiveness more than anything else that fascinated him. The way she looked, the way she walked, compelled attention. Pass her in the street and you'd pause to watch her go by. Beautiful? Of course. But something else, too, a sense of detachment, a sense of not quite belonging to the busy clutter of anyone else's life. Whether or not this apartness was a front, a carefully rehearsed pose to keep the world at arm's length, Winter didn't know. Last night, in her flat, she'd seemed almost normal. Real bruises. Real pain. But the closer he'd come to her, the stronger grew his conviction that the real Maddox, whoever she might be, was still under lock and key. Naked, she was available to any man with eight hundred quid to blow. But even for that kind of money you'd get scarely a glimpse of the genuine article.

This notion of a counterfeit personality stirred him in all kinds of ways, some of them deeply personal. Winter knew a great deal about the business of camouflage, of adapting his accent, his manner, even his body language, in order to make himself at home in someone else's head. That was the way you coaxed a man towards confession and a ten-year sentence, and it helped immeasurably if you could pull off the trick without a moment's self-doubt or compunction. A good detective could ghost his way into anyone's life, and last night, for the first time, he'd realised that he shared this talent with the likes of Maddox. They both knew how to dissemble, how to bluff, how to hide. And they'd both, for a price, screw more or less anyone.

'Did you?' It was Jimmy Suttle. He had a pint of lager in one hand and a copy of the *News* in the other. He pulled out the other chair with his foot and sat down.

'Did I what?'

'Shag her? Last night?'

'Might have done.' Winter speared the last cube of beef. 'What do you think?'

Suttle swallowed a mouthful of lager. The best part of a day with Richardson's DVDs had given him some extremely intimate glimpses of Maddox in action and he still couldn't picture Winter's bulk on the receiving end. For one thing, Winter was far too mean to pay for it. For another, Maddox didn't look like the kind of woman to offer him a freebie. Which probably meant a stand-off.

'You didn't,' he said at last. 'But you're regretting it.'

'Close.'

'You did. And you're regretting it.'

'Afraid not.'

'What, then?'

'You want the truth? We watched a couple of French movies and talked about a bloke called Arthur Rimbaud. She told me a bit about herself and then put me to bed.'

'At her place?'

'Of course.'

'And kissed you goodnight?'

'Maybe.' Winter reached for the paper napkin. 'Maybe not.'

Winter had never done coy before, emphatically not with Suttle, and the young DC couldn't believe it. Whatever spell this woman cast, she certainly had the measure of Paul Winter.

'She's in there, isn't she? Under your skin?'

'Bollocks.'

'Proves it.' Suttle began to laugh. 'Look at you. French movies? Arthur Thingy? This is student talk. Whatever happened to the fanny rat we all know and love? Talk any woman into bed? Where did all that go?'

'Good question.' Winter pushed his plate away and glanced at his watch. 'I talked to Cathy Lamb this morning. She's happy we go after him.'

'Who?'

'Who?' Winter looked up in surprise. 'Wishart, of course.'

Ten minutes on the internet had already given Winter a business address for Simulcra. Wishart ran the company from an office in Baltic House, an unlovely modern colossus at the motorway end of Kingston Crescent. The fact that Wishart was less than a minute's walk from the nick that housed the Pompey Crime Squad Winter viewed as an exceptionally good omen.

Simulcra was on the seventh floor. An outer office was manned by a middle-aged woman with brutally cropped hair and an expensive tan.

'Been somewhere nice?' Winter had already pocketed the warrant card.

'Bali.'

'OK, was it?'

'Lovely. What can I do for you, Mr Winter?'

'I'd like a word with Mr Wishart.'

'I'm afraid you can't.'

'Why's that?'

'He's in Poland.'

Winter was looking at the framed photo on the wall behind her. Half a dozen men in dinner jackets were seated at a circular table at some function or other, beaming at the camera. Winter recognised a member of the Shadow Cabinet plus a female TV reporter who'd made her name in the first Gulf War. Maurice Wishart was sitting between them.

A phone began to ring. The woman behind the desk was still looking up at Winter. Was there any way she might be able to help him?

'Not really.' Winter nodded at the single door that must have led to Wishart's office. 'When's he back, then?'

'Thursday.' The woman reached for the phone. 'Late-morning flight out of Warsaw.'

Suttle stayed in the car while Winter sorted out a search warrant. The duty magistrate was evidently an easy sell because Winter was back behind the wheel within minutes.

'Showed her the SOC report on Camber Court, plus the arrest docket on Singer. Evidence of cocaine seizures both times. Is it reasonable to conclude that Mr Wishart may also be using the white powder?' Winter lodged the warrant on the dashboard with a satisfied nod. 'We think yes.'

Port Solent was tucked into a northern corner of

Portsmouth Harbour. On Friday, at Camber Court, Wishart had supplied an address in the big horseshoe-shaped block of flats that dominated one end of the marina. Winter picked his way through the thin drift of midday traffic and joined the motorway out of the city. To the left, across the grey expanse of the harbour, Suttle watched the tiny white sail of a yacht tacking towards Spithead and the open sea.

'Bit harsh, isn't it?' Suttle reached for the warrant. 'All this for a toot or two?'

'Cathy's up for it. She's been talking to Alcott. The suits are pissed off about *Tumbril* and want to make a point or two about all those fucking Rotarians who think they're beyond the law. Nicking Singer chuffed Alcott to bits.' Winter nodded. 'Payback time.'

Suttle scanned the warrant. Operation *Tumbril* had become the talk of every canteen in the county, a million quid's worth of covert investigation that hadn't produced a single arrest. There were accountants and solicitors in Pompey who were still raising a glass to Bazza Mackenzie for seeing off the *Tumbril* squad.

'We think Wishart's linked to Mackenzie?'

'I doubt it. If he uses charlie it may ultimately come from Bazza but that's not the point. It's broader than that. Put twats like Singer and Wishart in front of the magistrates and you'll get front page in the *News*, guaranteed. These guys aren't immune. That's Cathy's line, anyway.'

'So we're sending a message?'

'Exactly.'

Winter brought his Subaru to a halt in the big car park at Port Solent, and opened the boot. A sledge-hammer lay inside, long-handled with tape wound around the shaft. These days, forcing an entry called for a battering ram, backup, gauntlets, a hard hat and half a day on the computer with the Risk Assessment form, but Winter had never seen the point of all these complications. Now, he lifted the sledgehammer out with a grunt and gave it to Suttle. The long curve of the apartment block loomed beyond the bars and restaurants that lined the marina basin.

Suttle shouldered the sledgehammer.

'Isn't this a bit hasty?' he queried. 'Shouldn't we at least knock first?'

'No point.' Winter was locking the car. 'He's not going to hear us in bloody Poland, is he?'

Wishart's flat was on the third floor. Winter led the way along the corridor, tallying off the numbers. Three doors from the end, he paused, rapped twice, waited for a moment or two, then stepped back to give Suttle the space he'd need.

'You want me to bosh it?'

'Yeah.'

Suttle eyed the two keyholes. Mortice locks were always trickier. Backing off from the door, he swung the sledgehammer. The first impact splintered the wood around the mortice. On the second, the door shifted slightly as the lock gave. The noise was deafening, echoing down the corridor. Already Winter could hear the rattle of nearby chains as other residents unlocked their own doors to investigate.

'Now the Yale.'

Suttle aimed the ram at the little brass disc. He was beginning to sweat with the effort. This time a single blow was enough. The door burst open.

'What on earth's going on?'

A woman in her sixties had appeared behind them in the corridor. She was wearing a turquoise shell suit and a pair of slippers. The Pekinese under one arm had a scarlet bow.

'CID, madam.' Winter gave the dog a tickle under its chin. 'Drugs Squad.'

Without waiting for a reaction, he waved Suttle into the apartment and pushed the door shut behind them. When it swung open again, he put a chair under the handle.

'Nice.' Suttle had dropped the sledgehammer on the sofa. Now he was at the window, checking out the view. 'You think he's got one of those?'

Winter followed his pointing finger. Dozens of yachts and motor cruisers stirred beside rows of wooden pontoons.

'Derek?' Winter was on his mobile to the Duty Inspector. 'DC Winter. Crime Squad. We've just done a door at Port Solent. You need to take a look for the damage report.' He gave the address and hung up before turning round to inspect the rest of the place.

The living room was generous and Wishart had been careful not to clutter the big, open stretch of cool grey carpet. The sofa occupied one corner, positioned for the view and the big digital TV, and there was a modest dining table against the wall opposite. Beside the sofa, magazines lay piled on a small occasional table, and Winter flicked through them. Copies of *The Economist, Jane's Defence Weekly* and *Flight International*. Night-time reading for the busy entrepreneur who couldn't leave his job at the office.

'Guess who . . .' Suttle had found a photograph, housed in a stand-up frame. Winter stepped across and took a look. Maddox.

'Where was this?'

'By the CD player.' Suttle nodded at the stack of audio equipment in the corner.

Winter was taking a proper look at the photo. Maddox was sitting at a restaurant table, surveying the remains of an elaborate dessert. An empty bottle of wine was upended in the cooler beside her tidied plate, and the photographer had perfectly caught the warmth of her smile as she raised her glass in a celebratory toast. Her other hand was draped around the figure beside her. Wishart had left his jacket on the back of the chair. The pale dead eyes were narrowed in anticipation of the flash and the expression on his face spoke of the deep pleasures of ownership. For the first time, to his intense disappointment, Winter began to question Maddox's account of the limits she set to her working life. She saw this man socially. She'd lied.

Winter turned the frame over and began to prise off the back. Suttle's grin grew broader.

'You really think he's hidden it in there?'

'Hidden what?'

Suttle stared at him, then began to laugh.

'What are you really after? What's all this about?'

Winter was looking at the photo again. Suttle circled round behind him.

'That's taken in the flat.' He pointed at the photo. 'Richardson's place.'

Winter felt the relief flooding through him. Then his eye was caught by a detail in the background. He was trying to visualise the layout at Camber Court. He remembered the dining table in the middle of the the huge living room, one end of the table close to the window, the other opposite the door.

'There's panelling on the wall here.' He touched the glass frame with his finger. 'I don't remember panelling at Richardson's.'

Suttle peered at the photo.

'You're right. So it's not the flat at all. It has to be some restaurant, right?'

'Right.' Winter's heart sank again.

'Is that a problem?' Suttle was watching him closely. 'It is, isn't it?'

'Not at all.'

'Yes, it is. I can see it in your face. She's a tom, mate. It's what she does for a living. For fuck knows how much, she lets him take her out before they get it on. How's that for a night's work? Decent meal? Quick fuck afterwards? And all on the meter?'

Winter had pulled himself together. He told Suttle to sort through the rest of the living room. After that, he wanted a proper search of the adjacent kitchen.

'And you'll take the bedrooms, eh?'

'That's right.'

Winter left the room before Suttle had time to protest. He still had the photo. The master bedroom lay at the end of the hall. Next door was a second bedroom that Wishart had converted into a study. Already Winter was dreading what he might find.

He started with the study, lowering the venetian blinds for a little privacy. A desk occupied most of one wall, flanked by a filing cabinet. Above the desk hung a calendar featuring a group of black women posing in some kind of zoo.

Winter fired up the PC and began to sort through the contents of an in-tray which lay beside it. Most of the stuff was domestic bills. Wishart was prolific with the heating, spent a fortune on his telephone, and used the Tesco Shop 'n' Drop service to keep his fridge stocked.

Towards the bottom of the pile Winter found last month's Amex account. The billing ran to three pages. Most of it was routine – rail fares, petrol, three-figure payments to a vintner – but a handful of entries caught his eye. Three were to Steve Richardson: £800 a pop for Maddox's services. Another was a £980 payment to the Chichester branch of Monsoon. The third showed the name of a restaurant in Petersfield, Mon Plaisir. The bill came to £113.56, exactly the kind of sum you'd end up spending for two people in an upmarket restaurant, and when he checked through the billing again he found three more entries for what sounded like a pub restaurant, with smaller sums that were still substantial enough to warrant a meal for two. The Humble Duck. Sidlesham.

Winter scribbled a note of the restaurant billings together with the dates. There were a million people in the world that Wishart might have invited for a leisurely pub supper. God, even Mrs Wishart might have driven down for an evening with her workaholic husband. But Winter was already haunted by the image of Maddox at the restaurant table and something told him that cosy get-togethers had been a regular feature of their life together.

The PC was live now. Slightly surprised to be spared the need for a password, Winter double-clicked on Outlook Express and waited for the rest of his delusions to crumble. Seconds later he was looking at a long list of messages. To his relief, scrolling backwards through the months, nothing had Maddox's name on it. On the contrary, most of the traffic seemed to be commercial, messages to clients or would-be clients, many of them abroad.

Dozens of the emails had pinged to and from West Africa – confirmations of flight bookings to Lagos, various addresses in Nigeria – and Winter found his gaze returning time and again to the calendar hung on the wall over the desk: the month of February overprinted on a huge colour photograph. He studied it for a moment or two, wondering exactly why Wishart should have given pride of place to a bunch of exuberant African women posed in front of a cage of lions. Then, struck by a sudden thought, he abandoned the emails and began to go through the first of the desk drawers. He found Wishart's address book under a brochure for Greek holidays. He went straight to M but drew a blank. Under R Wishart had scribbled Steve Richardson's details – the Camber Court address, a phone number and an email listing. Beneath, in the same scribble, was a circled M.

Winter peered at the details that followed, making notes of a landline number plus a mobile. The email address was Hararian@bt.co.uk. Returning to the PC, he looked at the emails again. Messages from Hararian appeared with depressing regularity. Winter stationed the mouse over one of them, wondering whether to pursue this search any further. What was he trying to prove here? Except that whores lied for a living?

He closed his eyes, knowing that he had to do it and knowing too that the next couple of seconds would lead to nothing but grief. For once in his life, much against his better judgement, he'd trusted somebody. And, to no one's surprise, he'd been royally screwed.

The message was brutally about 'Fantastique, eh, mon ours?' Winter hadn't a clue what ours meant but the rest was only too obvious. Did Wishart have to buy compliments like these? Were these extras on his account for which Maddox charged premium rates? He suspected not. Scrolling onwards, he steadied the pointer over the most recent email. Maddox had written to him ten days ago, a message that simply confirmed some arrangement they'd made. 'As usual I'll be late. As usual you'll be pissed off. And as usual we'll be wonderful,' she'd written, sealing the missive with a line of crosses.

Winter stepped away from the computer, wondering

quite what to do next. A phone console lay next to the PC. Winter picked up the receiver and pressed the PLAY button for messages. There were five. None, to his relief, were from Maddox but the last voice confirmed a booking for Friday night, earlier than usual, seven o'clock, table by the window. The accent might have been French. Winter keyed 1471 for the last incoming number and listened to a line of digits. 01730. Petersfield. He jotted down the rest of the number. The phone directory was on the floor beside the desk. 762398 was Mon Plaisir.

Winter went to the window, opening a gap between the blinds, glad of the thin sunshine on his face. Any minute now he'd develop another headache. He knew it. Should he bother with tearing the bedroom apart? Should he challenge his own frail chemistry with a sackful of porno shots, Maddox giving Wishart his money's worth, teasing the slack-faced bastard with yet another variation on a weekly theme? Might there be love letters in there? Clinching proof, if he needed it, that Maddox's warped take on relationships some-how extended to bizarre games like these?

He lingered by the view, unusually oblivious to a well-built blonde woman scrubbing the foredeck of one of the yachts below, then returned to the Amex statement to make sure he hadn't got it wrong, but the payments to Steve Richardson were there in black and white, £2400 in the last month. So why was Wishart still spending that kind of money if Maddox was so keen? And, more to the point, why should any of this bullshit matter to Winter?

He closed his eyes a moment, remembering the scalp massage she'd given him last night, the scent of the oils she'd used, the way the pressure of her fingertips seemed to build a dyke against the recurrent pain that had begun to alarm him so much. He'd pay good money for treatment like that, be glad to, and the very thought brought a wry smile to his face. Maybe, after all, he was no different to Wishart and the rest of the clientele at Camber Court. Maddox didn't deal with real people at all, only punters.

'Well?'

It was Suttle. He'd found nothing next door, either in the living room or the kitchen, and he wanted a steer on just how serious this search was supposed to be. Should he start giving the cupboards a proper seeing-to? Should he be lifting the fitted carpet and digging around behind the skirting board? Only he had a bit of a lower back problem, recent squash injury, and if they were up for the full nine yards then someone should be making a call for reinforcements.

Winter barely heard him. Another entry on the Amex billing had caught his eye. £4299 to a travel agent in Southsea. Was this business? Some kind of family holiday? Or was Maddox extending her favours to some exotic location, courtesy of the man who paid her bills? The fact that he didn't know, and shouldn't be bothered, simply compounded his frustration. Something was happening to him, deep inside his head, only this time it had nothing to do with the pains that had been plaguing him for weeks. What was at stake this time was his judgement. Suttle was right. He'd completely lost it.

'Well, boss?'

The young DC sounded almost sympathetic. Winter looked at him, despairing.

'Fuck knows,' he said.

Eight

Tuesday, 24 February 2004

'Why don't we get her down to take a look at the body?'

Faraday had been exploring exactly the same proposition a couple of hours earlier. A positive ID from Unwin's mother might save a great deal of time. Now, easing the Mondeo down Bath Road, he glanced at Barber and shook his head.

'I need to talk to the pathologist first. The body's in a real state. An ID could be tricky.'

'Birthmarks? Something personal only a mum would recognise?'

'I doubt it. Four months in the oggin and there's bugger all left.'

'Yuk.' Barber was scanning the numbers on her side of the road. 'There, look. The one with the fridge in the front garden.'

Faraday braked. Number 267 was a narrow, bay-fronted house with a loop of TV aerial hanging from the roof. A poster in the front window advertised a pre-Xmas anti-war rally in the Guildhall Square.

Faraday found a parking spot at the end of the street and they walked back to 267. Barber's knock brought a woman to the door. She was in her early twenties, slightly built, bare feet, jeans, hooded top with 'Penn State' across the front.

She peered at Barber's warrant card.

'Police?' she said blankly.

She invited them in. The narrow hall was in semi-darkness. Faraday squeezed past a mountain bike and followed her into the kitchen at the back. Potato peelings lay heaped on the kitchen table and a copy of *Socialist Worker* was open at an article on the landed gentry. A big pot of lentils bubbling on the stove did nothing to disguise the heavy scent of marijuana.

'And you are?'

'Marie.'

'Marie who?'

'Marie Grossman.' She folded her arms and perched herself on a battered stool. 'What's this about?'

Barber explained about Chris Unwin. She had grounds to believe he might be living here.

'Chris?' Marie shook her head. 'Haven't seen him since . . .' she frowned '. . . back end of last year.'

'You know him, though?'

'Yeah.'

'He lived here with you?'

'He lived here, yeah. Not with me, though. I had another place. Kind of squat, really.'

'So how well do you know him?'

'Chris? I suppose I know him like everyone else knows him. Same pubs, same gigs, know what I mean?' She studied her bitten fingernails a moment. 'Actually, he's a bit of a dickhead. I know I shouldn't be saying it, especially not to you lot, but he is.'

'Dickhead how?' Faraday asked.

'He can be a bit mad. And silly too. Pulls daft stunts; thinks he's the business. One time he tried to get me over to France with him. Terrific, I said, so where are we kipping? He hadn't got an answer to that so it had to be the back of his bloody van.'

Faraday wanted to know more about the van. Did it belong to Unwin?

'Haven't a clue. He always makes like it is but that doesn't count for anything, not with Chris.'

'What kind of van are we talking about?' Barber had produced her pocketbook.

'A white one.'

'Make?'

'Dunno.' Marie shrugged, reaching for a packet of Rizlas. 'Is he in trouble or something? Is that why you're here?'

'Why do you ask that, Marie?' It was Faraday this time.

'Dunno. But it's not a social call, is it?'

Faraday conceded the point with a nod, then pressed her further, trying to build a fuller picture of Unwin: the names of people he mixed with, where he might be living, the pubs he used, whether he ever talked about trips to the Isle of Wight, how many times he went over to France, what he might be doing there. Only the last question sparked any kind of response.

'He's after furniture,' Marie said. 'He goes to auctions in these little villages, gets the stuff for a song, then brings it back and flogs it to antique dealers. I nearly had a big old bed off him once, lovely thing, but he wanted silly money.'

'Where are these antique dealers? Here? Pompey?'

'No.' She shook her head. 'He won't touch the local dealers. He always says the real money's out in the country. Don't ask me where though. I never asked.'

Faraday changed tack.

'Does he have a girlfriend that you know of?'

'No idea. Probably not.'

'Why do you say that?'

'Because he's so –' she frowned '– immature. He

might find himself some fifteen-year-old, some kid he could impress with his crap French and his Led Zeppelin CDs, but anyone with half a brain wouldn't give him the time of day.'

'You think he might be gay?'

'I doubt it. He wouldn't have the imagination.'

The comment brought a grunt of laughter from Tracy Barber, then she exchanged looks with Faraday. For the second time today they seemed to be getting nowhere.

'So there's nothing left of him here?' Faraday gestured back towards the door. 'He didn't leave anything behind? Clothes? Knick-knacks? Nothing with his photo in?'

'Definitely not. There's five of us living here at the moment and believe me we don't have that kind of space.' She concentrated on the roll-up for a moment or two, and reached for a box of matches. Then she looked up again. 'Is that it?' She nodded at the lentils on the stove. 'Only I'm the one who's cooking tea today.'

It took Paul Winter most of the evening to decide what to do about Maddox. Finally, from a bar in Gunwharf, he dialled her number. As the number rang he picked his way between the tables and pushed out through the big glass doors. Across the harbour, the lights of Gosport.

'Maddox? It's Paul Winter.'

'Hi. I've been worried about you.'

'Yeah? Why's that, then?'

'Your head. It needs fixing.'

Winter could only agree. He hadn't been in a state like this since a long-ago fling with a woman called Misty Gallagher. Like Maddox, she had a body to die for. And like Maddox, she didn't seem to care who she shared it with.

'What do you want to do then?'

'Come round.'

'Why?'

'Because I've got something to show you.'

Winter could think of a thousand reasons why this was a thoroughly bad idea but knew he was lost. This was a game they were playing and the best he could do right now was try and understand the rules.

'Give me ten minutes.' He began to button his car coat. 'Some more of that brandy might be nice.'

She was waiting for him when he tucked the Subaru into a space across the road outside the flats, a tall angular silhouette in the tenth-floor window. She gave him a wave as he looked up, then pulled the curtains with a flourish. Lost, thought Winter again.

The flat felt warm after the chill of the wind off the sea. Maddox was wearing a long silky kaftan in a rich dark blue. She took his coat and led him by the hand towards the sofa. The swelling on her face had begun to subside and Winter could smell mint on her breath.

'Whatever you like.' She was looking down at him. 'On the house.'

'I'm not with you.'

'I'm offering you sex. All you have to say is yes.'

'Just like that?'

'Just like that.'

Winter could only stare at her. He'd thought of nothing else all day. Yet here it was, the bluntest of proposals, and he knew he couldn't do it. Not like this.

'Is there a problem?' Maddox had settled herself beside him.

'Yeah. There is.'

'What is it?'

'You.' He frowned. 'Me. Everything.'

'You prefer we talk first?'

'I prefer you stop treating me like a punter.'

'You're not a punter.'

'What am I, then?'

The question surprised even Winter. It cut through all the clutter in his head. It was perfectly phrased.

Maddox knew it, too. She withdrew slightly, appeared to have trouble framing an answer.

'Listen.' Winter looked at her. 'We don't need any of this stuff, we really don't.'

'What stuff?'

'You coming across like that. I haven't a clue what made you do it but to tell you the truth you shouldn't have bothered. I've been around a bit, my love. And I know when people are faking.'

'You don't fancy me?'

'I think you're gorgeous.'

'Is it this?' She touched the fading bruise that pouched her left eye.

'Not at all. It's this.' He nodded at the kaftan. 'And that little pantomime when I was down in the street there.' He gestured towards the window. 'You've got the wrong bloke, Maddox. If I want to go to the theatre I'll buy a ticket.'

'You think I'm acting?'

'Yeah. And I think you probably never stop. In my game you get to recognise the symptoms. You know the surest sign of all?'

'Tell me.'

'People get themselves into trouble, often physical trouble. They play a part, push it too far, and end up in the shit. Sometimes it's overconfidence. Sometimes it's crap judgement. Sometimes they're pissed out of their heads. Sometimes they're just being a prat. Either way, they end up in a situation they can't control.' He nodded at her face. 'Know what I mean?'

'Yes.' She nodded. 'I do.'

'Honestly?'

'Yes.' She smiled at him. 'And I like you, too. A lot.'

The simplicity of the confession stopped Winter in his tracks. This was the Maddox he'd met last night, the woman who'd taken care of him, the black sheep banished by her mad aristo family, the slim-hipped vision who screwed fat cats for a great deal of money and spent her spare time with the ghost of a burned-out French poet. He loved all that, loved it. Worse still, he wanted to believe it was true.

Maddox had folded her long legs beneath her. She hadn't taken her eyes off Winter's face.

'Tell me what you're thinking,' she said at last.

'OK.' Winter fingered the hem of the kaftan, trying to work out how to put it. Finally he looked up at her. 'You want to keep me, don't you? You want to hang on to me?'

'Yes.'

'Otherwise you wouldn't have come across like that.'

'Yes.'

'So what I'm thinking is we should be straight with each other.'

'Really?' She threw back her head and stared up at the ceiling. 'But what would happen then?'

'I've no idea.' Winter reached for her hand. 'You want to give it a go and find out?'

It took Faraday the best part of an hour to read the letters. He'd got home late after clearing his desk of paperwork and found a Jiffy bag waiting for him on the front-door mat. His name was misspelled again,

'Farraday', and he knew at once where it had come from. Karen Corey must have driven round and left it earlier. In barely forty-eight hours he'd forgotten all about Sunday's celebrations and the square-faced figure in the curling wartime snap.

Oddly pleased to be entrusted with something so personal, Faraday emptied the letters onto the kitchen table. They were all handwritten, page after page of painstakingly neat script, and he sorted quickly through them, checking the chronological order.

Harry and Madge seemed to have met at a Saturday night dance. Harry had been with a mate called Bob. Madge was with her sister Daisy, and they'd made a foursome. Afterwards Harry had walked Madge home through the blackout. Where she lived, he wrote, had been a street he'd often visited as a kid. His best pal Michael used to be at number 4, right opposite. Wasn't that strange?

As the relationship developed, the letters got longer and more intimate. Harry was a Royal Marine. He and Madge had courted through the spring and summer of 1943, meeting whenever Harry could wangle a railway warrant up from the West Country, where he seemed to be based. They went to the flicks. They saw Anne Ziegler and Webster Booth, the Sweethearts of Song, at the Empire in Edinburgh Road. They peered through the barbed wire at the beaches on the seafront and tried to remember what it was like to run down the pebbles and plunge in.

One July weekend, glorious weather, Harry borrowed a bike and they rode together up to a part of the hill that wasn't wired off. Harry described the view, the Solent black with ships, and then the ride down into the country beyond. They'd found a lane that led to nowhere. There'd been an old flint wall, shelter from the wind, and they'd sat with their backs to the wall in the hot sunshine, dreaming of what the world would be like once the war was over. 'Did you mean what you said?' Harry had written. 'About having four kids? Only four's my lucky number, and that might have to include us.'

Afterwards, he'd picked poppies for her, and then they'd pushed their bikes round the edge of a field, looking for a different way home. A pub at the foot of the hill had taken the last of his money – a lemonade and a bottle of light ale – but Madge wasn't to mind any of that because, said Harry in a rare flourish, she'd made him the richest man in the world.

Faraday eased back on the kitchen stool, wondering whether Gwen owed her sixty years to that summer excursion, but then he did the sums and concluded that she must have been conceived earlier, around April, unless her real birthday was much later than Sunday's celebration suggested. Either way, Madge and Harry had very definitely become a couple, and by the turn of the year Harry appeared to have proposed marriage. 'Pompey or Plymouth?' he'd written. 'If we can choose where to live, my darling, which will it be?'

Then, abruptly, came a three-month silence. No letters. No news from the West Country. No cheerful digs about the weight that Madge was putting on. Finally, in mid-March 1944, a hastily written two-page scribble arrived, quite out of keeping with everything Faraday had read before. By now Madge must have given birth. Harry had enclosed money for the baby and said he loved the name Gwen. He also thanked Madge for the watch and told her it was the best Christmas present he'd ever had. Rarely needed winding up. Always kept perfect time.

In closing, he wrote that it was impossible to get

back into Pompey for a while but that he hoped to see her before too long. Life, he said, was a bit difficult just now but it wouldn't be this way forever. She was to take the greatest care of herself and the baby and make sure that she got a fair share of the family ration book. One day soon they'd be on the beach together, all three of them. They'd have ice creams. They'd take the steamer to the Isle of Wight. He'd teach his baby daughter how to swim. And when the sun went down, they'd go home, their own little place, with absolutely nothing in the world to worry about.

The letter was signed, as usual, with a carefully drawn H. The row of kisses extended across the page with a cartoon explosion where the last one hit the edge. With space for a PS, Harry had written, 'Remember how much I love you. And remember that nothing else matters.' Squeezed below it, a second PS: 'Bob sends his best, too.'

Bob? Faraday leafed back, remembering the name from an earlier letter. Bob had been Harry's pal the night he'd first met Madge. He'd partnered Madge's sister Daisy, and had reappeared a couple of times in subsequent letters. Whatever Harry had been up to during the winter of 1943, Bob had obviously been with him.

Faraday left the letters on the kitchen table and went through to the lounge. He'd remembered a trailer for a concert on the radio and if he turned it on now he might still be in time to catch the final movement. He bent to the hi-fi, and then pulled the curtains against the windy darkness, recognising the slow swell of strings towards the end of the Berlioz *Requiem*. Sitting with Madge and Faraday in the church hall, Karen had mentioned some kind of top secret outfit to which Harry had belonged in the months before D-Day. She had had no details of what they did or where they were based, but Faraday had come away with the impression that it must have been connected to the preparations for D-Day.

Back in the kitchen he tidied the letters, wondering yet again why he'd been asked to read them. In one sense, it didn't matter. Indeed, he rather enjoyed the opportunity to peer through this tiny keyhole at a world which seemed so far removed from the chaos and clamour that – on the grimmer days – threatened to overwhelm every copper he knew.

Strange, he thought. Back in 1943, with half the planet at war, there was still a bedrock of decency, a web of relationships, that more or less everyone seemed to take for granted. People led their lives with modest expectations and a cheerful determination to make the best of it. This resilience, this wonderful mix of optimism and fortitude, was there in every paragraph of Harry's letters. Getting by was physically tough, money was chronically short, the Germans were itching to kill them all, yet life somehow went on regardless.

Faraday smiled, imagining this sunny couple pedalling up the slopes of Portsdown Hill and into the country beyond. Sixty years later, pleasures that simple seemed infinitely rarer. People were wealthy now. They had cars, mobiles, limitless credit. They could eat all year without once peeling a spud. They could switch on the telly, surf the internet, and spend an hour on the phone to Australia for the price of a pint. But what did all that technology, all that conversation, really boil down to? Were people any wiser now? Any happier? Any more deserving? Would Harry recognise the world he'd fought to save?

Faraday bundled the letters together and tried to

squeeze them into the Jiffy bag but they kept snagging on something inside. Abandoning the letters, he felt in the bag and extracted a single sheet of paper. The official-looking letter had come from the War Office. It was addressed to Madge Corey. As nominated next of kin, she was the person entrusted with the news of Cpl Harry Jennings's death. He'd been killed in action on 28 March 1944. The undersigned, a Captain Barraby, offered his regrets. There were no further details.

Faraday stared at the letter, then reached for the Jiffy bag again. There was still something inside. Slowly, he upended the bag and gave it a tiny shake. A watch slipped out. He turned it over. Sixty years had taken the shine off the metal casing but he could still read Harry's name engraved on the back. Faraday gazed at the watch, fingered the cracked leather of the strap, tried to imagine the circumstances in which it had last been worn. Then he turned it over again, checking the time.

Just gone midday, he thought. Or five past midnight.

Paul Winter let himself into the silence of the bungalow at Bedhampton, glad of the chance for a decent think. He'd left Maddox where he'd found her, tucked into one end of the zebra-skinned sofa. They'd talked for a couple of hours, mainly about her, a conversation that had swirled and eddied around her life, giving Winter a richer understanding of the path that had taken her to Camber Court.

In her late teens she'd wanted to be an actress. She'd failed to get into RADA or the Central School of Drama, but a combination of family money and a wild interpretation of Anya in *The Cherry Orchard* had won her a place on a three-year course in Manchester.

She'd loved the city but within a year realised that her career on the boards was going nowhere. She didn't have the self-discipline to submit herself to someone else's direction. She quarrelled with other people's interpretation of the parts that came her way. And she loathed the slightly camp cliquishness that seemed to go hand in hand with the business of being an actress.

A change of course, and another large cheque from her father, took her to Bristol. This time she was reading English and from the moment she plunged into the nineteenth-century novel she knew that she'd at last made the right decision. Winter had never come across George Eliot or Ivan Turgenev but the way Maddox described the excitements of that first year made perfect sense. Every novel, she'd said, was an undiscovered room in the biggest house in the world. She'd unlock the door, creep in, meet the tenants, listen to their stories, admire the view from the window, and then move on. These were imagined worlds. You explored them on your own terms. They existed in the deepest silence, yet the voices, if you chose to listen, were unforgettable. They were there for her, and her alone.

Did she miss the thrill of live performance? Yes. Did she miss the company of her fellow drama students? Emphatically not. Did she regret abandoning the prospect of a working lifetime waiting for the big break? Again, no.

A decent degree at Bristol had brought her to Portsmouth. Philippe, her father's *bête noire*, had made his brief appearance. Disinherited and reduced to living on her modest savings, Maddox had one day bumped into Steve Richardson. She'd known at once, she'd told Winter, that Steve was a fellow-traveller in life. He'd worked for a time in television, producing pop shows, and had shagged the arse off a string of big-name boyfriends. He'd been a DJ on commercial radio, hosted end-of-pier beauty contests, co-written a musical about Noel Coward that had flopped within weeks. He'd been involved in every kind of madcap financial punt – from Anatolian-themed restaurants to a travel company specialising in gay tours abroad – and had finally been declared bankrupt. Only his long-time buddy, Ali Hakim, had kept him afloat.

Hakim had a great deal of money and it was Hakim – on Steve's prompting – who had invested in the apartment at Camber Court. The gentlemen's club had also been Steve's idea, and Ali had come up with the funds to make it happen.

Steve, said Maddox, had always been undaunted by the small print of business. He might have been useless with cash-flow projections and downside risks but he cooked like an angel, knew his way around a wine list, and – most important of all – understood exactly how much you could screw out of grown men for the right kind of sex. When he and Maddox met, he was looking for a couple of quality girls. They had to be classy in every respect. Cécile, a Latvian blonde with a qualification in sports physiotherapy, was already on the books. Maddox would complement her perfectly.

Winter, intrigued, had wanted to know exactly how Maddox had dealt with this suggestion. Maddox had laughed.

'We were pissed in a bar in Winchester,' she said. 'And I thought it sounded interesting.'

Steve had phoned her within the week. He was already living in Camber Court and the decorators had finished the bedrooms. One of Steve's many friends ran a restaurant in Gunwharf; he was wealthy, driven, and was happy to buy sex rather than invest precious time in all the preliminaries. Maddox was waiting for him at Camber Court the afternoon he'd found an hour to spare.

'What was it like?'

'Fine. He was a nice guy. You take charge.'

'How?'

'Run the shower, have the oils ready, all that. I'd psyched myself up for it. Told myself it was motherhood without the nappies. Men need a bit of looking after.'

'And the sex?'

'No problem. He was mad about oral and he was very unselfish. I wasn't complaining. Far from it.'

'And did he come back?'

'Every Wednesday. Half past two to half past three. Back then Steve charged him six hundred and kept a hundred for himself. Within a couple of weeks he'd come up with two other guys. One was an American on attachment to IBM. He could only manage the evenings. The other was a property developer, young guy, pleasant enough but completely screwed up. I think he only wanted me so he could bitch about his wife. Easiest five hundred pounds I ever earned.'

'And no reservations? No scruples?'

'He didn't care. He hated her.'

'I meant you.'

'None.' Maddox had laughed. 'But then I've always been lucky because Steve's extremely choosy. Cécile and I never have more than half a dozen clients on the go. Most of them have been with me for a while. They become friends. They trust me and I trust them back.'

The conversation, as Winter had planned, led inevitably back to Wishart. He'd become a member of Steve Richardson's gentlemen's club at the start of last year. He knew one of Cécile's clients socially, an accountant with a forty-foot motor cruiser on a mooring at Port Solent, and the accountant had mentioned Camber Court. Intrigued, Wishart had been invited down for supper.

'You met him at the flat?'

'Yes. His accountant friend was there as well, with Cécile. I don't think Maurice quite understood the set-up to begin with but the moment you walk in it's obvious.'

'He rose to the challenge?'

'Couldn't keep him down. We had a meal first, few drinks, then Cécile and I left them to it so Steve could talk business. We were in bed within ten minutes.'

Winter hadn't wanted the details. Instead, he'd asked about ground rules. What happened if a punter like Wishart fell in love with you?

'It doesn't happen. What Maurice wants is control. That's not the same as falling in love.'

'How do you know?'

'Because you can tell. I'm a trophy as far as Maurice is concerned. I'm a piece of art he's bought at an auction. He wants me hanging on his wall, and his wall only. He's not into sharing.'

'You knew that from the off?'

'I sensed it, yes. He'd ask me about the other guys, how they were with me, what I did for them.'

'How they compared?'

'Exactly. Most men never put it into words but Maurice did.'

'So what did you say?'

'I didn't. I claimed client confidentiality. He had the grace to laugh.'

Over the spring and summer Wishart became a regular punter. His business was expanding rapidly and he was approaching the point where he had to make a decision about going public. In bed, he'd plot out various strategies with her, share his hopes, map pathways into the future. There were strokes he'd pulled, she said, of which he was especially proud – stuff that sounded illegal but gave him a flying start on the opposition. He ran his business, she said, the same way as he made love – with fierce disregard for anyone else involved. What mattered was the outcome. Everything else was niff-naff.

'You liked him?'

'He amused me.'

'How? Why?'

'Because he's so much the prisoner of his nature. I suppose we all are. But Maurice seems to have more of it than anyone else.'

Winter wandered into the kitchen and poured himself a hefty Bell's from the bottle on the side. He stood by the window, gazing at his own reflection in the glass – overweight, thinning hair, slightly bemused expression – wondering quite what Maddox really made of him. He'd pushed her harder on Wishart, asking that same question – how do you keep him out of the rest of your life? And she'd repeated that it hadn't been a problem, not until recently when he'd become obsessed by the need to lock her away for himself.

'Have you encouraged him at all?'

'How do you mean?'

'Do you see him out of hours? Off the premises? Meet for a drink?' Winter had shrugged. 'A meal, maybe?'

'Never.'

'Do you ever phone him? Drop him the odd note? Send him a text? Anything like that?'

'No.'

'Has he been here? Apart from the other night?'

'God, no.'

'Have you been to his place?'

'Absolutely not.'

'So he's no reason to think you might be up for what he wants?'

'Not unless he's blind and deaf. But that's the problem, you see, because Maurice only hears and sees what he wants to hear and see. Everything else, all the other little signals, get filtered out. He knows what he wants and the rest is . . .'

'Niff-naff?'

'Exactly. He just won't bloody listen.'

Winter had accepted this version of events with a wry shrug. None of it was true but listening to her Winter had begun to ask himself why she'd chosen to complicate her life in this way. The damage to her face was incontestable. He'd no real evidence that Wishart had been responsible but he was prepared to give her the benefit of the doubt that he'd beaten her up. If that was true, it would certainly have made a difference. She'd be scared. Wishart was an animal. It might well happen again. Just how could she put this man back in his cage?

The answer seemed equally incontestable. In the shape of Winter, she'd come face to face with a real-life detective. Winter might be the answer to her dreams. He had clout. He represented authority. He could be signed up for the cause. Winter, in short, might be a way of fending Wishart off.

Now, in the silence of the bungalow, Winter drifted back to the lounge, nursing his glass, curious to understand how he'd let this situation develop. The more time he spent with Maddox, the more she got under his skin. Yet the more he listened to her –

watched her face, her easy smile – the more he knew she was lying to him. She might never have made the grade at drama school but she was still a performer and, to Winter at least, a bloody good one. The lies were fluent. The story made sense. Only the visit to Wishart's apartment had told him the whole thing was bollocks.

And yet. And yet.

Winter sank into the armchair beside the mantelpiece. He hadn't bothered with a real fire for years but the sight of the plastic flowers that filled the empty gape of the fireplace was beginning to depress him. He stared at them for a moment, wondering about another Scotch before bedtime, then he became aware of a red light winking on his answering machine.

He struggled to his feet, wondering who was mean enough not to get through on the mobile. He picked up the receiver and pressed the PLAY button. It was a woman's voice. She was phoning from the GP's surgery. A cancellation had come up with the neurological consultant. Apologies for the short notice, but could Mr Winter manage Wednesday afternoon?

Winter stared down at the phone, aware of a sudden churning in the very pit of his stomach. He'd forgotten about the consultant. He'd almost forgotten about the pains in his head. But here was his mortality again: a stranger's voice on the telephone, a reminder that his immediate future might well rest in someone else's hands.

He reached for the telephone, then hesitated. He knew the number by heart. And more than that, he knew there was no one else he wanted to talk to. He looked up at the ceiling a moment, his eyes brimming, then shook his head and returned to the kitchen. An hour later the bottle was empty.

Nine

Willard had been at his desk for a couple of hours by the time Faraday appeared at his office door. A stack of cleared paperwork was awaiting collection by one of the Management Assistants and his fourth cup of coffee was cooling beside the phone.

'Well?' Willard wanted an update.

Faraday propped himself on the edge of the long conference table. He'd been up since before dawn, striding north through the puddles on the path that skirted the harbour, marshalling his thoughts for exactly this moment.

He told Willard about the interviews with Pelly and Gary Morgan. Pelly, he said, was a loose cannon, extremely volatile and clearly capable of inflicting considerable physical damage. Gary Morgan had been on the receiving end of Pelly's wrath and obviously had a score or two to settle. Evidence for the altercation between Pelly and the missing Chris Unwin rested squarely on Morgan's word, and he – in turn – was pointing the finger at Lajla, Pelly's Bosnian wife. She was the one who'd overheard the row in Pelly's office.

'What's her version?'

'Don't know yet. She wasn't there yesterday.'

Willard grunted and scribbled himself a note. Then he looked up again.

'What about Unwin?'

Faraday listed the measures he'd taken to try and find him. Tracy Barber had started a trawl on the Police National Computer via the PNC bureau at headquarters in Winchester. Had Unwin surfaced over the last couple of months – on a stop/check, say – then the details should have been logged. If Unwin had any kind of encounter with the police from here on in, then his name was flagged with a priority phone number. Should Unwin prove to be alive, then Faraday wanted to be the first to know.

Tracy Barber was also in the process of trying to get a judge's order before submitting Unwin's full name and date of birth to the major clearing banks in the hope of identifying some kind of account, and if that happened then they'd be able to check for recent transactions. A formal notification had gone to the immigration authorities at the local ferry port should Unwin suddenly reappear, and Barber was awaiting word back from Portsmouth-based ferry companies in the event that they had records of vehicle bookings in Unwin's name. Either P & O or Brittany Ferries might have taken him to France; Wightlink would certainly have carried his van to Fishbourne. One way or another, these searches might yield a registration number for the van, and maybe even some CCTV footage, a big step forward.

Willard made another note.

'What about DNA? You've got an address for Unwin?'

Faraday described the interviews with his mother and the woman in Bath Road. Unwin, he concluded, was a gypsy – not much liked, no close friends, always on the move. Even without Pelly's assistance, he told

Willard, he seemed to have a talent for vanishing without trace.

'So how do you rate the chances?'

'Of finding DNA?' Faraday was still hoping to get his hands on a toothbrush or a couple of hairs from a comb.

'Of getting a match.'

'I don't know, sir. The ages seem to tally, same height and build, both white-skinned, both male. But to be honest I think we need a second PM. We still can't prove foul play. The missing head will be the clincher.'

Willard nodded.

'I agree. What did the pathologist say?'

'She said the head could have sheared when he hit the rocks if he came off the cliff, but there's no indication of other impact injuries so we're thinking he was washed ashore. A proper look at the spinal bones might tell us a lot.'

Willard swivelled his chair from side to side, deep in thought. A second post mortem would be expensive, no change from £2000, but the topmost cervical bone would be separated from the spinal column and subjected to microscopic analysis, and if there was evidence of tiny saw or cut marks, then the specialist experts at the Forensic Science Service would find them. On the other hand, as Faraday pointed out, there could still be a million other explanations for the body's sudden appearance, none of them deserving the attentions of the Major Crimes Team.

Willard thought otherwise.

'Do it,' he said. 'What else?'

'We might take a look at Pelly's boat.'

'He's got a boat?'

Faraday hadn't mentioned it. He gave Willard the

details. Pelly used it for fishing plus the odd spot of people smuggling. So Gary Morgan claimed.

'How big's this thing?' Mention of the boat had put a gleam in Willard's eye.

Faraday was trying to visualise the photo Blu-tacked to the wallchart in Pelly's office. He estimated around twenty-five feet.

'That's big. It's got accommodation? Some kind of cabin?'

'I think so, yes.'

'Then bosh it, for sure. Christ, it's all beginning to slot in, isn't it? If you can establish motive then the rest of it writes itself. He's pissed off with Unwin. He's a headcase when it comes to violence. He gives the bloke a leathering. Things get out of hand. He finds himself with a body; knows a thing or two about ID procedures; saws off the head; dumps the evidence way out to sea; doesn't allow for expanding gases or tidal currents or any of that stuff, and hey presto . . .' He held up both hands. 'We find the rest of him on the rocks.'

Willard was pleased with himself. In ten brief minutes between phone calls he'd identified the prime suspect, figured out a sequence of events and cracked the case single-handed. All that remained was the tiresome business of putting Pelly in front of a jury.

'You really think we should treat the boat as a crime scene?'

'Of course.' Willard nodded.

'And his house? The premises? The old folks' home?'

'Yeah. If he was killed at the home, there'll be DNA. Bosh whatever car he drives as well. Bodies leak in transit.' He gazed up at Faraday a moment. 'Why am I having to tell you all this, Joe?'

'Because I'm not sure we've got the grounds yet. All

188

we have is a toerag of an informant. Pelly's right about Morgan. The man might be telling us what we want to hear but I don't believe a word he says.'

'You're being too clever. Sometimes the truth stares you in the face.'

'Yes, sir, and sometimes it doesn't.'

'My money's still on Unwin.' Willard was turning this into a pissing contest. 'Rule him out and I'm open to other suggestions. Use your judgement. You're closest. But a favour, eh Joe? Don't use my precious bloody budget to hedge your bets. If it looks like a duck, it is a duck.'

'So where are we with the second PM?'

'Commission it if you think it's necessary. But why not get Scenes of Crime to take a look at the boat first?'

There was a longish silence. Willard was seldom this bullish. Normally he insisted on keeping every lead open until the overwhelming weight of evidence indicated a name at the end of a proven chain of events. Anything else, as he often pointed out with some force, would only come unstuck in court, an outcome he viewed as unforgivable. Now, Faraday wanted to know why he was casting caution to the winds like this, piling all his investigative chips on a single name.

'Talked to Nick Hayder recently?' Willard nodded at the pile of newspaper cuttings on the conference table, all of them about the double killing in Newbridge. 'He's still sorting the small print but it turns out we've got a TV star in the frame, bloke they were about to chop from the series. These people are off their heads. They live in a different world. Another twenty-four hours, and we'll probably have the bloke charged. Imagine that, eh?' He grinned, relishing the thought. 'Every front page in the country.'

Faraday's first call went to Colin Irving on the Isle of Wight. The DI's Scenes of Crime unit was based, conveniently enough, at Shanklin. Faraday passed on Mr Willard's compliments and said he'd be glad of SOC's services on the Tennyson Down incident. As of now, Major Crimes were treating the headless body as a suspicious death. Faraday's little operation even had a codename – *Congress*.

'Do you have a search warrant?'

'Not yet. We'll need to sort one out.'

'So when do you want to box this thing off?'

Faraday glanced at his watch. 09.55. Favourite would be a search warrant from a Pompey magistrate, minimising gossip on the island. Say an hour and a half to secure the warrant, plus thirty minutes for the journey time across the Solent, and they could be over on the island by half past twelve. Given a one o'clock start at Bembridge Harbour, they'd still have three and a half hours' daylight for the SOC team.

Faraday enquired about a car to meet them in Ryde. Then he was struck by another thought.

'How about someone to bring Pelly over from Shanklin? He needs to be there when your lads do the business. He'll also have a key to the boat. I'll meet Pelly on site with the warrant. He's bound to kick up.'

'No problem. Do you want to fire up the MIR? Only they might be redecorating at the moment.'

The Major Incident Room on the Isle of Wight was at Ryde police station. It had a bank of computers with the latest HOLMES software and room for a dozen or so DCs.

Faraday had become aware of Tracy Barber standing at the open door. He gestured her inside. Irving was asking about the MIR again. Faraday bent to the phone.

'It's still early days, Colin. If we get a result on the boat, we'll probably bring Pelly back here while we put the SOC boys into the Shanklin place To be frank, we're a bit stretched at the moment. One thing and another.'

He could hear Irving laughing. The New Forest killings were all over the morning papers and the island DI had just had his wife on the line, demanding the inside story.

'That's your lot, right?'

'Yeah. Nick Hayder's deputy SIO.'

'To?'

'Who do you think?'

Faraday brought the conversation to an end, then glanced at his watch again. This time of year the hovercraft left every half-hour. He looked up at Barber and asked her to organise a warrant at the Magistrates' Court. After that he wanted her back at Kingston Crescent, working the phones to try and lay hands on Unwin. He'd call her from the island if he needed her to come across.

'You'll pick the warrant up from the magistrates?'

'Yeah. En route to the hovercraft. I'm going to try for the 12.45.'

Faraday got to his feet. He had a long list of other chores that awaited his attention but most of them could wait. Barber was still standing at the door. He shot her a smile. Days like this, on his own, working against the clock, made him feel like a detective again.

He was in Ryde by one o'clock. First in the queue off

the hovercraft. Faraday had been half expecting to be greeted by Darren Webster but the DC waiting at the hovercraft arrivals door was a large man in his late forties, Frank Newbery. He accompanied Faraday across the bridge to the car park by the bus station. Courtesy of DI Irving, he'd be available for as long as required.

Newbery produced the keys to an unmarked Fiesta. They drove up the hill out of Ryde, the rows of terraced houses washed in thin sunshine. A quarter of an hour later they were descending towards the gleaming blue spaces of Bembridge Harbour. The agreed rendezvous was the marina tucked into the north-west corner of the harbour, a couple of acres of pontoons and waterside properties with a curiously unfinished air. Pelly had already arrived. He was sitting in the back of an area car and appeared to be asleep. Faraday stood beside the Escort, gazing down at him. The PC in the front wound down the window.

'You want him out? Only we've got his inflatable in the boot.'

Pelly opened one eye. He was wearing a thick ribbed sweater under a blue fleece and the jeans looked new. Recognising Faraday, he held his gaze for a long moment before clambering out of the car.

'I knew it would be you. Can't leave it alone, can you?'

Without another word Pelly joined the PC at the open boot and hauled out a tightly wrapped bundle of rubberised grey fabric. A foot pump came with it. Faraday looked at the bulky parcel that lay on the ground between them.

'How long have you had that?'

'Couple of months. Little Christmas present to

myself. On offer at the chandlery over the other side of the harbour. Still got the receipt if you're bothered.'

The sheen on the pebbles told Faraday that the tide was falling and he stood for a moment beside the bleached ribs of a long-abandoned rowing boat, watching Pelly as he began to stamp air into the inflatable. A picturesque flotilla of houseboats nosed against the causeway that carried the main road across the harbour, while out on the water dozens of craft lay at their moorings, swinging gently as the tide sucked out towards the long sandy bar that marked the harbour entrance.

Faraday took stock. In addition to the houseboats, the foreshore was overlooked by a block of flats beside the main road. Hardly the spot you'd choose to manhandle a body out of a car and row it across to a waiting fishing boat.

'What did you use before you got this?' Faraday nodded down at the little dinghy, fast taking shape.

'I had another one. Totally knackered. So many holes I had to bin it. Look at this lot.' Pelly dug a toe into the pebbles. 'Kids are out of control. Fucking glass everywhere.'

Faraday had turned his attention to a sturdy, twin-hulled boat riding at a buoy out in the harbour. Bright yellow, he recognised it from the photo he'd seen in Pelly's office.

'You want to check the warrant?'

'Not fussed.' Pelly was kneeling beside the inflatable, adjusting the air valve.

Faraday took a tiny step back. After yesterday's interview, compliance was the last thing he expected. The PC beside the Escort was shouting his name. The SOC lads were on their way. They'd be here in ten.

The message drew a snort of laughter from Pelly.

'Hope they're not mob-handed,' he said. 'This thing only takes two.'

The Scenes of Crime team arrived minutes later, a white van that turned off the main road and came bumping across the marina car park. The DS acting as Crime Scene Manager was a ruddy-faced Yorkshireman with a gouty limp and laugh lines round his eyes. He sat in the van with the door open, breaking the seal on a pack that contained a new one-piece forensic suit. Newbery introduced Faraday, who nodded down at the beach where Pelly had nearly finished inflating the dinghy.

'He's the guy with the boat. He'll take you out there.'

The DS was scanning the harbour. Faraday pointed out the distinctive twin yellow hulls a hundred metres or so from the shoreline. Earlier, on the phone, he hadn't gone into any detail, simply asking for tests to establish the presence of blood, tissue or other body fluids.

'What's the story?' The DS was on his feet now, struggling into the suit.

Faraday patched in some of the background. They were dealing with a Misper. One candidate had disappeared around October and there was a possibility that Pelly might have been involved. He used the boat for fishing trips; took blokes way out and charged them for a day at sea. If the Misper was down to him, he might have used the boat to dispose of the body.

The DS nodded and walked round to the back of the van. A DC acting as Crime Scene Investigator was already checking a couple of grab bags of equipment.

'October, you say?'

'There or thereabouts.'

'That's a while. And the boat's been in use since?'

'We assume so.'

'Blokes tramping on and off?'

'Bound to have been. The boat's used for charter parties, like I said.'

'What about the dinghy?' The DS nodded towards the waterline.

'Pelly says it's new. Christmas. I'll check it out before you're through.'

'So just the boat, then?'

'Yes. Probably.'

The two men exchanged glances. Faraday had been in this situation a thousand times before, relying on forensic science to reconstruct a crime scene, but he knew there were limits to the magic these blokes could conjure from their chemicals and paper filters. The winter would have given Pelly every chance to tidy up the evidence and his purchase of a new dinghy was, on the face of it, suspicious. As far as the fishing boat was concerned, a couple of gallons of bleach might work wonders for a man's sense of guilt, and the weather on an exposed mooring like this – months of rain and seawater – might well have done the rest.

'We'll do our best, eh?' The DS picked up one of the bags. They'd take a preliminary look first, assess the scale of the job, then call for reinforcements if needed. With a full four-man team, they might be here three days. Depended.

Faraday took him down the beach to introduce Pelly. The two men shook hands. They obviously knew each other.

'All right?' The DS was gazing down at the inflatable with its pair of tiny oars. 'Can't you do any better than this?'

Pelly laughed and gave the dinghy a kick.

'I'd have brought the outboard if I'd known it was you,' he said. 'Except the bloody thing's bust.'

They manhandled the inflatable into the water and Pelly held the painter while the DS clambered in, pulling up the hood on his suit against the chill of the wind that cut across the harbour. Watching them as the little inflatable nosed out towards the fishing boat, Faraday asked the DC about Pelly's reputation.

'Everyone knows about him.' The DC was decanting clear fluid into a plastic bottle. 'But that's the thing about this place. Even a bad bastard like Pelly can't hide.' He grinned, looking up at Faraday. 'One happy family, that's us caulkheads.'

Caulkhead was island-speak for a native.

'Bad bastard how?'

'Throws his weight around. Doesn't care who he upsets. Me and Dave –' he nodded at the DS crouched in the stern of the inflatable '– we quite like him but he's certainly got himself a reputation, especially with the women. Serial shagger. Puts it around a bit.'

'What else?'

'Word is, he's into people smuggling.'

'True?'

'Aye. Says me.'

'So why hasn't anyone boxed him off?'

'Fuck knows. Leads a charmed life, our Rob. Always has done.'

Minutes later Pelly returned in the inflatable for the DC. Faraday had walked back to the van. He'd spotted a pair of binoculars tucked into the glove compartment and found himself a perch amongst a stand of marram grass across the road from the harbour, protected from the icy wind. All he could do now was wait for word on how the search was progressing.

Inland from the harbour lay Brading Marsh, an area of wetland recently declared an official RSPB site. Faraday and J-J had scouted the marsh years ago, spending the best part of a freezing December day taking their first look at water rail, a small, shy, stalk-legged bird that haunted the edges of the reed beds and squealed like a piglet at the least sign of danger. Deaf to the bird's cry, J-J had nonetheless loved the way it emerged to poke around in search of food, stabbing at the rich mud then beating a rapid retreat in a flurry of wing beats.

Now, hoping for another glimpse of the little bird, Faraday worked the focus ring on the binoculars until the blur of greens resolved itself into a distant reed bed. At this range he knew he'd be lucky to spot anything at all but there was an excellent website that tallied monthly sightings for Brading Marsh and the last time he'd looked, back before Christmas, the longish list had included a merlin.

The merlin was the smallest of the falcons, and another of J-J's favourites. They'd first set eyes on one during an expedition to Dungeness, and J-J – barely nine – had clapped his hands in delight, watching the little hawk putting a flock of sparrows to flight. Faraday could remember the moment now, the merlin bouncing along, a flurry of quick wing beats then a fleeting glide, twisting and turning in pursuit of its prey. This little drama, all too predictably, had ended in a distant explosion of feathers, and J-J had returned to the Bargemaster's House that night to rummage through Faraday's growing library of bird books. For weeks afterwards, drawings of the merlin appeared in odd corners of J-J's bedroom, carefully executed studies in brown and yellow crayon, and a couple of years later, when J-J's interest had begun to extend to the Battle of Britain, his depiction of 1940 dogfights had always included a lone merlin entangled with the Spitfires and Messerschmitts, the plucky little hawk often badged with the RAF roundel and a helpful squadron number.

Faraday smiled at the memory, turning his attention back to the harbour itself. Fifty metres away, drifting peaceably amongst a cluster of moored boats, he spotted a small flock of teal. Some of them were asleep, their heads tucked beneath their wings, and Faraday watched them for a moment before easing the binos to the left until they settled on Pelly's boat. Pelly himself was back on dry land now and Faraday could see the bulky shapes of the DS and DC working inch by inch over the exposed decking around the wheelhouse. Already the sun was beginning to dip towards the rising ground beyond St Helen's and Faraday wondered whether they'd have enough time to complete the preliminary search in daylight. Whatever happened, Faraday suspected he'd be leaning on Colin Irving for an overnight watch on the boat.

Was Pelly himself the least bit concerned? Faraday thought not. The area car that had brought him down from Shanklin had long since disappeared, but with Newbery's blessing Pelly had made himself comfortable in the back of the unmarked Fiesta. The car was barely thirty metres away and through the binoculars Faraday had a perfect close-up view of Pelly sprawled across the rear seat.

He was absorbed in a book, a paperback. He read quickly, nodding from time to time when a particular passage caught his eye, not remotely concerned by the small drama playing itself out on the nearby harbour. Once, as Faraday watched, he laughed out loud, throwing back his head with an abruptness that

Faraday remembered from yesterday's interview, and Faraday began to wonder again about the reputation that this man had acquired for himself amongst the locals.

On paper, Willard was undoubtedly right. It was easy to plot a sequence of events that would make Pelly responsible for Unwin's disappearance. He was impatient. He was outspoken. And he almost gloried in settling quarrels with the brisk application of violence. That much, with Morgan's help, they could evidence.

On the other hand, though, Pelly seemed a more complex proposition. His affection for his elderly charges, most of them adrift in a foggy old age, was – in Faraday's judgement – unfeigned. He appeared to be fond of these women and he might well do a good job of looking after them. Likewise, his anger at the irritations of daily life – the incessant inspections, the size of his tax bill, plus all the other hoops that the bureaucrats obliged him to jump through – was probably shared by every other self-employed adult in the UK. In a larger sense, Pelly clearly viewed the country as a lost cause. Family life had become a footnote in the history books, and in the shape of eighteen elderly cast-offs Pelly had living proof that society's glue was becoming unstuck. Quite where this kind of rage might lead was anyone's guess but Faraday couldn't help recognising in himself a flicker of solidarity. The investigation of major crime took working detectives into ugly territory. What people did to each other these days, especially in a city as claustrophobic as Portsmouth, sometimes defied description.

Faraday was still looking through the binos, still wondering about the title of Pelly's paperback, when a shadow fell over over him. It was Newbery. He was in radio contact with the SOC team on the boat and he had a message to pass on.

'They've found blood, sir. Asked me to let you know.'

Winter was on his third issue of *OK! Magazine* by the time the nurse called his name. He'd always hated hospitals. He resented the way they took charge, the way they seemed to rob you of control, and forty minutes spent trying to interest himself in the sex lives of C-list celebs had left him feeling even more combative than usual.

'How's it going?' The consultant was a small, neat man with heavy-rimmed glasses and perfect nails.

Winter sat down in the chair in front of his desk. He felt like a candidate in an interview, summoned to justify his fitness for the job on offer. Fail this, he thought grimly, and the consequences won't bear thinking about.

'Fine,' he said at once.

The consultant looked surprised. His eyes strayed to notes that must have come from Winter's GP.

'Severe headaches?' he queried. 'Pains behind the eyes? Problems with your vision?'

'That's right.'

'But not at the moment? Is that what you're saying?'

'Exactly.'

'Good.' The consultant got up and circled round the desk until he was standing behind Winter. Winter could smell the soap he must have used to wash his hands after the last patient.

'Does this hurt at all?'

Winter could feel the light touch of fingertips at his

temples. If anything, it was a pleasant sensation. In fact it reminded him of Maddox.

'No,' he said.

'And this?' The pressure increased, easing slowly across his forehead until the fingers met above his nose.

'No.'

'Or this?'

The side of his neck this time, the consultant probing upwards until he was feeling under the ledge of Winter's jawbone.

'Afraid not.' Winter was beginning to feel a fraud.

A series of reflex tests followed. Then the consultant sat down and picked up a pen.

'Are you allergic to anything that you know of?'

Winter laughed. His list of acute allergies extended from the breed of earnest young infants who toed the constabulary line and dared call themselves detectives to elderly couples who dawdled round Sainsburys on Saturday mornings and ended up buying a trolleyful of pink loo roll. Neither appeared to be an immediate threat to his health so he shook his head again.

'Nothing in the way of food or drink?'

The mention of drink put Winter on guard. He knew what was coming next and when the consultant asked him about his average weekly alcoholic intake, he had the figures ready. These guys always doubled what you told them so he took the real figure, halved it, then halved it again.

'Maybe a couple of Scotches a night. Say half a bottle a week.'

'Beer at all? Lager? Wine?'

'The odd Stella. I've never gone in for wine.'

'And that's it?'

'Yeah.'

If there'd been a window in this airless office, Winter would have been gazing out of it. As it was, he favoured the consultant with a cheerful grin.

'What d'you think, then? Only I'd hate to be wasting your time.'

'Not at all, Mr Winter.' He was frowning at the notes. Then he looked up. 'Describe the pain.'

The question was so direct it took Winter by surprise. He began to fumble his way towards an answer, then realised that this might be his one chance of coaxing some kind of result from the system.

'It's not like a normal headache at all,' he said carefully. 'We're not talking hangover here. It's really intense, really painful. In fact it's bloody unbearable. You end up feeling like an animal, banging off the walls, trying to get away from it.'

'That's good.' The consultant seemed pleased. 'Very good. And your vision?'

'Goes haywire.' Winter looked round. 'Take the floor, there. Or your tabletop. Or the wall. Or the screen over by the bed. Any flat surface.'

'And?'

'And it's like you're underwater. Stuff bubbles up. I told the GP. It's the weirdest feeling, like you're watching a film.'

'You say you went blind a couple of times.' The consultant had one finger in the notes. 'How long did that last?'

'A minute or so. Really scary. That's when the pain was beyond belief. I thought the inside of my head was going to burst. I can't do it justice, can't describe it. I'd like to say it frightened me but it's worse than that. It's not just thinking I'd had it but being glad it might soon be over. Anything to stop it hurting. Know what I mean?'

'Hmm . . .' The consultant studied Winter for a moment or two, then turned to his PC and entered a couple of keystrokes. 'Diagnosis is never easy, Mr Winter. We'll need to conduct some tests. Maybe a scan. You'll have to bear with us, I'm afraid. It may take a week or two.'

'What would a scan tell you?'

'It'll give us a picture of the inside of your head.'

'And what will you expect to find there?'

'I'm afraid I can't answer that question.'

'Yes, you can. You're an expert. That's what we pay you for.'

'You pay me for trying to get you better, Mr Winter. And if that means getting to the bottom of whatever's wrong with you, then that's exactly what we'll do. Speculation isn't helpful at this stage.'

'Yes, it is. From where I'm sitting it is.'

The consultant appeared not to be listening. There was a grid of some sort on his screen. He ran the end of his pencil along a couple of lines, tapped in some more commands, then scribbled a note to himself.

Finally he looked up at Winter again.

'We have a slot on the CT schedule next Monday at half nine. Could you manage that?'

It was dusk when the DS on the boat put through another call to Newbery. They'd done as much as they could for this afternoon and they needed Pelly to come and get them. Newbery walked across to the Fiesta and tapped on the window. Pelly abandoned his book and pushed the inflatable onto the darkening harbour. On the ebbing tide, the mooring was only an hour or so from drying out and it took only a couple of minutes before Pelly returned with the DS.

Faraday accompanied him up towards the van as Pelly returned to the boat for his colleague.

'What's the score, then?'

The DS dumped the holdall at the back of the van and fumbled for his keys.

'We've got blood from the rear decking, and from the cabin forrard.'

'Lots of blood?'

'Yeah. Congealed, of course, but definitely blood. It could be fish, of course. The swabs have to go away for analysis. It'll be days yet.' He was peering towards the road, watching a pair of headlights slow for the turn into the marina car park. 'There's a bit of a galley down below, nothing elaborate but a couple of cupboards and a work surface, and a basin and two-ring stove. We'll have to have that lot out, and the floorboards up as well. That's where you find the real evidence. The rest, to be truthful, has been trampled to death. The boat looks pretty new to me but it's obviously been used recently. We'd have trouble in court with what we've got so far.'

Faraday nodded, wondering about the implications. The inflatable was on its way back now, and he could hear the steady *splash-splash* of the oars as Pelly pulled for the shore. Should he arrest him on the basis of the afternoon's tests? Or was it wiser to wait until the SOC team had stripped the boat to its bare bones?

Undecided, Faraday left the DS to load the van and walked down the beach. Pelly was dragging the inflatable up the pebbles towards the Fiesta. He needed the headlights. The last thing he wanted to do was to deflate the dinghy in the dark.

'We need to talk,' Faraday said. He nodded at the car.

'Can't it wait?'

'No.'

Pelly looked at him a moment, then shrugged. They both got in the car, Faraday behind the steering wheel. He read Pelly the formal caution, then produced a pocketbook.

'That boat out there, it's yours. Am I right?'

'Yeah.'

'Since when?'

'Since I ordered the fucking thing.'

'When was that?'

'Dunno . . .' Pelly was staring out at the last of the light, a steely gleam on the water. 'March, April last year. I can't remember.'

'OK.' Faraday jotted down the dates, then looked across at Pelly. He'd tucked the paperback into the pocket of his leather jacket. The author's name was Fitzroy Maclean. 'The SOC team have found traces of blood aboard. Do you have any comment?'

'SOC?'

'Scenes of Crime.'

Pelly began to laugh.

'We catch fish,' he said softly. 'What kind of crime's that?'

'You're telling me it's fish blood?'

'I'm telling you we've been out pretty much every week for the past month or so. Sometimes it's me on my jack. Sometimes we're mob-handed. But however many rods we're carrying we never fail to land fish. And what do we do with these fish? We gut them. And what happens when we gut them? They bleed. You ought to have asked me earlier. Saved yourself a lot of time and money.' At last he looked across at Faraday. 'Whose blood did you think it was, as a matter of interest?'

205

A knock on the window brought the conversation to a halt. It was DC Newbery. He wanted a private word.

Faraday got out, annoyed at the interruption, aware of the shape of another car alongside the SOC van.

'DC Webster, sir. Says it's urgent.'

Faraday hesitated a moment, then told Newbery to get in the car with Pelly.

'Keep an eye on him,' he said. 'I'll be back.'

Faraday walked up to the car park. Darren Webster was deep in conversation with the DC from Scenes of Crime. At Faraday's approach he broke off. Faraday studied him for a moment.

'This had better be good,' he said.

'It is, sir. Or at least I think it is.'

'How did you know we were out here?'

'I'm using the same net.' He nodded towards his car. 'Have been all day. I put two and two together, had a word with the assistant at Scenes of Crime.' He broke off to peer into the darkness of the harbour. 'That's Pelly's boat you've been sorting out, right, sir?'

'Yes.'

'That's what I thought. Problem is, he's only had it on the water since the end of last month.'

'Really? So how come he's just told me it's been his since March?'

'That's when he must have ordered it. It's brand new. He got it off a firm in Ventnor, Cheetah Marine. They started to fit it out against a five-hundred-pound deposit, then he dicked them around on the progress payments so the build got delayed and delayed. They delivered three and a half weeks ago.'

'You're sure about this?'

'Positive, sir.'

Faraday was doing the sums. Unwin seemed to have gone missing in early October. The gap between then and the moment when Pelly finally laid hands on his new boat was at least four months. No one hung on to a body for that long.

'How come you know all this?'

'Because one of the laminator guys is a mate of mine. He'd mentioned it before because Pelly pulled every stroke to get it earlier and apparently it started to get nasty. I belled my mate again at the weekend. He confirmed the dates.'

'So Pelly never had a boat before this one? Is that what you're telling me?'

'Not at all, sir. I checked that out, too. He had a beaten-up old Tidemaster – GRP thing, same mooring. Had it for years.'

'And what happened to that?'

'Good question.' Faraday caught the gleam of a smile in the darkness. 'Sir.'

Ten

Wednesday, 25 February 2004

Faraday finally got hold of Willard on the third attempt. He could hear laughter and the chink of glasses in the background. His irritation at the afternoon's developments, already acute, began to harden into anger.

Willard was asking whether he was anywhere near a television. Nick Hayder had tipped off the BBC ahead of the arrest he'd ordered and the pictures were all over the early evening news. The TV presenter had been taken to Alton nick to meet his brief and early reports from the interview room suggested he wanted to get the thing over and done with. Forensic evidence from the scene would bind him hand and foot. A decent amount of cocaine seized from his bathroom offered a clue to his state of mind. The only remaining puzzle was motive. Do you really batter someone to death because they've decided to replace you on the series with someone younger? And, even more bizarre, do you have to do it *twice*? Helping yourself was one thing, greed on this scale quite another.

Faraday waited for Willard to finish. From the darkened car he could see the bulk of the Boniface Nursing Home across the road beyond a thick laurel hedge. There were lights on upstairs. A couple of minutes ago a young carer had hurried away down the road, her shift evidently over.

'So how did the boat go?' Willard had returned to planet Earth.

'It didn't.'

Faraday briefly took him through the events at Bembridge Harbour. The SOC swabs had already gone off for analysis but even the DS in charge admitted that Pelly might well be right. The tests simply registered the presence of certain proteins. It would be days before they knew whether they were human or not.

'And you're thinking . . . ?' Willard must have stepped out of the celebrations. The laughter in the background had gone.

'I'm thinking it's fish. Pelly didn't turn a hair all afternoon. No man has blood pressure that low. Not if he'd had a body on board.'

'So what now?'

Faraday itemised the steps he wanted to take. Number one, a second post-mortem. Number two, more hands to the pump.

'How many?'

'Half a dozen at least. We've started a number of LOEs but we need to nail them down. Take Unwin for starters. We haven't a clue where the guy might be and the only sensible thing to do is blitz it.'

'You want to use the MIR at Ryde?' LOEs meant Lines Of Enquiry.

'Yes.'

'Full HOLMES?'

'I'll let you know tomorrow, sir.'

HOLMES was the computer software that had freed complex investigations from a mountain of paperwork.

'So what makes you so sure you're on to something?'

'Because Pelly had another boat before the one he's

got now. I talked to the harbour master about an hour ago. We've got to harden this up but he thinks the boat was on the mooring until around October time. Then it disappeared.'

'And Pelly?'

'We're about to tackle him. He left the scene last thing this afternoon. As far as I know, he's back here at the home.'

'And the woman? His wife?'

'Her, too. Separate interview.'

'Good. And not before bloody time.'

Willard was back with the revellers. Faraday looked at the phone a moment, then ended the conversation in disgust. Tracy Barber stirred beside him. She'd come over for the interviews. Her day in the Major Crime Suite at Kingston Crescent had taken them no closer to Chris Unwin.

'They're buzzing on the Newbridge job,' she said wistfully. 'Wall-to-wall champagne. Do you lot always push the boat out like that?'

Faraday didn't answer her. He was staring at the house across the road, thinking of Pelly in the car. He knew all the time, he thought. And just let us make fools of ourselves.

According to the woman at the door, Mr Pelly wasn't in. Wednesday nights he normally went over to Ventnor on business. Should be back within a couple of hours. Faraday asked for Mrs Pelly. Said it was important.

'Lajla?'

'That's her.'

The woman disappeared. An elderly resident drifted down the hall towards them, a thin, stooped figure in a threadbare cardigan. Spotting something in the open doorway, she shaded her eyes, gave them a bewildered smile and a little wave, then came the shuffle of her slippered feet and the *clack-clack* of the Zimmer frame on the bare lino as she changed course and disappeared.

Moments later another figure appeared, hurrying towards them, barefoot, much younger, slight, black jeans and a dark T-shirt. She stepped into the spill of light from the carriage lamp above the door. She had a narrow face, sallow complexion, wonderful bone structure, but it was her eyes that compelled attention. They were a vivid green, flicking quickly from one face to another. Morgan was right, Faraday thought. This was someone you'd enjoy getting to know.

'Mrs Pelly?'

'That's right.'

Faraday introduced himself, showed her his warrant card. Tracy Barber nodded a greeting.

'You're police?' The word carried a heavy foreign inflection. She looked instantly alarmed.

Faraday did his best to soften the moment with a smile. Lajla asked what they wanted. It was her busy time. She had food on the stove. Her daughter was doing her homework.

'I'm afraid it's important. We won't stay longer than we have to.'

She looked at them a moment, those big green eyes, then shrugged and invited them in. She lived at the back. They were to follow her. Faraday and Barber retraced their steps past Pelly's office. The door was open, the light off. A corridor beyond it echoed to Faraday's footsteps. Lajla had paused in front of a door at the end. Faraday could hear pop music, suddenly louder as Lajla opened the door, and then a whispered conversation in a language he didn't recognise. The music stopped. Lajla glanced over her shoulder.

'Moment, please.' She forced a smile. 'My daughter.'

She disappeared through the door, then the music began again, less loudly. A minute or so later Lajla was back in the corridor, telling them to come in.

The flat was bigger than Faraday had expected. A spacious living room lay at the heart of it. There were smells of cooking through an open door on the far side and a table beside the window had been laid for two. The window was curtained, a blue fabric with a subtle grey pattern, and this colour scheme was echoed in the sofa and single armchair. The walls looked newly painted, a shade of cream that reminded Faraday of Eadie's bedroom, and the carpet underfoot was spotless. After the dowdiness of the rest of the home, the flat came as a surprise. Take a photo of this room, Faraday thought, and you'd be looking at a shot from a style magazine.

Lajla asked them to sit down. A blonde girl had appeared at the other open door. Faraday recognised her face from their first visit to the home.

'This is your daughter?'

'Fida? Yes. Please . . . come and say hello.'

The girl did what she was told. The touch of her hand was icy cold. Tracy Barber gave her a smile. She didn't smile back.

'We're sorry about your tea.' Barber nodded at the table. 'We won't be here long.'

The girl looked at her, didn't say a word.

'You've got homework?'

'Yes.'

'Lots of it?'

'No.'

Lajla interrupted, told her daughter they'd be busy for a while. The girl nodded, obviously reluctant to leave, then finally turned on her heel and disappeared into the room across from the kitchen. Faraday glimpsed a big double bed before the door banged shut.

'How can I help you?' Lajla had taken a seat at the table, preserving a space between them. She sat bolt upright, perfect posture, her arms folded over her chest.

Faraday began by asking her where she came from.

'Bosnia. I'm Bosnian.'

'Have you been here long?'

'Yes.'

'How long?'

'Since 1993. Why do you ask?'

'It's just routine, Mrs Pelly. Getting the facts straight. Were you married to Mr Pelly when you came here? Or was that something that happened afterwards?'

'Afterwards.'

'When?'

'1994. The next year.'

'And your daughter? Fida?' Faraday nodded towards the bedroom door. 'Mr Pelly is her father?'

'No.' She shook her head. 'I don't know why you ask these questions.'

Tracy Barber was studying her notebook. It was obvious that Lajla was extremely nervous about this sudden intrusion into her life and, like Faraday, Barber was curious to know why. The temperature in the room seemed suddenly to have plunged. She felt like someone who'd brought the worst possible news.

'We've received some information . . .' she began. 'And we have to make some inquiries. It may be that

you can help us. We'd be glad if you could.' Lajla
nodded, said nothing. 'You have a resident here called
Mrs Unwin. Is that right?'

'Mary.' Lajla nodded. 'Yes.'

'Has she been here long?'

'A long time, yes. Lovely lady. Important.'

'Important?'

'From a good family. How do you say? Proper?'

Barber made a note of the word, amused, then
looked up again.

'Mrs Unwin has a grandson, Chris. Am I right?'

'Chris, yes.'

'He comes and sees Mrs Unwin. He comes in a van,
a white van. Yes?'

'Yes.'

'What's he like, Chris Unwin?'

The question seemed to throw Lajla. Faraday was
watching her carefully. She frowned, relaxed a little,
then she began to finger a fleck of something on the
tablecloth.

'He's –' she shrugged '– a young boy, my age maybe.
He comes like you say for Mary, only he calls her
Belle. What's he like? He's OK. He smiles a lot, brings
her presents, us too sometimes. He's nice. We all like
him.'

'He comes often?'

'Not so often. He comes when –' she brushed the
fleck away '– he can.'

'When did you last see him?'

She looked up. The question had come from
Faraday. She said she couldn't remember. A long time
ago.

'Before Christmas?'

'Yes.'

'Was that strange?'

'I don't understand.'

'Did he normally come at Christmas? Did he come last Christmas and the Christmas before?'

'Of course, like I say, with presents.'

'But this Christmas he didn't?'

'No.'

'Did that make you wonder why not? Why he didn't come?'

'No.' She shook her head. 'Christmas is very busy. We get children up from the school, from Fida's school. They sing to the old people. We have cakes and the children dance. We have a tree, too. We make it very nice.' She risked a small smile. 'Very special.'

'I'm sure you do, Mrs Pelly. I'm just trying to ask you about Chris Unwin.'

'You think something's happened to him? Is that why you're here?'

'We don't know. It's possible.' Faraday gestured at the space between them. 'That's why we have to try and find out.'

She nodded, looking down at the tablecloth. Her arms were folded again. Tracy Barber had spotted the bedroom door. A tiny crack had opened. She caught Faraday's attention, her eyes flicking left to the door.

Faraday nodded, adjusting his weight in the chair. Like everything else in the room it felt new.

'Do you know a local man, Gary Morgan?'

Mention of the name brought colour to Lajla's face. 'No.' She shook her head. 'Not really.'

'What do you mean, not really? Have you ever met him? Is he known to you?'

'Yes. We . . .' She studied her fingernails, refusing to go on.

'We what?'

'We . . . nothing. I met him a couple of times. It was

215

wrong. I . . .' She tipped her head back, looked up at the ceiling, pursed her lips, then shook her head. Whatever line of questioning she'd been dreading, it wasn't this. 'He came to the home sometimes. He knew one of the girls. We talked. He was nice. He said he had some Turkish friends. Maybe I'd like to meet them.'

'And did you?'

'I tried. I went down to the pub. There were no Turkish friends.'

'Why not?'

'I don't know. He said they didn't come. Not that night.'

'You tried again?'

'Once. My husband was very angry. We were in the pub again. He took Gary outside . . .' She turned her head away, evidently distressed.

Barber was watching her carefully.

'Is your husband a violent man, Mrs Pelly?' she asked at last.

'Only sometimes. Then he was. Outside the pub.'

'What about here? In the home?'

'Never. He's never touched me. He wouldn't.'

'What about other people.'

'Other people? I don't understand.'

'Gary Morgan says you told him about a row, a fight, between your husband and Chris Unwin. Do you remember telling him that?'

'Yes.'

'Was it true?'

'Yes. There was no fight. Just a row. Rob was very angry.'

'Do you know why?'

'Yes. Chris said that some of the carers, some of our girls, were being cruel to Mary. It wasn't true. Mary, she makes these things up. She makes everything up. She's like a child. She likes the attention. It's a game.'

'And Chris Unwin didn't understand that?'

'No. He said he was going to complain. Get the inspectors in. Rob told him to take Mary away, find somewhere else for her if it was that bad. They were shouting at each other. It upset lots of us. I made them stop.'

'And that was it? Finished?'

'Of course.' She seemed surprised by the question.

'Your husband didn't talk about it afterwards?'

'No. It was nothing. Nothing to talk about.'

'Is Mary still here?'

'Of course.'

'And Chris? Her grandson?'

'I don't know. Maybe he's scared to come back.'

'Why would he be scared?'

'Some men are like that. My husband . . . he can make people afraid. It's nothing, nothing serious, but we do our best for our old people, we really do, and Chris was wrong to say the things he did. He should trust us more.'

Faraday was watching the bedroom door. The crack, if anything, had got bigger and he could just make out the shape of Lajla's daughter inside, stock-still, listening to every word.

At length he turned back to Lajla.

'Gary Morgan says your husband beat him up. Is that true?'

'Yes.'

'Is your husband a jealous man?'

'Jealous?'

'Does he hate you being with other men?'

'Yes.' She nodded. 'Always.'

'Why?'

Her head tipped back again and her eyes closed, and watching her body begin to rock back and forth in the chair Faraday knew he wasn't going to get a reply. Then he heard footsteps coming down the corridor, louder and louder, someone in a hurry. The door burst open. Pelly.

'What the fuck is this?' He kicked the door shut behind him with his heel.

Faraday was on his feet, looking him in the eye. Pelly shaped for a headbutt. Serious violence was seconds away.

It was Tracy Barber who forced herself between them.

'Boys, boys . . .' she murmured, easing Faraday back towards his chair. By the time she turned to deal with Pelly, he was bending over his wife, asking her whether she was OK, checking that everything was all right.

'You're sure?'

'*Da.*' She struggled upright, off the chair, and buried her face in his chest. She was sobbing uncontrollably, an almost animal noise that came deep from within. Finally she surfaced, her face shiny with tears. '*Hvala,*' she kept gasping. '*Hvala.*'

Pelly had found a tissue from somewhere, dried her eyes.

'See what you've done?' He was looking at Faraday again. 'Go on, take a look. Does that warrant of yours cover this? Does it?'

Faraday knew it was pointless trying to explain. Fida was in the room now, circling the grown-ups in the middle of the floor. Her mother blew her nose, then whispered something and extended a hand. Moments later the three of them were locked together, swaying gently, while Pelly told Faraday to get the fuck out.

'I have some more questions, Mr Pelly.'

'Wrong, pal.'

'Not for your wife. For you.'

'Wrong again. This is still a free country. You want to talk to me you'll have to arrest me. Your fucking choice. And even then I wouldn't give you the time of day. Why don't you come back tomorrow, eh? Give my wife a chance to feel like a human being?'

Faraday became aware of the lightest pressure on his arm. It was Tracy Barber. She was nodding towards the door. Faraday resisted for a moment and then, with the greatest reluctance, followed her out of the room. Behind him he could hear Lajla crying again.

She was saying something in her own language, something urgent; then Pelly's voice, same language, trying to calm her down.

Faraday had paused in the corridor. Barber came back for him. He looked at her a moment. He couldn't remember when he'd last felt so helpless, so frustrated.

'You understand any of this?'

'No.' Barber took his arm. 'And unless your Serbo-Croat's better than mine, we're out of here.'

Maddox had never been to the Churchillian in her life. A favourite haunt of Winter's in his more sentimental moods, the pub lay on the crest of Portsdown Hill with sensational views out over the city.

'How's the steak and kidney?'

'Brilliant.' Maddox waved her fork at the roomful of busy diners. 'They must make this stuff in industrial quantities. Still tasty, though. Very clever.'

Winter grinned at her, then drained the last of his Stella. Maddox had opted for red wine and Winter had bought her a bottle. Three glasses down, she'd finally mustered the courage to take off her dark glasses.

'There. Tell me the truth. Go on.'

Winter gazed at her a moment, then reached out and turned her face towards the view. Reflected in the window, against the blackness of the night, the bruising was almost invisible.

'You look great,' he said. 'See for yourself.'

She laughed at him, told him he'd missed his vocation. Nurse, maybe. Or full-time liar. Winter scoffed at the thought. Nothing felt more natural than Maddox in this mood. To his immense satisfaction, he knew he could ask her anything.

'Tell me more about Wishart. You say he's had dealings in Africa. What's all that about?'

'I haven't a clue. I know he's been there a lot. Nigeria, mainly. It must be on business, must be. Maurice wouldn't go anywhere for anything else.'

'What's he selling?'

'I don't know. Like I said, he got involved with those chums of his on the Hamble, the ones with the construction yard. It was Maurice who persuaded them to try their hand at the military market, just in a small way. He showed me some of the advertising once. Sweet they were, these little boats. Like something my brother used to play with in the bath. Tiny things. Cut-price gunboats. Perfect for the Affs, apparently.'

'So who gets to buy them? He ever give you names?'

'Never. And to tell you the truth I was never that interested. But I'm sure he'd sell them to anyone. In fact he'd sell anything to anyone. Life's just a series of dots to Maurice. The buzz comes from trying to join them all up.'

Winter smiled at the image. He'd once said something very similar himself, in answer to some prat question about the job. The real scalps, he'd pointed out, fall to the guys with the straightest rulers. Connect the right dots in the right order, and you've got yourself a result. Simple.

'When's he back, then?'

'Tomorrow. He phoned this afternoon, says he needs to talk to me.'

'To apologise?'

'To explain. Maurice doesn't do apology.'

'And what did you say?'

'I said there was nothing worth explaining. He'd lost his rag and that was that. I told him I didn't want him in my flat ever again and that Camber Court wouldn't feel the same without Steve Richardson.'

'We bailed Richardson,' Winter pointed out. 'He'll be back in residence.'

'Of course, but I think he's lost the taste for it. Whoever put the fear of God in him, it worked. He's low, really low. The last thing he wants is another knock on the door.'

'So Wishart's got nowhere to screw you?'

'Exactly. And he's not best pleased. He even offered to up the money. A thousand and not a penny to Steve. We could go to a hotel. His place. Mine. The back of the car. Anywhere. The man's crazy for it. Couldn't understand why I wouldn't say yes.'

'It's not it, my love. It's you.'

'I know. And that's why I don't have a choice. I have to put him out of his misery.'

'How?'

'By saying no.'

'He won't believe you.'

'He doesn't. And that's another problem. Just how

do you tell a man you've never really fancied him? To Maurice, it's simple. He's spent a fortune on me so the argument's over. I've become an investment, a kind of bank account. He's God knows how much in credit so he can just take what he wants when he wants. Then he gets little me on the phone like he did this afternoon and it all kicks off again. I don't want him screwing me; I don't want him giving me money; I don't want ever to see him again. End of story. Does he listen? Does he ever . . .'

Winter gazed out at the view a moment, the island shape of the city etched with street lights against the blackness of the Solent beyond. In less than a day, he thought, Wishart will be returning to the remains of his front door, crudely secured by the firm Hantspol retained for forced entry. Inside, he'll find a calling card from DC Paul Winter and a photocopy of the magistrate's warrant. No illegal substances had been found on the premises, neither was there a scrap of evidence to suggest they ever would be, two points Wishart would doubtless be making to his powerful friends at headquarters.

'Is he a vindictive man?' Winter enquired.

'Totally. He once told me he'd been crossed in business, badly stitched up. And you know how he sorted it out?'

'Tell me.'

'He had the man killed. Bought a contract. Paid the going rate.'

Winter blinked. For once three pints of Stella suddenly seemed a bad idea.

'He did *what*?'

'Had the guy murdered.'

'This was abroad?'

'God no. It was here.'

222

'In England?'

'In Portsmouth.' She paused, suddenly concerned, reaching for his hand. 'It's come back, hasn't it?'

'What?'

'The pain.' She gave his hand a squeeze, then touched his forehead. 'I think we should go.'

Faraday and Tracy Barber sat in an Indian restaurant on Ryde High Street. Earlier they'd booked into a small hotel down near the Esplanade. Tomorrow morning, Willard would be sending half a dozen DCs across, bright and shiny after this evening's ongoing celebrations over the Newbridge job.

Tracy Barber had already said her piece. They'd stepped into a domestic set-up they couldn't possibly understand. She'd no idea whether Pelly slept with his wife or not. All the gossip suggested that he had trillions of other women on the go but what she didn't question for a moment was the closeness of their relationship. He was deeply protective where Lajla was concerned. He cared for her. In return, she very obviously depended on him. Was that kind of dependence fuelled by sex? Had it ever been? She hadn't the remotest idea.

Listening, Faraday could only agree. The more time he spent with Tracy Barber, the more he warmed to her. She was very robust, very straightforward, and yet she had a woman's intuitive feel for the nuances of relationships, for the patterns iron filings made when they were drawn to a force more powerful than themselves. In this sense she reminded him a little of Eadie. The same comforting certainty in her own judgement. The same courage to step in when she felt it was necessary.

'She must have phoned him when we first arrived

tonight,' Faraday said. 'You remember how we waited outside in the corridor? While she was supposed to be sorting out her daughter?'

'Sure.' Barber was demolishing the last of her prawn korma. 'And what does that tell you?'

'That she couldn't handle us by herself. Where she comes from, people like us are probably bad news.'

'Sure. That's why she needed Pelly back in a very big hurry. He's the prop. He's her shield. When we were there alone with her, she was just lobbing the answers back, one-word stuff, ping-pong, waiting for him to walk in the door.'

'You don't think she's got a problem with the language?'

'No, she's been here too long for that. Ten years in a country, you should be pretty fluent.'

'Maybe she doesn't get out enough.' Faraday was determined to test every excuse. 'Maybe you don't get a lot of conversation out of gaga eighty-somethings.'

'No.' Barber shook her head. 'It's more complex, I know it is. She was petrified tonight; couldn't wait for Pelly to come to the rescue. The little girl felt it as well, didn't you notice?'

Faraday nodded. Fida, too, had been in tears by the time they'd left.

'So what are we looking at?'

'I don't know. Except that I don't buy the stuff about Unwin. You've been right about Morgan all along. The man talks bollocks. My bet is Morgan got that little story about the row out of her, gossip really, and then built on it. The little shit wants to screw Pelly, get his own back. Spot on, sir.'

Faraday permitted himself the beginnings of a smile. His day could use a little TLC.

'So where are we?' he asked again. 'You're telling me it isn't Unwin in the fridge?'

'I've no idea. It might be that Morgan is righter than he knows. It might be that Unwin and Pelly have been in business together. Maybe people smuggling, maybe drugs, maybe double glazing, God knows. It might be that the falling-out went way beyond the scene in the office. Whatever happens, we're certainly looking at one big coincidence: Unwin disappearing, a body turning up, and now all this stuff about the two boats. But all I know for sure is that Lajla wasn't lying tonight when we mentioned Unwin. She hadn't got a clue what we were on about. Genuinely.'

'Pelly could have killed him without her knowing. Makes perfect sense to me.'

'Sure. Of course.'

'He needn't have done it at the home. In fact he'd have been mad to have done it at the home.'

'Where, then?'

'On the boat, the old boat. Or maybe somewhere out in the country.' He paused, trying to imagine the circumstances. 'Say he lured Unwin into the country on some pretext or other, battered him round the head, then shipped him aboard. No . . .' He frowned, then shook his head. 'The boat, definitely. Has to be the boat – a lot less hassle. Why give yourself problems with a dead body when you can take the bloke to sea, kill him when it suits you, then get rid of the evidence overboard?'

'With or without a head?'

'Without. You saw it off. Presumably on board. Which is why we're going for the second PM.'

'OK.' Barber pushed her plate away. 'So he's dumped the body. Dumped the head. What happens to the boat?'

'You've got a problem. Major crime scene. Lots and lots of blood. You clean it up. Get rid of it. Dump it. Set it on fire. Whatever.' He looked up at her, smiling. 'Then you buy a new boat.'

'But you told me he'd had the boat on order since March.'

'Sure. But he hadn't been able to pay for it. And by the time that happened, Unwin may well have been dead.' He paused, gazing at her. 'Yes?'

'Exactly.' She was smiling. 'So where did he get the money?'

Suttle was asleep when Winter rang. The young DC rolled over, groped down on the floor for his jeans, extracted his mobile.

'Who is it?'

'Me. Listen. What are we supposed to be doing tomorrow morning?'

Suttle was still trying to read his watch. 01.56. Unbelievable.

'Court first thing.' He rubbed his eyes. 'Then Cathy wants an update.'

'On?'

'*Plover*. The ACC's down on a state visit. Cathy needs to know how we're doing in case he presses her on the detail. Shouldn't take long, eh?'

There was a silence. Then, very faintly, the sound of a woman's voice in the background.

'What's going on?' Suttle was properly awake now. 'What is this?'

Winter, back on the phone, ignored the question.

'Eight o'clock,' he said. 'Usual place.'

Eleven

Jimmy Suttle was deep in the paper by the time Winter turned up for breakfast. Pete's Place was a hugely popular cafe wedged into one of the arches beneath the viaduct that carried trains in and out of the harbour station. Winter had always loved this slice of Pompey life – the rattle of carriages overhead, the dense fug of steam and roll-ups, the fruit machine winking in the corner, the woman behind the counter who always gave him an extra egg in his full English. This was one of the urban burrows where people like Winter could slip behind a table at the back and keep the lowest of profiles. No matter how busy it got, he'd never once been bothered.

This morning, though, the cafe was empty. Just Jimmy Suttle, in his court suit, reading the sports pages of the *Daily Mail*.

Winter took his coat off and shook the rain onto the greasy linoleum. Suttle came here on sufferance, one of the generation who would never dream of touching coffee unless it arrived in a Starbucks mug with a fancy name at a silly price.

'You ordered yet?' Winter exchanged a wave with the woman behind the counter.

'I had something at home.'

'Couldn't wait?'

'Wouldn't take the risk.'

'Bless you, son.' Winter gave him a pat on the shoulder, signalled for the usual, and settled himself on the other side of the table.

'How was she?' Suttle didn't look up.

'Fine. Sends her best. Asks to be remembered.'

'Very funny. As if I'd ever forget.'

'Listen.' Winter reached across, folded Suttle's paper, and put it to one side. 'There's something we ought to talk about.'

'Sure. You want to get this over with? Fine by me. I can take humiliation.'

'No, son, you've got it wrong. That's the trouble with you lot. You think there's never more to a relationship than shagging. As if I'm that stupid.'

Suttle gazed at him a moment, then shook his head in wonderment.

'I was right,' he said. 'You *are* in love.'

'Don't be silly. We're good friends, that's all. She's terrific, a one-off. You remember Wishart? The punter she was sorting out?'

'Sure. Sad old bastard.'

'Right.' Winter grinned. 'Rich old bastard, too. Turns out he's gone soft on her. Wants to tuck her up. Insists, actually.'

'Insists how?'

'He turned up and gave her a slapping the other night. Scared her witless.'

'Really? And is that where you come in?'

'Naturally.'

'To keep Wishart off her?'

'Yeah.'

'For a price?'

'For conversation, son.'

'Oh yeah?' Suttle was laughing now. 'You're telling me you talk a lot? In between times? That's nice.

Women like that in a man. Shows respect. Not just fanny, is it? Not when it's the real thing?' Suttle reached for the paper and got up. 'I've got some calls to make. I thought we were here to talk business, not your fucking love life. My mistake.'

'This *is* business.' Winter nodded at the seat. 'Sit down.'

Suttle eyed him for a moment, realised he was serious, resumed his seat.

'Go on, then.'

Winter told him a little more about Wishart. How successful the guy had been. How he'd built one business on another. How he was still turning out go-fast patrol boats but expanding into future-forecast military simulations. How he was now on the verge of going public.

'This is a guy who thinks he's got it made. Not just thinks, knows. Maddox says he talks in phone numbers, silly money.'

'Eight hundred pounds a trick? She's right.'

'Peanuts, son. If the listing goes through, he'll be sitting on the thick end of fifty million quid. Most of that is to fund an expansion in the boatbuilding business. According to Maddox, he's talking to a yard in Gdansk.'

'Where's that?'

'Poland. Cheap as chips. They'll build them for fuck all. Wishart flogs them wherever he can. Then he'll be looking at even more dosh.'

'Doesn't this bloke ever stop?'

'Never. And no one ever gets in his way.' Winter leaned back as his breakfast approached. 'And you know why? Because he won't let them.'

Suttle eyed the brimming plate. Winter was dotting

his eggs with brown sauce. At length, he tucked a paper napkin into the collar of his suit and dug in.

Wishart, he said, was the kind of animal who could never leave Maddox alone. If it wasn't sex, then it was money. If it wasn't money, then it was a series of other little hints about just how powerful and successful he'd become. Most of the boasts simply passed her by. To be frank, she'd told Winter, she found all the name-dropping – regular Concorde trips, privileged access to MoD ministers, lunch at the Savoy with visiting Pentagon three stars – a bit wearying. But something Wishart had said recently, within the last month, had stuck.

'What was that, then?'

'He said he'd had someone killed.'

'Seriously?'

'Serious enough for him to be dead, yeah.'

'And she believed him?'

'Yeah. She said he was a bit pissed at the time . . . but yeah.'

'Did she say who?'

'No.'

'Does she know who?'

'She says not.'

'Do you believe her?'

For the first time Winter faltered.

'Yes,' he said at last. 'Of course I bloody believe her. Even Wishart wouldn't be crazy enough to give her chapter and verse. But he did tell her it was local.'

'Here? Pompey?'

'That's what Maddox is saying.'

'Do we know when?'

'Recently.'

'Motive?'

'Fuck knows. Business? Bound to be.'

Suttle was gazing at Winter's empty plate.

'Cathy's hoping we might have turned some more charlie up,' he said at last. 'What a nice surprise.'

'Yeah, but . . .'

'But what?' Suttle had reached for one of Winter's slices of toast.

'Just think about it. I tell Cathy what's happened. I explain we're looking at a suss homicide. She gets on the phone to Willard and by lunchtime the whole thing's shipped off to Major Crimes. Is that what we want?'

'Maybe she doesn't get on the phone to Willard. Maybe she's as keen to hang on to it as we are.'

'She has to tell him, has to. That means it's his decision, not hers. Do we take that risk?'

'What's the alternative?'

'We freelance it.'

'Like how?'

'I get time off. Just now that's not a problem.'

'It isn't?'

'No. I don't want to go into it all, but no.'

'What do you mean, no?' Suttle was frowning, wanting to know more.

'Doesn't matter. Let's pretend I'm on the sick. That gives me plenty of time to run around. What I'll still need is someone on the inside, someone to make the phone calls, bell PNC, do the stuff I couldn't.'

'And that's me?'

'Yeah.'

'But you'd carry the file?'

'Yeah.'

'And take a bow at the end?'

'Of course not. Team effort. You and me.'

Suttle finished the toast, taking his time. At last he licked his fingers and looked up.

'You're talking bollocks, mate. I vote we front up to Cathy, tell her everything. Tenner says she lets us run with it. And you know why? Because she's got the ACC up her chuff and she badly wants to keep impressing him. All this other stuff just complicates it.'

Winter did his best not to look impressed. He'd known Suttle for just over a year. The lad came from the depths of the New Forest, a huge family in a tiny village near Brockenhurst. A couple of years in uniform had largely been spent in Andover. Neither CID politics nor the city of Portsmouth had ever figured in his brief career and this was the first time Winter had realised just how much he'd taken in. It wasn't Winter's deviousness that had put Jimmy Suttle off. It was the fact that there was a better way of achieving the same result.

He pulled the napkin out of his collar and wiped his mouth.

'You think I'm losing it?' he muttered, getting up.

St Mary's Hospital lies on the main road out of Newport, an impressive-looking complex with fine views of Albany prison. Faraday got to the mortuary in time to meet the Home Office pathologist before he began work on the contents of fridge 2, drawer 4.

Simon Pembury was sitting in a side office studying the first post-mortem report. He was a thin, freckle-faced man in his late forties with a hobby farm near Dorchester and a daughter called Susie on whom he doted. He'd come over on the ferry from Southampton first thing, and the plate of custard creams beside the cup of coffee was evidently a substitute for breakfast.

The two men shook hands. Faraday had known Pembury for years and liked him. His work was meticulous. He never committed himself beyond the reach of the known facts and cheerfully resisted every attempt to shape his conclusions to time or any other investigative pressures. He was also deeply impressive in the witness box.

'Susie OK?'

'Never better. First year at Durham. Absolutely loves it.' He brushed crumbs from the PM report, found his place in the dense lines of text. 'This looks like it might be challenging.'

Faraday could only agree. He briefed Pembury on what little progress the inquiry had made to date. One possible lead on a name, and perhaps a time frame, but little else.

'When are you thinking?'

'Round October. If we're looking at the right person.'

'Age?'

'Twenty-eight.'

'Anything else?'

'Not really. We've talked to his stepmother but she was pretty clueless. We've yet to trace an address. Friends are thin on the ground. It's a puzzle, frankly.'

'No impact injuries . . .' Pembury's finger was back in the PM report. 'Shame.'

'Quite. If he'd come off the cliff, we'd at least be looking at a sequence of events. The way it is, he has to have been washed up.'

Faraday offered the thought as a speculation. Pembury nodded his agreement.

'But no head,' he said.

'Exactly.'

'Hmm . . .' He reached for another custard cream, then nodded at the report. 'This looks pretty thorough to me. Any length of time in the oggin, you're going to have problems with appendages. Fish eat the dangly bits. Crabs, too, if he ends up in the shallows. No identifying marks, I see. No tattoos, no scars, no evidence of stab wounds or contusions. So . . .' He looked up. 'What's your thinking about the head?'

'We need to know whether it was removed.'

'Of course. And we'll do our best. But why remove the head and leave the hands? Prints would be as useful as dental ID.'

'I know. And I can't explain that. Not yet, anyway.'

'OK.'

Pembury got to his feet and glanced at his watch. One of the technicians had appeared at the door with word that the body was ready on the slab. There was more coffee if Pembury needed it but they had a traffic jam of routine post-mortems already delayed until the afternoon, and the technician would be grateful for an early start.

Pembury accompanied Faraday into the corridor that led to the post-mortem room. The cervical bones, he said, might offer evidence of cut or saw marks. They'd need to be detached, cleaned and then subjected to detailed examination under an electron microscope. The process would take at least three days.

'That's fine. We're still waiting on the tox results.'

Liver tissue, residual urine and stomach contents from the first post-mortem had been sent away for toxicological analysis. The results wouldn't be back for another week.

Pembury stepped into the changing room, leaving Faraday in the corridor. The soft whirr of the extractor fans and the sharp acid smells of disinfectant never failed to put him on edge. Faraday must have attended more than a hundred post-mortems in his career, from cot-death babies to pensioners battered to death for the price of a bus fare home, but he was still fascinated by the skills which people like Pembury brought to the gleaming metal slab.

Standing at the open door, Faraday could see the grey bulk of the corpse that had been hoisted from the foot of Tennyson Down. For the rest of the morning it would be Pembury's job to try and tease a story, a narrative, from the handful of anatomical clues that awaited him, to reduce flesh, sinew and bone to the bare lines of clinical data that might propel the investigation forward. With luck he'd find the telltale marks on the bones of the neck that would trigger microscopic analysis. The evidence might finally be strong enough to support speculation about the kind of knife or saw that Faraday's team should be looking for. Fingers crossed, the next couple of hours would take the inquiry into a new phase.

Behind him Faraday heard a door open. Then came the elastic snap of latex as Pembury adjusted his surgical gloves. He accepted a mask from the waiting technician, then eyed Faraday for a moment before nodding at the body on the slab.

'Shall we?'

DI Cathy Lamb, as Suttle had predicted, was delighted by Winter's news.

'How firm is this?'

'He definitely told her. The guy became a problem. The problem had to be resolved. Resolved as in sorted. Resolved as in dead and buried. That's what money's for.'

'This is verbatim?'

'Near as.'

'So how come she's telling you?'

They were sitting in the DI's office in the Ports-mouth Crime Squad suite at Kingston Crescent. The Major Crimes set-up was only a floor above but Winter could sense already that DI Lamb wouldn't be climbing the stairs for an appointment with Detective Superintendent Willard. At least not yet.

'Well?' Cathy was still waiting for an answer.

'She trusts me.' Winter flashed her a smile. 'We have a relationship.'

'Appropriate, I hope.'

'Completely. She tells me all about her punters. I wonder whether she'll accept post-dated cheques. If it was closer to Christmas, I'd be hopeful. She strikes me as a generous woman.'

Cathy knew better than to press Winter. There'd never been the remotest possibility that he'd garnish meetings like this with the truth about the many short cuts he took, and she'd long since abandoned any attempts to enquire further. You judged Winter by the scalps he left at your door. Quite how he came by them didn't bear contemplation.

'You'll start with the Coroner's Officer?'

'Of course, boss.' Suttle was studying his pocket-book. 'I put a call in just now. He's ringing back.'

Lamb nodded, running through the other options in her head. Every detective carried a subconscious tally of dodgy deaths, bodies found in circumstances that might warrant a question or two, and just now she couldn't think of anything recent that fitted the time frame.

'We're sure about October?' She was looking at Winter.

'That's what she said. He told her just before Christmas, referred to a couple of months ago. That's October on my calendar.'

'And she's absolutely certain he wasn't –' she frowned '– just making it up?'

'She says not. Richardson had laid on a special pre-Yuletide spread. They all got a bit more pissed than usual.'

'Wishart told *everyone*?'

'No, no. He and Maddox were in bed afterwards. He'd bought her a ring for Christmas – huge diamond; must have cost the earth.'

'You've seen it?'

'She showed me. She still keeps it in the box, never wears it.'

'Why not?'

'She won't. She thinks he's trying to lock her away. She's not having it.'

'And it was this particular night he mentioned killing someone?'

'Buying a contract, yeah. I think that's what got to her. Wishart's playing Santa, gives her this monster ring, and then tells her what happens to people who don't quite see things his way. He was sending a message. That's her take on it.'

'Wishart tried to frighten her? Is that what you're saying?'

'Yes.'

'And succeeded?'

'Obviously.'

'Why obviously?'

'Because she's now told me.'

Lamb brooded for a moment. Winter had been saving Wishart's assault on Maddox until later but now began to wonder. Suttle spared him the effort.

'Wishart beat her up,' he told Lamb. 'At the weekend.'

'Badly?' Lamb was looking at Winter.

'Badly enough,' Winter conceded.

'And you don't think that's germane? You don't think the girl's after a little revenge? Shit, Paul. What else haven't you told me?'

Winter threw his hands up, the soul of injured innocence. Suttle was right. Wishart was extremely heavy, jealous as fuck; wanted to spend his life writing Maddox huge cheques in exchange for sole ownership. He was also someone who was used to getting his own way; didn't take no for an answer.

'And Maddox?'

'Is still saying no.'

'To sex?'

'To becoming Wishart's property. The sex isn't a problem but Wishart wants all of her, no other punters on the side, exclusive access.'

'And you?'

'Me?'

'How do you fit into her life? Getting all this stuff out of her?'

'I don't, Cath. Maybe I'd like to, but I don't. She's damaged goods. She's brainy, she's beautiful, she's reckless as fuck, she gets off on playing Mata Hari three times a week, but deep down I don't think she's got a clue who she really is. She started this thing as a game. She wrote the rules. She thought the punters did her bidding. But with Wishart it's not like that at all. The bloke's a monster. I told you. He scares her shitless.'

Even Winter was surprised by the vehemence of this little outburst. He sat back in the chair, eyeing Cathy Lamb, annoyed with himself for letting Maddox get to him like this. For her part, Cathy let the moment pass. With all her reservations about Winter, she recognised when something really mattered to him. Just now, for whatever reason, that something was Maddox, and if he was right, if a homicide charge lay at the end of whatever happened next, then she was prepared – as ever – to take him on trust.

She looked at him a moment longer, then nodded at the door.

'Go for it,' she said. 'But no surprises, eh?'

Faraday was at Newport police station by early afternoon. He found DI Colin Irving in his office, bent over the quarterly overtime budget. Faraday settled himself in the chair across the desk, aware that he still carried the smell of the mortuary.

'Has Willard been on?'

'Yes.'

'About Darren Webster?'

'Yes.'

'Do you mind?'

'Of course I bloody do.' Irving still didn't look up. 'He's in the CID office. Awaiting your instructions.'

'Thanks.' Faraday got to his feet, then paused by the open door. 'It's Operation *Congress*, by the way. For when you put the invoice in.'

Webster was ready to leave at once. He followed Faraday down the rear stairs and out to the car park at the back. A ledge of thick cloud to the west carried the promise of yet more rain.

'Where to, sir?' Webster was trying to sort out the seat belt in Faraday's Mondeo.

'Ventnor. That mate of yours at Cheetah Marine.'

'Dave Parncutt? No problem.' He finally managed to strap himself in. 'By the way, sir. I owe you an apology.'

'You're right.' Faraday nodded. 'You do . . . Detective Constable.'

*

Ventnor lies at the bottom of the Isle of Wight, a once-genteel Victorian spa resort curtained from the rest of the island by the dramatic fold of St Boniface Down. In the tourist brochures the town laid regular claim to being one of the UK's sunniest spots. It boasted some fine Victorian terraces, a brace of folksy museums, atmospheric beachside pubs and a botanical garden that turned all that sunshine into a display of blooms unrivalled on the south coast. Webster, who'd been born in neighbouring Bonchurch, had a different story to tell.

'Cowboy town.' He was grinning. 'You want anything from serious gear to ripped-off antiques, this is the place to come. The rest of it is packaging.'

'You like it?'

'Love it. Always have.'

They were coasting down the zigzag that plunged towards the sea. Beneath them the crescent of pebble beach was dulled by the blanket of cloud that now shrouded the entire island. On a sunny day, thought Faraday, this view would be sensational.

'The main factory's back on the industrial estate.' Webster nodded over his shoulder. 'But we need to go to the farm. That's along at Bonchurch.'

Faraday was still looking at the beach. A tiny curl of breakwater, a carefully dumped jumble of huge rocks, reached south into the sea. A second arm completed the harbour. The work looked new, construction still under way.

'Ventnor Haven.' Webster glanced at a text on his mobile. 'We used to have a pier down there, sweet little thing, but you can't move for developers these days. If there's money in it, it'll happen.'

Faraday was thinking about Pelly's boat. Apart from the yachtie madness of Cowes and the picturesque little harbour at Yarmouth way over to the west, Bembridge was the island's only anchorage.

'There'll be moorings here?'

'Pontoons, more like. Cost you an arm and a leg when they get round to sorting out a tariff.'

'And Bembridge?'

'There's a marina there as well. In fact there are two. But it's way cheaper to buy a mooring on the harbour itself.'

'How much?'

'Depends.' He glanced at Faraday. 'You mean Pelly?'

'Yes.'

'Hundred and fifty a year. He'd never come here. Not with half the town watching his every move.'

Faraday saw the point. Ventnor was built like a Victorian music hall, tier after tier of terraced houses rising from the promenade, every window offering a perfect view of the beach and the new anchorage. If you were after sharing your secrets, you couldn't do better than this claustrophobic little spa. If you wanted something more anonymous, you'd undoubtedly settle for the wider spaces of Bembridge Harbour.

They were in the town centre now, Faraday following Webster's instructions as they picked their way through a maze of narrow streets towards neighbouring Bonchurch. En route from Newport the young DC had been enthusing about Pelly's new boat. Dave Parncutt was a laminator with Cheetah Marine as well as a hang-gliding fanatic, and Webster had accompanied him on a couple of proving trials back last summer when the first of the 7.9-metre boats had put to sea. Faraday was soon lost in the blizzard of technical detail but it seemed that Pelly had made a perfect choice. Symmetrical planing hulls. Low wash characteristics. Steep dead rise. Plus the use of ultra-light building materials that coaxed a great deal of power from the twin 225 hp outboards. With a dozen or so asylum seekers aboard, said Webster, Pelly's pride and joy could do in excess of forty-five knots, comfortably outrunning anything else in the Channel. Not only that, but the twin-hull design enabled him to run the boat directly onto a beach, giving him a huge choice of landing sites. For a people smuggler who also ran fishing charters, it was near-on ideal.

'How much?' Faraday had asked.

'Dunno.' Webster had grinned again. 'But if I had that kind of money, I wouldn't be doing this job.'

The smaller of Cheetah Marine's factories lay beside a smallholding at the end of a narrow track on the outskirts of Bonchurch. Faraday parked and left Webster to sort out the interviews while he contacted Tracy Barber. For the time being, until one of the Major Crimes DSs shipped across from Pompey, she was holding the fort at the incident room they'd taken over at Ryde police station. Her extension was engaged and Faraday tried another line, getting through to DC Bev Yates. He'd just returned from a visit to the Bembridge harbour master but his news could wait until the evening debrief.

'Get Tracy to ring me on the mobile when she's got a moment.' Faraday was watching Webster as he re-emerged from reception. 'Nothing urgent.'

Webster accompanied him back to reception. A small, cluttered office beside it had been hurriedly cleared to make space for an extra chair. A poster on the wall featured a blonde in a blue bikini draped over the latest Cheetah offering, and there was a pinboard beside it covered with press cuttings from the last

Southampton Boat Show. Looking at the poster, Faraday recognised the distinctive yellow hulls. Bembridge Harbour, he thought. Barely twenty-four hours ago.

'This is Sean. Dave's down in Ventnor sorting something out.'

Sean Strevons co-owned the firm. He was a cheerful-looking thirty-something with a paint-stained fleece and an impressive dangle of blond dreadlocks. He apologised for the state of the place and hoped Dave wasn't in too much trouble. Through the thin partition wall Faraday could hear the *thump-thump* of a hammer drill.

'It's not about Dave,' Faraday said at once. 'It's in relation to a customer of yours. Rob Pelly?'

Mention of the name drew a sigh from Strevons. Faraday asked why.

'It's difficult.' He looked from one face to the other. 'Is this off the record? Only the island's a tiny bloody place.'

Faraday told him to go ahead. He wasn't after a formal statement, not yet anyway.

'What does that mean?'

'It means that you can tell us what you like. We may come back to you for a statement. It's your right to refuse to make that statement. Though naturally we'd be curious to know why.'

'What is this?' Strevons was seriously concerned now.

'DI Faraday's from Major Crimes,' Webster reminded him. 'I told you just now.'

'Yeah, but what kind of major crimes?'

Faraday just looked at him, made no attempt to explain.

'Tell me about Rob Pelly,' he said at length. 'I understand he's bought a boat.'

'He has, that's right.' Strevons swivelled the chair and nodded at the poster. 'He's had one of those off us. Brand new 7.9. Nightmare, to tell you the truth.'

'Nightmare how?'

'Bloke didn't have the money.'

Pelly, he explained, had given them a ring back in the spring of last year. He'd heard rumours of the new design and wanted more details. Sean had invited him down from Shanklin and shown him the plans.

'We were laying down the moulds by then. We gave him the full tour.'

The new 7.9 series had a basic hull shape with a variety of add-ons. Customers could stipulate exactly what they wanted, from the size of the wheelhouse to the power of the engines aft.

'What did Pelly want?'

'He wanted the biggest engines, the basics down below, stainless steel rails all round . . .' He frowned, trying to remember, then rummaged in a filing cabinet beside the window. At length, one finger anchored in the file, he sat down again. 'Full lighting fit – internal, after deck, the lot – plus hydraulic steering and a gantry for the roof mast. When I asked what he wanted the gantry for he said he might be after a radar. We don't get that very often, believe me.'

Webster had produced his pocketbook and was scribbling notes.

'Cost?' asked Faraday.

Strevons consulted the file again.

'I quoted him £36,000 plus VAT for the hull. Add another £24,500 for the engines, fitted. That's without VAT. All in, you're looking at just over seventy grand.'

'You ask for a deposit?'

'Five hundred pounds.'

'What about the rest?'

'Three stage payments. A third when the building starts. A third when the engines go in. The rest before we deliver.'

'And Pelly?'

'He came up with the deposit OK. That was back in June. Then we sent him an invoice for £23K in August because we wanted to start the build. That's when the problems kicked off. He kept coming up with excuses. Told us to start regardless; he'd sort out something for next week. Basically, he hadn't got the money.'

'And had you started?'

'Yes. He said he was negotiating a remortgage, even showed me some of the correspondence. I believed him.'

'Was the correspondence forged?'

'I dunno.' He shrugged. 'But we never got the money, not then anyway, and he got quite nasty.'

'Threats?'

'Implied threats. Told us the country was full of greedy thieving bastards who needed sorting out. Not us, of course, but we all knew what he meant.'

'You stopped the build?'

'Of course. It wasn't a catastrophe. We simply used the mould on another order. Told him we'd start again the moment we saw the money.'

'And when was that?'

His eyes flicked back to the file. The cheque for £23,333 had cleared on 11 October. By that time there was a waiting list for 7.9s, but Pelly wasn't having it. He needed the boat asap and wasn't in the mood to wait.

Faraday was watching Webster's racing pen.

'How did you get round that?' he asked.

'We didn't, not to begin with. He even offered us an extra five grand to queue-jump but we weren't really sure about his money by then so we were a bit wary. Oddly enough we had a couple of cancellations so he was lucky. The build started the third week in October. He paid the second instalment after Christmas. Then the rest when we delivered towards the end of January.'

'No problems?'

'None. He even sent us a thank-you card.'

'Have you seen him since at all?'

'No. But then I'm not sure we'd want to.' He shut the file and tossed it on the desk. 'Most of the people we deal with are fine. Pelly, excuse my French, was an arsehole.'

'Did he ever say why he wanted the boat? What he might be using it for?'

'Fishing. He said he wanted to take charters out. That would make sense, a fit like that, except for the radar.'

'Did you install a radar?'

'No, but then we don't. You haven't got the height really, not for decent coverage, not unless you're only interested in ten or fifteen miles out.'

'And you think he was?'

'Must have been. Otherwise he wouldn't have asked for it.'

Faraday was trying to remember whether Pelly's new boat carried a radar sweep. He thought not.

'So what else do you know about Mr Pelly?'

'Nothing.'

'You never asked around? When things were getting sticky?'

'There's gossip, obviously, but –' he shrugged '– there's gossip everywhere, place like this.'

'What does the gossip say?'

'I'm not sure I can tell you that.'

'Why don't you try?' Faraday offered him a chilly smile. 'I wouldn't ask you if it wasn't important.'

'No . . .' Strevons swivelled the chair again, avoiding Faraday's gaze. 'I don't suppose you would.'

At length he said he'd heard rumours of people smuggling. The property Pelly was trying to remortgage was in Ventnor. Strevons knew it well.

'And?'

'It's full of foreigners. It's the talk of the local pubs. I'm talking proper foreigners. Not blokes from the mainland.'

'You think Pelly brought them in?'

'I don't know. It's gossip. Like I say.'

'Of course. But let's assume the rumours are true. Let's assume he has a boat already. A . . .' Faraday shot a look at Webster.

'Tidemaster.'

'Tidemaster. Let's pretend he wants something better. What would he buy?'

Strevons looked at him for a moment, recognising the corner into which he'd just been backed. Then he had the grace to smile.

'You're right,' he said softly. 'One of ours would be perfect.'

Twelve

Thursday, 26 February 2004

The Coroner's office was on the third floor of Portsmouth's Guildhall, a monumental piece of Victorian architecture that dominated the busy square at the city's heart. One of the three Coroner's Officers was a bulky curmudgeon called Bill Prosper. Prosper was an ex-policeman, and an old enemy of Winter's. They'd been on the same relief together way back and as a direct consequence Prosper viewed Winter as a permanent stain on the force's reputation. If he'd found Winter in the laundry basket, he'd once told a colleague, he'd have taken him to the dry cleaners for a thorough going-over.

'This is Jimmy Suttle.' Winter knew exactly how to wind Prosper up: 'I'm teaching him how to be a proper detective.'

Prosper threw a look at Suttle and then nodded at a desk in the corner of the big open-plan office where a significant bundle of buff files awaited their attention.

'Sixty-seven and counting,' he said. 'And that's only October.'

'You've got coffee here?'

'There's a machine in the passage. Help yourself but go easy on the milk.'

Winter and Suttle exchanged glances. Winter had already been on the phone to Prosper, wanting a steer on those October fatalities that might warrant further attention. Prosper, whose working life had long adjusted to the glum excitements that followed a sudden death, had accused him of having a laugh.

Every day the office was dealing with seven or eight deaths uncertified by either a hospital or a GP. Some of them were down to drugs or alcohol. Others were industrial accidents, blokes who'd ignored safety regulations and paid the price, or broken bodies recovered from the pavement after taking a header from a tower block or a multi-storey car park. A handful, especially in winter, were scooped up from some beach or other, their dead lungs full of water. Each of these bodies was subjected to post-mortem examination. Most turned out to have died from natural causes or because the individual concerned had decided to throw in the towel. A tiny handful were flagged by the pathologist for further police investigation but no one during October qualified for this select little file on Prosper's computer screen. Mere Coroner's Officers, though, could always be wrong. So drop by, he'd told Winter, and help yourself.

Winter divided the files in half while Suttle sorted out the coffees. For the rest of the morning they worked slowly through their respective piles, an increasingly dispiriting task. Early on, Suttle discovered a woman of forty-three who'd been found naked and lifeless on the stairs by her suspiciously unmoved partner. Turned out she'd been a junkie for half her life and had choked to death after a syringeful of especially potent smack. Winter, meanwhile, briefly pondered the case of an eighteen-year-old scaffolder who'd visited a number of Fulham pubs after a Pompey away win, necked half a bottle of Jim Beam on the journey home, and celebrated by opening the door and hanging out as the train sped through Rowlands Castle station. A

London-bound express on the other line had taken his head off.

Neither victim seemed to offer any conceivable link to Wishart and nor did any of the other deaths that had required the attentions of the duty pathologist. By lunchtime Winter was back at Prosper's desk.

'You want September or November?' Prosper was enjoying this. 'Only I've had a quick shufti through both.'

'And?'

'Bugger all.'

He was right. All afternoon, case by case, Winter and Suttle hunted for any trace of a contract hit. Most of these people, all too obviously, were predisposed towards an early end, either because of self-abuse or inattention or recklessness, or the kind of enveloping despair that led to suicide. Others, in the considered view of the Coroner, were simply in the wrong place at the wrong time. It wasn't the North End mother of three's fault that the driver of an Astra lost control after a tyre burst, mounted the pavement, and wiped her out. Nor could the Filipino sailor at Flathouse Quay, who turned out to be deaf, have been expected to hear the warning *peep-peep* of the 38-tonne artic that crushed him to death as it reversed. These bad-luck fatalities were regrettable, tragic even, but of absolutely no use if you were looking for evidence of body parts from the grenade that Maddox had so casually lobbed into Operation *Plover*.

'You're sure she's not making this up?'

Suttle and Winter were walking back to the car park. Winter had another headache coming on.

'Positive,' he said. 'She doesn't piss about. Not with stuff like this.'

'How do you know?'

It was a good question and Winter pondered the merits of an honest answer for long enough to give Suttle the opening he needed. They were halfway up the dank staircase that led to Floor E in the multi-storey. Suttle caught Winter by the arm as he turned for the next flight of concrete steps.

'Listen,' he said. 'You remember you once gave me a bollocking about getting involved with the punters?'

'The what?' Winter was out of breath.

'The clientele? Young Trudy? Remember what you said?'

Winter wouldn't meet his gaze. Trudy Gallagher was a nubile seventeen-year-old, the love child Bazza Mackenzie had always called his own. Last year Suttle had given her a knobbing and paid the price.

'That was different,' Winter muttered.

'Different how?' Suttle had backed Winter against the wall. From several storeys below came the squeal of a door opening and then womens' voices echoing up the stairwell.

'Screwing Trude was totally out of order. You were bloody lucky they only put you in hospital.'

'And screwing Maddox? Some fucked-up tom with more money than sense?'

'Different,' Winter insisted. 'For starters I'm not screwing her.'

'I don't believe you.'

'Well you should, son.' Winter at last looked him in the eye. 'If I could, I would. Truth is, I can't.'

'Why not?'

'I don't know.' Winter shook his head, aware of the swelling cackle of conversation as the women mounted the stairs below them. 'It just doesn't happen.'

'Why not?' Suttle's concern was genuine. 'Love job, is it?'

'Christ knows. If I could remember what love felt like, I'd tell you. Just now . . .' He shrugged, gazing at the wall opposite, trying to focus on the zigzags of graffiti behind the curtain of bubbles, trying to rescue some shred of self-respect from this small moment of truth.

'Trust me.' Suttle's face was inches from Winter's. 'I'm trying to help.'

'Help? Help how?'

'You're sick, mate. I can see it. Something's happened, something's gone wrong, and I just want to know what. Maybe I can help. Could you handle that?'

Winter could feel the knobbly chill of the concrete on the back of his head. The women were in sight now, three of them staring up through the banisters, laden with shopping, not knowing what to do. Suttle was still in Winter's face, still demanding an answer. Winter summoned the beginnings of a smile, pushing him gently away.

'Thanks for the thought, son.' He fumbled for his car keys. 'Maybe you'd better drive, eh?'

Faraday and Webster were back at Ryde police station by late afternoon. After the interview at Cheetah Marine Webster had given Faraday the tour of Pelly's alleged properties on the eastern side of the island, the list of half a dozen addresses he'd acquired from the informant, Gary Morgan. For the most part these were modest red-brick terraced houses tucked away in side streets, and Faraday had been surprised by the evidence of Pelly's care for the properties. In every case the exterior woodwork – front door, window frames – had been repainted, always in the same shade of green. Every window was curtained, and the tiny rectangles of front garden were free of the usual debris of spilling refuse bags and sodden mattresses. There was even a new-looking satellite dish bolted onto the front wall of each house a foot or two beneath the eaves.

Parked opposite a house in the back streets of Sandown, watching a couple of men emerge from the front door, Faraday had speculated on the implications of this little surprise. He'd never heard of a man in Pelly's situation going to such lengths. For someone allegedly making a fortune from other people's misery, he was certainly spending a bob or two keeping his empire in good shape, a hint of philanthropy that sat uneasily with accusations of ruthlessness, violence and naked greed.

'If he's making so much money, how come he couldn't afford the new boat? To begin with, at least?'

'Dunno, sir.' Webster was still watching the two men. 'Maybe it's a timing thing. Maybe he only got these places very recently. The boat he's using now, he could bring dozens of blokes in.'

'But he's only had it a month.'

'I know.'

'So it doesn't make sense, does it?'

Faraday carried the thought with him to Ryde. Tracy Barber was up in the Major Incident Room, deep in conversation with two of the DCs Willard had shipped over as reinforcements. She broke off, accompanying Faraday to the SIO's office. Faraday gazed round. He found the bareness of the desk oddly comforting. It suggested, at this stage in the investigation, a sense of limitless possibility.

'Well?'

Barber began to tally the day's developments. On Faraday's instructions she'd dispatched a couple of DCs to Midhurst to trawl the antique shops for word on Chris Unwin. If it was true that he'd been shipping furniture over from France, then it made sense that he'd look to West Sussex for the best prices. Marie Grossman had seemed pretty certain that Midhurst had figured in their conversations, and by now the DCs would have had plenty of time to turn up a lead or two.

'They belled me this afternoon.' Barber had settled herself in the spare chair across the desk. 'They got a result in two shops, one at either end of the main drag. Both times the owners recognised the name, said that Unwin turned up with bits and pieces he'd bought at auction in French villages – big heavy stuff, wardrobes, beds. Apparently you had to watch him on price. He'd be asking silly money.'

'Was this a regular run?'

'No. And he never phoned ahead. Just drove over and wandered in. We get the impression he wasn't too organised.'

'So how often do they see him?'

'One bloke reckoned every five or six weeks, roughly. The other guy thought that sounded about right.'

'OK.' Faraday nodded. 'So when did they last see him?'

'Late September. We've even got a date. One guy looked in his petty cash ledger. September twenty-seventh. Two hundred quid. Unwin never took cheques.'

'And the other guy?'

'The same. Hand on heart he couldn't be certain, but he thought early autumn.'

'Do they have an address for him? Mobile number?'

'Nothing. You remember Marie's take on Unwin? A bit of a dickhead? These people thought the same.

254

Rick thinks they're far too well bred to say it but that's the impression they're giving. Unwin was all mouth. Pretended he could speak French, claimed to have all kinds of contacts, asked them what they wanted for his next trip over, but never turned up with the right gear. Some of the stuff he brought over was OK, no problem, but he never listened.'

'And the van?'

'White. Old model Transit. Loads of rust round the sills and the bottom of the rear doors.'

'Reg number?'

'One bloke thought M reg but wasn't really sure.'

'And no word since September?'

'No. Not that they were surprised . . . but no.'

Faraday went through the drawers until he found a pad. Scribbling himself a note, he listened to Barber detailing the rest of the day's developments. An application had been made for a Judge's Order to pursue enquiries on Unwin's name with the major banks. Wightlink had made available CCTV video recordings on the car ferry crossing to Fishbourne. P & O and Brittany Ferries were combing their customer databases for bookings in Unwin's name, a line of inquiry that should, in theory, yield a home address plus a registration number for his van. So far nothing had turned up and *Congress* was further hampered by the fact that no one had a clue what the man looked like.

'I talked to Media Services this morning,' Barber added. 'If we can come up with a photo, the *News* will stick it in the paper. Waifs and strays column. Return to owner asap.'

There was a single knock at the door. It was Bev Yates. He had a woman on the phone for Tracy. Sounded urgent.

Barber got up and left without a word. Faraday nodded at her empty seat. He'd worked with Yates for a couple of years now and had a great deal of respect for his judgement. At forty-four, Yates was still as bewildered as ever by the challenges of his private life, but a young wife and two squalling kids had done nothing to hamper his effectiveness on the job. This morning Faraday had asked him and his oppo – Gerry Mulligan – to scout the marina and boatyards around the edges of Bembridge Harbour in search of more information about Pelly. Specifically, he wanted to know about Pelly's previous boat.

'Tidemaster 21.' Yates sat down. 'I've even got a shot.'

He slipped a photocopied sheet from the back of his pocketbook. Faraday unfolded the sheet and studied the grainy black and white photo. It had come from the For Sale pages of a magazine and showed a sturdy working boat with a wheelhouse midships. The text below detailed the features on offer. Perkins diesel. VHF radio. Colour fish finder. Two bunks, self-draining deck, plus nav lights. 'Good clean sea boat,' the ad ended. '£9000'.

'This was Pelly's?' He returned the photocopy.

'Afraid not but he had one just like it.'

'Who says?'

'Bloke I talked to at one of the boatyards.' Yates glanced down at his pocketbook. 'Mark Sprake. He owns the yard and some of the moorings. Pelly's had one since 1995. Started at a hundred and twenty-five quid a year, now it's up to a hundred and fifty. The Tidemaster has been on the mooring for the last couple of years. Before that Pelly had something a bit smaller.'

'So what happened to the Tidemaster?'

'Sprake doesn't know.'

'What do you mean, doesn't *know*?'

Faraday didn't bother to hide his irritation. He was still smarting from yesterday's abortive SOC search, Pelly letting them waste an entire afternoon in the knowledge that they'd chosen the wrong boat.

'You think he sold it?' Faraday was still looking at the ad.

'It's possible.'

'What does Sprake think?'

'Hard to say. I get the impression they're all a bit careful about Pelly. If he sold it, then it certainly didn't happen locally.'

'Did he ever ask Pelly?'

'He says not.'

'So the boat's there one day, gone the next, and no one wondered why?'

'That's right.'

'What about the rent on the mooring?'

'Pelly still paid it. Made no difference. Then a couple of months later the new boat turns up. This one's bigger than the Tidemaster so Pelly's up for a few more quid. End of story.'

'I don't believe it.'

'Neither did I.'

'And?'

'We asked about. The key is the date, right? That's the crippler. If we can come up with a date when the Tidemaster actually went, then we've got the beginnings of some kind of timeline. One old guy we found was a fisherman, used to do it commercially, now just potters about. Got a little boat of his own; keeps the freezer full. We met him lunchtime, in the pub down there, The Pilot. The old guy says Pelly got shot of the Tidemaster around the end of September, beginning of October.'

'How does he know?'

'It was his wife's birthday. There's a fancy caff on the other side of the harbour, Baywatch on the Beach, and they put a special spread on for her at lunchtime. Coming round on the harbour road the old guy had a good view of Pelly's mooring. It was a Friday, and he remembers the Tidemaster wasn't there.'

'Maybe Pelly was out fishing.'

'Not on Fridays apparently. He never took the boat out on Fridays. Over the weekend the old guy kept his eyes open. No Tidemaster. Soon after that he bumped into Pelly at Tesco up in Ryde; asked him about the boat.'

'And?' Faraday, at last, was smiling.

'Pelly said he'd sold it on. Someone he'd met in France had come over with a trailer and carted it off. Seemed happy as Larry about it.'

'Did Pelly give a date for all this?'

'No. Just referred to last week. The old guy thought that was odd. He lives and breathes the harbour; he's down there every day. Nothing gets by him. Hauling a boat that size out is a bit of a performance. If it had happened, he says he'd have seen it.'

'Excellent. You statemented this old guy?'

'Going back tomorrow, boss. He said he wanted a bit of time to think about it. Shame. Another pint and there wouldn't have been a problem.'

'And the date? The wife's birthday?'

'October third.'

Faraday was already drawing a timeline. Around March Pelly expresses interest in one of the new Cheetah 7.9s. In June he comes up with the five-hundred-pound deposit. By August he's struggling to find £23,000 to start the build and Cheetah assign the hull to another customer when Pelly's cheque doesn't appear. At the end of September Chris Unwin makes final visits to Midhurst, Southsea and the Boniface Nursing Home to see his ancient Nan. After that he disappears. On 3 October an eagle-eyed local notices that Pelly's Tidemaster has also slipped its moorings. Three days later Cheetah Marine clears Pelly's cheque for £23,333.

Faraday asked to see the Tidemaster ad again. £9,000.

'Was Pelly's boat the same age as this one?'

'I've no idea, boss. The old guy in the pub said it was pretty knackered.'

'No more than nine grand, then?'

'Probably not.'

Faraday gazed at his pad. The timeline was perfect but the sums didn't begin to add up. The door opened again. It was Tracy Barber. She shut the door with the back of her foot and consulted a slip of paper.

'I've had Marie Grossman on the phone. She thinks she may be able to lay her hands on a photo of Unwin.'

'How come?' Faraday was still staring at the pad.

'There's a Pompey pub called the Speke Arms. They have local bands in on Sunday nights, plus the odd out-of-town muso when they can afford it.' She glanced down at Bev Yates. 'Ainsley Lister?'

'R and B.' Yates nodded his approval. 'Nottingham boy. Brilliant on a good night.'

'Well, the last time Ainsley was down, Marie and Chris Unwin happened to be in there as well. Apparently Unwin's a big fan. He got hammered that night and insisted on having his photo taken with the star. Marie remembers it like yesterday; didn't know where to hide herself. Said the guy with the camera was a local, another big fan of Ainsley's; might well still have the shots.'

Faraday was still trying to place the pub. Bev Yates came to the rescue.

'The Speke's in Fratton. Half of Paul Winter's dodgy snouts drink in there. Maybe you should give him a ring.'

Winter, nursing yet another headache, was contemplating an early exit from the squad office at Kingston Crescent when Faraday came through on his mobile. He hadn't seen Faraday for the best part of a year, not since *Tumbril* had hit the buffers. He'd done the DI a favour then, trying to help him out of the enveloping disaster, but it was obvious at once that Faraday hadn't called for a cosy chat.

'You know the Speke?'

'In Fratton? Of course I do.'

'We need a bit of help. Bev Yates says you're the man.'

Faraday outlined the message from Marie Grossman. It seemed that Winter had contacts who practically lived in the place. One of them might remember an R and B singer called Ainsley Lister and have the photies to prove it. Winter settled back in his chair, rubbing his eyes, trying to concentrate. A couple of calls would sort the information Faraday needed but first he wanted to know more.

'What's this about, then?'

Faraday said nothing for a moment, then he explained briefly about the headless body and about the missing Chris Unwin. Nothing was certain in this world but the two ends of this particular inquiry might well meet in the middle.

Winter was alert now. Even the numbing thump of the headache seemed, for a moment, to ease.

'When was this, then?'

'What?'

'This body of yours. When was it recovered?'

'Ten days ago.'

'You've done the PM?'

'Of course.'

'So how long had the guy been dead?'

'Hard to say. Could be three months, could be longer. The timeline we're looking at says early October if it's Unwin but we've nothing to stand it up.'

'Fine.' Winter shut his eyes a moment, willing himself to concentrate as the pain sluiced through his head. 'I'll make some calls; give you a bell later.'

Snapping the mobile shut, he got to his feet and walked unsteadily towards the door. One of the management assistants, watching him reach for the handle, wondered whether he'd been reckless enough to risk a heavy session at lunchtime. Then, without warning, Winter stumbled and fell. The management assistant was by him within seconds. His eyes were closed and his face felt clammy to the touch. A thin trickle of blood was threading down his temple from the impact with the door frame.

'What's going on?'

Cathy Lamb had appeared at her office door. Seeing Winter, she hurried over. On her knees beside him, she cradled his head for a moment, and then told the management assistant to help her turn him into the recovery position. Winter weighed a ton. By the time he was lying on his side, Cathy had found a tissue.

'You OK, Paul?' She dabbed at the blood.

'Fine.' Winter looked up at her a moment, and then began to vomit.

Cathy signalled for more tissues. Winter was still throwing up.

'Easy, Paul. Go easy.' She held his head again while

Winter emptied his stomach onto her skirt. His embarrassment was acute. He was struggling to get to his feet.

'I'm fine,' he kept saying. 'Just fine.'

Cathy calmed him down. A couple of passing PCs from Traffic saw what was happening and stepped in to lend a hand. They eased Winter away from the door and propped him upright against the wall. Winter couldn't take his eyes off Cathy Lamb's skirt.

'Shit,' he kept saying. 'I'm sorry.'

'No need. Just take it easy.'

'Yeah?' Winter was looking around now, alarmed. 'Where's Jimmy?'

'Haven't a clue, Paul. You need a doctor?'

'No.' He shook his head and then wiped his mouth with the proffered tissue. 'I'm OK now. Seriously. Just . . .' He shut his eyes and then squeezed hard. Red lights flared out of the darkness, bolts of raw pain. When he opened his eyes, Suttle was standing between Cathy Lamb and one of the blokes from Traffic. Draped over them, a curtain of bubbles. Winter reached up for Suttle. He was sweating again. He'd never felt worse in his life.

'Do us a favour, Jimmy?'

Suttle caught his hand and helped him to his feet. Cathy Lamb, after a moment's indecision, told him to stay put and then headed for the washrooms at the end of the corridor. On Suttle's arm, Winter made it back to his desk. One of the Traffic PCs had managed to find a first-aid box. Winter looked up at Jimmy Suttle.

'There's been a development,' he mumbled. 'You free tonight?'

Suttle drove Winter home. By the time they got to Bedhampton it was dark. Suttle walked him slowly up the garden path towards the squat bulk of the bungalow. Winter was breathing hard, like a man halfway up a mountain, and seemed to have difficulty remembering where he'd left his house keys.

'Trouser pocket,' he concluded.

Suttle recovered the keys. The fourth one fitted the front door. Inside the narrow hall he fumbled for the light switch. The house smelled damp and empty. This is where old people live, Suttle told himself.

Winter wanted a drink. Suttle headed for the kitchen, leaving Winter in his favourite chair beside the gas fire.

'Scotch.' Winter called him back and pointed at a glass-fronted cabinet on the other side of the room. 'There's ice in the fridge. You have one too but go easy, eh?'

'Why's that?'

'You're driving me.' Winter managed a grin. 'Chauffeur job.'

Suttle hesitated by the door, not at all sure where his real responsibilities lay. Everything told him that Winter should be in hospital, or – at the very least – in bed. Yet the conversation in the car had already convinced him that nothing short of handcuffs and a three-man escort would get the man anywhere near a doctor. He'd always been headstrong, even reckless, yet the longer Suttle worked with Winter the more he recognised how shrewd the man could be. He took risks, in fact he thrived on them, but they were finely calibrated and he seemed to have an instinct, an inner compass, that rarely let him down. Show Winter the toughest knot in the world and he'd somehow tease it out.

'You really think this bloke on the island is our

man? The guy with no head?' Suttle was back from the kitchen.

Winter stared up at the teacup, ignoring the question.

'What's that you've got?'

'Scotch. I couldn't find a glass.'

'Top cupboard on the left. I'm not drinking Scotch out of that.'

Suttle beat a retreat. Seconds later he was back. He gave the glass to Winter and watched him swallow the first mouthful. Almost at once he began to look better. There was colour in his face, even the beginnings of a smile.

'The bloke in the sea . . .' Suttle tried again.

'Has to be.' Winter's head was tipped against the back of the chair. 'The timings fit, the guy's the right age, and it was obviously a professional hit. Who else goes to the trouble of taking the head off? Eh?' He turned his head sideways, eyeing Suttle. 'Another thing.'

'What's that?'

'Wishart has access to boats. In fact he makes the fucking things. So tell me this. If you've got a body and nowhere to dump it, what do you do? Easy. You stuff it in a boat, drive into the middle of nowhere, and chuck it overboard.'

'So who is this guy?'

'God knows. They're saying Unwin, whoever Unwin is. He's a runner, definitely.'

'You want me to go down to the Speke? Talk to some of your guys?'

'No.'

'No? I thought we were after a photo?'

'We are, son. Or we will be.' Winter's eyes strayed

to the clock on the mantelpiece. 'There's a restaurant in Petersfield. Mon something. You know it?'

'Mon Plaisir. What about it?'

'We need to be there by seven.' Winter glanced down at his empty glass. 'Just time for the other half.'

By the time they got to Petersfield Winter seemed to have recovered. Mon Plaisir was a much-reviewed restaurant that occupied the bottom of a half-timbered house in a corner of the town's main square. According to Suttle, it specialised in French provincial cooking and three-figure bills. He'd been out with several local girls who were dying for a trophy meal there and one day, if he could raise a mortgage, he might give it a try himself.

He found a parking space with a perfect view of the restaurant and switched off the engine. So far Winter hadn't said a word. He sat in the passenger seat, slowly working his way through a packet of Werther's Originals, scanning the square for signs of life. At this time of night on a Thursday the middle of Petersfield was dead.

'Now what?'

'We wait.'

They sat in the half darkness for nearly an hour. Once, Suttle tried to start a conversation about Winter's state of health, suggesting a check-up might be a wise move, but Winter ignored him. Around 19.40 it began to get seriously cold and Suttle switched on the engine and turned up the heat but Winter wasn't having it. The engine off again, Winter peered across at the restaurant.

'He's late,' he muttered.

'Who is?'

'Wishart.'

'*Wishart?* We're waiting for Wishart?'

Again, Winter said nothing. Then a cold hand gave Suttle a pat on his thigh.

'You're a good lad,' Winter grunted.

Gone eight o'clock, Wishart finally arrived. The Jaguar coasted past them, a gleam of metal under the sodium lights. Wishart was behind the wheel, even bulkier in a heavy black coat. Beside him was another figure, slighter. Wishart found a parking space near the restaurant and got out, his breath clouding on the chill night air. The passenger door opened.

'Fucking Maddox.' Suttle threw Winter a look. 'You knew about this?'

'Yeah.'

'Set it up?'

'No.'

'But I thought he'd given her a slapping?'

'So did I.'

'So how come?'

Winter shook his head, refusing to go further. Wishart had taken Maddox by the arm. They paused briefly by the parking meter while he checked that they didn't need a ticket, then they kissed, a long kiss, his gloved hands cupping her battered face. Mon Plaisir lay across the road. Minutes later, without their coats, they were sitting in the window, bent towards each other in the flicker of candlelight across the elaborate table setting.

'What's she doing? Your eyes are better than mine.'

'She's talking to him. She's smiling. He's lighting a cigarette for her. She's laughing now. Christ knows why, state of her face.'

It was news to Winter that Maddox smoked. Another betrayal, he thought grimly.

'And Wishart?'

'He seems pretty relaxed. It's hard to tell from this angle. I can see her better than him.'

Drinks arrived. Maddox proposed some kind of toast. They touched glasses, kissed again. Then Wishart's hand disappeared into his jacket pocket.

'He's got a present for her. She's taking the paper off. It's some kind of jewellery box, long thing, maybe a necklace. Yeah, a necklace, definitely. She's looking at it, holding it up in the candlelight. Now she's trying it on. He's telling her something. She's laughing again.'

'And?'

'She can't get the thing on properly. He's got up. He's sorting out the clasp for her.'

Winter's eyes were closed now. Slumped in the passenger seat, he sucked on a Werther's, listening to Suttle's muttered commentary. He wanted it all, every last detail, every last particle of evidence proving that he'd got this woman so utterly wrong. She'd told Winter she wanted nothing more to do with this man. She'd said he'd chased her, harassed her, beat her, frightened her. She'd asked for Winter's protection. She'd wanted a sentry at her door. Yet here she was coiled around Wishart's little finger, his every last wish, another trophy in the big glass-fronted cabinet that was his life.

'What's happening now?'

'You don't want to hear this.'

'Tell me.'

'She's giving him a kiss. Must be the necklace. Now he's looking at his watch.' Suttle began to laugh. 'Maybe they'll skip the meal. Get right down to it. Who needs fancy cooking when it's already on a plate, eh?' Suttle glanced across the car at Winter. 'You OK?'

'Never better, son.' Winter struggled upright in the seat, pulled his coat more closely around him, then nodded at the clock on the dashboard. 'That thing right?'

'Yeah.'

'Good.' Winter smothered a yawn, no longer interested in the peep show across the road. 'You know how to find the Speke?'

Thirteen

It was Faraday's decision to press Willard to escalate *Congress* to a full HOLMES-based investigation. After a night back on the mainland for a meeting with a CPS lawyer on a previous job, he'd taken an early hover-craft, walking the half-mile from the Esplanade to Ryde police station. At this hour the Major Incident Room was still empty. Collecting the key from the front desk, Faraday took the stairs to the first floor and let himself in.

Already, the SIO's office had attracted a light snowfall of paperwork. Faraday made himself com-fortable behind his desk and sorted through the messages that had come in since he'd bailed out the previous evening: a formal list from the Land Registry of island properties owned in the name of R. Pelly; a scribbled note from Tracy Barber confirming a meet with an expert in tides and currents from Southampton University; a photocopied blow-up map of Bembridge Harbour, with properties warranting a visit edged in green highlighter; and a tally of bookings over the last eighteen months on P & O ferries in the name of Chris Unwin. The latter had come with a vehicle registration number and a Southsea residential address, 267 Bath Road.

Faraday gazed at it a moment, knowing another visit would be pointless. Unwin had long since moved on from Bath Road. The vehicle registration, on the other hand, was a breakthrough. Tracy Barber had already accessed the details of the van from the Police National Computer and would be circulating them to all forces first thing.

Faraday's gaze drifted back over the rest of the messages. Barely a day of serious legwork had already produced a good deal of information. Each of these lines of enquiry would generate further contacts, yet more interviews to be actioned, transcribed and added to the rapidly growing body of evidence that might make a second interview with Pelly a very different proposition. So far the investigation had been exploratory and therefore paper-based. Without the HOLMES computer program, software that would file and cross-index every scrap of information, *Congress* was already in danger of overlooking a vital lead.

Willard, still at home in Old Portsmouth, was halfway through his breakfast. Faraday talked him through yesterday's developments and the Detective Superintendent agreed at once to escalate the inquiry to HOLMES. They had a headless corpse and a possible ID. In the shape of Pelly they were looking at a prime suspect with means, opportunity and the first shadowy hint of motive. Pelly and Unwin had certainly fallen out. Pelly was a man who carried a grudge. The hunt now was for evidence of how lethal that grudge might have been.

'Back-record conversion.' Willard was thinking aloud. 'How many indexers will you need?'

Faraday had already decided on six. Three would be inputting current intelligence while the rest would be playing catch-up.

'DCs?'

'As many as you can spare, sir.' Faraday was looking

at the highlighted map. 'We need to blitz the area around Bembridge Harbour. That's serious house-to-house.'

Willard grunted something about the New Forest job that Faraday didn't catch. Then he was asking about what else Faraday had in mind for the Outside Enquiry Team. Faraday touched all the obvious bases. He wanted detectives into all of Pelly's properties. He wanted interviews with whoever lived there. He wanted to know where they'd come from, how they'd travelled, and what part Pelly played in their lives. At the nursing home itself he wanted further interviews with staff and residents. It might be asking a lot of a gaga eighty-year-old, but the inquiry team had already anchored a timeline on early October, and he needed every scrap of information to try and build a picture of what might have happened over that first week.

'How about SOC?'

'On Pelly's place? I'll be talking to the Shanklin boys this morning. Pelly's had four months to tidy up but you never know your luck.'

'You'll need to raise an intelligence cell. You want Imber again?'

'Please.'

'OK.'

Brian Imber was an ultra-fit 54-year-old DS who'd carved out a force-wide reputation for himself in the war against drugs. A brilliant intelligence analyst, he'd be the key to fleshing out the rumours about Pelly's people-smuggling activities. In all probability, he'd bring someone with him, maybe one of the Hantspol Field Intelligence Officers.

Willard had evidently finished his breakfast. He said he'd be in the office by half eight. Nick Hayder would fight like a terrier to retain at least a couple of bodies for the clear-up on the New Forest job, but with one or two exceptions on the leave roster the rest of the Major Incident Team had nothing seriously pressing to do. With luck, by lunchtime, Faraday should be looking at an Outside Inquiry team of around a dozen DCs, with a DS in charge back in the incident room, plus another DS to sieve the incoming material as it began to flood in.

'So who do you want as Statement Reader?'

'Dave Michaels.'

'You're telling me he's cracked HOLMES Two?'

'Of course.'

'Good fucking luck.'

Willard barked with laughter and rang off. The statement reader was a key part of the team, scanning incoming interviews for those all-important titbits that flag the path to a successful conviction. The original HOLMES package was hard copy – mountains of paper – and Dave Michaels had been an artist with the ruler and the felt-tip pen, somehow able to keep the ever-growing jigsaw of inquiries intact in his head. HOLMES Two, on the other hand, now put the whole process on screen, and the DS was famously ham-fisted when it came to key strokes. Not only that, but he had a murderous temper. The last time Faraday and Michaels had worked together on the updated software package, the DS had been briefly hospitalised after putting his fist through his PC screen.

Faraday reached for a pen and circled Pelly's name. The investigative machine he was about to lead had an awesome reach. Hundreds of man-hours, umpteen databases, forensic tests so precise they could put a name and a date of birth to a three-cell smear of DNA, all of this lay in wait for the gaunt, driven shadow who'd so far kept them all guessing. The man had a certain presence. He made no secret of the short cuts he was prepared to make. When necessary, he dealt in the currency of violence. But was that really enough to drive him to homicide?

Something told Faraday that it wasn't but, try as he might, he couldn't explain why. Maybe it was his relationship with Lajla, his so-called wife. Maybe it was something buried in the image that Faraday had carried away from the home the last time he'd been up there: the three of them, Pelly, Lajla and the girl Fida, locked in an embrace, holding each other, comforting each other, keeping the world away from their door. Every investigation has a series of special moments, Faraday thought, when the truth begins to reveal itself. And he had a growing conviction that this was one of them.

'Sir?'

Faraday looked up to find Bev Yates at the door. He'd slept badly, been roused by an obscenely early call.

'Winter,' he explained briefly, 'thinks he's laid hands on a photo of Unwin.'

Winter was back at the wheel. A good night's sleep and a fistful of painkillers had routed the demons in his head and he felt immeasurably better. In an early phone call to Cathy Lamb he'd promised to settle her dry cleaning bill, go easy on the liquid lunches and consult his GP. The fact that he hadn't touched daytime alcohol since the weekend didn't matter. Better that his DI put yesterday down to a bucketful of Stella than he bother her with the truth.

He took the slip road off the end of the motorway, and slowed for the big roundabout that fed traffic into the continental ferry port. Suttle was up at the *News* centre in Hilsea, talking to a reporter about putting Unwin's photo in the paper.

Last night, at the Speke, they'd scored a result within minutes. Friday evenings featured R and B bands, and one of Winter's army of informants was best mates with the bloke who sorted out the audio rig. He, in turn, knew exactly who took all the photos and pointed him out in a gaggle of drinkers arguing the toss about Pompey's chances in tomorrow's away game. A word in his ear, a drink for himself and his girlfriend, and Winter was on a promise to accompany them both home at closing time for a browse through the photograph album. Suttle came too, and he was the one who spotted Unwin.

'Has to be him. Complete dickhead. Look.'

He was right. Chris Unwin was on the right in the photo, a tallish, gangly figure with an inane grin and a leather jacket that was several sizes too big across the shoulders. One arm was around a startled-looking guitarist and in his other hand, elevated for the camera, he held a crudely lettered sign that read 'The A-Lmighty'.

'Get it?' Suttle asked Winter. 'A-L-mighty? A-insley L-ister?'

The photographer from the Speke confirmed Suttle's hunch. He'd included the shot in his album because he said it summed up the freakiness of that particular night. Lister was playing Southsea after an embarrassment some months earlier when he'd forgotten to turn up. This gig was a freebie for the benefit of his many fans and none of them had been disappointed. He'd played four sets in all, each progressively wilder, and the evening had ended with a hard core of doped-out R and B fans holding an impromptu whip-round to buy their star a diary and an alarm clock. Never again did they want their expectations raised in vain. Ainsley, like the poster said, was God Almighty.

Winter circled the ferry port until he found a parking spot within walking distance of the Immigration office. Last night's ID parade had developed into a bit of a session. An evening on quality skunk had stilled any doubts Winter's new friend might have had about the company he was keeping, and he'd willingly offered some thoughts about young Chrissie. Unwin, he'd said, was a liability. Tell him anything and it'd be round the town in half an hour. He was a lunatic that way, trading rumours and gossip for some half-arsed notion that he might win himself friends, and what made it especially sad was his constant habit of boasting about the strokes he'd pulled abroad.

Unwin, according to the photographer, was a part-time people smuggler. He had a toshed-up old van, and a million contacts in the world of French country auctions, and on some trips he quadrupled his winnings by stuffing the wardrobes in the back of the van with asylos he picked up in Cherbourg. There was a place he knew where they waited for a crossing. Lots went on fishing boats and somehow made it to the Isle of Wight. Some, lucky enough to meet our hero, shipped in through Pompey. Never had he been stopped. Never had he made less than one fifty a head. Hence the wad in his back pocket just begging to buy the whole fucking world a drink.

Winter, checking that he still had the original photo, could well believe it. What never failed to surprise him was how obvious most crime was, and how retarded most criminals. 'These people are shit,' he'd once told Cathy Lamb. 'They're inbreds. We ought to remember that.'

'Mick Kingston about?' Winter was standing in the tiny reception area, eyeballing a tall blonde behind the desk. Immigration officers were never less than hostile and this woman, although pretty enough, was no exception.

'Who wants him?'

'DC Winter.' Winter flipped his warrant card. 'Remind him he owes me.'

The woman checked the card longer than was strictly necessary, then disappeared through a door at the back. Seconds later she returned.

'He says to go on in.'

Winter stepped round the counter and through the door. The office, part of a Portakabin, had seen better days. Mould was growing on the damp stains beneath the window and the desk was sagging where one of its legs had collapsed. Pervading everything was the heavy fug of tobacco smoke.

'All right?'

Mick Kingston was demolishing a doughnut from a paper bag. There was a light dusting of sugar on his chin and a smear of jam around the corner of his mouth. His uniform jacket hung on the back of the door.

'Mr W.' He got up and wiped his hand on his trousers. 'Who do we blame for this pleasure?'

Winter produced the photo.

'Him, since you ask.'

'Who's that?'

'Bloke called Chris Unwin.' Winter wrinkled his nose. 'Don't you lot ever open a window?'

'No point. Heating's fucked. Open the window and you'll freeze your arse off.' He was still looking at the photo. 'Bloke on the right?' Winter nodded. 'Why him?'

'Suss people smuggling. Said to come through here regularly.'

'Yeah?'

Kingston got to his feet and bent to a computer at the other desk. A couple of key strokes took him into a database. He began to scroll through.

'Unwin, you say?'

'Yeah.'

'No.' He shook his head. 'He's not on the name manifest.'

'What's that? Some kind of watch list?'

'Yeah. We keep an eye on the obvious ones. The older the van the bigger the interest. Establish a pattern and – bingo! – full turnout. Dogs, scanners, black magic, the fucking works, mate. Blokes like him, no chance.'

'But he's not on your list.'

'That's right.'

'So what's gone wrong?'

'Where do you want to start?' He returned to the armchair and the rest of his doughnut. 'Number one, we don't have the blokes, not any more. Number two, this is a full EU port, the punters just sail through. You sure he used Pompey? Only Poole would have been even better. It's unmanned most of the time and word's been out for months.'

'You're kidding.'

'Afraid not. Fortress Britain?' he began to laugh. 'Believe that kind of crap and you'll end up in politics. Listen, leave me a note of the name. Write it down or something. I'll see what we can do next time he comes through.'

'I'll spare you the trouble.'

'Why's that?'

'He's probably dead.'

*

Willard was as good as his word. By lunchtime the MIR at Ryde police station was filling with personnel. DS Dave Michaels had been one of the first over, accepting Faraday's invitation to set up base camp in the bigger of the two squad rooms. From here he organised the trickle of indexers who arrived off the hovercraft or the Fast Cat, civilians from Basingstoke and Southampton who'd responded to Willard's bugle call, packed their bags, and headed south. One by one they settled behind the computer screens that lined the walls of the incident room, working their way through yesterday's statements, opening files, inputting data, readying the system for the flood of information to come.

Faraday, meanwhile, briefed the other of the two DSs, a bright high-flyer called Pete Baker who was to be in charge of the Outside Inquiry Team. Baker had been on Major Crimes for less than six months but already he'd won glowing reports from Willard. To the Detective Superintendent Baker embodied exactly that blend of sharp intelligence and thrusting ambition that badged a man for glory. Faraday, who'd seen Baker wilt under less than extreme conditions, wasn't quite so sure. Baker certainly talked a good war but from Willard's eminence it was all too easy to mistake presentational skills for something else entirely. In Faraday's view, the DS role on Major Crimes was the hinge of the whole operation. Unless he had a talent for hard graft, for insisting on scrupulous standards of evidence-gathering, for keeping the troops up to the mark, then *Congress* was in trouble.

'Boss?' It was Brian Imber.

Imber, too, was a DS but on this occasion he'd been shipped in by Willard to head the intelligence cell. A year ago, on Operation *Tumbril*, he and Faraday had nearly come to blows as a year's worth of work disintegrated in less than twenty-four hours. Both men had observed a decent period of mourning – no phone calls, no face-to-face contact – but a chance meeting on a Waterloo-bound train had healed the deeper scars, and now they were back on the best of terms. Imber had just run his farewell marathon, a murderous twenty-six miles around the Peak District, and couldn't resist showing Faraday the snap his wife had taken as he crossed the line.

'Three hours nine.' He pointed at the wiry, mud-splashed figure, both arms raised. 'Not bad for a geriatric.'

Faraday called for Tracy Barber and then went hunting for an extra chair. Most of the morning, off and on, he'd been devoting some thought to this conversation. In his experience intelligence fuelled most successful inquiries and *Congress* would surely be no exception.

'DC Barber's ex-SB.' Faraday found a space for Imber.

'I know.' Imber sat down. 'I was talking to Six this morning. Paula Adamson. She sends her regards.'

Mention of the name brought a blush of pleasure to Barber's cheeks. Six was police-speak for MI6. Access to their intelligence files was heavily restricted. Uniform or CID didn't have a prayer. Only Special Branch were in the same loop.

Imber was still looking at Tracy Barber.

'What else have we got?'

'Not much.' Barber ducked her head. 'Lots of local scuttlebutt, whispers mainly, but nothing you could take to court. I understand we've got Pelly's lodgers on today's outside inquiries list. That's a good place to start.'

Faraday nodded. The full *Congress* team should be in place by late afternoon, and he'd launch this stage of the investigation with a squad meeting. He'd begin with a detailed background brief, the story of the inquiry to date, and then call for Pete Baker to allocate tomorrow's actions. These would concentrate on house-to-house inquiries around the edges of Bembridge Harbour, with a smaller team handling staff and resident interviews at the Boniface Nursing Home.

Imber wanted to know more about Pelly's lodgers.

'Are these guys legal?'

'He says yes. And most of them work for him through an agency.'

'He takes a percentage? Charges bed and board?'

'Exactly. This time of year it's mainly grading and packing for the supermarkets. That and casual work in the catering trade. We think he also ships some of his guys off the island and up to the north. In fact the bloke in the frame for the body may have been driving the van.'

'You've got a name?'

'Chris Unwin. No one's seen him since October. There's other stuff fits the timeline.'

Faraday took Imber through the known chronology. Imber, to whom this kind of narrative was meat and drink, was impressed.

'That's in two days?'

'Three.'

'You've done well. What else do we know about Pelly?'

Faraday told him. Pelly appeared to have served in the army. He may have met Lajla in Bosnia during the war. Either way, she'd come to the UK in 1993 and married Pelly soon afterwards. She had one daughter, Fida.

'Pelly's?'

'She says not.'

'Do we have a unit for him in the army? Anyone looked up his record?'

'No.' Faraday shook his head. 'He's got an SAS tattoo on one arm but that might mean anything.'

Imber smiled, familiar with a world where men lived out their fantasies and sometimes paid the price.

'What's he like then, this Pelly?'

Faraday and Tracy Barber exchanged glances.

'He's strange.' It was Barber this time. 'Extremely volatile. Extremely chippy. Bitter, even. Lots of mouth. Easily wound up. Allegedly violent. Bit of a piss artist, according to some. On the other hand –' she frowned '– he seems pretty genuine around the old folk in the home, and sounding off at the state of the nation's no crime.'

'He does that a lot?'

'All the time. Press the right button and you get both barrels. He hates the place – us, taxmen, the weather, you name it. It might be a blind but I doubt it. The English are shit. Official.'

'Bitter sounds about right.'

'Yeah.' Faraday leaned forward. 'But it's more than that, Brian. I can't put my finger on it, not yet, but there's something else going on there. He's a bad boy. I'll put money on it. But the real question is why.' He looked up, catching Imber's eye. 'Am I making any sense?'

Winter was parked up on the seafront when he finally got through to DI Cathy Lamb. From fifty metres, he had perfect line of sight on Rose Tower. Maddox's flat was up on the tenth floor. Early afternoon, the windows of her bedroom were still curtained, an image that caused Winter physical pain.

'Paul?' Cathy sounded equally harassed. 'Where are you?'

'South Parade. About to interview a witness. Jimmy and I have come up with a possible hit. Bloke called Unwin.'

He began to explain about the headless body recovered from the Isle of Wight but Cathy cut him short. She'd had Terry Alcott on. The ACC was under fire again from Wishart. He'd returned from abroad to find everyone talking about a visit from the Drugs Squad and a botched repair on the remains of his front door. Alcott wasn't bothered about Wishart's threats to go to the Police Authority and his local MP. Just wanted assurance that inquiries were on track and likely to be productive.

'Productive?' Winter hadn't taken his eyes off Maddox's flat.

'He wants a result, Paul, and the faster you turn this round the less chance I have of referring it to Major Crimes. You with me?'

'Of course. Does Alcott think we're still chasing Wishart on drugs charges?'

'For the time being, yeah. But there are limits, Paul. As ever.'

Lamb rang off. Winter had been dreading the moment Cathy Lamb picked up the phone to Willard and surrendered control of *Plover* but for now he seemed to have won a stay of execution. He studied his mobile a moment, wondering why Suttle hadn't been in touch, then keyed in his number.

Suttle was still at the *News* building, up in the north of the city. Winter wanted to know why.

'Tell you later.'

'You alone?'

'No.'

'Tricky, is it?'

'Very.'

Winter ended the conversation with a grunt and pocketed the phone. Outside, standing on the pavement, the wind was icy. Winter buttoned his car coat and walked across to the flats. Up on the tenth floor the carpeted hall was empty. Winter paused briefly beside a vase full of roses on a table beside the lift. A single touch told him they were artificial. Fitting, he thought grimly, heading for Maddox's door.

She answered on the third ring. Her face was pale but the worst of the bruising had gone. She was wearing a man's shirt, the lightest blue, not much else. Her bare feet curled on the cold cherrywood floor.

Winter pushed past her without a word. What he really wanted to find was Wishart in her bed. He wasn't at all sure where a scene like that might lead but it would certainly spare him the chore of trying to screw the truth out of someone he'd thought he could trust.

Maddox's bed was empty. A paperback lay open on her pillow and there was a writing pad on the floor with an uncapped fountain pen beside it.

'Where have you been?' Maddox was standing in the doorway, her long body propped against the jamb.

'Working. Where do you think?'

'I've been worried about you. How's the head?'

'Better. Since you ask.'

'Better how?'

'Clearer.' He managed a chilly smile. 'You mind getting some clothes on? I'll wait next door.'

He stepped past her without waiting for an answer. She joined him on the sofa, tucking her knees under her chin. She looked calm, not the slightest evidence of guilt or embarrassment. She wanted to know what had happened.

Winter gazed at her, knowing already that resolution and willpower weren't enough. Maddox cast a spell he simply couldn't fathom. In barely a minute she'd turned him back into an adolescent. He couldn't remember feeling so helpless, so angry, so betrayed.

'*Happened*? What is all this shit . . . ?' He looked away, wondering where to start. Maddox saved him the trouble.

'Is it about last night?'

The question floored Winter. He stared at her, uncomprehending. She offered the briefest smile.

'Petersfield. The square outside the restaurant. You were in the car with the other guy. The young one.'

'You saw us?'

'Of course. You gave me a lift back here the other day. Same car. Subaru. Remember?'

'Yeah. I do.' Winter nodded. 'Of course I do. What about Wishart?'

'What about him?'

'Did he see us?'

'No.'

'You didn't tell him?'

'Of course not.'

'So what was all that about? The necklace? The meal? You all over him?' Winter fought to keep himself under control. 'Isn't Wishart the guy who drops by on a weekend and gives you a smacking? Isn't he the bloke you're trying to get rid of? Or am I missing something here?'

'You're missing nothing.'

'So explain it. Pretend I'm even thicker than I look. Pretend I haven't sat up half the night wondering what kind of prat you really take me for. Just pretend for a moment that any of this matters.'

'Any of what?'

'This. Us.'

'You think it doesn't?'

'Jesus.' Winter was on his feet now. 'You want the truth? I don't know what to think. I'm here on a job. I'm a working cop. I've come with a list of questions and a photo I'm going to show you but before we get round to any of that I'd quite like a steer on where you're coming from. Wishart beat you up, or that's what you told me. Barely a week later you're telling the guy to help himself. That's pretty subtle, isn't it? Too fucking subtle for me.'

'You want to sit down? Talk about it?'

'No. I want you to explain. Not lie. Not fanny around. Not treat me like a punter. Just explain. Call it a favour. Call it whatever you like. But just tell me the way it is.'

'OK.' Maddox held Winter's gaze. 'He phoned.'

'When?'

'Yesterday afternoon. He'd flown in from Warsaw, gone straight back to Port Solent. He was spitting nails. Someone had broken into his flat.'

'That would be me.'

'I know. You'd left a card. He told me.'

'And?'

'He wanted to drag me out to dinner.'

'Really?'

'Yes.'

'First time was it? Bit of an adventure?'

'Not at all. We've done it before. Quite a lot.'

'I thought you told me it was strictly business? Camber Court? Couple of hours in bed and leave your cheque on the pillow?'

285

'I was lying.'

'Why?'

The question had been a long time coming but Winter sensed that she must have anticipated it. Her head went down. She began to pick at a loose thread on the hem of the shirt. She's acting, he thought. Again.

'There was a time when I thought it might work,' she said quietly.

'Did you encourage him?'

'I didn't say no.'

'But were you keen? Did you –' Winter shrugged, remembering every word of the emails '– ever write to him?'

'Yes.'

'Make him feel . . .' Winter had done his best to avoid the word. 'Loved?'

'Yes. And I might even have meant it too. He's a powerful man. Powerful men can be sexy, believe it or not.'

'So why didn't you tell me this before?'

'Because I needed him off my back. The thing had become impossible. Like I said, he just wanted too much of me. I told him that but he wouldn't listen. When he lost his temper, when he hit me, I knew I had to find a way out of it. Then you turned up.'

'Yeah.' Winter nodded. 'Mr Gullible.'

'Not at all. Most men I know would have tried to shag me and then moved on. You've gone way past that.'

Winter permitted himself a rueful smile. Maddox was more right than she knew.

'Tell me about last night.' He returned to the sofa, sat down. 'We didn't stick around.'

'Shame. You missed the best bits.'

'Really? And you expect me to believe that?'

'Yes.' She nodded. 'Because it's true. I'd agreed to the meal because I had to tell him it was over. The only way you do that with someone like Maurice is dress it up. They can't handle rejection. There has to be another way.'

'So what did you tell him?'

'I told him about you. I said we'd become friends. I said you cared enough to want to look out for me.'

'You think that's true?'

'Yes, I do.'

'How did he take it?'

'Badly. We never got as far as the main course. The management had to call a cab.'

'Why?'

'Ask them. They were brilliant.'

'Wishart got stroppy again?'

'Ask them,' she repeated. 'The *patron*'s a Mr Lawrence – Tony Lawrence, ex-navy, just like Maurice. Thank God he was there.'

Winter kept telling himself this was bullshit. All the same he badly wanted it to be true. At length he produced the photo from the Speke Arms, Chris Unwin alongside Ainsley Lister.

'The bloke on the right.' He touched the grinning face. 'Ever seen him before?'

Maddox spent a moment or two looking at the photo. Then she shook her head.

'Never,' she said. 'Why?'

Winter explained about the body on the Isle of Wight. If Wishart had meant what he'd said about a contract hit, then Chris Unwin might well have been the target. Maddox's gaze returned to the photo. Then she looked up at Winter.

'Strange,' she said.

'Why?'

'Because all of that came up last night. In fact that's what set Maurice off. I'd had a go about last weekend, what happened up here, how horrible he'd been. When that made no difference, I reminded him about what he'd told me before Christmas. He frightens me, he really does, and I was honest enough to say so.'

'And?'

'He just laughed. Told me it was nothing. Little game, that's all.'

'He denied it?'

'Not at all. To Maurice, getting rid of someone's no big deal. He admits it, even boasts about it. He says it's just business. Needs must. Means and ends. His words, not mine.'

'And you?'

'I told him I couldn't cope with all this stuff. In fact it was worse than that. I'd had a bit to drink by then and I gave him a choice. Either he left me alone, got out of my life, or I'd take it further.'

'Take what further?'

'The stuff about the contract, having this person killed.'

'And how would you do that?'

'By telling you.' She reached for his hand. 'That's when he threatened to kill me, too.'

Fourteen

Faraday sent a Scenes of Crime team into the Boniface Nursing Home in the early afternoon. He attended with the warrant himself, all too aware of Pelly's likely reaction, but the proprietor's absence spared him a confrontation at the front door. Instead, Faraday found himself trying to explain the situation to Lajla.

'We have to conduct a search.' He indicated the activity behind him. 'It may take some time.'

'How long?'

'Two days? Maybe three?'

Lajla was staring at the vehicles occupying the half crescent of gravel that served as a parking area at the front of the house. The DS in charge at Shanklin had decided on a forensic team of five. As well as a Crime Scene Manager and a couple of investigators, he'd attached a scientist and a photographer. Already, they were pulling on their grey one-piece suits.

'What are you looking for?' Lajla's voice was low.

'I'm afraid I can't discuss that. For the time being we'll be limiting the search to you and your husband's private accommodation. Do you have a garage at the back? Some kind of workshop?'

'A garage, yes.' Lajla was transfixed by the sight of an Alsatian emerging from the back of a van. Faraday had asked for an initial drugs sweep in case Gary

289

Morgan had been right about Pelly importing narcotics from France.

'And a workshop? Outhouse?'

'Yes. Come.'

Faraday followed her round the corner of the
building. Twin ribbons of concrete led to a double
garage. Beyond, adjoining the garden, was a low
timber-framed building that reminded Faraday of a
miniature cricket pavilion. The single door had
recently been repainted and the padlock looked new.

'What's in here?'

Lajla's bare arms were goose-pimpled with cold.

'All kinds of things. Old furniture. Boxes. Tools for
the garden'. She shrugged. 'You know.'

'And you always keep it locked?'

'Of course.' Her eyes flicked left and Faraday turned
in time to see the Crime Scene Manager approaching
with one of the investigators. The CSM needed to be
clear about the search parameters. Cleaned-up crime
scenes were never less than challenging.

Faraday explained about the garage and the outhouse. Then he turned back to Lajla. She was shivering
with cold.

'How many cars do you have?'

'Me?'

'You and your husband, between you.'

'Just one.'

'And he's out in it at the moment? Mr Pelly?'

'Yes.'

'Is it a new car?' It was the Crime Scene Manager.

'New? I don't understand. Nothing we have is new.'

'What about the boat?'

'The boat?' Lajla was beginning to panic. Faraday
and the CSM exchanged glances. Then Faraday
pressed the point.

'We searched your husband's boat yesterday. I understand it was brand new.'

'Yes, of course.' Lajla nodded. 'I forget.'

'So what about the car? Is that new as well?'

'No. It's old, an old car.'

'How long have you had it?'

'I don't know. It's hard. I can't remember. You must ask my husband.'

'But have you changed it recently? You must be able to remember that, surely.'

'No.' She looked from face to face to face, hunted, miserable. 'We had another car. Now we have this one. It's bigger, better. Rob goes to the cash and carry.'

'But when did you get it? Before Christmas?'

'Yes.'

'How long before Christmas?'

'Please.' She took a tiny backwards step. 'My English isn't so good.'

At Faraday's prompting they went indoors. An entrance at the side of the house led to a corridor Faraday recognised from his previous visit. Once again, he found himself in Lajla's sitting room.

'You share all this with your husband?' Faraday nodded towards the adjoining bedroom.

'No.' Lajla shook her head. 'Rob has his own rooms. Fida and I, we live here.'

'Where are they, your husband's rooms?'

'Upstairs.'

'May we see them?'

'Of course but . . .' Her head went down. 'He locks them.'

'They're locked now?'

'I think so.'

They all went upstairs. The narrow corridor at the top was poorly lit. Faraday tried the first of three doors, then the rest. Lajla was right. They were all locked. In the gloom the three men blocked Lajla's retreat to the head of the stairs, the unvoiced question hanging between them. What kind of a marriage allowed for a set-up like this? Separate accommodation, everything of Pelly's locked?

Faraday stepped aside, letting Lajla hurry past them. There was a row of black and white photos, nicely framed, hanging on the wall between two of the doors. Faraday paused, inspecting the first of them. It was a view of a valley. In the foreground, beyond the fire-blackened ruins of a farmhouse, an orchard of fruit trees was frothing with blossom. A track wound past the orchard and down to an ancient bridge over a sizeable stream. The centre of the bridge's arch had collapsed, and the water bubbled and pleated around the fallen stones. In the distance appeared the swell of the encircling mountains, black against an ominous sky. It was a curiously wistful shot, Faraday thought; paradise smudged by the hand of man.

The CSM and the investigator were waiting for Faraday at the foot of the stairs. Of Lajla, there was no sign. Faraday detailed the areas he wanted searched. The CSM nodded, scribbling himself a note, then indicated the still-open door to Lajla's apartment.

'Someone's been in there with the paintbrush.' He glanced back at Faraday. 'You notice that?'

Faraday nodded.

'I did.' He glanced at his watch. 'And the carpet's brand new, too.'

Winter had collected DC Suttle at the *News* building at the top of the city. Now they were heading north up the motorway towards Petersfield. Winter wanted to know what had prompted Suttle to spend an hour or so leafing through back numbers of the city's daily paper when they had a ready-made fall guy for Wishart's ever-open chequebook.

'Unwin? I just don't buy it. You were there last night. The guy's a wide boy. Say it's true about the asylos. Say he's bringing them in by the vanful. What's that got to do with Wishart? The man's a suit. He owns companies, does deals. Unwin isn't in his league, unless he tried to flog him the wrong French wardrobe. And you wouldn't take out a contract for that, would you? No matter how much you hated the fucking colour.'

In spite of himself, Winter laughed. There were days when Jimmy Suttle reminded Winter of his own CID apprenticeship. When the lad bothered to concentrate, he had the makings of a reasonable detective.

'OK,' Winter conceded. 'Let's pretend you're right. Let's just say it's one big coincidence. Who else we put in the frame? Got a name, have you?'

'Yeah, matter of fact.'

'Like who?'

'Not saying, not yet.'

'*What?*' Winter began to laugh. The parallels were even closer than he'd thought. 'We on the same side here? Same job? Same pay grade?'

Suttle didn't respond. He'd helped himself to one of Winter's Werther's Originals and he sucked on the sweet as the Waterlooville exit sped past. A mile or so later he turned in his seat, favouring Winter with the widest of grins.

'All that bollocks yesterday morning,' he began. 'In the Coroner's office.'

'What about it?'

'We were looking in the wrong area.' He reached for the bag again. 'Turns out it wasn't Pompey at all.'

*

The restaurant at Petersfield was closed. Winter eyed the *Fermé* sign on the door and rang the owner on his mobile. Within a minute Tony Lawrence had appeared on the pavement, a lanky sallow-faced individual who clearly resented this abrupt intrusion in his well-ordered day.

'I thought you said two o'clock?'

'Got delayed. My apologies. You mind if we talk inside?'

With some reluctance, Lawrence led the way into the restaurant. The dozen or so tables were already laid for dinner. Behind the tiny bar a door led to an office. There was only room for a desk and a couple of chairs. Suttle stayed on his feet, inches from a calendar advertising wines from the Médoc. He'd no idea what an apple-cheeked blonde with an enormous chest had to do with *appellation contrôlée* but he wasn't complaining.

Winter wanted to know about two of last night's guests. They'd been sitting at the table in the window, a middle-aged man and a younger woman.

'Maurice Wishart.' Lawrence cut him short. 'Is that what this is about?'

'You know Wishart?'

'Very well. Have done for years.'

'He's a friend?'

'I like to think so.'

'And the woman he was with last night? You know her too?'

'Not really.' Lawrence frowned. 'Why?'

Winter ignored the question. He'd had a formal complaint about a scene in the restaurant last night. The woman was alleging that Wishart had threatened to kill her.

'Maurice lost it.' Lawrence was dismissive. 'It happens sometimes.'

'Do you know why he lost it?'

'Haven't a clue. Domestic tiff? Some kind of argument? I run a restaurant, Mr Winter, not a therapy group.'

'I understood you had to intervene.'

'That's true. I called a taxi for the young lady.'

'Were there other guests?'

'Yes. We had half a dozen covers last night. Naturally, we try and avoid giving offence. In this case there wasn't a problem. Maurice flared up, went too far, behaved like a prat. I had a call from him this morning. Mea culpa. Full apology.' He offered Winter a chilly smile. 'Case closed.'

'Did he hit her?'

'I think he tried, yes.'

'You think . . . ?'

'One of the waitresses came to find me. That's when I stepped in.'

'And what did she say?'

'She said that Maurice . . .' He shrugged. 'Listen, Mr Winter, it was nothing, absolutely nothing. It warrants neither your time nor mine.'

'Maurice what?'

Lawrence shook his head, refusing to go any further. At length Winter produced a pocketbook. He wanted a name and contact details for the waitress. He might also want to interview guests who were in a position to supply witness statements. Lawrence looked at him a moment longer, not bothering to hide his irritation.

'It seems he got her by the throat. There was a necklace of some kind. God knows. As I just tried to explain, Maurice is an old friend. We go back a long way. I'm sure he meant no harm. Maybe he'd had one too many. Maybe this woman had spoken out of turn.'

'Out of *turn*?' Winter began to laugh. 'What kind of relationship are we talking about here? You invite someone to dinner and they have to have permission to speak? Out of *turn*?'

'Wrong phrase. Badly put. Maybe she wound him up. Christ knows.'

Winter nodded, seeming to accept the explanation. Then he asked what happened after the woman had gone.

'Maurice and I had coffee.'

'What did he say?'

'I can't remember.'

'Was he upset?'

'Not particularly. He's a busy man, Mr Winter. Lots on his mind. I offered to call him a cab as well but he chose to drive. Like I say, it was a tiny incident. I'm sure the lady will get over it. Frankly, I've no idea why you're here.'

Winter began to ask another question, this time about previous occasions when Wishart may have dined with the same woman, but Suttle intervened. He wanted to know whether Wishart was a regular guest at the restaurant.

'Yes.' Lawrence stared up at him. 'Is that some kind of crime?'

'Not at all. Does he bring business contacts here? To your knowledge?'

'Yes, I'm sure he does. In fact I know he does. We open for lunch during the summer. I think he finds it a convivial setting.'

'And do you –' Suttle smiled at him '– get to talk to any of these people?'

'From time to time. *En passant . . .*'

'Would you remember names? Faces?'

'I'm not with you.'

'Wishart's a friend of yours, Mr Lawrence. He drops in here socially. He uses the place to wine and dine people he wants to impress. You'd notice them, remember them.' Suttle paused, aware of Winter beside him. 'So my question is this. We're talking last year, maybe the summer, maybe lunch. Did Wishart ever turn up with a black guy? Mid-thirties? Maybe in naval uniform?'

There was a long silence. Lawrence held Suttle's gaze, his face betraying nothing. Finally, he shook his head.

'No,' he said softly. 'I don't remember anyone like that.'

Faraday was back from Shanklin by mid-afternoon. Most of the indexers had arrived by now and were bent over keyboards in the Incident Room, punching in data from the investigation's opening days. At his desk at the other end of the room DS Pete Baker was deep in conversation with a couple of DCs who'd just stepped off the hovercraft. Their overnight bags were stacked with the others in the corner, and one of them was making notes while Baker briefed them on the details of a particular action.

Faraday watched them for a moment, aware of the sheer reach of the investigative machine under his command. On division, as a DI, you were a firefighter, tackling outbreaks of minor crime day after day, throwing a DC or two at a shoplifter, or a walk-in artist, or some scrote who made a bob or two by flogging contraband lager round the estates. Here, by contrast, you could afford to focus enormous resources – forensic, house-to-house, intelligence – on a single event, tracking backwards through hundreds of statements and thousands of words until you'd teased out a motive, and a means, and some semblance of explanation for a man's death. As an intellectual proposition major inquiries had never failed to fascinate Faraday. Now, as conductor of this orchestra, he found them faintly daunting. So many options. So many false leads. So many opportunities to drop the baton and lose the beat.

En route to his office, Faraday was intercepted by Dave Michaels. The DS had been talking to the enquiry teams working their way through the properties Pelly owned in Shanklin and Ventnor. Written statements would follow but already a pattern was beginning to emerge.

'We're talking Balkans. Bosnians mainly but Kosovans too. The blokes can't believe it. None of them's got a bad word to say about the man.'

'Who?'

'Pelly.'

Michaels settled himself in Faraday's office. The DS was a squat, cheerful forty-two-year-old who'd swapped a promising CID career in the Met for the subtler comforts of life on the south coast. His wife, once a WPC in Balham, had long since abandoned the job to look after a brood of football-crazy kids, but nothing would keep Michaels away from serious villainy. Ending up as DS on Major Crimes, he'd once told Faraday, was as close to perfect as any man had a right to expect.

Now, he was speculating about Pelly. His tenants evidently regarded him as some kind of saint. How did that fit with his current status as prime suspect in a homicide?

'Saint?' Faraday was speed-reading a list of messages on his desk.

'Yeah. According to our blokes, they say he can't put a foot wrong. Decent place to live, OK jobs, wages paid on the nail. Christ, he's even lent one of them his Steve Earle CDs. I know they're crap but does that sound like extortion?'

Faraday looked up.

'What about the paperwork?'

'Kosher. They all check out.'

'So how did they get here?'

'Pelly brings them in. Just like that. Totally up front. He's running a service. It's like National Express. They raise the money, bung him the fare, and he takes care of the rest of it. All they need is the right story.'

'Meaning?'

'Meaning they have to convince him they're having a hard time. Do that, and they're on the bus.'

'Are we sure Pelly isn't writing their lines?'

'That was my question but the lads won't have it. Every single interview they do, it's the same story. Pelly's tough as fuck. If they step out of line – don't turn up for work, let things get out of hand – he chucks them out. No fannying around, no appeals; they're on the street. But if they keep their noses clean, fair day's work, no problem. One bloke was apparently a bit of a poet. Said Pelly had the soul of a peasant, the stamina of a goat and the brain of a fox. Said he belonged in the mountains. Thought the world of him.'

'So where does that leave us?'

'Dunno, boss. But from where I'm sitting, the guy's halfway to being Mother Teresa. Seems he speaks a bit of Serbo-Croat: sees through the bullshit if they ever try and snow him.'

Faraday put the paperwork to one side and turned to face Michaels. He was still unclear about Pelly's role in bringing in these refugees.

'You're telling me he goes over there on recruiting drives?'

'Good as. The stuff our lads are coming up with, he has contacts with various agencies, Bosnian mainly; knows where people are having a hard time. He goes over to the Balkans, interviews them, makes some kind of case-by-case assessment, then gets them back over here.'

'For money?'

'Definitely. But none of them have a problem with that. Compared to most guys in the business, Pelly's an angel. Plus he knows what'll wash with the Immigration people over here. If they get past Pelly, they know they'll be odds-on for a permit this end.'

'And he registers them on arrival?'

'Within a day. As required. Every time. He books them in at Southampton, then brings them back over here.' Michaels nodded at the phone. 'I checked the process out with the asylum people at Croydon this morning. Totally kosher. Turns out they've even heard of Pelly. The famous Mr P. The guy who spares them all the hassle of finding a hostel and trying to keep these people alive. Few more of him, and the bloke I was talking to thinks he'd be out of a job.'

Faraday brooded for a moment. Try as he might he couldn't rid himself of the image of Pelly and his strange little family locked together as Faraday and Barber beat a retreat. What fuelled a man like Pelly? What fed the obvious anger within him? And, most important of all, what might have driven him to murder?

Michaels checked his watch and stood up. The

squad meet was booked for six o'clock. Pete Baker had put the word round the outside inquiry teams and the CSM would be making an appearance for an early update on progress at the nursing home. Rooms had been found at a modest hotel off the seafront and Michaels had sought local advice on an Indian for the post-meet wash-up.

'The Koh-i-noor.' He grinned. 'All you can trough for a tenner a head.'

At the door he found DC Webster lurking in the corridor.

'You after Mr Faraday, son?'

'You, skip. Though the boss might be interested, too.'

'What's that?' Faraday looked up from the number he was trying to dial.

'It's about Pelly. I got a call from the bloke we talked to at Cheetah Marine. Heard a rumour he thought he ought to pass on. Turns out it's true.'

'And?'

'Pelly's had enough. I talked to the estate agent. He's trying to sell up.'

Cosham police station lies on the mainland, barely a mile north of the muddy creek that serves as Pompey's moat. From Cosham, a fair-sized army of uniforms keeps a wary eye on the estates that sprawl over the lower slopes of Portsdown Hill. It was nearly five by the time Winter and Suttle made it to the front desk.

'Sergeant Brothers at home?' Suttle flipped his warrant card.

The clerk disappeared to check. Seconds later, he was back.

'Over the courtyard.' He nodded at the door. 'He'll meet you on the steps.'

Ivan Brothers was a sergeant in Cosham's Traffic department, a towering, rather intense ex-motorcycle cop with a reputation for plain speaking. According to Suttle, he'd been cagey on the phone, refusing to discuss details of the case on anything but a face-to-face basis. When Winter had enquired further, demanding to know the name and circumstances that made a visit to Cosham nick so pressing, Suttle had once again told him to be patient. He didn't want this thing to go off at half-cock. Rabbit from the hat, thought Winter, following Brothers and Suttle into the DI's vacant office.

Brothers stamped his authority on the meeting at once. He was due home to take his wife shopping at six. This time of night, he'd be leaving at half five. Suttle therefore had thirty minutes to make his case. He plainly hated CID.

'Victor Lakemfa.' Suttle was reading the name from his pocketbook. 'October twenty-first last year.'

'That's right. Hit and run. File is still open.'

'We're talking that little road on the back of Portsdown Hill. Yeah?'

'Correct. Crooked Walk Lane.'

'You put out a press appeal the following day. Witnesses. Anyone who might have been in the area around half eight, nine. The *News* carried a report. Lakemfa was a Commander in the Nigerian navy, over here on a course at *Dryad*.' Suttle folded his pocketbook shut and laid it on the conference table. 'That's pretty much all I know.'

Winter eyed the pocketbook. Mention of the Nigerian navy had aroused his interest. HMS *Dryad* was a naval shore establishment tucked away beside the village of Southwick. The command and control courses it offered attracted officers from countries all

302

over the world. Wishart, Winter thought. And all those visits to Lagos.

Brothers was being difficult. Road deaths sparked an exhaustive investigation, a procedure as complex and painstaking as anything CID could muster. As lead officer on this particular job, it had been Brothers's responsibility to drive the inquiry forward. To date, unusually, they'd made virtually no progress. Divulging details of the case required clearance from the Traffic Inspector, who was acting as SIO.

'Where is he?' It was Winter.

'On leave. In Florida.'

'And when's he back?'

'Week after next.'

'What about his deputy?'

'Flu. Probably back Monday.'

'Can't wait that long, skip. Not with the ACC breathing down our necks.'

'That would be Mr . . . ?'

'Alcott. DC Suttle mention *Plover* at all? How your lad Lakemfa might tie in? Only Mr Alcott's giving *Plover* top priority.'

Brothers stole a look at his watch, then asked Winter to shut the office door.

'So what's *Plover*?'

Winter was back at the table, shedding his car coat, savouring this small moment of triumph.

'Can't say, I'm afraid. Not without the say-so from my guvnor.' He beamed at Brothers. 'You want to tell us about Lakemfa? Only time's moving on.'

Brothers conceded the point with a weary sigh. Lakemfa, he said, was a thirty-four-year-old commander in the Nigerian navy. He'd already spent six months on one *Dryad* course and had returned last year for another. He lived in a rented flat in Port Solent and travelled to *Dryad* most days by bike, returning in the evening. The route he favoured took him to a narrow country lane that wound up the rear face of Portsdown Hill. Traffic was normally limited to the odd tractor or locals taking the short cut back to Southwick. On the night of 21 October a woman returning home found a body sprawled beside a bike near the top of the lane. There was blood still seeping from his nose and ears.

'Lakemfa?' Suttle was making notes.

'Correct. He was wearing proper riding kit, Lycra stuff, high-vis vest, helmet, the lot. We found ID in his day sack, temporary *Dryad* gate pass.'

Damage to the rear wheel of the bike suggested a hit and run but there were no skid marks on the road, and no witnesses. Forensic tests on the bike recovered microscopic flakes of black paint which may or may not have been evidentially material but exhaustive inquiries in the area failed to flush out a vehicle.

'I take it Lakemfa was dead.'

'Very. The PM showed skull fractures, probably from impact with the road.'

'Even wearing a helmet?'

'Sure. It happens.'

'But you're saying he wasn't run over?'

'No. We set up an incident room down the corridor there, ran a paper-based inquiry, blitzed it for a week or so, team of five. The guy's nationality was a bit of a drama because it turned out he was quite highly placed back home. Had the ear of the President. Tipped for stardom.'

'Who told you that?'

'We went through the intel boys, put it in the hands of ILET.'

Winter nodded. The International Liaison Enquiry

Team were stabled at the force intelligence HQ, a featureless office block on an industrial estate off the M27. They had a direct feed to Special Branch and links into all the major embassies. On a case like this their involvement made perfect sense.

'So what happened?'

'Very little. The media appeals produced virtually nothing. Witness boards on surrounding roads, crap response. Incidents like these, we often get the driver in over the next day or two, once the booze has worn off, but no bugger put his hand up. On fatals we run a seventy-two-hour review. Turned out to be one of the shortest meetings on record. We had zilch. Most unusual.'

The following week, he said, they kept plugging away, but the investigation was hamstrung by the sheer absence of leads. The divisional source handling unit tasked a number of informants to keep their ears to the ground. Word was passed to the fire service to be especially vigilant for burning cars. Finally, with the Nigerians pressing for return of Lakemfa's remains, a second PM was commissioned in the event of defence lawyers one day demanding an independent report. Then, towards the end of November, Lakemfa's body was flown to Lagos.

'End of story?' Winter couldn't keep the smile off his face.

'I sincerely hope not. The Coroner has yet to set a time limit on the investigation. As far as we're concerned, the file remains open.'

Mention of the Coroner prompted Winter to ask about jurisdiction. Crooked Walk Lane, it turned out, was the Winchester Coroner's turf. Hence the blank they'd drawn earlier with the Pompey deaths.

'What else did you recover from Mr Lakemfa?'

'We left his apartment to the MOD police. They sorted out his possessions.'

'I meant the day sack.'

'Ah . . .' Brothers looked up at the ceiling a moment, ordering his thoughts. 'Address book, mobile, assorted paperwork.'

'You still have them?'

'No. But we do have the billing on the phone. Standard procedure. If the guy's on the phone when he gets himself killed it gives us a starting point.'

'You still have the billing?'

'Of course.' He hesitated. 'You want to see it?'

Brothers left the room. Several minutes later he returned with a big plastic box full of files. In one of them, amongst the PM reports, press cuttings and policy logs, Brothers finally located the call billings on Lakemfa's mobile. Winter asked for a photocopy.

'The lot,' he added. 'Please.'

Brothers left the room again. From the office next door came the whirr of a photocopier. Three sheets of paper, still warm.

'Is that it?' Brothers hadn't sat down.

Winter was scanning the numbers. The records went back to early July. Finally he looked up.

'Good work, skip.' He pocketed the billings. 'You'll be the first to know once we've cracked it.'

Fifteen

The first of the *Congress* squad meetings was over by half past six. Dave Michaels had finally mustered a full house – all thirteen DCs plus support staff – and Faraday had spent a brisk ten minutes tracing the operation back to the moment when a birder had spotted a body wallowing amongst the rocks beneath Tennyson Down. Putting Chris Unwin's name to the headless corpse was still, he emphasised, a supposition, but the sheer weight of circumstantial evidence was beginning to make the link all but irresistible.

No one had seen Unwin since early October. At about the same time Pelly's old boat – the Tidemaster – had also disappeared. After failing to come up with the money to fund the build for a replacement, Pelly had suddenly produced a cheque for £23K, money it might be possible to link back to Unwin. Most significant of all, there was first-person evidence that the two men, Unwin and Pelly, had been involved in some kind of row.

Whether this was connected to their shared business interests wasn't clear. There may also have been a dispute about the treatment of Unwin's cherished nan, Mary. Either way, Pelly had a reputation for escalating petty slights and routine disagreements into something far more violent, as one local informant had found to his cost. Homicide, all the same, remained a large step for any man to take. At this, one or two of the older DCs exchanged glances. A couple of decades in the job taught you that the price of a life could be absurdly cheap. These days, especially, kids of eighteen were pulling knives and using them on the slightest provocation. A spilled drink? An unwise glance at someone else's woman? Better to do the bastard than bother with conversation.

Before winding the meeting up, Faraday summarised the thrust of tomorrow's actions. DS Pete Baker would be tasking the bulk of the Outside Team with house-to-house enquiries around the margins of Bembridge Harbour. Because it was Saturday, there'd also be an opportunity to talk to anglers, birdwatchers, walkers, and maybe even the more intrepid dinghy sailors – anyone, in short, who regularly used this stretch of water. Pelly himself had already told one witness that he'd sold his Tidemaster to a French buyer who'd trailered the boat and driven it away. A Tidemaster was a sizeable craft. DS Baker had a stack of photocopies to show around. Had anyone seen a boat like this being winched onto a trailer? Could anyone remember when this might have happened?

With the harbour flooded with detectives, Faraday also intended to put a handful of DCs into Pelly's nursing home. There were eighteen registered residents, all of them women. Some of them were gaga. One or two were terminally ill. All of them were seriously old. Few of these ladies would cut the mustard in the witness box – indeed, most of their testimony might well be inadmissible – but patience and a listening ear could conceivably offer ammunition for the moment when Faraday decided to pull Pelly in for interview. That moment had yet to come, but when it did Faraday wanted as many court cards in his hand as possible. Pelly fancied himself as a poker player. So far, in Faraday's judgement, he'd been bluffing.

Returning to his office, Faraday found Willard sitting at his desk, paging slowly through the Policy Book. He'd just stepped off the Hovercraft in the middle of a cloudburst and was trying to dry out.

'How's it going?'

Faraday summarised progress to date. Willard didn't look up. The Policy Book served as an ongoing record of Faraday's stewardship of the inquiry. He carefully logged every decision he made, together with an explanation to which he might have to return months later.

Willard's finger was anchored on one of this afternoon's entries.

'Why the HSU?'

The Hampshire Surveillance Unit was based at Totton, the other side of Southampton. Specialist detectives were available for tasking, should an inquiry warrant their help.

'We need to keep obs on Pelly. When we turn up at the home he's never there. Be nice to know where he gets to.'

'What are you thinking?'

'I'm thinking he's got a lot of bases to cover. The big one is the boat he used to have. We've yet to talk to him but I'm betting a sale to some mystery French buyer is bullshit. The man needs to cover his arse.'

'I'm not with you.' Willard had abandoned the Policy Book.

Faraday perched himself on the edge of the desk. Down the corridor, he could hear a cackle of laughter from Dave Michaels.

'Pelly has definitely moved the boat from the

harbour. That we know. He may have taken it somewhere else. Or he may have sunk it.'

'Because it's a crime scene.'

'Exactly. He's got a body to dispose of. If he's taken the head off on board, then he's up to his knees in DNA. Whoever did that body, assuming foul play, was forensically aware. Answer? Scuttle the boat.'

'So how does he get back?'

'My question exactly. A decent way out to sea, he'd need another boat. And someone on board to drive it. That someone becomes a material witness. As Pelly will obviously know. Pelly being Pelly, he's bound to pay him a visit.'

Willard nodded, glancing at the Policy Book again. 'And the HSU?'

'The guys are coming over tonight. They'll rotate with a back-up team for a couple of days. With luck we may have cracked it by then.'

'You think so?'

'Why not?' Faraday smiled. 'If Nick Hayder can get his name in the papers, it can't be that hard.'

A tap on the door brought DS Dave Michaels into the office. The Crime Scene Manager had failed to make it to the squad meet and had phoned in to apologise.

'How are they doing?'

'Nothing so far. Place is clean as a whistle. But they've seized a load of Pelly's paperwork – financial records, personal stuff – and they've taken his computer as well. What do you think?'

Faraday directed the question to Willard. The force computer crime department was currently swamped with work. The waiting list for hard disk analysis now stretched to seven months. Not until May could they begin to recover deleted emails and other files. The alternative was to outsource the job to a private firm, a decision that carried a £2,500 price tag. Minimum.

Willard dismissed the cost implications. He was looking at Faraday.

'You think it's worth it?'

'I think it might be. This is a guy who covers his tracks.'

'Then do it.' Willard had noticed another entry in the Policy Book. 'What about the second PM?'

'Pembury phoned through this morning. He's prepared the neck bone for electron microscopy. Should have a result by tomorrow. The tox is back from the first post-mortem, though.'

'And?'

'The guy was pissed, whoever he was. Twenty-nine millilitres of alcohol, still there in his liver,' said Faraday.

'That's the best part of a bottle of Scotch.' Michaels was laughing again. 'At least he died happy.'

'Anything else on the tox? Drugs?'

'Traces of paracetamol. Pembury's seen the results, too. The guy might have been on medication for anything, but flu could be a runner.' Faraday paused, remembering Webster's earlier news. 'There's something else you ought to know about Pelly. He's trying to sell up. Dave?'

Michaels nodded. DS Baker had dispatched two DCs to check out the estate agency and they'd returned with the full story. Pelly had first approached them in November last year. He'd said he'd had enough of tucking old ladies up at night and wanted out. The property market was still buoyant. There'd never be a lack of demand for a decently run home. Anyone fancying a new life on the Isle of Wight, plus a lifetime's supply of incontinence pads, no problem.

'Has he found a buyer?'

'One or two nibbles but nothing firmed up. He started at £550,000 but he's dropped twice since then so he must be keen to get shot of the place.'

'Any clue where he might be off to?'

'I asked that. It was the lad Webster again. Said the estate agent hadn't a clue, except it wouldn't be anywhere English. Apparently Pelly gave him a volley. Told him the country was shit. Anyone with half a brain should be queuing for the ferry.'

'No bloody wonder. If you've just killed someone.'

'Exactly.'

Another figure, slighter, had appeared in the corridor behind Dave Michaels. DS Brian Imber. Faraday gestured for him to come in. He needed a bigger office.

Imber found a space beside the wall board, pushing the door closed with his foot. Willard looked up at him, expectant. Imber rarely bothered with impromptu meetings like this unless he had something worth sharing.

'Well?'

'I've been taking a look through Pelly's bank statements. The seized material includes his business account plus a private account he runs through NatWest. Remind me about October the third.' Imber was looking at Faraday.

'That's the day the Tidemaster had definitely gone.'

'You can evidence that?' Willard wanted to know.

'Yes, sir.' Faraday nodded. 'We've found an old boy who keeps an eye on the moorings, knows all the boats by heart. October the third was his wife's birthday. Pelly's boat had gone. He thought it was odd because Pelly never went to sea on Fridays. Something to do with wages day at the home. The old boy ran into Pelly soon afterwards, at Tesco. That's when Pelly told him about the French guy.'

'OK.' Willard turned back to Imber, 'So what does the bank statement tell us about the third?'

'Pelly made a couple of transactions. One of them happened every Friday, like Joe says. Cash withdrawal on the business account to pay the wages. The other one was a bit special.'

'Like?'

'Like he handed over thirty grand.' Imber offered a thin smile. 'In cash.'

'Shit.' Willard was delighted. 'Really?'

'Yes, sir. And it gets better. Ten days later, the thirteenth, he pays in another whack. £124,567.'

'Cash?'

'Yes. I phoned the bank this afternoon. They won't discuss Pelly's affairs without a Production Order but the guy made a big point of telling me they always file a report on cash transactions over ten grand, so we assume they passed Pelly's name on. This time next year someone might get round to actioning it.'

Willard was still smiling. All kinds of financial institutions were now obliged to report suspiciously large cash transactions, part of the government's crackdown on money laundering. Great idea, except that the regulators were drowning in an ocean of paperwork and follow-up inquiries were grinding to a halt.

Faraday was pursuing the timeline. The cash deposit presumably funded the first instalment on the new boat from Cheetah Marine. Few companies were happy to accept a five-figure sum in cash. But why would a man like Pelly, so careful, so paranoid, leave so obvious an audit trail with the second cash deposit?

Willard looked blank. Michaels hadn't a clue.

Everyone looked at Imber. He was, as ever, word perfect on both sums and dates.

'Forty-five grand of that money stayed with Nat-West. On November sixteenth, they processed a money transfer, £80K, to a foreign bank where he was setting up another account.'

Michaels was frowning. 'November, Pelly went to the estate agents, decided to sell up,' he pointed out.

'Exactly.'

'So where was the foreign bank?'

Imber glanced at Faraday a moment.

'Sarajevo.' He smiled. 'Bosnia.'

Winter sat at home, the curtains drawn, the modest lounge in semi-darkness. He'd never bothered with a new PC, making do with Joannie's big old laptop. The internet had never appealed to him, either. He'd used it on the rare occasions he fancied a cheap flight to Malaga or Rhodes, a week by himself in the sun watching the Brits pissing off the locals, and there'd been the odd moment when he'd had a wallow in the gamier porn sites, marvelling at dexterous Californian blondes with limitless appetites for oral sex, but by and large he resisted the temptation to bury evening after evening drifting from site to site. Surfing, he told himself, was for losers.

Tonight, though, was different. Suttle, bless him, had very probably scored a result with Commander Victor Lakemfa, and before Winter decided where to take *Plover* next he needed to know a great deal more about the Nigerian navy.

Google threw up a list of websites. Methodically, Winter began to work through them. After the best part of an hour, comparing one specialist report with another, he'd settled on an image of the country that would, he thought, have offered someone like Wishart the perfect target.

Like most of Africa, the place was falling apart. Ninety-five per cent of government revenue came from oil, a heavy crude pumped from wells in the Niger Delta. The locals, poor by the standards of most Nigerians, were understandably fed up with losing their inheritance to the fat cats in Lagos, and the area's youth in particular had gone in for a spot of direct action. Oil platforms had been hijacked. Foreign workers kidnapped. Supply pipelines blown up. One of the navy's own patrol boats stolen at gunpoint. Late last year, in an incident that had surfaced in the *Daily Mail*, a sizeable Russian oil tanker, impounded by the Nigerian authorities after allegations that it was carrying contraband crude, had simply disappeared from a guarded berth in Lagos docks. One evening 100,000 tonnes of oil tanker lay alongside. By dawn next day it had gone.

Winter grinned. Pompey, on a good weekend, also had plenty of potential for anarchy but he couldn't remember the local kids ever nicking anything on this scale. So just how would the likes of Commander Lakemfa cope?

The answer, in a word, was badly. Most Nigerian navy vessels had once been high-tech. The Nigerians had paid a fortune to European shipyards for missile-carrying frigates but had never got on top of the training to make them properly operational. Nowadays, most of them never left harbour. The weapons systems didn't work, the spares situation was a joke, and if you were lucky enough to have a helicopter on the back end, the thing would be too knackered to fly. Year after year, money got tighter and tighter. Thanks to lousy wages, below-decks morale had hit rock-bottom. The Nigerian navy, in short, was stuffed.

Winter wandered through to the kitchen and poured himself a Scotch. In any inquiry rule one was to put yourself in the heads of the villains, and in this respect *Plover* was no different. The Nigerians had, at all costs, to keep the oil flowing. With their navy in the knacker's yard, they surely wanted something simple, something matelot-proof, to put the fear of God up the bad boys in the Niger Delta. Winter had already paged his way through Wishart's company website, and knew that the eleven-metre Marauder was probably the answer to Nigeria's prayers. The Marauder, in company-speak, could deliver a great deal of fire-power, at great speed, in water as shallow as a metre and a half. They zipped around at forty knots and a driving licence would probably qualify you to command one. At $1.7m each, they were a steal.

Winter stood at the kitchen window, staring into the darkness. Barely half an hour in Wishart's apartment had offered ample evidence to link the man to Nigeria. Emails confirming flight bookings to Lagos. Messages addressed to the higher echelons at the navy's Eastern Command HQ. Even the 2004 calendar on the wall over his desk, an arresting shot of a group of black women decked out in green and gold, sharing a joke beside a cage full of lions. From memory, Wishart's last visit to Africa had been back in late September. Since then, according to Maddox, the trips to Nigeria seemed to have ceased.

Winter reached for the bottle of Scotch. Say the guys in the Road Deaths Investigation Unit were right. Say Victor Lakemfa really did have the ear of government. Wouldn't that make him an obvious target for Wishart's heavy guns? Wouldn't he bombard the Nigerian with hospitality? Gifts? Straight bribes? Anything, in short, to smooth the path to a big, fat contract? And if, for some reason, Lakemfa hadn't been able to deliver. Or if, even better, he'd turned Wishart's courtship into some kind of blackmail demand, extorting ever-larger sums of money for the price of his own silence, wouldn't that turn him into the kind of threat that Wishart couldn't afford to ignore?

Winter smiled, tipping his glass to his own reflection in the window, only too aware of the dangers of putting speculation in front of hard evidence. At this stage he still needed to cement the link between Wishart and the luckless Victor.

Back in the lounge Winter sorted through his briefcase until he found the billing on Lakemfa's mobile. Already, he'd isolated a dozen or so numbers that had been regularly accessed between July and late September. Some of them were working hours only. Three. Lakemfa had also phoned in the evening. Winter scribbled down the numbers, then emptied his glass and checked his watch.

The big double bedroom lay at the front of the bungalow. Winter padded along the hall and eased the door open. In the spill of light he could see the long shape of Maddox's body under the duvet. She appeared to be asleep.

Winter sat on the edge of the bed and touched her cheek with the back of his hand. Moving out of her apartment at Rose Tower had been Winter's idea, strictly precautionary, but it hadn't taken much for her to say yes. After this afternoon's visit to Mon Plaisir, Winter was at last convinced that Maddox really did want Wishart out of her life. Not only that, but she obviously believed his threats were genuine. He'd attacked her twice now within the space of a week. Who on earth would need more evidence than that?

She struggled upright in the bed, rubbing her eyes. Winter's 'Viva Magaluf' T-shirt was several sizes too big.

'What's the time?'

'Half ten. Where's your mobile?'

She peered at him a moment then fumbled in a bag beside the bed. Winter punched in the first of the numbers from Lakemfa's billing. At length a woman answered, a language he didn't recognise. Winter grunted an apology and rang off. The second number began to ring. Then came a voice Winter recognised, languid, thickened by a lifetime of cigars and good living.

'Sweetheart . . .' Wishart sounded amused. 'You've come to your senses—'

Winter rang off again, no apology this time. Maddox was staring at the phone.

'That's a private number. Where did you get it?'

'We raised a billing. Wishart's number was on it. The phone's registered in the name of Lakemfa.'

'Victor?' A smile ghosted across Maddox's battered face. 'Sweet man.'

'You know him?'

'Of course. He was over here last year. Black guy. Naval officer. Very smooth. Played the gallant. Very funny too.' She was still looking at the phone. 'So why did you need the billing?'

Winter ignored the question. With Maddox, life was infinitely simpler if he stuck to being a detective.

'How come you ever met?' he wanted to know.

'Victor's a chum of Maurice's. I've never got to the bottom of it but it must be business. There's no other reason he'd spend that kind of money.'

'Who?'

'Maurice. It must have cost him thousands.' She frowned. 'Steve Richardson would know.'

'Lakemfa used Camber Court?'

'Yes.' She nodded. 'Back in the summer. Maurice stood him a couple of freebies. You'd be amazed how much Krug those Muslims can handle.'

'And afterwards?'

'That, too.'

'Who with?'

'Me.' She reached for Winter's hand. 'Maurice could occasionally be very generous that way.'

Faraday walked Brian Imber the length of Ryde Pier for the 23.15 Fast Cat back to Portsmouth. Imber was due before a circuit judge in Winchester at nine fifteen next morning in order to acquire the Production Order that would unlock Pelly's army service record. In the meantime, as he'd confided to Faraday in the Indian restaurant, he'd been chasing the secretary of Pelly's regimental association, a phone number he'd picked up from paperwork seized at the nursing home.

'The guy didn't actually serve with Pelly but he put me on to someone who did.'

'A mate?' Faraday was nervous of word getting back.

'Christ no, far from it. The only reason I phoned him was the fact that Pelly didn't seem to have any mates. The guy that organises the regimental jollies has him down as a loner, real oddball, someone you'd never want to get close to.'

'He said that?'

'Good as.'

Faraday came to a halt, his attention caught by a sudden flap of wings overhead, and the two men lingered for a moment. Beyond the berthing arm and railhead at the pier's end Imber could just make out the lights of the approaching catamaran. Five miles away, across the blackness of the Solent, the busy glow of Portsmouth.

Faraday pulled his anorak tighter against the bitter wind. He wanted to know more about Pelly. Imber dug his hands in his pockets, started to walk again.

'The guy I talked to obviously hated him. They'd fallen out big time over something or other and he didn't have a good word to say about Pelly. These were early days in Bosnia, remember. All the locals at each others' throats and our lads in the middle. Scary stuff if you've just shipped in. You know what the word Balkans means in local parlance?'

'No.'

'Blood and honey. Says it all.'

Faraday nodded. Despite the SAS tattoo on his arm, Pelly had in fact been in the Royal Engineers, part of a team of sappers attached to the Cheshire Regiment. The supply lines stretched into the mountains from the coastal port of Split, and Pelly had found himself constructing a secure billet for the Cheshires in a disused secondary school at Vitez.

'Apparently he loathed it,' Imber said. 'And he was really vocal. It wasn't the work so much, not the graft, just the set-up. We were part of the UN force, remember. We were peacekeepers, piggies in the middle. Most of the guys out there found it pretty frustrating but Pelly went over the top. Crap blue beret. Crap rules of engagement. Crap everything. After a while he started keeping a list of local heavies he wanted to slot. These were real animals, guys who got off on the violence. Everyone knew who they were but it was Pelly who wanted to take them out.'

'And?'

'He got warned off. Not just the company sergeant major but the locals too. It seems that Pelly had picked up a bit of Serbo-Croat; got stuck in where he shouldn't. Bloke I talked to mentioned a particular bar in Vitez, basement place. Pelly was mates with the guy who owned it, a Bosnian, and did him a couple of favours when his pipes burst. The one thing our lads avoided like the plague was taking sides. Bosnian? Croat? Serb? It made bugger-all difference. Pelly ignored all that and didn't care who knew it. As far as he was concerned the politics were black and white. The Serbs and the Croats were carving the place up between them. The guys on the receiving end were the Bosnians.'

Faraday paused again, hearing the burble of the approaching ferry. His knowledge of Balkan politics was sketchy at best but Bosnia seemed to be figuring more and more in this investigation. Lajla was Bosnian. Many of Pelly's refugees were Bosnian. Pelly himself might well be feathering a nest over there. And now, thanks to the indefatigable Brian Imber, Faraday was beginning to understand why.

'How long did the war last?'

'Three years.'

'And Pelly was there for the duration?'

'Yeah, but not in the army. You won't believe this but the MoD had been caught on the hop. By the time we put our lads in theatre, they were in the middle of a huge cost-saving exercise. Five months into the deployment blokes of Pelly's rank were offered the chance to bin it.'

'Bosnia?'

'The job. What we're talking here is voluntary redundancy. The terms were quite generous. Pelly put his hand up like a shot. Bloke I talked to said everyone celebrated on the strength of it – glad to get rid of the bastard, beers all round.' Imber chuckled.

'But you're telling me he stayed on?'

'Yeah. I don't know the details yet but he seems to have started some kind of charity. Blankets for Bosnia, humanitarian relief, whatever.'

'But why didn't he join one of the existing outfits?' Faraday had a dim memory of news footage of lorries grinding through the snow, aid convoys manned by a ragtag army of volunteers.

'Because Pelly's not the joining type. It's his way or nothing.' Imber glanced across at Faraday. 'This can't be news to you, surely.'

'Absolutely not.' Faraday was thinking of the first time he and Barber had met Pelly – the tautness in the face behind the desk, the way he lashed out at any passing target. 'What about these reunions? Does Pelly ever go?'

'God no. They were glad to see the back of him. He's only on the mailing list because the rules say he has to be.'

They walked on in silence for a while. The odd car drove past, taxis meeting passengers off the late-night crossing. Finally Faraday asked Imber for an opinion. He'd worked with the DS for years now. There were very few others whose judgement, at this early stage, he'd trust.

Imber took his time to frame an answer. Then he tried to put it all together: the timeline, the missing Chris Unwin, that long list of coincidences that seemed to bind Pelly to the headless body at the foot of the cliff. In theory it looked compelling, but there was something, Imber said, that didn't quite fit. Pelly, without doubt, was a man who carried a grudge. But his story plainly didn't end there.

'What makes you say that?' Faraday was intrigued.

'The conversation I had on the phone.' Imber was searching in his wallet for the Fast Cat ticket. 'The guy said Pelly was a pain in the arse but he also said something else. Of all the people he knew who were out there at the time, Pelly was the one who really brought it home with him. Why?' He offered Faraday a bleak smile. 'Because the bloke genuinely cared.'

It was Maddox who coaxed Winter out of his pyjamas.

'I'm going to take it personally,' she said, 'if you don't get rid of these things.'

'What's the matter with them?'

'Nothing. I adore paisley winceyette. But just now I've got a bit of a problem with self-esteem. Don't you fancy used goods? Have you got a thing about fading bruises? You're a detective. Just give me a clue.'

She was stretched full length on the bed, propped on one elbow, sipping a glass of Sainsbury's Pinot Noir that Winter had liberated from Joannie's little cellar under the stairs. Naked below the T-shirt, she'd already suggested a break from Winter's unending list of questions.

'Not a break exactly. Call it therapy. Call it anything you like. Am I *that* unattractive?'

'You're lovely. I told you.'

'Thanks . . . but that's not it, is it?'

'Not what?'

'Not what's keeping you –' she nodded '– in those things.'

'You're right. It's not. Listen. Tell me something. You were fucking Victor. Wishart's idea, his treat.'

'Sure. And mine.'

'What does that mean?'

'It means I enjoyed him. Not the screwing necessarily but the guy himself. Africans are like kids. They can be dizzy, off the planet. Some of them are seriously arrogant. But they've got something we haven't. Is it sunshine? Is it the Rift Valley? Is it the music?' She beckoned Winter towards her, kissed him on the lips, unbuttoned the pyjama top and gently traced a line between his nipples with a moistened fingertip. 'Have you ever been to Africa?'

'Never.'

'We should go. Soon.'

'We?' Winter barked with laughter. This woman was like a crime scene. She had to be controlled, taped off, analysed, understood.

'Yes . . .' She was evidently serious. 'We. You needn't sleep with me. You needn't feel threatened. But you're a bright man. Africa will teach you stuff you never even dreamed about. You want me to tell you about Rimbaud? You think it might be time for that?'

Winter hadn't a clue what she was talking about. Rimbaud was a face on a T-shirt.

'Your Victor . . .' he began.

'. . . was a great shag.' She eased herself away from him. 'You want me to be honest? A *really* great shag.'

'You told Wishart that?'

'No, but I bet Victor did. Maurice didn't have much time for competition. Still doesn't.'

'So why did he. . . .' Winter was struggling to find the right phrase '. . . buy you for him?'

'It was a boast. Fake solidarity. What's mine is yours. Except it didn't work out because I quite liked Victor.'

'More than Wishart?'

'Maurice was powerful. Is powerful. Like I've told you, that has its charms. But Victor's funny and Maurice doesn't do funny.' She studied him a moment, her head cocked to one side. 'You know something most men never understand? Laughter is the real turn-on, the real aphrodisiac. Show me a man who can make me laugh and I don't care what size dick he's got. Victor was perfect.'

'I bet.'

'Don't be neurotic. Listen, we were talking about Africa. I've still got a bit of money tucked away. We could do it – take a flight, couple of weeks, whatever you can manage. Change your life, I promise.' She reached for him again, cupping his big face in her hands. 'Those headaches of yours? Gone. Blown away. New perspectives. Lots of laughter. Lots of everything. Does that sound too daunting? You think you could cope?'

Winter gazed at her for a moment. He'd slept in this bed for the best part of twenty years. It held all kinds of memories, not all of them happy. There'd been nights, too many nights, when he'd roll back in the early hours, reeking of booze and cheap perfume, oblivious to the pain these small acts of treachery might inflict on the woman beside him. From time to time Joannie would erupt, retire to the spare bedroom, threaten divorce, tell him he was a greedy fool, but the marriage had somehow survived. Since she'd gone, to his bewilderment he hadn't touched another woman. The opportunity had been there, all too often, but in ways he still couldn't fathom it had become impossible to betray her. Married, he'd cheerfully shag anything. Alone, a widower, any kind of relationship seemed fraught with menace. Now this.

'Let me . . .' Maddox took his hand. Instinctively, Winter recoiled.

'Lakemfa pissed Wishart off,' he said. 'I need to know why.'

'Ask Victor. I'm sure he'll be delighted.'

'I can't.'

'Why not.'

'He's dead.'

The news silenced Maddox. She asked if Winter was joking. Winter shook his head. Maddox stared at him for a long moment, then plucked at the sheet and covered herself. Winter explained the circumstances as gently as he could, but when it came to the hit in the darkened lane the best he could manage was a cold recitation of the facts. Lakemfa had nearly made it to the top of the hill. Someone had hit him from behind. Falling, he'd fractured his skull. End of story.

'And you think Maurice did that?'

'I think he probably paid for it.'

'Bastard.'

'Exactly. But I need to know why.'

Maddox was shaking her head. Her eyes were moist in the semi-darkness. She began to say something about Victor Lakemfa, about how considerate he could sometimes be, but the memories overwhelmed her. She reached for Winter again, then changed her mind and rolled over.

'Fuck,' she whispered.

Sixteen

Saturday, 28 February 2004

Ryde Esplanade was busy on a Saturday morning. Already, barely nine o'clock, shoppers were spilling off the buses in the seafront terminal and there was a queue of cars waiting to drop passengers for the hovercraft crossing to Portsmouth.

Faraday paused to check his ringing mobile in the bright, cold sunshine. It was a number he didn't immediately recognise though the voice, when he finally answered, put him in a position of some embarrassment. The woman who'd given him a lift home from last weekend's celebratory wake, the woman whose mother had sent him Harry's letters. But what on earth was her name?

'It's Karen Corey.' She spared him the trouble. 'I thought it'd be better to leave this call to the weekend.'

'Oh?' Faraday had stopped on the seafront, arrested by the sight of a huge container ship nosing up the deep-water channel towards Southampton. 'How can I help you?'

'It's about those letters. Mum wondered whether she could have a word.'

'Now?'

'We were thinking tomorrow if you could spare the time. Mum goes to the spiritualist temple at ten. Maybe the afternoon?'

Faraday apologised. He'd be tied up all weekend

and probably most of next week too. Might he give her a ring when things had eased up a little?

'Of course. I'm really sorry to have bothered you. Mum'll be mortified.'

'That we can't meet?'

'That I called you. To be honest, all of this is my idea.'

'All of what?' Faraday was on the move again, looking for a break in the traffic to cross the road. Despite the pressures of *Congress*, Karen Corey had aroused his interest. Again.

She was still apologising. She was sorry to have disturbed him. Best to leave the next call to Faraday.

'But what's this about?' Faraday asked again. 'Just give me some kind of idea.'

With some reluctance Karen began to talk about Harry. There were one or two issues her mum wanted to resolve. For Madge's sake, and for her own.

'But why involve me?'

'Because you're a detective.'

'Are we talking something criminal here?'

'I don't know. None of us do. But that's the point, really. We're after advice and little me thinks you're the man who might be able to help. How's that for cheeky?'

Faraday thought about the proposition for a moment or two. He could see the turning that led to the police station now, up at the top of the High Street.

'I'll be in touch.' He glanced at his watch. 'And it's Joe, by the way.'

The Major Incident Room at Ryde police station was up on the first floor. DS Pete Baker met Faraday at the top of the stairs. The outside inquiry teams, he said, had already been dispatched to Bembridge. He'd gridded the edges of the harbour and the rising ground behind and assigned the house-to-house calls accordingly. DCs Barber and Webster, meanwhile, were already interviewing residents at the nursing home in Shanklin.

'Pelly?'

'Good as gold. Met them at the door, even offered a pot of tea.'

'How about Scenes of Crime?'

'Ongoing, sir. Webster says they're starting on Pelly's own quarters this morning. Then it'll be the garage and the rest of the stuff outside. They're estimating getting shot of the bulk of it by close of play Monday.'

'Anything to show for it so far?'

'Not yet, sir.'

Faraday and Baker were joined by DS Dave Michaels. He'd been downstairs, talking to one of the desk clerks.

'There's an old boy came in a couple of minutes ago. Name of Castle.'

'Wally Castle?'

'That's him. We tried for a statement first thing but he wasn't interested. Not unless he could have a word with the guvnor. The lads drove him over. Thought it might be important.'

'Of course. Give me ten minutes, eh?'

Faraday walked down the corridor towards his office. Wally Castle was the fisherman who'd first noticed that Pelly's old boat had gone. What else might he have dredged up from those October days? Faraday stepped into his office. Amongst the messages awaiting his attention was an earlier phone call from Brian Imber. The circuit judge in Winchester had fallen ill overnight and been carted off to hospital. Imber was having to make other arrangements to acquire the Production Order but had meanwhile taken a call from another ex-squaddie who'd served in Vitez. This man, a sapper like Pelly, was only too pleased to mark Imber's card but had no interest in committing himself to a written statement. Under the circumstances Imber had decided it was worth a trip to London. If Faraday thought that was a bad idea he had until half nine to head him off. Otherwise, the meet would go ahead.

Faraday lifted the phone. Imber answered on the second ring.

'Do it,' Faraday said. 'We'll sort out a statement as and when.'

'Fine.' Imber was evidently already on the train. 'That's what I thought you'd say.'

Faraday hung up. The first of the HSU teams had left a report on his desk. Pelly had spent the night at the nursing home. The surveillance teams changed shift at 05.00 and the lads on the next watch would doubtless be in touch.

Faraday studied the report for a moment or two, then reached for the Policy Book, wondering whether the expense of the HSU was really justified. Everything he knew about Pelly told him that the man was all too aware of the investigative options at Faraday's disposal. Letting the SOC team waste the best part of an afternoon boshing the wrong boat had been a classic spoiler. Would someone as vigilant as Pelly really be reckless enough to pay a visit to a key potential witness?

There came a knock at the door. Faraday looked up to find Dave Michaels with an elderly man who peered at Faraday with some interest.

'You the boss, then?'

'Mr Castle,' Dave Michaels explained. 'Come down specially.'

Michaels stepped out of the office and shut the door. Faraday extended a hand. Castle ignored it. With his bright eyes and shock of snow-white hair, he reminded Faraday of a bird. An egret, maybe. Faraday judged him to be at least eighty.

'You mind?' Castle found himself a perch on the chair Faraday kept for visitors. 'I was in half a mind not to come but what's the harm, eh?'

Faraday offered tea or coffee. Castle said no to both. He wanted to sort out this business about Pelly. He'd no intention of keeping Faraday long. He plucked at the creases in his trousers, big raw-knuckled hands, joints swollen with arthritis.

'Well?' he demanded. 'What's the bugger done?'

'I'm afraid I can't tell you, Mr Castle, not until our inquiries are complete. It may turn out to be nothing. Who knows?'

'Serious though, eh? You don't put this many men on the ground. Not on a Saturday. Not without good reason.'

'Indeed.'

'Still not going to tell me?'

'No.'

'Hmm . . .'

For a moment Faraday thought the old man had finished. He'd simply come over to find out what Pelly had been up to. Once a fisherman, always a fisherman.

'You know Mr Pelly well?'

'No.' The shake of the head was emphatic. 'Nobody does.'

'But you see him around?'

'Of course. Even at my age, you take an interest. Always have, if you want the truth.'

331

'And what do you see?'

The old man was gazing up at the wall board. Imber had brought over one of J-J's colour shots from Faraday's Pompey office, a little domestic gesture that Faraday had found oddly comforting.

'Gannets.' Castle nodded in approval. 'Saw a couple once, off the back of the Wight. Bloody rare though, round these parts. Keen on birds, are you?'

Faraday nodded. Nothing would have pleased him more than a leisurely chat about the RSPB reserve that stretched south from Bembridge Harbour but he knew this was neither the time nor place.

'I understand you've something to tell us, Mr Castle. Am I right?'

The old man's gaze returned to Faraday. He wanted to be sure he wasn't going to land anyone in trouble.

'Like who?'

'Can't say. Not without you telling me it's all OK. That's the point, see?' He jabbed a bent finger in Faraday's face. 'You get my drift?'

'No.' Faraday shook his head. 'I'm afraid I don't. This is a major inquiry, Mr Castle. You have my absolute assurance that we take everything in the way of information extremely seriously.'

'That's as may be but it don't answer, does it? See . . .' He bent forward and tapped Faraday on the knee. 'What I'm saying is this. I can tell you something about somebody and that somebody might not thank me for it. Especially since he's my nipper.'

'We're talking about your son?'

'We might be. Depends. You tell me it's going to be OK with him, and I might see my way to telling you one or two things. Now then.' He leaned back and folded his arms. 'What do you say?'

'Does he know you're here? This boy of yours?'

'Never.'

'You think you might get him into trouble?'

'Dunno. Might, I suppose.' He shrugged. 'You fellas would know best.'

Faraday eyed the old man for a moment, trying to gauge what kind of deal he was after. Finally, he suggested they talk in confidence.

'What does that mean?'

'You trust me.'

'And that son of mine? You'll see him right? Handle it personally? Yourself?'

'Depends what he's done.'

'He's done nothing, see? Just a favour, that's all.'

'A favour for who?' Faraday paused, beginning to sense the drift of this strange conversation. 'Pelly?'

The old man nodded, his eyes bright.

'That's the one,' he confirmed. 'Damn fool that he is.'

Winter woke up late, knowing he was going to be violently ill. The experience of the last couple of months had prepared him for thudding headaches and a blinding pressure behind his eyes but nothing as unbearable as this. It began above the bridge of his nose, a small, intensely hot bubble of pain that spread with the quickening rhythm of his pulse until it seemed to fill his entire skull. It had an almost liquid quality and when he shut his eyes, hunting for images that might offer some kind of relief, all he could picture was a swamp of molten lava, viscous and evil, flooding into the deepest recesses of his brain.

He reached out; found Maddox still beside him; tried to get out of bed. Seconds later he was sprawled on the carpet and she was kneeling over him, slipping a pillow under his bursting head then heaving his body onto one side as he started to throw up. She stripped off the T-shirt and used it as a bib, catching most of the vomit. Winter was gasping for air, for distraction, for a way out, for anything.

'Bathroom cupboard,' he managed at last. 'Bottom shelf.'

She brought the painkillers back with a glass of water. He swallowed three, then threw up again.

'You need a doctor.' Maddox was hunting for her mobile. 'Where do I find the number?'

Winter was past caring. He clawed at the bed. Sleep. Oblivion. An early grave. Whatever.

'Here.' She wanted him to drink more water, try again with the tablets. This time he managed to keep them down.

She got him back to bed and he managed to doze for a while. When he awoke, she was still there, bent over him.

'You told me you were going to see the consultant.'

'I did. I'm up there again on Monday.' Winter tried to get her face into focus. 'Don't leave me, eh?'

'Leave you?' She kissed him. 'As if.'

She adjusted the curtains against the bright sunshine, then slipped between the sheets again, her long body wrapped around Winter's ample frame. With his face nestled between her breasts, he could hear the steady thump of her heart. The pain had seemed to ease a little.

She began to murmur to him, something in French, nothing he could remotely understand. Then she slid away again, returning with a bowl of water and a flannel she used to bathe his face. She knew of a friend's weekend cottage out in the country. She'd stayed there often, entrusted with the key and the occasional company of a stray cat that lived in an outhouse at the bottom of the garden. The cottage was down a lane, she said, miles from anywhere. The nearest pub was a forty-minute walk through woods and across a field. This time of year the fields were full of brent geese and you could lie awake at night listening to the wind in the trees and the dormice under the thatch, and the distant honking of the geese. Beyond the fields lay the salt marsh and a tiny patch of harbour and then the open sea. She'd never had much faith in paradise, she said, but this was pretty close.

The thought put a wistful smile on Winter's face.

'Take me there?'

'Today, my love. Now. Just as soon as you can manage it.'

'You mean it?'

'Yes.' She kissed him. 'Funnily enough.'

She began to caress the swell of his belly, paused when his hand caught hers.

'No? You don't want to?'

'Not like this.' Winter managed a grin this time. 'You'd see me off.'

'Later, then. When you're feeling better.'

'Whatever.' He closed his eyes and winced. 'Just give me time.'

Faraday took Bev Yates with him to Bembridge Harbour. A glorious day had brought out the weekend drivers, and Faraday's borrowed Fiesta crawled up the hill towards the village of St Helens that overlooked the water below. Wally Castle sat in the back, supplying directions, one gnarled old hand shading his eyes against the low slant of the sun.

'Here,' he said at last. 'One on the end.'

Faraday coasted to a halt beside a modest semi-detached house, red brick with a tiny patch of front garden. A battered Land Rover was parked outside, both windows down. As he got out, Faraday glimpsed lobster pots in the back. The old man had produced a key. Faraday was still inspecting the contents of the Land Rover.

'He's a fisherman? Your boy?'

'Plays at it. Kids himself.'

The old man led the way to the front door. Before he managed to insert the key in the lock, the door opened.

'What's this?'

The old man mumbled something about an earlier phone call. The barefoot figure in the dressing gown at the door was evidently his son, Sean.

'Fucking *law*?' Sean looked far from pleased.

DC Yates flipped his warrant card and introduced Faraday. They'd welcome the chance for a brief chat. 'Mr . . . ?'

'Castle. Same as him, daft old bugger. You'd think one was enough, wouldn't you?' He looked at Faraday. 'What's this about, anyway?'

Faraday said he'd explain inside. After a moment's hesitation Castle held the door wide while they stepped past. The house looked like a building site. The wall at the end of the tiny hall had been reduced to rubble. Beyond the twin Acrows supporting the floor above, there was a kitchen in a similar state of chaos. The old units had been ripped out. Pipes sprouted from the bare boards. Wires hung from the ceiling.

'Got a bit of work on.' Sean was rolling himself a cigarette. 'Make yourself at home.'

Faraday heard someone moving around upstairs. Then came a woman's voice, asking what was going on.

'Tell you later. Go back to bed.'

'Who else lives here?' Yates had his pocketbook out.

'Mandy. My other half. Get any sense out of her after last night and you're a better man than me.' Sean asked his father for a light, then turned back to Faraday. 'What's this about?'

Faraday briefly explained. He was investigating the disappearance of a Portsmouth man. He had reason to believe a row might have got out of hand. Did Sean know a Rob Pelly?

'Yeah.' Sean nodded. 'For sure. Owns a nursing home. Shanklin way.'

'He's down here a bit too.' Faraday nodded towards the harbour. 'Is that right?'

'Yeah.'

'Doing what? Exactly?'

Sean was looking at his father. Later, there was clearly going to be a conversation.

'Bits and pieces. Fishing mainly. He's got one of those fancy Cheetahs – brand new, nice bit of kit. Must be money in old folks' homes.'

'You said "mainly"'. It was Bev Yates this time. 'What does "mainly" mean?'

'It means he works as hard as every other bugger. Then pushes off for a bit of fishing. Me? I do the reverse.'

'But you said "mainly"', Yates insisted. 'What else does he do with the boat?'

'Dunno. Ask him.'

'OK.' Yates scribbled a note, then began to prowl round the kitchen. 'Must cost a bit, all this.'

'Like you wouldn't believe, yeah.'

'The fishing game see you right, does it?'

'You have to be fucking joking.' Faraday and Yates spun round. A woman was standing in the wreckage of the hall. She was wearing a cardigan that was several sizes too big for her, unbuttoned at the front, and not

337

much else. For someone closing on middle age, she was in extraordinary shape.

Faraday glanced back at Sean. His eyes were shut and he was shaking his head. A bad morning had just got abruptly worse.

'And you are . . . ?' Yates was smiling at her.

'Mandy. What's it to you, then?'

Yates dug out his warrant card again. She barely spared it a glance.

'Ask him what we do for money.' She was pointing at Sean. 'Ask him who has to put out to pay the bloody supermarket bill. Go on. He won't bite.'

'Mr Castle?' Yates was beginning to enjoy himself.

'Pay no attention.' He sounded weary. 'She's been pissed since the Christmas before last. Most blokes wouldn't give her the time of day.'

'Wouldn't they?' She stepped between the two detectives and thrust herself in Sean Castle's face. 'How's that then? When half the fucking island can't wait to shag me?'

Faraday noticed that the old man had crept away. Under the circumstances, he didn't blame him.

Mandy hadn't finished. She was sick of living in a tip, sick of getting by on chip butties, sick of all Sean's banging on about the money he was going to make. Proper men, real men, knew how to look after their women. Not cart them round Lidl like some trophy shag.

'What about you, then?' She'd turned on Yates. 'Married, are you?'

'Very.'

'Yeah? What a fucking waste. Me? I'm out of here.'

She disappeared down the hall. Moments later Faraday heard the tramp of footsteps overhead, then a door slammed and with it came a brief moment of silence.

'Well, son? You going to tell them or shall I?'

It was the old man. He was back between the Acrows.

'Tell them what? She's on the Jim Beam again. You can smell her from the top of the hill.'

'I meant Pelly. The boat. They're going to find out anyway. Best you get it off your chest.'

'Boat?' Faraday's interest had quickened.

Sean was examining the remains of his cigarette. Finally he shot his father a withering look and told Faraday it was nothing, just a favour.

'Yes, but what boat?'

'Mine. Back last year Pelly wanted a charter. I know he'd asked around and no one was very keen. In the end he came to me. He knew it would cost him but he didn't turn a hair.'

'How much?' It was Yates.

'Five hundred.'

'What kind of boat are we talking about?'

'An Aquabel Sports.'

'Yeah, but what's that? Big boat?'

'Twenty-seven foot.'

'And how long did he want it for?'

'A night.'

'A *night*? For five hundred quid?'

'Yeah. He knew it was over the odds but it made no difference. He was in a hurry. He even paid on the spot. Cash. Full whack.'

Faraday propped himself on the table. At last, he thought.

'So why would he need this boat of yours?'

'He never said and I never asked. That kind of money, you don't want to know.'

'What do you *think* he wanted it for?'

'I haven't a clue.'

'Did he take it out himself, your boat?'

'Yeah. That was my only condition. He knows what he's doing in a boat, Pelly. I showed him the ropes and off he went. There's no way I was having some stranger at the wheel.'

Yates was busy scribbling notes. Faraday still wasn't clear why Pelly hadn't used his own boat. At first Sean wouldn't answer. When Faraday put the question again, he dug his hands deeper into the pockets of the dressing gown and looked him in the eye.

'His own boat went out the same night. They left in convoy, him and another bloke. High tide was around eight.'

'We're talking the Tidemaster?'

'Yeah.'

'So who was it at the wheel?'

'I've no idea. Honest to God.'

'You didn't see him at all?

'Not properly. Not close up. A young-looking guy? Tallish? I don't know. It can get really dark out there.'

Faraday let the silence stretch and stretch. The old man was looking happier.

'So when did all this happen?' Faraday asked at last.

Sean Castle had stepped over to the window. He wiped off the condensation with his sleeve, then peered out.

'October time, beginning of the month. I was down on the harbour next day. Pelly gave me the keys back.'

'OK was it? The boat?'

'No, it fucking wasn't. Couple of bloody great gouges out of the gunnel on the starboard side. Told me he hadn't a clue how it happened. Nerve of the guy.'

'What kind of gouges?'

'So big.' Castle held his thumb and forefinger apart, the width of a cigar. 'Looked to me like he'd taken a swing or two with an axe, but the bugger wasn't having it.'

Faraday nodded, exchanged a glance with Yates.

'And Pelly's own boat?' Yates enquired. 'The Tide-master?'

'Dunno. Never saw it again.' He shrugged, pulling the dressing gown more tightly around him. 'Five hundred quid, you don't ask too many questions.'

Winter was still in bed when Suttle finally turned up. Winter made it to the front door, pausing in the hall to catch his breath. Suttle stared at the paisley pyjamas.

'What's the matter? You look crap again.'

'Long story, son. Come in.'

'I thought we were going down to see Cathy Lamb? I thought you wanted a lift?'

'Later.'

Suttle's car was parked outside, door open, engine still on. He locked it and returned to the bungalow.

'Through the back?' Suttle nodded down the hall.

'No.' Winter indicated the adjacent door. 'Come in here.'

The bedroom couldn't have been changed since the death of Winter's wife. Suttle tried to take it all in. No man would have chosen this wallpaper, these curtains, this particular brand of carpet, all of them studies in pink and powder blue. Waking up in a room like this, thought Suttle, would be like drinking tea with four sugars. You'd spend the rest of the day getting over it.

Heaped on the floor beside the bed was a pile of clothes. Since when had Winter taken to wearing lacy black knickers?

'Maddox,' he said briefly.

'She's here?'

'Gone to Sainsbury's.'

'Shit. No wonder you're looking so rough. Sort you out, did she?'

Winter let the comment pass. He'd phoned Cathy Lamb and asked for an urgent meet. Before they drove down to Kingston Crescent, they ought to be sure what they wanted out of it.

'Wishart, for starters,' Suttle suggested. 'You had a good look through the billing?'

'Yeah.' Winter eased himself back into bed and reached for the flannel. 'One of the numbers was his. I checked it out. Lafemka was on the phone to him most days. The last call he made to Wishart was after lunch the day he died.'

'OK.' Suttle perched himself on the edge of the bed, stirring the heap of clothes with the toe of his trainers. 'So we can definitely link the bloke to Wishart. It's not enough, though, is it? Not if we're right about a hit?'

'No. I've got a couple of numbers you might like to phone. Blokes you ought to talk to.' Winter dug under the pillow and tossed over a mobile. Suttle didn't pick it up.

'Are these guys snouts of yours?'

'Yeah.'

'So why don't you do it?'

Winter eyed him for a moment, then collapsed back against the pillows. This was the moment he'd been avoiding for the last couple of months. Suttle, like most detectives, rarely noticed the obvious. Until now.

Winter rubbed his eyes. 'I'm not too well, if you want the truth.'

'How's that, then?' Suttle looked startled.

Winter told him about the headaches, about the

moments when he thought he was going blind, about this morning.

'You were sick again?' Suttle was looking hard at the carpet. 'Like the other day?'

'Yeah. But worse.'

'Why didn't you tell me? Shit . . .' He shook his head. 'Does Cathy know any of this?'

'No.'

'Then tell her. Else I will. You shouldn't be working at all. You need a doctor.'

'I've got one. And a consultant. And another bloody appointment, Monday morning as it happens. We should get rat-arsed Sunday, just in case.'

'You're kidding.' Suttle reached for the mobile. 'You think it's that bad?'

'Yeah.'

Suttle shook his head, sobered now, and scrolled through the list of numbers until Winter told him to stop. He scribbled down a couple of names; looked up. A car had come to a halt outside. Suttle got to his feet. Maddox was unloading shopping from the boot of Winter's Subaru. Suttle watched her for a moment or two as she pushed in through the gate.

'So where does she fit in to all this? Give us a clue.'

'Wish I could, son.'

'You mean that?' Suttle glanced round.

''Fraid so.' Winter shut his eyes, wincing with pain. 'Toms I can handle. Wives, no problem. Maddox? You tell me.'

'Nice, though, eh?'

'Very.' His hand clawed towards the strip of tablets on the duvet. 'As if that helps.'

Maddox took the shopping straight through to the kitchen. Already, to Winter, the house felt different, warmer, shared. He listened to Suttle listing all the

343

clever ways Wishart had distanced himself from the hit. Payment would have been in cash. The car would have ended up on some industrial estate in Manchester or Newcastle, just another torched statistic. The hitman, with every incentive to keep his mouth shut, would have banked his money and gone to ground. Wishart's fingerprints would be invisible.

'So what's the problem?' Maddox was standing at the door. She'd evidently overheard everything.

'We need to put him away. Evidence would be nice.' Pursuing this thought was more than Winter could manage. He lay back again, shading his eyes against the noonday sun.

Suttle nodded. A mobile billing was a start, he said, but no jury would convict for taking regular phone calls.

'You need to hear it from the man himself . . . *n'est-ce pas?*'

'That would be favourite.' Suttle grinned at her. 'Think you can manage it?'

'Yes.' Maddox crossed the room and bent over Winter. 'I think I can.'

Seventeen

Faraday was on the phone to Willard when DS Dave Michaels appeared at his office door. DC Barber needed to speak to him. It sounded urgent. Faraday nodded, bringing the conversation with his boss to a close. Willard had just received a supplementary estimate for the analysis on Pelly's hard disk, £3,500, a lot of money for a punt that might take the investigation nowhere. How was the rest of the case shaping up?

Faraday mentally reviewed the facts he knew he could rely on. Apart from Pelly's cash windfalls and his subsequent purchase of the new boat, it amounted to very little. The charter of Sean Castle's fishing boat might yet prove a breakthrough but Castle himself had no interest in making a formal statement. Computer analysis, on the other hand, was regularly proving to be an evidential gold mine. With luck, the techies might turn up something priceless.

Willard agreed.

'We'll do it,' he said. 'Ring me if anything develops.'

Michaels disappeared to transfer Barber's call to Faraday's extension. The DC was still at the nursing home.

'How's it going?'

'Slowly. They're sweet, some of these old dears, but you wouldn't set your clock by them.'

345

'Anything useful?'

'Quite a lot about Pelly's so-called missus. She's a bit of a favourite here; the oldies adore her. Apparently she helps out all the time, really hands-on. And you pick up the feeling she doesn't get out much, her choice as far as I can gather. This is her bit of England. She doesn't seem that keen on the rest of it.'

'Is that you saying that?'

'No, there's one old lady who really dotes on her, thinks she's wasted running around after a bunch of geriatrics. She thinks Lajla pines a lot for home. Apparently she's very close to her brother; gets regular letters.'

'From Bosnia?'

'Berlin. He's a mechanic. Shares a flat with their father; just had a baby himself. He sends his kid sister piccies and Lajla shows them round.'

'What about the relationship with Pelly?'

'Father–daughter. That's what this same old lady thinks. Actually she's a youngster, spring chicken, barely seventy. Keeps her eyes open. She says Pelly's got a regular girlfriend, big woman. Often spends the night. As far as Lajla's concerned, Pelly seems to play the protector. Maybe brother–sister, not father–daughter.'

Faraday shut the office door with his foot. Gary Morgan had mentioned a local woman Pelly was seeing. Must be one and the same.

'So why the call?' Faraday asked.

Barber took her time explaining. She and Darren Webster had agreed that the key interviewee would be Mary Unwin, Chris Unwin's treasured granny. They'd put her top of the list but getting anywhere near her had been a bitch. First, she'd alarmed the care staff by not eating her breakfast. Then she'd felt giddy and retired from the shared lounge to take a nap. Finally, after lunch, there'd been yet another problem. She always watched *Neighbours*, never missed an episode, couldn't possibly be disturbed. Finally, half an hour ago, Tracy Barber had practically forced her way into Mary's tiny bedroom. She'd found her reading a copy of *Woman's Weekly*. The TV, when she tried it, didn't even work.

'So who kept you out?'

'Pelly. He's been around all day. Nice enough with everyone else but in this case a pain in the arse.'

'And Mary? When you talked to her?'

'Genuinely off the planet. She must read *Woman's Weekly* for the pictures. Her hearing's not too great either, so you have to shout.'

Barber described the course of the interview. With every new conversation, she and Webster had tried to establish the pattern of visits from Chris Unwin. They had copies of his photo and most of the old dears recognised him. Yes, he used to drop in to see his nan. Have a cup of tea with her in the lounge, clown around a bit, make everyone laugh. And no, they hadn't seen him recently, not since way before Christmas.

'And Mary?'

'She wasn't sure. One minute she knew him, the next minute she didn't. Then she wrecked the whole thing by asking whether he was still delivering the papers every morning. Turned out she'd got the wrong bloke, complete muddle.'

'Useless then. Is that what you're saying?'

'Well, no, it's not. That's why I called. This is going to sound freaky.'

Barber, it transpired, had been on the point of giving up the interview with Mary Unwin. Nothing she said made any sense. She had a real problem with time: kept talking about the war as if it was yesterday, couldn't remember what she'd had for lunch. Then, unprompted, she'd suddenly started talking in sign language.

'*Sign?*' Faraday blinked.

'Yes. It was definitely sign language, the full repertoire: different shapes with her fingers, lots of gesturing, touching her elbow, shoulder, forehead, the lot. If I knew sign, I'm sure she would have been making perfect sense.'

'No clues at all?'

'Just one. She kept pulling her finger across her throat and then pressing her hands together, like she was praying. She must have done it half a dozen times. She was always looking over towards the door too, as if she half-expected someone to be outside.' Barber hesitated. 'You understand sign, sir. I remember you telling me. That son of yours, J-J . . .'

'That's right.' Faraday glanced at his watch. 'You want me to come over?'

'Might be a good idea, though I'm thinking we ought to be putting a camera on this. Just for the record.'

Faraday nodded. Interviews with vulnerable witnesses were frequently recorded on videotape, a precaution to head off charges of harassment. He said he'd bring a camera over and then brought the conversation to an end. The longer Tracy Barber was on the team, the more she impressed him. Like the best detectives, she was constantly thinking ahead, arranging and rearranging the available bits of the jigsaw, hunting for the bigger picture.

Faraday found Ellie Unwin's mobile number in the Policy Book. She was stuck in a traffic jam on the outskirts of Eltham. Faraday explained Tracy Barber's problem with Mary. Did Ellie's mum often abandon conversation for sign?

Faraday could hear Ellie laughing.

'Often,' she said. 'She does it when she gets excited. Or distressed. Chris is the one you should talk to. It's always fascinated him.'

'How come she learned it in the first place?'

'She worked with deaf mutes when she was younger. Before I was born, actually. Gave it up when my dad came along.'

It was Winter who spotted Terry Alcott's silver Land Cruiser in the car park at Kingston Crescent police station. Hauling in the ACC on a Saturday afternoon was a sign that *Plover* was getting itself a reputation. Winter, despite his thudding head, was impressed.

Alcott was occupying the chair behind the desk in Cathy Lamb's office. He was an imposing man, physically big, and carried his authority with an easy wit. He lived out in the Meon Valley, a two-acre spread with river frontage, and had been down in Southsea since mid-morning. His eldest son played prop forward for the Hampshire Colts and Alcott rarely missed a game. Out of uniform, thought Winter, he looked almost human.

'Afternoon.' He gave Winter a nod and then glanced up at Suttle. 'And you are . . . ?'

'DC Suttle, sir.'

'Good. Excellent. Find a seat. DI Lamb's gone AWOL for a couple of minutes. Bring me up to speed.'

Winter summarised *Plover*'s progress as best he could, knowing that Alcott would already have been briefed by Cathy Lamb. That was the way officers of his eminence always operated, comparing one account with another, looking for daylight through the dodgier joins.

Winter began with Singer but Alcott shook his head.

'Singer can wait,' he said. 'Tell me about Mr Wishart.'

Winter nodded, concentrating on the last twenty-four hours. With the mobile billings he could evidence the link between Lakemfa and Wishart. He knew from his brief trawl through Wishart's emails that the businessman had been in regular touch with the naval high command in Nigeria. And he had Maddox's word that she was one of the sweeteners Wishart had tossed to Commander Lakemfa. Wishart, he said, surely had his eye on a big fat contract from the people in Lagos. Why else would he be spending all that money on someone he barely knew?

'And you're telling me it all went pear-shaped?'

'Yes, sir. We haven't got the details, not yet, but the story writes itself, doesn't it? Either Lakemfa didn't deliver or he got greedy and tried to put the squeeze on Wishart, or maybe he had other contractors in mind and started to play them off against each other. Everything we know about Wishart says this guy doesn't understand the word no. Plus he hates being pissed around.'

'So he puts out a contract on our Nigerian friend? Bit radical, isn't it?'

'Means and ends, sir. We're probably talking millions if the contract worked out. What's seven grand to some psycho in Paulsgrove?'

Alcott wasn't convinced. He looked up at Suttle. There had to be more.

'We've got a triangle here, haven't we?' he suggested.

'I'm not with you, sir.' Suttle was frowning.

350

'The man Wishart. Our Nigerian gentleman. And then this Maddox woman. Am I right?'

'Of course, sir, yes.'

'And DI Lamb gives me the impression that Maddox may now be having a problem with her client. Mr Wishart wants more than his entitlement. Insists, in fact. Tricky situation, that. Most women I know would start looking for a little protection. No?'

Suttle glanced at Winter, only too conscious of where this conversation might lead. Alcott was extremely shrewd. Uncomfortably so.

Winter agreed that jealousy might have been a factor in Lakemfa's death.

'You say that with some conviction, DC Winter.'

'I think it's possible, yes.'

'You know this woman?'

Winter didn't answer. It was a Saturday. He felt extremely ill. The last thing he intended to offer Alcott was a glimpse of the bewilderment that passed for his private life.

'I've formed an opinion, sir,' he said woodenly.

'Based on?'

'Conversation.'

'And?'

'She's extremely attractive. You'd have to be blind or mad not to want to . . .' He shrugged, leaving the sentence unfinished.

'And afterwards?'

Winter pretended not to understand, trying to fend off Alcott's relentless probing. Afterwards was exactly the question he'd have put. Afterwards was the essence of Maddox. Afterwards, the way Winter saw it, had probably robbed Lakemfa of his life.

'I haven't been there myself, sir. If that's what you're asking.'

'You haven't?'

'No.'

'Why on earth not?'

The question, voiced with guileful innocence, hung in the air. The two men gazed at each other. Winter was angry now, and disinclined to take this conversation any further. Suttle, embarrassed, tried to help him out.

'Maddox came up with a suggestion, sir. I don't know what you'd think.'

'Try me.' Alcott was still looking at Winter.

'She says she's happy to string Wishart along. Wear a wire.'

'You mean take him to bed? Record the proceedings?'

'Yes, sir.'

'And you think it would be worth it? Evidentially?'

'She says yes. She says she can get anything out of him. If he really did put a contract out on the Nigerian guy, she says Wishart will give her chapter and verse.'

'Why would he do that?'

'Because that's the way he is. Just like Singer. Can't resist a boast.'

Alcott nodded, considering the proposition. His eyes returned to Winter.

'And what do you think?'

Winter had seen the question coming. This time he was ready.

'Jimmy's probably right, sir. Definitely worth a shot.'

'But what do *you* think? Would you be comfortable with something like that?'

'Of course, sir.' He returned Alcott's amused gaze. 'Why wouldn't I be?'

*

352

It was the first time that Faraday had taken a proper look at the interior of the nursing home. He sat in the residents' lounge with Tracy Barber, waiting for word that Mary Unwin was ready for the interview. The big lounge was L-shaped, an uncomfortable space created by the forced marriage of two rooms. Armchairs of all shapes and sizes were arranged around the walls, unholstered in shiny greens and browns and occupied by elderly women. Most of them sat immobile, either asleep or staring into the middle distance, entombed in a world of their own.

A pile of audio cassettes lay on the table beside Faraday's chair. Curious, he sorted through them. 'Hey Diddle Diddle'. 'Georgy Porgy'. 'Rock-a-Bye Baby'. He looked up again, catching Tracy Barber's eye. With the big TV at the end of the room tuned to the cartoon channel and the cassettes awaiting the evening sing-song, the place felt like a cross between a kindergarten and a station waiting room. No wonder Mary Unwin spent so much time on her own.

Her bedroom was up on the first floor, next to the lift. There was space for a single bed, a small dressing table, an armchair and a tiny wardrobe. The portable TV on the dressing table was flanked by family photos, most of them either black and white or sepia, and Faraday searched in vain for anyone who bore the slightest resemblance to Chris Unwin. The young care assistant who showed them up asked whether they'd like tea or coffee. Of Pelly there was no sign.

Tracy Barber stood beside the door while Faraday set up the tiny video camera and then perched himself on the bed, bringing himself comfortably into Mary Unwin's eyeline. She was a frail-looking eighty-seven but had clearly made an effort to brighten herself up. Her scalp shone pinkly through the billow of newly permed curls and a slash of scarlet lipstick hinted at the woman she must once have been. Whenever anyone paid her attention, she had a habit of plucking at the loose bottom of a hand-knitted cardigan. Fine-boned, bird-like hands. Beautifully shaped nails. A single ring, gold, with a striking diamond in a nice setting.

Faraday introduced himself and thanked Mary for her time. On the basis of DC Barber's notes, he asked her again about her grandson. He'd been a regular visitor. Then he'd stopped coming. Did Mary know why?

The question appeared to confuse her. Barber told Faraday to raise his voice. He tried again, then a third time. By now he was practically shouting.

'Who, dear?' She leaned forward, worrying at an old stain on her skirt.

'Chris. Your grandson. Here.' Faraday showed her the photo.

She peered at it in a vague kind of way, then smiled, her whole face transformed. She said she loved sprouts. Could never have too many of them. In the life to come she'd have them for breakfast.

Life to come? Sprouts? Faraday stole a glance at Barber. The DC was half turned, her shoulder resting on the wall beside the door. She offered Faraday a tiny shrug. Exactly as she'd warned, nothing made much sense.

Faraday tried again. He asked Mary how long she'd been at the home, where she'd lived before, whether or not she'd ever been married, trying to get a fix on exactly how much of her past remained intact. Within minutes he knew it was hopeless. The further back he went, the foggier her life became. The only fact she seemed sure about was her affection for the Isle of Wight.

Faraday leaned forward, warmed the space between them with a smile.

'I lived on the island myself,' he signed, 'when I was much younger.'

She stared at him, trying to follow his hands. Then she began to sign back. A couple of the gestures Faraday recognised. The sign for ice cream. A gesture towards the ceiling that might have signalled sunshine.

'I think she's talking about holidays she had as a kid,' Barber murmured. 'We went through all this before.'

'You came over here as a child?' Faraday signed.

Mary was nodding, her eyes bright.

'Nicer, then.'

'Nicer than what?'

'Nicer than . . .' Her eyes strayed to the door but she didn't complete the sentence. Faraday noticed the thin hands gripping the arms of the chair and it occurred to him for the first time that something must have happened, something specific, something recent.

'What is it?' He was leaning forward now. 'What are you trying to say?'

Mary shook her head. Her eyes were closed. She'd had enough. Faraday glanced across at Barber. Barber drew one finger across her throat and then nodded at Mary. Faraday hesitated a moment, unsure how this interview would play if the videotape ever got into the hands of a defence lawyer. Then, casting caution to the winds, he leaned forward again, putting his hand lightly on Mary's knee. Her eyes opened at once and she watched as Faraday repeated Barber's gesture. The effect was instantaneous. She pressed her hands together, a prayerful gesture, and pointed at the door again.

'What happened?' Faraday followed the wavering finger.

Mary had begun to take tiny shallow breaths. She looked up at the ceiling, shut her eyes again, hugged herself, began to sway.

'Please tell me.' Faraday was on the very edge of his chair. 'Please tell me what happened.'

Her body stilled. Immobile, she blinked up at him. Her eyes were the palest blue. Then, without warning, she erupted in a flurry of sign. Faraday, knowing this was as close as they'd probably come, did his best. In sign, the gesture for 'Again, please' is two fingers in a scissor shape dipped twice, followed by a tiny tilt of the chin. Faraday tried it three times. On each occasion Mary simply stared at him. Then there came a tiny choking noise before she shut her eyes and pressed her hands together.

'Just tell me,' Faraday begged. 'Whatever it is.'

The long moment of silence stretched and stretched. Then she began to tremble.

'Horrible,' she whispered.

Jimmy Suttle dropped Winter off at Maddox's flat on Southsea seafront. Maddox had kept the Subaru. Late afternoon, she'd suggested they drive out to the cottage, spend the weekend there. With a handful of CDs, a bottle or two of wine and the remains of Winter's tablets, they could – she'd said – bury the weekend.

The choice of verb had disturbed Winter. More and more, if you knew where to look, there were signs of his own frail grasp on life: billboard ads for holidays he'd probably never take; pre-positioned ambulances, part of a new strategy to improve response times; even the ugly sprawl of the scrapyard beside the stretch of motorway that funnelled traffic out of the city, a final resting place for rusting submarines and knackered tugs. These were signposts he'd passed every working day of his life. Only now did he realise what they were telling him.

Saturday afternoon, traffic on the motorway was heavy. Maddox slipped into the outside lane, pursuing a big Mercedes estate. There were kids in the back, three of them in a line on the bench seat, taking it in turn to blow bubbles. The little girl in the middle had the pot of suds and she dipped the plastic hoop in the solution then passed it sideways. The kids blew the bubbles towards the rear window, a piece of impromptu theatre for shoppers heading back to the suburbs on the mainland, and Winter watched the bubbles burst, one after the other, no survivors. That's me, he thought. Absolutely no fucking chance.

As they crossed the top of the harbour and joined the east–west motorway Winter gazed back at the sprawl of rooftops, at the distant tower blocks, at the square-shouldered bulk of the naval dockyard. Pompey had never had the looks of calendar cities like Winchester or Oxford. No one had ever bothered to put it on boxes of chocolates and pretend it was Olde England. But that, in a way, was its charm. To Winter's delight, it had always resisted attempts to pretty it up. On the contrary, no matter how much money you poured in, it remained what it had always been: ugly, vigorous, stoic, a city that limped gamely on from war to war, wrapped up in its own preoccupations, its back firmly turned on the rest of the world.

Winter had always enjoyed it, savoured it, appreciated its funny little ways. He liked to think he was fluent in Pompey, liked to tell himself he'd made a decent career here, felt a few collars, taken a few scalps, understood the way the place worked. But only now, suddenly confronted with a parting that might be all too permanent, did he realise the depth of the loss he'd face.

They sped east, towards Chichester, the light draining from the sky. Maddox, sensing his mood, glanced across and extended a hand. Winter held it briefly, then looked away, his eyes filling with tears. Not in a million years would you ever have thought it. Not this. Not now.

DS Brian Imber returned to the island in time to catch the end of the evening squad meet at Ryde police station. He eased himself into the crowded Major Incident Room, listening to Faraday tally the handful of small victories his army of DCs had managed to post.

The house-to-house teams, equipped with shots of the Tidemaster, had turned up a number of locals for whom Pelly was a dirty word. Some called him an oddball. For others he was a loner. One leisure fisherman, a newcomer to the island, had stopped Pelly back in mid-October and enquired about the Tidemaster. He hadn't seen the boat for a while and wondered whether it was out of the water for repair. If so, he'd be glad of the chance to inspect it because it was exactly the kind of boat he himself fancied taking on. The enquiry, he said, had been genuine but Pelly's reaction had amazed him. The boat had gone abroad. It was history. So mind your own fucking business.

The story raised a chuckle in the MIR. Collectively, these men and women were drawing a bead on Pelly, agreeing that the timeline and the circumstantial evidence which surrounded it were beginning to harden into a half-decent narrative. No one was more aware of this than Faraday but for the time being he withheld mention of his own visit to Sean Castle. The fact that Castle had chartered his own boat to Pelly and could even pinpoint a date was a major breakthrough. Tomorrow the outside enquiry teams would be tasked to expand the house-to-house parameters, pushing slowly up the hill towards the village of St Helens, and one of the questions on their list would be about Sean Castle. Faraday wanted intelligence on the man – gossip, rumour, anything he could use to pressure him for a statement. Conspiracy to murder was a serious charge. As his solicitor would doubtless explain.

The meet ended with Faraday offering a brief summary of other lines of enquiry. The Scenes of Crime search at the nursing home had so far revealed nothing beyond evidence of the wholesale redecoration of the sitting room in Pelly's wife's accommodation: new carpet, new wallpaper, fresh gloss paint on the skirting and doors, plus a brand new armchair. The Volvo estate Pelly had owned for a couple of years had been sold in early October to a cash buyer from somewhere up north. A couple of DCs were trying to trace the vehicle for forensic examination but DVLA still had Pelly as the registered owner. Pelly himself admitted to once having had the new owner's details but now claimed to have lost them.

The Home Office pathologist, meanwhile, had confirmed traces of saw marks on the exposed vertebra from the headless corpse and was hopeful that further analysis might even offer a lead on the kind of saw used in the dismemberment. This piece of evidence alone, murmured Faraday, was useful ammunition in

Willard's ceaseless negotiations with headquarters. There were certain individuals higher up the force who were already questioning the value of spending so much precious resource on a drunken sailor who might have fallen off a passing boat. The fact that someone had definitely taken the bloke's head off was final confirmation that they were involved in a homicide inquiry.

The meeting over, Imber accompanied Faraday back to his office. Imber wanted a word with DC Tracy Barber.

'She's gone to London,' Faraday explained. 'Pressing social call. Back first thing tomorrow.'

'You've got her mobile number?'

'Of course.'

Imber was standing beside Faraday's desk. A pile of photos lay next to the phone.

'D'you mind?'

'Go ahead.' Faraday was still hunting for Barber's number.

Imber began to leaf slowly through the photos. One in particular drew a shake of his head.

'Where did you get these?'

'They came out of Pelly's flat at the nursing home. Scenes of Crime gave them to us this afternoon. It's like a museum up there. They took me up and showed me.'

'Museum?' Imber was still studying the photo.

'Maps on the wall. Posters for commemorative exhibitions. Couple of flags. And pinboards full of stuff like that.'

Faraday scribbled Barber's number on the back of an envelope and gave it to Imber. Then he circled the desk and studied the photo over Imber's shoulder. It showed women and children trudging away from a line of coaches. There was snow on the ground and the women's breath was clouding in the cold air. Some of them were struggling with bulging suitcases, others had pots and pans on lengths of rope around their necks. One or two, empty-handed, were staring numbly at the camera, while an older woman, alone in the snow, had her hands to her eyes, weeping.

In the background, lounging around the coaches, were soldiers. They were wearing baggy olive great-coats, belted at the waist. Big knives hung from the belts in scabbards, and every man carried an assault rifle. Many of the soldiers appeared to be sharing a joke. One, with a full beard, was pointing at the women as they filed past the camera.

Imber turned the photo over. The ink had smudged over the years but the date was still legible. February '93.

'Pelly must have taken these.' Imber was leafing through the rest of the shots.

'How do you know?'

'Guy I went to see today served with him out in Bosnia; gave me the full picture.' Imber dropped into the spare chair and dug around in his briefcase. 'I've brought a map.' He shook it open and laid it on the desk. 'It's now rather than then but I thought it might help.'

Faraday stared down at the map. It showed the whole of the Balkans from Slovenia in the north to Macedonia in the south, a patchwork of tribal states reaching inland towards the border with Romania. Imber bent to the map, finding the Adriatic port of Split, and Faraday followed his finger as he traced the road that Pelly would have driven time and again, trucking heavy engineering materials through the mountains to the town of Vitez.

It was here, said Imber, that the Cheshire Regiment had established their battalion headquarters, fortifying an abandoned school. The Brits had arrived under a UN mandate, protecting the supply lines that kept tens of thousands of refugees in Central Bosnia alive.

'The guy I met this morning was a loggie.' Imber glanced up at Faraday. 'That's a Logistics Officer. Dealt with the likes of Pelly every bloody day. Pelly was a corporal, 42 Field Squadron, Royal Engineers. It was blokes like him who had to get accommodation for the squaddies sorted before the winter came. They started with the school. Then the Serbs got stroppy out towards Banja Luka and the whole thing kicked off.'

He returned to the photos, picking a different shot this time – the coaches more distant, the women visibly exhausted, their kids hollow-eyed with fear. Mountains pressed in on the valley, folds of snow speared with fir trees.

The women and kids, said Imber, were Bosnian refugees, Muslims driven from their villages by the Serbs and dumped at the border. The border was at a place called Turbe. The townships of Travnik and Vitez lay down the valley. This was territory controlled by the Croats and they too had no love for the Muslims.

'So what happened to these people?'

'The UN built a refugee centre in Travnik. There were hundreds of women and kids in there. They had shelter and food and water and somewhere to shit but that was about it. Pelly would have lent a hand.' He tapped the photo. 'No question.'

Faraday gazed at the photo, at the blank hopelessness on these women's faces, at the faltering progress they made from shot to shot, struggling away under the eyes of the watching soldiers. He began to lay the photos out on the map, side by side, the grimmest testimony to an almost-forgotten war.

'And their men?'

'Driven into camps. Killed. Tortured. Starved.' Imber's finger found a particular group of soldiers. 'We're talking ethnic cleansing. According to the loggie the Serbs were world class. These guys happen to be regular troops. The worst of the lot were the paramilitaries, football thugs and criminals bussed in from Belgrade, out of their heads most of the time on plum brandy. They'd move from village to village, drag the men away, rape the women, nick everything that moved, then torch the houses. This particular day they'd had enough of the women and packed them into coaches and drove them to the border. The Croats could sort them out. Or maybe the UN.' He paused, fingering another grinning face. 'The Serbs even charged a fare. Eighty Deutschmarks each to be dumped in the snow. Welcome to Croatia.'

Faraday was trying to imagine what scenes like these would do to serving soldiers to someone like Pelly, trained for a very different war. He'd once heard the Bosnian conflict described as medieval. Now, however dimly, he began to understand why. Blood and honey, he thought. Life reduced to the very basics.

'Tell me more about Pelly.' He sank into the chair behind the desk, reaching for a separate set of photos.

Imber obliged. Pelly, it seemed, had joined up in his teens. At twenty-one he'd been in the Falklands, part of the task force that landed at San Carlos Water and fought their way to Stanley. Afterwards, for at least a couple of years, he had stayed on as part of the sapper team dealing with the hundreds of live minefields left by the vanquished Argies. The start of a new decade found Yugoslavia on the point of collapse. The Croats and the Serbs wanted to divide the spoils. The losers would be the Muslims. And so two years later Pelly found himself in Vitez, with his blue UN beret and his Minolta compact, and a passion to help that quickly soured into anger and disgust.

'The loggie said he became obsessed. Most of the blokes managed to cope. Pelly couldn't.'

'And you think he definitely took these?'

The second stack of photos featured more of the refugees from the coaches. By now they'd made it to makeshift accommodation in the ruins of some kind of factory and Faraday found himself looking at a tight semicircle of women huddled around a fire of smashed-up wooden pallets.

'That would be the camp at Travnik,' Imber confirmed.

He wanted to know the date. Faraday turned the photo over. Same handwriting.

'March ninety-three.'

'Spot on.'

'Why?'

'That's the month the MoD asked for voluntary redundancies. Gave Pelly the perfect out. By then he'd had enough of taking orders; wanted to do it his way. The loggie said the blokes thought he was crazy. Same story as before. Pelly took it too personally. They were glad to see the back of him.'

'So he left Bosnia that month?'

'Far from it.' Imber was eyeing the rest of the photos. 'What else have you got there?'

Faraday sifted quickly through the pile. There must have been nearly a hundred shots. After a while Pelly had put the woodsmoke and the squalor of the refugee camp behind him. Instead he was in a valley. The snow was thinning on the mountain slopes and there was a greenness to the landscape that spoke of spring. Half close your eyes, thought Faraday, and this could be Switzerland or Austria: high Alpine meadows, wild flowers underfoot, eagles and kites riding the first thermals as the air slowly warmed beneath them.

Then, with a fierce abruptness, came a shot of a still-burning house. The place looked new, an upmarket chalet with a brick drive and a double garage and space on the lawn for a modest swimming pool. But most of the roof had gone, and there were scorch marks around the windows where the glass had blown out, and on closer inspection Faraday could see pockmarked areas of white stucco where bullets had hit. He reached for another photo, then a third. More houses, equally ruined. Family cars – one of them a Ford Mondeo – put to the torch. Pets – a cat, a pair of Alsatians – butchered in the snow. And finally a line of corpses, possibly a whole family, lying where they must have fallen, their arms outstretched, bags nearby, each head with a neat bullet hole and a spreading crimson stain beneath.

Faraday, who'd seen hundreds of photos from the Scenes of Crime reports, couldn't take it in. One moment this village must have been every estate agent's dream. The next, it was a charnel house.

At the very bottom of the pile, beneath the burned-out mosque and the blackened remains of someone who'd been burned to death, was a photograph of a horse. Pelly must have come across it in the meadow behind the houses. It was standing in bright sunshine, head down, munching grass, totally untroubled by the carnage beyond the distant curtain of drifting smoke.

Faraday passed the shot across, saying nothing. These were images from a nightmare, all the more powerful for being so recent. No wonder Pelly was so wound up. An experience like this would stay with you forever.

'Place called Ahmici.' Imber was collecting the photos. 'Little village near Vitez. Pelly was one of the first in. Did the recce. Took the shots. The Croats and the Muslims had been at each others' throats for weeks. The Croats thought a massacre might sort it out. Staked out the village at dawn. Cut off the escape routes. Then the death squads went in. Killed each family as they made a run for it. First the men. Then the male children. Then the rest. Very Balkan.'

'And Pelly?'

'Released some of these shots to the press. His bosses didn't get the joke. He was out of uniform within a month. Redundancy package, the lot. Apparently they couldn't understand why he didn't become a plumber in Swindon. Probably still don't.'

Faraday sat back in the chair. Images like these would haunt any man. Ten years later Pelly was still living with them. Literally.

'So where does this take us?' he asked at last.

'Dunno.' Imber was still looking at the horse. 'The bloke I met this morning was lucky enough to be flown home. Copped a nasty wound and never went back.'

'Someone shot him?'

'No, he hit a local car on a mountain road. Head-on. Bloke only had one headlight. You know what the squaddies used to call those?' He laughed softly. 'Bosnian motorbikes.'

Eighteen

Some sixth sense told Faraday not to expect good news. He fumbled for his mobile in the gloom, wondering what could warrant a call at half past seven on a Sunday morning. It was Dave Michaels, already in his office at the MIR. He'd just had a bell from one of the Crime Scene Investigators up at the nursing home. The CSI had been making an early start on the garage round the back and had been curious about the presence of an ambulance in the front drive. One of the staff had told him about a fatality during the night. Woman by the name of Mary Unwin had just been discovered dead in bed. Ring any bells?

Faraday was already on his feet.

'Anything else? Any details?'

'None. The CSI didn't even know if it was of interest. Just trying to be helpful.' Dave Michaels knew all about Mary Unwin because Tracy Barber had fed him a full account of yesterday's interviews.

Faraday was heading for the little en suite bathroom. Still on the mobile, he filled the basin and reached for the soap. He told Michaels to contact the mortuary at the hospital and then sort out a Home Office pathologist for the post-mortem. Last night's actions for the outside inquiries team would have to be revised. He wanted a couple of DCs into the home for interviews with night staff, residents and anyone else who might have anything useful to say about Mary Unwin's movements over the last twelve hours and about her general state of health. The latter should involve the GP who regularly visited the nursing home. Was there any kind of pre-existing condition? Had she been feeling ill? What had she eaten or drunk?

Faraday mopped at his face with a wet flannel, each successive question prompting another, overwhelmed by the sense that *Congress* had just arrived at an important crossroads. Make the wrong decision, take the wrong turn, ignore an important lead, and the consequences didn't bear contemplation.

Finally, his checklist exhausted, Faraday waited for a response.

'Pelly?' Michaels queried.

'Check with the Surveillance Unit. Find out if he's still at the home.' Faraday reached for a towel. 'Ever get the feeling he's winding us up?'

DC Tracy Barber was already at her desk in the Major Incident Room by the time Faraday arrived. He called her along to his office. Dave Michaels had passed on the news about Mary Unwin and Barber closed the door before turning back to Faraday. She'd been thinking, she said, about yesterday's interview at the home.

'You remember the way it was? You on the bed? Me by the door?'

'Yeah.'

'The door wasn't quite shut. I'm sure someone was out there in the corridor.'

'You're telling me you saw someone?'

'No, but I had a sense – someone moving, footsteps, a presence. Eavesdropping would have been a doddle, the way you had to shout.'

Faraday nodded. Barber was right. Anyone with an interest in his conversation with Mary Unwin could have picked up the drift from several rooms away.

'Who do you think, then?'

'No idea. Pelly was out, according to the surveillance log. I checked it first thing, as soon as Dave Michaels told me.'

'Out for sure?'

'Out as in doing the weekly Tesco shop. Eighteen loaves of Mighty White and a trolleyful of Complan. He didn't come back until gone five.'

'Lajla?'

'Could have been. She's light on her feet. But then it could have been anyone.'

A knock on the door brought Dave Michaels into the office. He'd just been on to the surveillance team trailing Pelly. The man was currently having breakfast with a middle-aged white male in the Farringford Hotel, in Freshwater Bay. Faraday knew the hotel well. It had once belonged to Alfred Lord Tennyson, a lovely confection in Victorian Gothic that nestled in the shadow of Tennyson Down. Odd, thought Faraday, that this investigation should come full circle. A body recovered from the foot of the cliffs. And now the prime suspect tucking into eggs and bacon barely a mile inland.

Michaels was still standing in the open doorway.

'PM?' Faraday queried.

'I phoned Pembury at home. He's duty call-out.' Michaels grinned. 'We just ruined his weekend.'

Winter had always hated Sundays. When Joannie was alive it was the one day of the week when she had tried to coax her husband into some kind of domestic routine. She'd ask him to drive her to one of the local gardening centres. Or they might visit her mum in Brighton. Or she'd draw up a list of DIY jobs around the house and threaten to call in a tradesman unless Winter rolled up his sleeves and did them himself.

Winter always succumbed to these chores with as much grace as he could muster but deep down he'd always thought of Sundays as the one moment in the week when real life let him down. He thrived on the small print of the job: on phone calls, meets, mischief, manipulation, business, the ongoing carnival that paid the bills. Sundays, unless he was on a job that spilled over the weekend, brought all that to a temporary halt. It was a different kind of time, dead time. Worst of all it made him stop and think.

At Maddox's insistence, they'd set out on a walk to the low line of trees that marked the distant edges of Pagham Harbour. She'd found him a pair of gumboots and a thick fleece, and she'd wound one of her own scarves around his neck. The weather was miserable, a thin grey light and a hard, bitter wind that scythed across the flat fields, and Winter's mood was soured further by the knowledge that the life he'd somehow taken for granted had so suddenly come to a full stop.

Cathy Lamb had phoned last night instructing him not to report for duty for at least a week. Jimmy Suttle had also been in touch, expressing a worryingly genuine concern about his well-being. All this sympathy was deeply touching but the last role Winter intended to play was that of the invalid. Being ill, he told himself, was a state of mind. You surrendered control. You relied on other people. You became a sitting duck for all that well-intentioned compassion.

Last night they'd gone to bed early, leaving the remains of a log fire in the grate. Tired to the point of exhaustion, Winter had followed Maddox up the narrow wooden stairs and collapsed into bed. The cottage was freezing, no central heating, and they'd hugged each other for warmth under the duvet.

Within minutes Winter had been asleep, his arms still wrapped around Maddox, and he'd woken hours later to find her looming over him, tented by the duvet, asking whether he was OK. Winter had grunted in the darkness, not knowing quite how he felt, and later, when she'd wanted to make love to him, he'd simply done her bidding, glad of her presence more than anything else. Afterwards, nose to nose, she'd asked him what else she could do to help.

'Nothing,' he'd muttered. 'Just be here.'

Now she walked beside him, aware of his darkening mood, her gloved hand tucked beneath his arm. They'd woken late. She'd made a huge pot of tea, laid a new fire in the hearth, fetched in a pile of extra logs for the afternoon. Down by the water, an hour's walk away, there was a pub that sold mulled wine and a thousand real ales. They did big Sunday roasts for lunch and with luck the weather would keep the yachties away.

Winter had sat in the kitchen, buoyed by a good night's sleep, marvelling at how pleasant a Sunday could be and trying to work out the catch. Now, with the pub finally in view, he realised what it was. He'd come across this place before. Just days ago.

'The Humble Duck,' he grunted. 'Come here often, do you?'

'Yes.'

'Alone?'

She glanced across at him.

'What kind of question is that?'

Winter didn't answer. The pub, at midday, was already comfortably full. Winter ordered drinks at the bar while Maddox found a table in the corner. There was a mirror behind the bar, and Winter watched the heads turn as she unbuttoned her long leather coat and draped it over the back of the chair. She was wearing jeans and a man's sweater she'd found in a drawer in the bedroom. She rarely bothered with make-up or jewellery, and she'd barely put a comb through her hair, but every man in the room was aware of her presence.

'You used to come here with Wishart.' Winter put the drinks on the table.

'How do you know that?'

'I'm a detective.'

'Very funny.'

'True, though, isn't it?' Winter could still picture the entries on Wishart's Visa statements. 'Couple of drinks. Bottle of wine. Big steak. Then back for an afternoon's screwing. Am I getting warm?'

'Yeah.' Maddox grinned. 'And was it like this?'

'This?'

'You and me? Last night? This morning?' She leaned forward and kissed him on the lips. 'The answer's no.'

'Why not?'

'Because we need each other.'

The simplicity of the answer caught Winter off balance. He looked at her for a long moment, then reached for her hand.

'Do me a favour?'

'Anything.'

'Then tell me how you really feel.'

'About?'

'Me. This. Us. The truth is I've got a problem with Wishart. You know why? Because I still can't work out where he fits. You fucked him for money? For love? For—'

'I don't fuck anyone for love.'

'Never?'

'No.' She shook her head. 'You love someone, it's different. It's not fucking any more. Fucking is theatre. Fucking is dressing-up. Fucking is performance. Fucking you pay for. Fucking buys me a place of my own and a nice view and space in my head where I can be me.'

'Lakemfa?'

'Was a sweet fuck.'

'Wishart?'

'*Un trou de cul.* An arsehole.'

'And this?'

'This, my love, is something else. And you know the irony?'

'Tell me.'

'That you should have walked into my life through a bedroom door. That I should owe this . . .' she grinned at him, then gestured at the space between them '. . . to fucking.'

Winter held her gaze for a long moment, gleefully aware of the listening ears around him. Then he fumbled for his mobile. Jimmy Suttle answered on the third ring.

'How are you?' Suttle asked at once.

'Never better.' Winter was still looking at Maddox. 'How are you getting on with those calls I asked you to make?'

'Good.' Suttle appeared to be driving. 'I've fixed to meet the Bone at two. Pub down in Copnor. Sends his best, by the way. You want me to bell you afterwards?'

Winter glanced at his watch. Lunch would take an hour or so. They should be back at the cottage by three.

'Forget it.' He reached for the menu and winked at Maddox. 'Best if I ring you this evening.'

By the time Faraday finally got through to Willard, it was mid-afternoon. The Detective Superintendent was in Bristol with his partner, Sheila. They'd spent a pleasant lunchtime with friends and now he was contemplating the journey home.

Faraday told him about Mary Unwin. He and DC Barber had definitely been close to a breakthrough. Trying to restore some kind of order to the wreckage of the old lady's memory was never going to be easy but in Faraday's view she definitely had something to say. He described her sign language, the finger across the throat, and her preoccupation with the world beyond the door. Maybe she'd stumbled across something. And maybe she'd paid for that knowledge with her life.

Willard didn't buy it. For one thing, she sounded like the perfect definition of the vulnerable witness. The interview Faraday had described was way over the top. If she'd ever made it into the witness box – itself highly unlikely – the defence would have crucified police conduct of the case. And besides that, most of what Faraday was saying was speculation. What *Congress* badly needed was fact, a body of evidence that would be one hundred per cent lawyer-proof in court. To date, most of what Faraday had put together totally failed that test.

Listening to Willard in this mood did nothing for Faraday's blood pressure. Just occasionally, after a good lunch and a glass or two, his boss confused leadership with statements of the blindingly obvious. Of course *Congress* was difficult. The Major Crimes team still lacked a name for the body and in the shape of Rob Pelly Faraday had taken on a formidable challenge. The man was forensically aware. He knew how to cover his tracks. He was obstructive in interview, had no time for the normal courtesies, and appeared to have spent most of his life making enemies. Nonetheless, the sheer weight of circumstantial evidence had now convinced Faraday that there was a link between the body at the foot of the cliffs and a set of events that had taken place back in early October. Piecing together that set of events, he told Willard, was the absolute priority.

'Fine, Joe.' Willard still sounded unconvinced. 'But just ask yourself how you're going to do it. You can't pull the guy in, at least not yet you can't. The PM on the old lady may throw something up but I doubt it. SOC are pissing in the wind. Where's the breakthrough?'

Faraday, more irritated by the minute, was about to tell Willard about the revelation from Sean Castle. Then came a knock at the door. It was Tracy Barber. She had a guest downstairs, someone who'd asked for Faraday by name.

'Who is it?' Faraday mouthed.

Barber grinned at him, then stepped across to the desk and wrote a name on the pad beside the phone. Faraday gazed down at it. *Pelly*.

Willard was talking money again. The budget was becoming a nightmare. He had to have solid progress to fend off the assassins in Resource Management. Faraday cut him short.

'Something's come up, sir.' He was already on his feet. 'Ring you later.'

Faraday knew at once that Pelly had been drinking. He sat on the bench by the front desk, his arms folded, his wet anorak unzipped and thrown open. The rain had flattened his hair against his skull, and the strip of scarlet ribbon that secured his pony tail hung limply down his back. He was wearing a scuffed pair of combat boots beneath faded jeans, and when Faraday stepped through the door his eyes glittered in the unshaven gauntness of his face. He looked like someone from a peace demo or a refugee from an all-night rock concert, and for a moment Faraday wondered what the staff at the Farringford had made of their unexpected breakfast guest.

Pelly got to his feet.

'Mr Faraday.' He swayed a little, corrected himself. 'Thought we'd have a little chat.'

Faraday took him upstairs to his office, told Barber to divert all phone calls, shook his head when she asked whether he needed a second pair of ears and shut the door.

Pelly was gazing at J-J's shot of the diving gannets on the wall board. Faraday settled himself behind the desk.

'I could take this personally.' Pelly was still looking at the gannets. 'In fact I have taken it personally. Blokes all over my house. Blokes all over my business. Blokes in my garage. Blokes up my arse. Where does it stop? Doesn't a man have rights here? Shouldn't you be giving me a clue?'

Faraday said nothing. Pelly, he'd decided, always opened a conversation at gale force. Best, under the circumstances, to bend with the wind.

'Anything else?' he said mildly.

'Fucking right. I go down to Bembridge, I pick up the phone to my nice friends at Cheetah Marine, I even waste a minute of my precious time trying to get some sense out of that arsehole Morgan, and what do I find?

What I find, Mr Faraday, is that your blokes have been there before me. They're everywhere, all over the fucking island. Some of them have funny suits and all those fancy chemicals. The rest keep knocking on other people's doors. A man has a reputation here. Just what am I supposed to have done?'

'That's what we're trying to establish.'

'So why don't you fucking ask me? Save yourself a lot of time? Eh?'

His face was pale with anger. Faraday wondered about offering coffee, decided against it. Anger was good. Angry people made mistakes.

'You drove over here?'

'Sure. You going to do me for that? Breathalyse me? Only I'm telling you now, you'd get a result.' He paused, nodding to himself, then looked up again, struck by another thought. 'And you know why I've had a drink or two? Because I've got a deal, because I've finally managed to shift the fucking place. But then I expect you'd know that, wouldn't you? Your blokes round the estate agents day and night. Eh?'

'You're selling up?'

'Of course I am. Who'd want to stay here? The best thing about the English are the old dears in my home. After that, you can bin it.'

'Sorry to hear about Mrs Unwin.'

'Yeah. Shame.'

'What happened?'

'Haven't a clue. She had a couple of Martinis last night. Happy as Larry. Next thing we know –' he clicked his fingers '– out like a light. Blown away. Gone. Happens all the time. Our business, we call it dying.'

Faraday ignored the sarcasm. He wanted to know

where Pelly was going once he'd sold the nursing home.

'Bosnia,' he said at once. 'Land of the free.'

'Why?'

The question hung in the air. A smile spread across Pelly's face. Partly disbelief, partly something close to contempt.

'*Why?* Have you looked around lately? Have you blokes got eyes in your heads? The state of the place? Kids bossing the streets? Crap schools? Foul-mouthed women? Tosspot politicians? Half the population pissed? The rest locked in at home watching crap TV? Is that where you want to live? Seriously?'

'But why Bosnia?'

'Because it's not here. And because my wife wants to go home. She misses it, Mr Faraday. Bosnia was a bad place once. Really evil. I brought her over here to get her away from all that. And you know what? Ten years of England and she can't wait to get back. You're talking about a woman who was gang-raped for three solid months. Who watched the Serbs beating her father up. Who lost her mother and a brother and the house she'd been born in and every other fucking thing to those goons. That leaves a scar or two, believe me, yet she can't wait to get back. So what does that tell you about England, eh?'

'You met her in Bosnia?'

'Yeah.' Pelly nodded.

'Travnik?'

Mention of Travnik put a new expression on Pelly's face and for a tiny moment Faraday saw the steel in the man. No matter how much he'd had to drink, there was still a sentry at his gate.

'You know about Travnik?'

'I know there was a refugee camp there. And I know

378

you were at Vitez. Engineers build things, mend things.' Faraday shrugged. 'You wouldn't have been short of work.'

'And I wasn't, my friend. Believe me. Anyone half decent . . .' He shook his head, his eyes brimming. 'Fucking unbelievable. The Serbs just dumped them. I saw it happen. Two feet of snow. Night coming on. These poor bloody women with nothing left in the world except their kids. And you know what those Serb bastards were saying? "So long! So long! Next time you die" I can hear them now. Cunts.'

'Was Lajla one of those women?'

'Yeah. And seven months pregnant. Came from a village up near Banja Luka. Lived there all her life. Fucking Serbs rolled them over. Took forty minutes. You ever hear of the camp at Omarska? No? Count yourself fucking lucky.' He eyed Faraday a moment, a man with a great deal of news to impart, then he made a visible effort, controlled himself, sat upright in the chair. 'What is this?' he said softly. 'What are you trying to get out of me?'

'I'm trying to understand the way it was.'

'For me? You're wasting your time. You should be asking about her. About Lajla. And about all the other Lajlas. You know the one thing you should never be in the Balkans? A woman. Not then. Not the way it was with the Serbs.'

When the Serbs cleared a village, he said, they started with the men and the boys – they went to the camps. Then they came back for the women. Lajla and her mother ended up in the same truck. The truck dropped Lajla at the school. She never saw her mother again.

'And at the school?'

'They'd cleared a classroom at the back. There were

379

stained old fucking mattresses on the floor – no sheets, no blankets, just the mattresses. The Serb boys spent fifteen days in the mountains, then they came back, six or seven of them at a time, one after another, cheering and clapping, making good little Serb soldiers. Can you believe that? In the classroom where this poor bloody girl had learned to *read*? Jesus.'

'And she got pregnant?'

'Yeah, just a bit. But you know the worst of it? She knew these animals. Christ, she'd even been to school with some of them. And there they were, just helping themselves.'

Faraday tried to imagine what it must have been like. For the second time in twenty-four hours he knew it was beyond him. More blood than honey, he thought.

Pelly was gazing out of the window. The anger had drained away. He looked almost sober.

'One thing I don't understand.' Faraday frowned. 'How come she wants to go back to this place? To this village? After all she's been through?'

'She doesn't. Not to her home village. We've got somewhere else in mind. The Jablanica Valley. Village called Celebici. Nice little smallholding near the lake – bit of ground, couple of goats, chickens, spare room for German tourists. Maybe a spot of freelance mine clearance if things get tight. Yeah . . .' He nodded. 'I can cope with that.'

Pelly lapsed into silence. Faraday was clearer now about what drove Pelly, about those months in the mountains that had changed his life. Any man who'd been through an experience like that would carry the images in his head forever. But what about Lajla? Gang-raped week after week? A woman who'd never know who'd fathered her child? How would you ever lay so many ghosts?

He put the question to Pelly. It drew an immediate shake of the head.

'She won't talk about it.'

'Not to anyone?'

'No. Not to me. Not to you. Not to fucking anyone.' He touched his head, then his heart. 'It's locked away. You'd be a brave man to even try and get at stuff like that.'

'Why?'

'*Why?*' Pelly threw back his head and laughed. 'Because she'd fucking kill you.'

Jimmy Suttle had never met the Bone. Winter, in odd conversations, had talked about the man's amazing prowess with the ladies, someone – he'd said admiringly – who could work his way down any street in Pompey and leave not a single taker with any complaints. His speciality was housewives and he went from door to door with a carpet-cleaning offer which was, to be frank, a steal. Once inside the house, he rarely left without a cup of tea and a biscuit or two and a sympathetic ear full of the local gossip. The Bone's ability to listen – to nod, to empathise, to agree – was the key, Winter had concluded, to his amazing tally of conquests. Women went to bed with him because he was a nice bloke. Not only that, but he shagged them witless.

Winter had described him as a Frank Skinner lookalike, and Suttle could see why. The same shock of blondish hair. The same open face. The same ready smile. He was sitting in a pub in the depths of Buckland, absorbed by the Pompey match report in yesterday's *Sports Mail*. This was a man you'd be happy to have clean your carpet.

Suttle muttered a greeting and asked whether he wanted to talk elsewhere. The Bone looked surprised.

'Here no good, mate?'

'Here's fine.'

Suttle bought drinks and found a table in the corner. The air was blue with roll-ups and a vocal semicircle of drinkers was glued to a telly in the corner. Everton 3 Tottenham 1.

'You follow the football?' Suttle had half an eye on Duncan Ferguson.

'Yeah. What's it with Mr W?'

'He's not well.' Suttle dragged himself away from the game. 'Hasn't been for several weeks.'

'Like bad, is it?'

'Dunno, mate. He's waiting for tests.'

'*Tests?* That's heavy shit, must be bad.'

Suttle studied him for a moment. He couldn't explain why but he was surprised at this man's concern. Either the Bone was a born actor or he really cared.

'You've known Winter long?'

'Yeah. Ever since he stitched me up on a handling charge. Well kippered or what? An hour in the cells and I would have sold him my mother. Hand it to the bloke. He's an artist.' He laughed at the memory, then raised his glass. 'To Mr W. Hope he gets better.'

Suttle explained briefly about Lakemfa. Black guy. Knocked off his bike the arse end of last year. Country lane, back of the hill.

'Mr W thinks you might be the man to know.'

'Know what, mate?'

'Who did him.'

'You're telling me he died?'

382

'Yeah. There's a bit of history here but I won't bore you. The point is someone did a wonderful job. No car ever discovered. No forensic. No witnesses. Just chummy in the road. Dead.'

'You're talking a hit, yeah? The kind of blokes I know, they normally take a couple of hundred to give a bloke a hiding, drink most of it, go over the top, kick the bloke to death and then get nicked at the end of it. Your guy's not like that at all, is he? Sounds a bit subtle for this city.'

'We're talking early October. Target was a Nigerian, naval guy. The way we see it, there was serious money involved.'

'How serious?'

'We think thousands.'

'Plural?'

'Yeah.'

'That *is* serious.' The Bone was looking thoughtful. 'Anything else to go on?'

'He was living in Port Solent. Had a rented apartment there.'

'Ah . . . housewives' delight.' The Bone was beaming. 'Leave it to me.'

It was dark by the time Faraday took Pelly back to the front office. He opened the door to the street and accompanied him onto the pavement. The rain had stopped by now and a creamy full moon was rising behind the shreds of racing cloud.

Faraday had spent the best part of an hour pressing Pelly on every aspect of his story. Under formal caution, with absolutely no doubt that anything he might say could be used in evidence against him, he'd freely admitted spending a financial windfall on buying the new boat. The money, he said, had come from foreign sources. It would all be declared in his tax return and he was under no legal obligation to explain further. As far as Sean Castle was concerned, he'd certainly chartered his boat but that, too, wasn't illegal. A mate he trusted had skippered the Tidemaster on its last outing and the boat had gone to a French buyer the following day. No, he hadn't got the French bloke's details. Neither did he know the whereabouts of the mate who'd taken the Tidemaster to sea. And yes, the same lack of interest applied to the northerner who'd given him a couple of hundred for his clapped-out old Volvo estate. Faraday, he said, was welcome to chase both buyers, and if he ever found the guy with the Volvo maybe he could return the set of titanium fish hooks Pelly had left under the front passenger seat. On Chris Unwin's mysterious disappearance he could shed no light. Bloke had done a runner. Happens all the time. End of story.

Watching Pelly cross the road to reclaim his new car, Faraday knew he'd been listening to a tissue of lies. More important still, he'd realised that Pelly himself understood this and wasn't much bothered. As long as the story held together, both men knew that Pelly would be home safe. His breakfast companion in the Farringford Hotel had funds available to buy the nursing home. Such was the depth of Pelly's disgust at the state of the nation, he'd agreed a silly price. By Easter, if the lawyers got off their arses, Pelly and his strange little family would be milking their goats on the shores of Lake Jablanica.

At the end of the interview Faraday had switched off the tape machine and sat back in his chair.

'Clever,' he'd said. And meant it.

Pelly drove into the night, giving Faraday a derisive farewell wave as he passed the police station. Faraday found Tracy Barber and Dave Michaels at the top of the stairs.

'Well, boss?' It was Tracy Barber.

Faraday looked at her a moment, then smiled.

'I think we're getting somewhere,' he said.

Nineteen

Monday, 1 March 2004

Winter drove himself to Portsmouth's Queen Alexandra Hospital. Maddox sat beside him as they turned off the motorway and climbed towards the distant sprawl of buildings that dominated the lower slopes of the hill.

Back at the cottage, Winter had woken early. He hadn't felt so cheerful for weeks and had toyed with cancelling the appointment at the hospital. Maybe good sex and a 4 a.m. discussion about Arthur Rimbaud had chased the demons away. Only Maddox's insistence that he give the medics a look inside his throbbing head had persuaded him to take the road back to Pompey.

The car park full, Winter left Maddox to find somewhere for the Subaru. His appointment card instructed him to report to the X-ray department on C level.

He made his way down the long corridors and followed the overhead signs until he found himself in a big reception area dominated by a framed photograph of a lighthouse under attack by the elements. The photo was a wild swirl of towering breakers and drifting spume, the sturdy granite thumb of the lighthouse dwarfed by the fury of the storm. Beneath the photo a line of text read *Avis de coup de vent*.

Winter studied the photo for a moment or two. Me, he thought.

The woman behind the desk consulted the morning appointment list and told him to take a seat. Winter wanted to know what *Avis de coup de vent* meant. She glanced up at him.

'Someone else asked that.'

'And?'

'Something about a gale warning. Heavy weather. It's French.'

'Yeah?' Winter looked back at the photo, then asked how long the scan would take.

'An hour or so. Depends.'

'On what?'

'How it goes.'

'Really?'

Winter gave her a look and then went through to the waiting area and found himself a seat before ringing Maddox. She'd found a parking spot round the back of the hospital and was watching a steady stream of patients labouring up the hill towards the A & E department. Why was everyone so fat in this city?

Winter smiled. She'd raised the same question last night, blaming his headaches on too much beer and too many burgers. He needed to lose a couple of stone at least and just then she'd been in an excellent position to judge.

'This lot's going to take a while,' he told her. 'I'll get a cab home.'

'OK.'

'You'll be there?'

'Probably not. I've got some stuff to do back at the flat. Hey . . .' her voice softened '. . . take care.'

'You too.' Winter ducked his head, overwhelmed yet again. How come this woman could breach his defences with such ease? How on earth would you put a life back together after something like this? Gale warning, he thought. *Avis de* whatever.

'Your name, sir?'

Winter glanced up. The nurse's face was a blur.

'Winter,' he said numbly.

She took him into the imaging area. The room with the CT machine was bigger than he'd thought, with radiation warnings on the door and a long glass panel offering a view from the control suite next door. Through the glass he could see two figures bent over monitor screens. Curiosity made him ask who they were.

'Radiographers, Mr Winter.' The nurse had a nice smile. 'Would you mind lying down here, please?'

She indicated a long couch at knee level. At the head of the couch was a big doughnut-shaped machine that dominated the room. Everything looked new.

Winter slipped off his jacket and lay full length on the couch. The nurse propped his head on some kind of support. He felt the clammy crinkle of polythene cupping the base of his skull. The nurse explained the procedure – a quick scouting shot, then another series of pictures, each requiring a tiny adjustment in the couch. At the most it would take a couple of minutes. She smiled again, and then disappeared.

Winter gazed up at the ceiling. He hated this. He hated the feeling that he was in some kind of queue. He hated the waiting, the anticipation, the lack of control, the knowledge that there were people next door, barely metres away, who were about to peer into the very middle of his brain. Life, for reasons he couldn't fathom, had turned the tables on him. Getting inside other people's heads was his job, his privilege. How come he was so suddenly on the receiving end?

His headache had got worse, throbbing and throbbing, and he began to wonder whether it might be connected with stress, and whether it would affect the images these quiet, efficient medics were bent on capturing. There was a smoke detector on the ceiling, directly in his eyeline, and he tried to concentrate on the tiny red light that winked and winked, on/off, on/off. Drive you mad, he thought. Looking at that.

Without warning the couch began to rise. Instinctively, like a kid on the Cresta Run, his hands tightened on the folds of blanket beneath him. Moments later he was going backwards, into the heart of the doughnut, a movie without a soundtrack, total silence.

Then came a voice – disembodied, firm.

'Nice and still in there, Mr Winter.'

He wondered whether to shut his eyes, decided against it. The couch had stopped. Immediately above him, inset into the inner surface of the doughnut, was a clear glass panel. There were red lights inside the panel and there came a soft whirring noise as the lights spun round and the couch eased his body out again. Then the couch stopped before sliding him into the doughnut again. More shots. Then it was over.

The waiting seemed to go on forever. Up on one elbow, Winter gazed at the figures on the other side of the glass panel. Two radiographers were studying an image on a monitor screen. One of them frowned, pointed at something, then nodded. Moments later the door opened and the nurse appeared. She had a syringe in one hand and a tissue in the other. She perched herself on the side of the couch. Another smile.

'Just a tiny injection, Mr Winter. Do you mind?'

Winter gazed up at her. He knew he'd had it. He knew with a terrible certainty that this was the figure of death. Not the Grim Reaper. Not the skull-faced guarantee that you were inches away from the grave. But a pretty girl with bobbed hair who was having trouble finding a vein in his forearm.

'What's this about, then?' Winter managed.

'Nothing really.' She'd practised the line a thousand times. 'Just a tiny definition problem with the machine. We're taking a couple more shots just to be on the safe side. There –' she beamed down at him '– didn't feel a thing, did you?'

An early lunch was Faraday's idea. He collected Brian Imber from the office that housed the Intelligence Cell and made his way downstairs. A pub round the corner on the High Street started serving at half eleven. Imber stood at the door, watching the barmaid wiping down the tables ahead of the lunchtime rush. Faraday was starving.

Away from the constant clamour of the Major Crimes machine, he needed time and space to review events. After the initial burst of energy, the *Congress* team was beginning to flag. Scenes of Crime and the house-to-house teams had produced very little. However hard they rattled Pelly's cage, nothing seemed to fall out.

'And Willard?' Imber was eyeing the menu chalked on the blackboard beside the bar.

'He's losing faith. There was a double murder in Waterlooville last night. Looks like a three-day event to me but I've lost seven DCs. The New Forest job was done and dusted in a week.' Faraday mimicked Willard's growl: 'And you lot haven't even got a bloody name for the body.'

'Unwin,' Imber said. 'Has to be.'

'Sure. But he wants it in writing. Like we all do.'

Faraday had just spent the best part of an hour on the phone to Willard, who wanted to scale down *Congress*. SOC had wasted a small fortune for absolutely no forensic return and the accommodation bills for the inquiry team were mounting by the day. The prime suspect had volunteered himself for interview but without solid evidence Faraday hadn't been able to lay a finger on him. In short, Willard was beginning to wish the bloody woman with the binoculars had done her birdwatching somewhere else. Another good blow and the headless body might have ended up on someone else's patch.

'He wants the HSU off the job, too. Doesn't see the point anymore.'

The surveillance teams had been shadowing Pelly since Friday night. Not once had anything remotely interesting appeared on their log.

'You fought him off?'

'Short term, yes. I told him that Pelly thinks he's got us shafted. In that kind of mood he might drop a stitch or two.'

'You think that's true?'

'Yes. The guy's strange. Yesterday I almost got to like him.'

'Great.' Imber looked less than impressed. 'So where does that take us?'

It was a good question. Faraday eased his chair away from the table. The pub was still empty.

'Bosnia's the key,' he said at last. 'I'm sure of it. Pelly still makes regular trips, brings blokes back, makes no secret of it. He's obviously got connections out there. In fact he likes it so much he's going to bloody live there.'

'You believe him?'

'Yes, I do. All that stuff we seized from his room –

the photos, the flags, the little souvenirs – it's got under his skin. If you're someone like Pelly, you need a good war. In fact you need more than that. You need a cause.'

'We're talking ten years ago. Different century.'

'I know, Brian, but mentally he's still out there, still in the trenches. Some blokes never let go and for my money he's one of them.'

'And Unwin?' Imber still wasn't convinced.

'I've no idea. Maybe he set up some kind of freelance operation. Maybe he got in Pelly's face. Maybe he became a threat of some kind, fancied Lajla, overplayed his hand. You know the way these things work. Someone like Pelly, it wouldn't take much.'

'No . . .'

The waitress arrived. Faraday ordered ham and eggs. Imber settled for pasta with salad. After promising himself he'd never run another marathon, he was back in training. The waitress gone, he turned back to Faraday.

'What about the PM on the old girl?'

'Pembury was duty call-out. He phoned me just before we left. Says he's going to buy a house over here, save himself the travelling.'

'And?'

'Nothing. He's putting it down to heart failure. Bit of arterial disease, bit of ischaemia, nothing you wouldn't expect in an eighty-seven-year-old.'

'No haemorrhages?' Imber touched his eye.

'Not a trace. And he looked bloody hard.'

Imber shook his head, as disappointed as Faraday. Given the possibility of yet another interview, they'd agreed that Pelly might have smothered Mary Unwin with a pillow. Had she put up a struggle, blood pressure would have burst some of the tiny vessels in her eyeballs, a telltale sign of suffocation. As it was, Pembury had attributed her death to natural causes, ending the Coroner's interest in the case.

'And the cervical bone from the corpse?'

'A result.' Faraday visibly brightened. 'He pulled in a skeletal specialist, guy from London. He's done a preliminary report and Pembury talked me through it.'

Microscopic cut-analysis, he said, had established that a handsaw had been used to decapitate the body at the foot of the cliffs. Each cut mark leaves a characteristic imprint in the bone, and from this evidence the specialist had concluded that Faraday should be looking for a handsaw with alternating offset teeth, probably a TPI of ten.

'Teeth per inch. I had to ask too. In plain English, we're after a Stanley Hardpoint or something similar. B and Q sell them by the thousand.'

'Scenes of Crime?'

'They found a brand new one on Sunday morning out in the back of the garage where Pelly has a workbench. There was even a receipt. You want to take a guess at the date?'

'October last year.'

'Dead right. The ninth. Pelly says there was a sale on. Binned his old saw because it was worn out and treated himself to a replacement.'

'Binned it where?'

'He says the dustmen took it with the rest of the rubbish. I've got a couple of guys working on where it might have got to but don't hold your breath.'

'Not looking good then, eh?'

'Afraid not. There's one possible, though. The computer analysis people were on this morning. Seems they're starting to get somewhere with deleted emails on Pelly's laptop. They haven't got the full story, not yet, but if Willard pulls the plug that's maybe all we'll have to go on. The outfit's based in Southsea. I said I'd come over.' Faraday, hungrier by the minute, was looking for the waitress. 'Fancy it?'

Winter had a key to Maddox's seafront flat. He paid off the cab and made his way across the road, glad he had someone to be with. Still numbed, he could only remember the face of the radiographer who'd intercepted him as he left the X-ray department. She must have known too. Why else would she check his phone numbers?

Upstairs, on the tenth floor, he knocked lightly at the door before letting himself in. To his surprise the flat was empty. Maddox's leather coat lay where she'd left it, draped over the sofa, and the kettle was still warm in the kitchen. He returned to the big living room and wandered across to the window. He felt utterly detached, completely alone, an audience of one queuing for a film he'd never wanted to see.

Brain tumour, had to be. In the cab he'd tried to visualise what it might look like, this stranger in his head. Was it dense? Hard? Spongy? Was it growing, day by day, hour by hour? Would the neurologist be assessing it even now, the contrast turned up on his monitor, a healthy lunchtime snack at his elbow? Winter didn't know, and the more he thought about it the less he was able to grasp what the next few weeks might bring. He'd never had much time for introspection and now he understood why. All this bollocks, he told himself, happened to other people.

He opened the tall glass door and stepped onto the balcony. Below, in the sunshine, a couple of girls were sprawled on the grass, enjoying the first thin warmth of early spring. Ladies Mile, the path across Southsea

Common, was bright with crocuses, and he fought hard to resist the thought that this might be the last time he'd ever see them. Was this the way it had been with Joannie? Had a five-minute diagnosis robbed her of everything she'd taken for granted?

He reached for the handrail that topped the glass screen and peered over the edge. The sheerness of the drop dizzied him. He could see cracks in the paving stones that stretched towards the kerb. He could feel the chill of the breeze on his face as it hit the front of the flats and eddied upwards. A couple of seconds at the most, he thought. Then oblivion.

For a second or two he toyed with the proposition. The ghouls at the mortuary would have a poke at his broken remains. The blokes on the squad might sink a commemorative jar or two and trade war stories. The *News* would doubtless run some wank feature on the stresses of modern police work. And then there'd come another day and he, like Joannie, would be history.

Winter shook his head, slipped out his mobile, stepped back into the living room. Suttle answered at once.

'How did you get on with the Bone?' Winter was eyeing Maddox's coat. 'We need to talk.'

Number 79 St Edward's Road lay on the margins of Thomas Ellis Owen's Southsea, an early Victorian development which offered naval officers a pleasing alternative to the teeming chaos of life within the garrison walls. This was as genteel as Portsmouth got, an area of sinuous tree-lined crescents and finely detailed terraces, though chaos of a different kind was now lapping at the edges of Southsea's pride and joy. Some of the gaunt Victorian villas in St Edward's Road had become residential homes for the elderly. Others housed single men in various stages of mental impairment, consigned to the tender mercies of community care. Number 79 had surrendered to multi-occupation.

Faraday and Imber paused at the gate. Instructions from DS Michaels had told Faraday to ring the second bell from the left. Faraday glanced at Imber. *Wowser* Productions?

The bell brought the clatter of footsteps up from the basement. The big front door was evidently double-bolted. Moments later Faraday found himself face to face with a pale thin-faced youth in jeans and a washed-out Ripcurl sweatshirt.

'And you are?'

'Meredith.' The youth gave Faraday's warrant card a cursory glance. 'I thought you'd be here earlier. Lucky to catch me in.'

The entrance hall was dark and smelled of cats. A newish-looking mountain bike was chained to the radiator, its fat tyres caked with mud. Faraday followed Meredith down a narrow flight of steps and through another door. The biggest of the basement rooms doubled as a workshop and bedroom. A sturdy bench ran the length of one wall with a shelf above it. Half a dozen PCs were networked together with a tangle of cables, while other uncased computers were strewn across the bare boards on the floor, their delicate electronic innards exposed in various states of undress. Imber was looking at the big double bed. The duvet was littered with invoices, magazines and sundry paperwork while a blizzard of yellow stickies covered the lower half of Miss July, the naked poster girl on the wall above.

'Why *Wowser?*' Faraday was looking at a pile of laundry in the corner.

'My dad's old dog. Cocker spaniel. He was really

cluey, fetch anything.' Meredith was squatting on the floor beside one of the computers. 'I'm in the retrieval business.' He grinned up at Faraday. 'Wowser Productions. Cool or what?'

Faraday fought the temptation to ask about security. There were bars on the tiny window at the front of the room and the front door had seemed sturdy enough, but he'd somehow expected something altogether more businesslike. Not this student doss.

Meredith had found a couple of stools. He perched on one and offered Faraday the other. The hard disk from Pelly's laptop lay on the workbench. Scribbled notes on the attached label recorded its progress from Pelly's desk in the Shanklin nursing home. Seized on the 27th. Logged in on the 28th. DBX files backed up and downloaded the same day. A cable snaked up from the hard disk to the nearest of the PCs.

'We dump everything onto this baby.' Meredith patted the PC. 'All the retrieval is downstream. That way we preserve the original evidence.'

Faraday was beginning to relax. Never be deceived by appearances, he told himself. The world belongs to the young.

Meredith switched on the monitor attached to the PC. He'd been briefed to explore the contents of Outlook Express. On the assumption that emails may have been deleted, he'd concentrated on the contents of the DBX file to which they would have been sent. He'd used specialist software to scan the file, slowly retrieving fragments of the original information. The process, he warned Faraday, was by no means perfect. At best, only fifty per cent of the recovered data would be coherent. But it might, with luck, offer *Congress* a clue or two.

'Who mentioned *Congress*?' Imber was looking alarmed.

'It was on the paperwork.' Meredith waved a thin arm at the enveloping chaos. 'Helps me to keep each operation separate.'

'You do lots of police work?'

'More and more. I've been vetted, if that's bothering you.'

'Good lad,' Faraday said drily. 'So what have you got for us?'

Meredith tapped at the keyboard. Lines of text appeared on the monitor screen. The detectives bent forward, mystified.

'It's Serbo-Croat,' Meredith explained. 'I was like you guys at first – thought I'd fucked up.'

'You know what it means?'

'Yeah, more or less. There's a Czech au pair down the road. Looks after a little girl, really sweet. She spent some time in Belgrade, speaks the language.'

'You *showed* her all this?' Imber again.

'I showed her hard copy. Told her it came from the friend of a friend. Got mangled en route. Social thing. She's cool about it.'

'And this is all you've got?' Faraday had so far counted what looked like five separate messages, islands of words in an ocean of white space.

'Yes. They're not complete, either. It's like one of those games. The trick is to fill in the gaps but I guess that's what you guys do for a living so . . .' he laughed '. . . over to you.'

He left the workbench and went across to the bed. Under a pile of invoices he found a battered-looking blue file. Inside, stapled to the covering note from SOC, was the au pair's translation.

Faraday studied it, Imber behind him. Not five

messages at all but bits and pieces from an ongoing email exchange. Meredith had disinterred another sheet of paper from the file.

'This is how it works date-wise,' he said. 'I can't guarantee it but it's the best I can do.'

Faraday scanned the dates. The first email had arrived on 14th July. It appeared to have come from a member of Lajla's family. There was a reference to 'Papa' never going out because of the summer heat. In another part of the message, after a series of blank spaces, a name: Dragan. Dragan, it appeared, wanted to get in touch with Lajla. He was due in Germany for a church conference. He might find the time to come to Berlin. The message, all too abruptly, petered out.

'Berlin?' Faraday looked up.

'That's where most of the emails come from. There's a registered domain name: Autos Bosna. You want the address?'

Meredith was looking pleased with himself. Even Imber was impressed. Another sheet of paper appeared from the file, a Berlin address, neatly typed.

'Muharem Mujajic?'

'He's the subscriber, owns the domain. He's also the one who sends the emails.'

'Lajla's brother.' Imber was peering at the translation. 'He's lived in Berlin with the father since they fled during the war. He must be running some kind of garage there. Germany's full of Bosnian refugees. Enterprising guy. Must be.'

'OK.' Faraday was trying to make sense of the next message. 'These are all incoming emails, right?'

'Yes.' Meredith nodded.

'Nothing from Lajla's end?'

'Not that I can find.'

'Why's that?'

'Dunno.' Meredith was scrolling through the text on the screen. 'I asked myself the same question. Maybe it's just a statistical quirk. The fifty per cent we can't retrieve just happens to include all her stuff.'

'Or she never replied at all.'

'Exactly . . . Look at this one.' Meredith had paused on the fourth message: 16th September. The sender this time had a different email address.

'Ba?' Faraday was looking at the suffix.

'Bosnia. There's no domain on this one. Just a subscriber address with an ISP. There's no way I can get past that. Maybe you guys have the right connections . . .'

Faraday and Imber exchanged glances. Prising subscriber information out of the likes of Freeserve or Yahoo often took months.

Faraday wanted to know which of his translations corresponded to the message on the screen.

'This one.' Meredith pointed out three lines near the bottom of the page. There were more gaps than words but Faraday could just tease out the essence of the message. The sender had obviously been trying to talk to Lajla by phone. She was never there – never at home, never returned his calls, never gave him an answer.

'To what?'

'Could be anything . . . look.' Imber was already on the last message. Muharem again, 27th September, and the message intact enough to suggest a tone of mild reproof. The priest's friend was a good man, he'd written. If you couldn't believe Dragan, then who in this world could you ever trust?

Dragan? The priest's friend? Lajla's evident reluctance to even acknowledge this series of messages?

Faraday got to his feet. He wanted to know how

much more Meredith thought he might be able to retrieve.

'Maybe another ten per cent. Maybe not even that.'

'So this is all we have to go on?'

'Afraid so. But the Berlin address must help, surely.'

Imber had slipped onto Faraday's stool. Now he reached for the mouse. Returning to the first message, he scrolled slowly down, trying to match the Serbo-Croat to the au pair's translation, hopscotching from one blank space to another. Finally, he folded the translation into his pocket and glanced round at Faraday.

'One question we haven't asked.' He nodded back at the screen. 'Just why would anyone want to delete these?'

Winter didn't bother Suttle with the details of his hospital visit. Denial, after all, had its uses. The Bone was waiting for them in a café-bar in Port Solent. He'd rung twice already, demanding to know where they'd got to.

La Esperanza offered five kinds of espresso plus designer lager at £3.50 a bottle. The view across the Boardwalk towards the yacht basin could have come straight from a brochure. Bit of decent weather, thought Winter, and he'd buy an apartment there himself.

The Bone was sitting alone at a table at the back. The tab for two beers lay beside his empty glass. Winter's shout.

'Got a name for us?' Winter wasn't in the mood for small talk.

'No, Mr Winter.'

'Why all the drama then?' Winter nodded at the mobile on the table.

'Just a little whisper I thought you might be interested in. I put the word out about your Nigerian friend. Manager in one of the pubs here told me the bloke had a bit of a reputation with the ladies. They thought he was a nice fella. Generous, too. Put lots of it around.'

'We're talking money?'

'Yeah. Plus he was shagging a couple of women round here. Showed them a really nice time. I've only talked to one of them but she was extremely pissed off when he died on her. She's got a house over the water there, part of a divorce settlement. She used to have chummy over for meals in the evening. Bit of a cook. Apparently she was on a promise of Christmas on the Virgin Islands. She'd even bought herself a new bikini.'

'What else did she say?'

'She told me he was wheeling and dealing. She thought it was drugs at first but it turned out he was shopping for boats – big stuff, some kind of bulk order. She hasn't got a clue about the details but she says he went to Norway a lot. Told her it was business. You can't move in the house for aquavit. Everytime he came back he brought her a bottle. It's everywhere. She hates the stuff. Never touches it.'

'How come she told you all this?' Suttle didn't believe a word.

'I said I was a mate of his. The bloke in the pub told me the Nigerian fella played five-a-side football, decent standard. Joined a team of locals; turned out every Thursday night. I told her I was on the team and she was kushti with that. Especially when I handed over the necklace he'd bought for her.'

The Bone produced a receipt and gave it to Winter. A silver cross with matching chain had come to £39.99.

'Special offer down Gunwharf.' He laughed. 'I told her I'd been trying to get her address for months. I'd had the key to his flat and nipped round before they cleared it out. I knew the necklace was for her because he'd told me about it. Made her cry when I gave it to her.'

Winter beamed at him. Lately, he'd been having his doubts about the Bone but a ruse this elaborate restored his faith. The man was a truly devious little shit.

'Anything else?'

'Nothing you'd want to know about.' He paused. 'Except one thing.'

'What's that?'

His eyes went to the receipt. Winter, with some reluctance, picked it up. When the Bone asked for readies, Winter counted out four £10 notes. For a moment Suttle thought he was going to ask for change.

'What about the beers?' The Bone pocketed the money.

'Jimmy'll settle up in a minute.'

'And a drink for afterwards?'

'Dcpends.'

The Bone looked at him a moment, then got to his feet. Winter caught him by the door, spun him round, marched him back towards the table. The girl behind the bar had turned away and was watching them in the mirror.

'Don't fuck around, son. Just tell me.'

The Bone looked hurt. He spent a while trying to restore the creases in his shirt. Then he glanced up again.

'This is the woman again,' he said. 'Couple of nights before the guy gets killed he tells her he's being watched. Bloke in a four by four. It's pitch bloody dark. The bloke's waiting for him in a lay-by down the other side of the hill, outside that village, Southwick. Follows him up the lane he takes home on his bike. Happened twice. Third time?' He clicked his fingers. 'Bingo.'

Twenty

Monday, 1 March 2004

The message was waiting for Winter when he got home. He stepped into the gloom of his bungalow, dumped his dripping coat by the door, and padded down the hall towards the living room at the back where he kept the telephone. The tiny red light was winking on the answerphone and he stood for a moment, paralysed by the remorseless pattern of events beginning to unfold. The red light drew him in, on/off, on/off, and he stared at it, unblinking, chilled by the comfortless knowledge that answering machines and smoke detectors would very probably outlive him. Had Joannie stood here? Anticipated the receptionist's voice? The abrupt summons to discuss whatever the radiographers had conjured from their CT scans? Had she felt like him? An otherwise cheerful bloke shafted by the traitor in his brain? Utterly fucking helpless?

He bent to the machine, pressed PLAY. It was Maddox. She wanted to know where he was, how it had gone. She was back in the flat. Ring me. *Please*.

Winter began to laugh. Minutes later, carrying the tray of tea back from the kitchen, he was still laughing.

He lifted the phone.

'Me,' he murmured. 'Why don't you come over here?'

She arrived within the hour with an armful of flowers

from a petrol station down the road. Already, in the shape of Jimmy Suttle and Cathy Lamb, Winter had sensed the shadow that serious illness casts around the invalid. People in the job, he thought, are tongue-tied, awkward; don't know how to voice their concern. Too many direct questions invite a conversation they don't want to have. Ignoring the subject completely is a bit of a cop-out. And so they tiptoe round you, over-cheerful, bright-eyed, burying their embarrassment under a mountain of clichés. It'll be OK. You'll survive. Just you wait and see.

Not Maddox. She put the flowers on the table, shed her coat and flung her arms around him. She wanted to know exactly what had happened at the hospital. She demanded a minute-by-minute account. With her bluntness and her curiosity, she made him feel he'd been somewhere immensely exotic, a traveller returning from a foreign land.

At the mention of the second set of scans, she looked troubled.

'That doesn't sound good.'

'No.'

'What do you think?'

'I think I'm fucked.'

'Does that bother you?'

It was a wonderful question. Winter found himself laughing again. He loved this woman and when she was around – this close, this honest – he didn't much care about anything else. The prospect of terminal disease, he thought ruefully, isn't just terrifying. It can also bore you to death.

He gave her a hug. She wanted to know whether his head still hurt.

'No.' He gave it an exploratory shake. 'Wouldn't fucking dare.'

'So what happens next? Only we've got some tickets to book.'

'You're serious?'

'Try me. We can fly Ethiopian Airways to Addis. It's buses from then on. Change your life.'

'So where are we going?'

'Harar. They used to call it the Forbidden City.'

The name triggered a memory deep in Winter's brain. Hararian, he thought. Maddox's email address. All those messages in Wishart's in-box.

'Arthur Thingy.' He beamed at her. 'Am I right?'

'Rimbaud.' She kissed him again, then tugged him off the sofa. 'You should be a detective.'

Later, with the steady drumming of rain at the bedroom windows, Winter asked Maddox about Wishart's wife. Where did she live?

'Wimbledon. They've just moved.'

'You know the address?'

'No, but I can tell you what the house looks like.'

Wishart, it turned out, had been looking for the right property since the back end of last summer. His wife, who was evidently well organised, had trawled the local estate agents, sending her busy husband a regular selection of likely prospects. These, Wishart would share with Maddox at Camber Court – part of the process, she now realised, of trying to get their relationship onto an altogether less professional footing.

'He wanted *you* to help him choose his next house?'

'It was a boast. Everything was a boast. It wasn't the look of the place or the number of bedrooms or whether or not it had matching saunas, it was the asking price. Maurice wouldn't give it a glance unless there were seven figures across the bottom of the page. A million pounds plus and he might be interested.'

'And you?'

'I played along. Told him what an amazing opportunity he had – all that choice, all those period features. In the end I think it was his wife who made the real decisions. Which is why he played fantasy house with me. People like Maurice are often less secure than they like to think. For eight hundred pounds I could turn him into Mr Powerful.'

'But he *is* Mr Powerful. Or that's what you've told me.'

'Overbearing, yes. Greedy, definitely. Impatient, irrational, single-minded – all those things. When you first get to know him, it all seems to add up, and that's definitely sexy, like I've said. But get to know anyone and you start to figure out the real picture. He couldn't handle this, for instance.' She touched Winter's head. 'Show him a hospital and he'd run a mile.'

'So would I. If I had a choice.'

'But you're different.'

'How do you know?'

'Because I do. Because I've sensed it from the start. In the end you think it's all nonsense, don't you? That's nice. That's me. That's why I'm here. The boat's gone down. We're on the same life raft.' She grinned at him, white teeth in the darkness. 'So how good is that?'

Winter was lost but she was right. It didn't seem to matter. He pulled her closer, felt himself stirring again. 'You never told me about that new house of his.'

'It's a big place: sweet dormers in the roof, lovely windows, three storeys. There's a wall at the front and big gates that he's just had replaced. The photo I saw must have been taken in spring. There's a huge chestnut tree in the front garden, lovely old thing, full blossom.'

'Wimbledon, you say?'

'That's right.'

'And the name of the street?'

'Home Park Road. He was always banging on about it. Backs on to the golf course.' She propped herself on one elbow, looked down at him. 'Why the questions?'

Winter looked up at her in the darkness. Putting Wishart away had suddenly become immensely important. The thought of him anywhere near this woman of his was unbearable.

'Nothing really.' He pulled her down again. 'Come here.'

For the first time in days Faraday spent the night at home. A phone call to Dave Michaels in the Ryde MIT had supplied an update on the afternoon's developments and he knew there was no pressing reason to hurry back. House-to-house calls with the reduced enquiry team were grinding on but the few trails Pelly had left simply petered out. Time and again, DCs returned with the same story. The man kept himself to himself. Provoked, he could be tricky. Give the bastard a wide berth. The surveillance team, meanwhile, were beginning to question the merits of sticking so close to their target. With the growing pressure of other claims on their time, they felt they might be better employed elsewhere.

The Bargemaster's House felt damp after all the rain. Faraday switched on the central heating, attended to his laundry, and found a decent concert on Radio 3 to fill the ticking silence. Brahms was an old favourite and tonight the gods had favoured him with a live performance of the German Requiem. He moved from room to room, afloat on the music, thinking vaguely about supper. Only in the flickering embers of the Requiem's end, still on the prowl, did Faraday notice the small brown envelope on the mat inside the front door.

The note was from Karen Corey. She apologised again for phoning him at the weekend. She'd like to buy him a drink. Under the circumstances it was the least she could do.

Faraday returned to the kitchen, the note in his hand. Oddly enough, he'd been thinking of her grandfather's letters only this afternoon. More and more, he sensed that Pelly's obsession with a Balkan war was the real key to *Congress*. Quite how it might have shaped more recent events was still a mystery but Faraday knew that war, organised violence on the grandest scale, cast a very long shadow.

A couple of years back the murder of a local prison officer had, it transpired, been rooted in an incident aboard a naval frigate ploughing south with the Falklands task force. Twenty years had done nothing to soften the anger and grief of those involved and only a great deal of painstaking historical research had finally unlocked the case. The Second World War, though even more distant, was doubtless still shaping thousands of lives. As Karen's persistence made only too plain.

Faraday had scribbled her number in the address book he kept by the phone. When she answered, he asked her whether she'd eaten.

'No.' She sounded surprised. 'I just got in from badminton.'

'Pasta and a bit of ratatouille? Only I've got an evening to myself.'

'Where?'

'Here.' Faraday smiled to himself. 'Compliments of the chef.'

She arrived within the hour, her face still pinked from the shower. Faraday had forgotten how attractive she was, with her snub nose and urchin hair, a figure that might have stepped jauntily out of a Dickens novel. In the classroom, Faraday thought, she'd be a natural: enthusiasm and good sense spiked with a hint of mischief.

The Jiffy bag containing Karen's grandfather's letters lay on the kitchen table. Faraday poured her a glass of Côtes-du-Rhône and then proposed a toast.

'To Harry . . .'

They touched glasses. Karen nodded at the Jiffy bag.

'What did you think?'

'I thought they were charming. It's hard, isn't it? Some things never change. Other bits . . .' He smiled at her. 'It could have been another world.'

'It was another world. Nan says so. That's what Harry can't grasp. That's what makes him so unhappy.'

Faraday blinked. Last time they'd talked Karen had mentioned the spiritualist temple. Her mum accompanied Madge every Sunday. Recently they'd been in touch with the long-departed Harry. These meetings apparently extended to conversation.

'She *talks* to Harry? Your nan?' Faraday wanted to be sure.

'Yes. Often. And not just at the temple.'

'And what does he say?'

'Well, that's the point really; that's why we thought of you in the first place.' Her head had gone down, her face flushed again, this time with embarrassment. 'This is going to sound weird . . . bizarre . . . truly daft.'

'Try me.'

'Are you sure?'

'I wouldn't have asked you otherwise.'

She looked at him a moment, a brief, searching glance that sought a certain assurance. She trusted him. She didn't want him to laugh at her. Faraday made a tiny gesture with his hand. Go on.

She reached for the Jiffy bag and emptied the letters onto the table. With them came Harry's watch and she held it for a second or two, perched on the kitchen stool, before dropping it into her lap.

'Harry was with a special outfit. It's not in those letters but Mum's checked it all out. A bunch of them volunteered for something called COPPS. That stood for –' she frowned '– Combined Operation Pilotage Parties.'

COPPS, she explained, were sent across the Channel in the winter of 1943–44 aboard midget submarines. Off the Normandy coast they'd swim the remaining mile or so under cover of darkness, crawling out of the surf to take core samples from the beach. Back home, these samples would be carefully analysed to gauge the load-bearing properties of the designated invasion beaches. Only if the underlying rock and sand were firm enough could heavy armour be shipped ashore.

'It must have been really dangerous.' Her eyes never left Faraday's face. 'There were Germans everywhere and getting caught would have been the end.'

'Why?'

'They'd have been tortured, for sure, and Madge says that no one could withstand that. So they each had a special tablet. Just in case. A suicide pill. Even back home they weren't allowed to tell anyone what they were up to. Can you imagine?'

Faraday couldn't. No wonder Harry's letters had so suddenly stopped.

'So what happened?'

'Harry apparently made half a dozen trips without any real problem. It was the last one that killed him.'

That night they were heading for a little coastal township called St-Aubin-sur-Mer. The beach there was codenamed Nan Red. Royal Marines and a Canadian armoured regiment were designated to storm ashore, provided the beach could bear the weight of the tanks. Harry and his oppo swam into the shallows. Waiting for the forty-five seconds of darkness between the regular sweep of the searchlights, they worked their way out of the shallows. It took about fifteen minutes to screw the core sampler down through the layers of sand. Then they eased themselves back into the water with their precious trophy, invisible against the blackness of the night.

'It was a good mile back to the submarine. Harry had a problem already. He'd done something to his shoulder a couple of days previously and he was getting bad cramps.'

'He was alone?'

'No. They always worked in twos. Kind of buddy system.'

'And Harry got back to the submarine OK?'

'No.' Karen's hand had found the wristwatch. 'Towards the end of the swim, Harry got really bad. His oppo was pulling him. It was quite rough. He could see the submarine but he was knackered. Whatever happened, Harry's oppo knew they both had to get back. If the Germans found a body in a wetsuit, there'd be all hell to pay.'

Harry's oppo, she said, had done his very best, but

413

by the time the submarine manoeuvred alongside Harry had gone.

'Apparently he was just floating,' she said. 'He'd probably died a while before. In a sea like that it must be hard to tell.'

Faraday reached for the bottle and refilled her glass. The ratatouille had been bubbling for a while. He turned it off.

'The men on the submarine got Harry aboard. I don't know whether they tried mouth-to-mouth and all that, but if they did, it didn't work. They brought his body back and notified Madge sometime later. They kept his body in one of the mortuaries under the hill. It was months before she could bury him.'

Faraday nodded. The chalk beneath Portsdown Hill was honeycombed with tunnels. An entire underground hospital had been constructed during the war years and even now there was a subterranean headquarters beneath one of the hilltop forts, a command centre for use in the event of nuclear attack.

'How was Madge?'

'It broke her heart. Mum was still a tiny baby. Madge wasn't even married but that didn't matter. All she wanted back was Harry. He meant the world to her. Read those letters and you can see why.'

Faraday sipped at his wine. So far it was a touching story, doubtless an echo of countless other wartime tragedies. But why, sixty years later, did it still matter so much?

Karen ducked her head. 'It was Bob, really. You remember Bob?'

Faraday nodded. Bob's name had appeared in the letters. He'd been Harry's best mate. They'd enlisted together, trained together, and they'd both ended up in COPPS.

'Bob stayed in touch?'

'Big time.' Karen nodded.

'And that was a problem?'

'Yes, it was. Madge had always had a feeling about him. He was a nice enough bloke, nothing horrible about him, but sometimes he let one or two things slip and Madge began to wonder.'

'How? About what?'

'About . . .' she ran a finger round the top of her glass '. . . everything really. Bob had been going out with Daisy for a while, Madge's sister, but we think Madge was the one he really . . . you know . . . fancied. He used to buy her chocolates sometimes, and pick bunches of flowers for her when there was really no need, and it was always when he knew Harry was away.' She lifted her head. 'You know what I mean?'

'Of course.'

'Well . . . when Harry had gone, and D-Day was all over and done with, and everyone knew the war was coming to an end, Bob came back to Pompey, made himself a real nuisance, wanting to take care of Madge and Mum. Madge said it was really awkward some nights. She was boarding with a family in Fratton and she'd get the baby down for the night and then there'd come the knock at the door and there was Bob. Chocolates again, and more bloody flowers. God knows where he got the money. It was embarrassing, too. The people Mum was boarding with were Methodists, really strict. They thought Madge . . . you know . . . she was a looker; I've seen the pictures . . .'

'How did she handle him?'

'She didn't. It was her friend, Grace, the woman you met a couple of years back. They were really close, Madge and Grace, and Grace was the kind who didn't put up with any nonsense from men. She was really bold that way. She'd been on the boats already, the liners across to New York, and she knew how to look after herself. So she saw Bob off, told him his fortune. You can imagine, can't you?'

Faraday smiled. Grace Randall, at eighty-four, had personality to spare. Faraday remembered her again from the previous inquiry, pencil-thin, racked with emphysema, but sharp as a tack. God knows what she must have been like in her prime.

'So what's the problem?' Faraday asked again.

Karen asked for another glass of wine. Then she cupped the glass between her hands as if she was trying to warm it.

'After the war one of the matelots off the submarine came and looked Madge up. He'd left the navy by now and he was working as a roofer building the new estate in Paulsgrove. He said he'd been with Harry the night he died. Turned out he was one of the blokes who hauled Harry out of the water.'

'And?'

'He said Harry was bleeding.'

'*Bleeding?*'

'Apparently, he had a stab wound, right through his rubber suit, just here.' She reached forward and touched Faraday's shirt above the waistband of his trousers. 'That's what had killed him. It wasn't exhaustion at all.'

'He'd bumped into a German? There'd been a fight on the beach?'

'That's what his oppo said.'

'And was it true?'

'No one knows.'

'What did the sailor think?'

'He said there was no way Harry could have swum a

mile with a wound like that. Harry bled to death. It wouldn't have taken long.'

Faraday tried to visualise the situation: a heaving swell, the black winter night, two men struggling back towards the dark bulk of the submarine, then a sudden flare of violence. The key issue, he realised at once, was motivation. Why would one man knife another when they'd just spent the last couple of hours cheating death?

He looked up at Karen. Her eyes were shiny.

'So who was in the water with Harry?' he asked.

'Bob.' She nodded. 'And he's still alive.'

Twenty-one

Tuesday, 2 March 2004

The *ping* of an incoming email awoke Faraday next morning. It was still dark. He swung his legs out of bed and fumbled his way through to the study next door to find a message from Eadie Sykes awaiting him.

Her schedule, vague as it was, suggested she should be in Melbourne by now, but for the time being she was hanging on in Sydney, pending news of possible backing for a film. A chance meeting in one of the bars up on the Macquarie campus had given her an introduction to a Pom anthropologist who was doing a PhD on the social impacts of the Pacific War on the native population of Vanuatu, and he appeared to be interested in turning his thesis into a movie.

Faraday scrolled on, recognising Eadie's limitless appetite for new projects, new faces, new departures. A sign-off paragraph offered an update on the rest of her social life. She'd looked up a couple of buddies from her own days at uni and made a mental note never to have kids. A nice American had taken her out on his yacht for a couple of days. And she'd even borrowed a bodyboard and hung out for a week on Manly Beach, making friends half her age and learning how to keep her mouth shut in the bigger waves.

Only at the end of the email, checking the address-ees, did Faraday realise that this message served as a chatty update for a wide circle of friends. He counted them. Including J-J and himself, the readership came to nineteen. Brilliant, he thought. The big relationship in my life, and I qualify for just over five per cent.

He got up from the desk and stood at the window for a moment or two. Dawn was spilling over the harbour, a cold, pale light that sharpened the low outline of Hayling Island. A raft of brent geese was floating gently seawards and he caught the black silhouette of a pair of cormorants, arrowing past in the same direction.

Twice in the night he'd woken up to thoughts of Karen and the luckless Harry. Two generations on his story still moved her but the real victim, she said, was her mum. Gwen somehow held herself responsible for what had happened. Without a young baby, she argued, Madge might have been less of a sitting duck for Bob's advances. Without the needful single parent in his sights, Bob might never have drawn the dagger in the first place.

Faraday, over supper, had been as gentle as he could. Recent conversations with Harry at the spiritu-alist temple might well have confirmed Madge's worst fears, and he believed Karen when she said that Gwen herself was only too prepared to go into the witness box, but the real issue here was evidence. The submariner was evidently dead. So was Harry. The rest, alas, was supposition. One day testament from beyond the grave might be admissible in court. But not yet.

Karen, three glasses down, had simply nodded. In her heart she'd known it was nonsense but she owed her mum and Madge everything. They'd been brilliant over her recent divorce and she could never do enough to repay the debt. So if they'd got themselves into a state about Harry, and if Grace Randall knew a man who might help, then who was she to call any of this stuff into question? Women can be crazy, she'd told Faraday, reaching for her coat.

Faraday had insisted on calling a cab. She could come back for the Renault in the morning. At the door, the cab waiting, she'd given him a hug and he'd held her for a moment longer before she'd turned away.

'Nonsense was your word, not mine,' he'd said. 'Give me a ring if there's anything else I can do.'

Now, he made his way downstairs. He'd run out of milk, but black coffee, he decided, might return him to the real world. He glanced at his watch, trying to remember the hovercraft schedule. 07.23. Later than he'd thought.

It was mid-morning before Winter felt well enough to think about getting on the road. He'd phoned Cathy Lamb at the squad office, uncertain whether he was on sick leave or not. Emerging briefly from a meeting, she'd told him to get a note from his GP and forget all about the job. Just now things were mercifully quiet. A long-running drugs operation, designed to disrupt one of the city's scarier supply chains, had been shunted into the sidings for a week or two and a bid to net half a dozen of the heavier football thugs was developing nicely. Neither initiative, she said, needed Winter's brand of detective work. Only seconds before she hung up did she mention Terry Alcott's decision on *Plover*'s next move. Accepting Maddox's offer to mount a sting against Wishart, the ACC had decided, was a non-runner. Too dodgy in practical terms. And a potential gift for the defence lawyers.

'Thank Christ for that,' Winter grunted.

She'd come into the bedroom seconds later with a handful of tablets and a cup of tea, demanding to know what Winter's DI had said. Winter told her.

'Why?' She frowned. 'What's wrong with a confession?'

'It's not that. It's the way we do it. There's a fine line. Alcott's talking entrapment. That might give us a problem in court.'

'So what do we do?'

The 'we' put a smile on Winter's face. He swallowed three of the tablets and sluiced them down with tea.

'We leave it to the professionals,' he said. 'Trust me, eh?'

Maddox left shortly afterwards, phoning for a cab down to Southsea. There was stuff to sort out at her flat and she needed a bit of time on the internet to find a decent deal for Ethiopia. If Winter insisted on driving to the GP's surgery, then so be it. She'd wrapped her arms around him and promised to be back by nightfall. In the meantime he was to take care.

By twelve o'clock Winter was north of Guildford. The *London A–Z* was open on the seat beside him. He'd found Home Park Road and circled it in red Pentel. The headache was beginning to ease but the pain behind his eyes still blurred his vision and twice he'd given overtaking drivers a bit of a scare.

On the Kingston bypass, he took a right. Ten minutes later, trapped in a queue of traffic, he was grinding slowly up Wimbledon Hill Road. Another right turn, narrowly avoiding an oncoming bus, and he was in a suburban street, nosing past parked BMWs, only too conscious of the sheer weight of money that had settled in this neighbourhood.

Home Park Road, on the map, stretched for maybe half a mile in a long gentle curve. Winter drove slowly, looking for a pair of new gates and a chestnut tree. Wishart had told Maddox about views of the golf course from the rear windows so the house had to be on the left. Finally, towards the end of the road, Winter found it. Three storeys. Grey brick with newly painted windows. The gates open and a fine view of a gleaming 4 × 4 in the modest sweep of gravel drive.

Winter parked across the road. The Crime Squad had a selection of digital cameras for situations exactly like this. He reached back, easing the neat little Olympus from the bag on the rear seat. The lens extended to 80 mm. Plenty big enough at this kind of range.

Five snaps were enough to capture wide shots of the property and a couple of close-ups of the SUV. The name of the house, newly plated on the pillar beside the gate, was Priory Lodge. The SUV was a Mitsubishi Shogun, black with tinted windows. Winter was debating whether to pop another tablet when there came a knock at the window behind him.

He looked round, squinting into the sunlight. A middle-aged woman was standing on the grass verge. She was small, blonde, still attractive. She was dressed with the kind of casual elegance Winter rarely met in Pompey and the dog beside her looked equally pampered.

Winter wound down the window.

'What on earth are you doing?' she asked.

Winter closed his eyes a moment, trying to squeeze the pain away, then got out of the car and flipped his warrant card. Already he suspected the worst.

'And you are?'

'My name's Wishart. Why do you ask?'

Winter looked at her a moment. He wondered where to start.

'Can we talk indoors?' He nodded across the road towards the house.

'Why? What do you want?'

'I think it's better inside, Mrs Wishart. Do you mind?'

Winter took her by the arm, felt a moment's resistance, then they were both walking across the road towards the house. The dog didn't know what to make of this sudden abduction. Useless, thought Winter.

The house was alarmed, with three locks in the big six-panelled front door. No wonder she needed a bag that size to carry the keys.

Inside, Winter found himself in a spacious hall. A staircase on the right was dominated by a huge oil painting. Winter recognised the jowly face, the set of the shoulders, the pale dead eyes that seemed to follow them as they stepped into the nearest of the reception rooms. Acres of blue carpet and a selection of carefully chosen antiques. Watercolours on the wall, individually lit. It was obvious at once that someone had put a lot of effort into this place. One day Wishart might even spend some time here.

Winter was looking round for somewhere to sit. Staying on his feet was becoming an effort.

'D'you mind?' He nodded at an occasional chair near the window, straight-backed, upholstered in blue velvet, edged in gold brocade. It was anything but comfortable.

So far Mrs Wishart hadn't said a word. Coffee would be nice, thought Winter, and maybe a biscuit or two.

'We're looking into the death of a Nigerian gentleman,' Winter began. 'Does the name Lakemfa mean anything to you?'

He knew at once that the drive had been worth it. She stared at Winter for a moment, then turned to shut the door.

'Are you from New Scotland Yard?'

'Portsmouth.' Winter offered her a chilly smile. 'Same gang, though. Same rules.'

'And this man Lak— whatever. You say he's dead?'

'That's right.'

She nodded, absorbing the news. A milk float whined by outside. Late, Winter thought. He looked up at Mrs Wishart again, trying to gauge her own take on this marriage of hers. Wedlock had clearly feathered her nest but there was something in the set of her face that spoke of disappointment. She knew a great deal, Winter decided, and most of it made her very unhappy.

'He came here . . .' She nodded towards the door. 'If I've got the same man. Maurice brought him home for the weekend. He was charming.'

'When was that?'

'Last summer. I can't remember the date. During the holidays, definitely. My son Charles was down from Oxford. He joined us for dinner that night.' She looked up. 'Dead, you say?'

'That's right.'

'When? How?'

Winter ignored both questions. He wanted to know where Lakemfa belonged in her husband's life.

'He was a business associate,' she said at once. 'My husband builds boats, sells them abroad – military kit mainly. I gather Mr Lakemfa was a potential customer.'

'Does your husband often bring clients home?'

'Not that often, no. To tell you the truth, we like to keep the two parts of our life separate. Maurice runs his business on the south coast. We hold the fort up here. It's not ideal but I must say it works.'

'We?'

'The family.'

'And Lakemfa? You made an exception for him?'

'As I say, he was charming. It was a pleasure. I gather he and Maurice were chums down in Portsmouth. Shared interests. You know what I mean?'

Winter nodded. I do, he thought grimly.

Mrs Wishart was asking again about Lakemfa's death. She wanted to know what had happened. Was it some kind of accident?

'He fell off his bike.'

'And died?'

'I'm afraid so.'

She looked down at him, trying to explore the implications of what Winter had just said. No policeman drove sixty miles because of a traffic accident.

'So what happened?' she said slowly.

Winter was looking at the window. A curtain of bubbles, thicker than ever, was rising between him and the view. He asked for a glass of water, wondered whether he still had the tablets in his jacket pocket. With some reluctance Mrs Wishart fetched the water. Winter swallowed the two remaining painkillers.

'Are you all right?'

'Fine.'

'So what happened to Mr Lakemfa?'

Winter did his best to concentrate. He normally excelled in these situations. He'd spent his entire career baiting traps and laying ambushes. With this woman he knew it would be no different. Yet all he felt was ill.

He drew a deep breath, looked briefly up at the ceiling. More bubbles.

'The vehicle outside,' he said. 'Is it yours?'

'Yes.'

'How long have you had it?'

'A couple of months. No, longer. Before Christmas. Is the date important? Do you want me to check?'

'Yes, please.'

She left the room again. Winter heard the sound of footsteps overhead. Then she was back with a manila file. Very efficient, he thought.

'October the sixteenth.' She was checking the date on the garage invoice.

'It was new?'

'Yes. One of Maurice's little surprises. He called it an early birthday present.'

'When is your birthday?'

'December the fourteenth.' She was looking worried now. 'Why do you ask?'

With some difficulty Winter got to his feet. He walked slowly across to the window and steadied himself against the frame. A Mitsubishi Shogun. Bull bars. Tinted windows. Black paint scheme. Just as he'd thought.

'What did you drive before this?'

'Exactly the same. A Shogun.'

'Same colour?'

'Yes. Same everything.'

'So why change it?'

'Good question. To tell you the truth, I was never quite sure. Maurice said there was a problem with the gearbox. He thought it was going to pack up on me, might be expensive.'

'Really?' Winter turned to face her. 'How did he know?'

'He'd borrowed it for a week. He said he needed a

four by four so we swapped cars. Have you ever driven a Jaguar? I didn't get on with it at all.'

Winter eyed her for a moment, knowing he was close now, a single question away. Dates, he told himself.

'You bought the new car on the sixteenth of October.' He nodded at the dealer invoice. 'When did your husband borrow the old one?'

'That's easy.' Her eyes drifted across to the window. 'It would have been the week before. He's impulsive that way, my husband. He makes a decision and then simply gets on with it.'

Faraday was in conference with Brian Imber when DS Michaels appeared at his office door. The surveillance boys had just checked in to say their goodbyes. There was an entry in the log that might be of interest.

Michaels made room at the door. One of the two DCs from the surveillance unit stepped into view.

'About eleven o'clock this morning, sir. A taxi turned up. We've got the firm and registration.'

'And?'

'A woman got out, middle-aged, white. She went into the home, stayed maybe five minutes, not much more. There was another guy in the back but we never got a good look at him.'

'So what's your point?'

'It's Pelly, sir. He obviously knew the guy in the taxi. Came out, chatted through the window.'

'Did this person get out of the cab at all?'

'No. That's the point, really. The whole conversation happened through the open window. Odd, we thought.' The second of the two surveillance DCs was beside him now, nodding in agreement. Might be worth following up, might not. Faraday's shout.

Faraday thanked them. Withdrawing the surveillance unit had, in the end, been Willard's decision and Faraday had expected little else. Major Crimes inquiries often relied on momentum. If you didn't break the case in the first three days, things could get sticky.

Faraday got to his feet. He thanked the two DCs for their help and there was an exchange of handshakes. Their departure left Dave Michaels in the open door.

Faraday sat down again.

'What do you think?'

'Worth a tickle. I know Barber and Webster are free. They were up here just now, cadging a coffee. I'll have a word with Pete Baker, yeah?'

Faraday nodded his agreement and Michaels went to find the DS in charge of outside enquiries. Imber reached for the door with his foot and pushed it shut.

'Have you talked to young Tracy recently?'

Faraday shook his head. The last time he'd had a proper conversation with Barber was over the weekend.

'She went up to town,' Imber said. 'She's got a girlfriend up there. Paula Adamson. Paula's well placed at Six, high-flyer, got herself involved in *Jetstream*.'

Jetstream, Imber explained, was the MI6 codename for intelligence operations mounted against our European allies. Some of their more ambitious initiatives extended deep into the Balkans.

'Paula and Barber have been a item for nearly a year. I gather the relationship extends to the odd professional favour.' Imber smiled. 'Barber wanted a steer on Pelly. Turns out he's cat three, starred.'

Faraday had only the vaguest notions about MI6 protocols. Category 3, it seemed, was a restricted access file. The accompanying star meant that there was no way Paula Adamson would impart its contents, not even to her very best friend.

'That means Six have taken a very great interest in Pelly. Quite why, I don't know.'

'Have taken?'

'Are taking. The file is still live. Barber at least got that far.' Imber got to his feet and checked his watch. 'It's just a thought, Joe, that's all. Bosnia might not be too far off the mark, eh?'

Winter found the dealership without difficulty. The last of the tablets, coupled with a large Scotch from a pub on Wimbledon Hill Road, had settled his stomach. The headaches he could cope with, just, but only he knew how close he'd come to throwing up over Mrs Wishart's nice new carpet. As it was, he'd been forced to beat a retreat, leaving an apprehensive figure framed in the downstairs window watching him make it back to the car. Only an empty Sainsbury's bag, hastily retrieved from the boot, had spared him serious embarrassment.

Now, he slipped the Subaru into a space in Customer Parking. The low glass sweep of the showroom was a showcase for a range of Mitsubishis. In the middle of the display was a brand new Shogun. For £32,499 Winter could join the rest of the Wimbledon housewives who needed four-wheel drive and desert-proof air conditioning to make it down to the shops.

Winter found a waste bin for the knotted Sainsbury's bag, then pushed into the showroom and began to prowl amongst the gleaming saloons. Within seconds a young sales executive was at his elbow.

'Can I help you, sir?' He smelled of aftershave.

Winter produced his warrant card. He was trying to trace a Mitsubishi Shogun taken by the dealership in part exchange for a new model. He had the registration number and the date of the transaction. Could the young man oblige with a couple of other details?

'Like what, sir?'

'Fetch the file and I'll tell you.'

The executive hesitated a moment, then disappeared into a back office. He returned minutes later.

'If you're after customer details, sir, there might be a problem. Under the Data Protection Act we—'

Winter cut him short. He'd already acquired current keeper details from Jimmy Suttle. PNC was giving a name in Kingston upon Thames.

'Jami Singh? Thirty-four Findon Way?' Winter was reading from his pocketbook.

The executive was deep in the file. A single glance told Winter the information was spot on. The executive looked up.

'What are you after then?'

'Number one, I need to know the state of the vehicle when you took it on. Number two, you can tell me what you normally do before you offer it for resale.'

'Like?'

'Like a bit of a scrub up.'

'Oh.' He looked relieved. 'I see.'

He went back to the file, flipped through it, then paused, his finger on a scribbled note at the top of the last page. He looked up. He seemed surprised.

'We normally give PX vehicles a proper going-over but on this one there was no need. The customer had given it the works already. Steam clean. Full valet. The lot.' He showed Winter the note on the file. 'The vehicle was pristine, saved us half a day in the car wash.' He glanced up. 'You've no idea how rare that is.'

*

The taxi firm operated from the lower half of premises two streets back from Shanklin's North Road. Darren Webster knew it well. On the wilder Saturday nights, he told Tracy Barber, he and his mates would abandon their cars and share a cab back to Newport. The firm offered police discount for off-duty coppers. Sweet deal.

Barber found a parking space across the road. Darren Webster pushed in through the boarded-up front door. A seating area at the front was empty except for an elderly woman with bleached hair and an enormous pile of shopping. Two controllers at desks behind the counter were working the taxi fleet. Barber looked round. According to Webster, this place had once been a greengrocer's, and she could still detect the faintest of smells. Onions, she thought. Or maybe leeks.

'Darren.' One of the controllers was young, no more than twenty. She abandoned her headphones and leaned over the counter to give him a hug. 'Where were you? Friday night?'

'Busy.' Webster shot a look at Barber. 'Murder job.'

'Really?'

She wanted the details but Webster shook his head. He was after a grey Peugeot, diesel engine. HN registration.

'That'd be Scottie.'

'Ran a fare up to Boniface? The nursing home? Round eleven this morning?'

'That's him.' The girl was consulting a log. 'Fare rang in from the station at ten forty-eight. Couldn't find a cab for love nor money. Scott took her back to the station afterwards.'

'You've got a name.'

'Yeah.' The girl ran her finger across the log. 'Unwin.'

Darren threw a look at Tracy Barber. Scottie, it turned out, was having a late lunch. The girl suggested they try Munchies Café on the seafront. Scott had a thing going with the woman who ran it and ate there most days.

It was a five-minute walk to Munchies. Barber counted the number of times Darren Webster met people he evidently knew. By the time they were in sight of the café, she'd concluded he was on nodding terms with half the island.

'Are you enjoying this? *Congress*, I mean?'

'Yeah, I am. It's not what I expected but –' he gave a passing motorcyclist a wave '– yeah.'

'What did you expect?'

'I thought there'd be more scope, you know, for doing stuff. On division you're on your jack. The boss hands out a list of jobs and off you go. This is different. Four, five actions a day? And no real idea how any of it fits together?'

'Maybe it doesn't.' Barber laughed.

'Yeah.' Webster had spotted Scottie in the window of the cafe. 'That had occurred to me, too.'

Scottie was a big man in his late twenties. An old rugby shirt stretched tight across his belly and he badly needed a shave. In a couple of years, thought Barber, he'll look twice his age.

Webster slipped into the chair across the table. Barber joined him. Scottie was chasing a curl of bacon rind with his knife. Webster did the introductions. Evidently he knew Scottie well.

'Copper too, are you?' Scottie eyed Barber. He had a lilting Welsh accent.

''Fraid so.'

'Fantastic overtime, the boyo here says.' He stabbed a fork in Webster's direction. 'Wouldn't mind a drop of that myself.'

Webster wanted to know about the fare Scottie had picked up from the station.

'Professional interest, is it?'

'Yes.'

'Why's that?'

Webster wouldn't say. Scottie folded a slice of bread and began to mop up the last of the egg yolk. A woman even bigger than himself was watching them all from the other side of the counter.

'Fare was a nice enough lady,' Scottie said at last. 'Just come down from London. Her mum died, see, and she had to pick up some bits and pieces. Amazing how often that happens. Relatives over for the leavings.'

'Was anyone with her?'

'Yeah, younger lad.'

'Get a name at all?'

'No. He didn't say much.'

'What about when you were waiting outside the home? Didn't Pelly come out? Have a chat?'

'Yeah, you're right, he did.' Scottie had abandoned the bread. 'How did you know that?'

'Doesn't matter. Just tell us what they said.'

'Can't remember, tell you the truth. I had the radio on by then. Just gossip, it was.'

'They knew each other?'

'I'd say so. Friendly enough, yeah.'

'And afterwards?'

'I drove them both back to the station. They weren't going home, mind, not to the mainland. They'd booked a room somewhere in Ryde, the pair of them. I got the impression the old girl wouldn't be ready until tomorrow.'

'Old girl?'

'The deceased. She's at some undertaker's in Newport, getting the treatment. They wanted to pay their respects, like, while they've still got the chance. Nice to hear that, these days—' he signalled the woman behind the counter for coffee '– eh?'

By the time Winter made it back to Bedhampton, he was on the point of collapse. Cheered by the sight of a light in the bungalow, he parked the Subaru and sat behind the wheel for a moment, mustering the strength to make it to the front door. For a moment or two he toyed with giving Maddox a ring on her mobile but decided that there had to be limits to this new dependence of his. He wasn't quite that helpless. Not yet.

She was sitting in the kitchen, rolling a joint.

'These are for you.' She nodded at the pile of doobies beside the kettle. 'Strictly medicinal. I thought they might help.'

She looked up at him. The light was dim in the kitchen, one of Joannie's forty-watt bulbs, and it was only when he swayed towards her, reaching for support, that she realised the state he was in. Seconds later she was making him comfortable on the sofa next door.

'Shit,' she said. 'I thought you went to the doctor?'

Winter shook his head. He'd been to London. Asked around.

'Asked who? Asked what?'

Slowly, Winter let the story spill out. He'd been following the wrong leads. He'd assumed a professional hit, a contract, a buffer between Wishart and the Nigerian charmer who'd somehow pissed him off, but all the time he'd been wrong. Wishart hadn't put a contract out at all. No, he'd done the fucking job himself.

'You can prove that?'

'No.'

'Why not?'

'Because I haven't got the evidence. I've got some old slapper up in Port Solent who was shagging the black guy. I've got her word that chummy was getting spooked by someone in a black four by four. And I've got Wishart binning his wife's Shogun within days. Was it black? Yes. Did he hose every last particle of DNA off it? Stands to fucking reason. But a file like that wouldn't even make it to the CPS. Let alone court.'

Maddox wanted to know about the CPS. Winter told her. Crown Prosecution Service. First of umpteen fences a successful operation had to hurdle. *Plover*, he concluded wearily, hadn't got a prayer.

'*Plover*?'

'Us. This. You. Wishart. Me.'

He lay back and closed his eyes. He seemed to have gone beyond the headaches, beyond the strange hallucinatory bubbles that curtained his vision, beyond any expectation that he might – one day – restore some kind of order to his life. All that was left, he told himself, was this small moment in time: Joannie's worn cushions beneath his bum and Maddox cross-legged beside him on the carpet, her face inches from his.

'They phoned,' she whispered at last.

'Who?'

'The consultant.' She frowned. 'Frazer?'

Winter nodded. His hand found hers. He didn't want to know any more.

With the *Congress* team depleted, the office in the Ryde MIR that served as a base for the inquiry's DCs was virtually empty. Darren Webster found himself a desk in the corner, hunted out a copy of *Yellow Pages*, and went to work.

His first call found the senior technician at the mortuary still in his office. Webster, who'd attended a number of post-mortems at St Mary's, wanted to know about a Mrs Mary Unwin. Her body had been shipped across from a nursing home in Shanklin a couple of days ago. The Home Office pathologist had completed his investigation within twenty-four hours. Where was she now?

'Gone.' The technician named an undertaker's in Newport. 'They collected her this afternoon.'

'Got the number there?'

'No problem.'

The undertaker's, too, were still at work. Young Mary was being prepared to receive visitors. The appointments book indicated a viewing in the Chapel of Rest at noon tomorrow. Name of Unwin.

'How many people?'

'One, as far I can gather. The daughter, we think. She wants to discuss arrangements for the funeral.'

Webster scribbled himself a note and turned to *Yellow Pages*. From 'Guest Houses, Hotels and Inns' he began to extract every accommodation address in Ryde, listing the names and numbers on a pad at his elbow. By the time he'd finished, he had twenty-eight. Call by call, he worked slowly down the list – always the same introduction, always the same question.

The seventeenth call went to a guest house a stone's throw from the police station.

'Ryde Haven Hotel. How can I help?'

'My name's Detective Constable Webster. I'm trying to trace a guest. Do you have a Mrs Unwin registered?'

'Hang on, I'll find out.'

Webster doodled on the bottom corner of the pad, waiting for a reply. The doodle, a series of cartoony hang-gliders, was beginning to spiral up towards his scribbled notes.

The receptionist was back. 'Mrs E. Unwin?'

'That's her. Is there anyone else sharing the room?'

'Not sharing, no. He's got a room of his own.'

'He? Do you have a name?'

'Hang on.'

Another wait. This time Webster left the doodle alone. Finally she picked up the phone again.

'Looks like Chris to me,' she said. 'Though the writing's terrible.'

'Chris who?'

'Chris Unwin.'

Webster thanked the receptionist and asked her to keep the call confidential. Then he put the phone down, sitting motionless, staring at the wall. Minutes later Tracy Barber put her head round the door.

'Boss wants to see you,' she said. 'Sharpish.'

Webster got up and hooked his jacket off the back of the chair.

'My pleasure,' he said, grinning.

Twenty-two

Faraday wanted to be sure. And more than that, before they moved to pull Unwin in, he wanted to plot exactly how they could extract the maximum value from this sudden windfall.

He'd convened an impromptu conference in the squad room used by the DCs. Dave Michaels was jubilant, Brian Imber less so, DS Pete Baker bemused. How come they'd spent two weeks attaching the wrong name to the body at the foot of the cliff? How come they'd fallen for a pattern of circumstantial evidence that had proved – in the end – so worthless?

A street map of Ryde lay on the table between them. The Ryde Haven Hotel was on one of the roads that climbed the hill from the seafront. A second call to the receptionist had established that both Mrs Unwin and her son were in their respective rooms. Faraday had dispatched Tracy Barber and Darren Webster, plus two other DCs, and they were covering both exits from the hotel. If mother and son left the hotel, they were to be detained.

Imber, ever the pragmatist, was unconvinced.

'We're going to arrest them?'

'Unwin, certainly. Unless he agrees to come down voluntarily.'

'On what charge?'

'Suspicion of murder.'

'That's a bit of a leap, isn't it?'

Dave Michaels broke in.

'The boss is right,' he said. 'We've been looking up the wrong alley. This is the first real break we've had. What if the guy declines our little invitation? Says he wants a night in with *Eastenders*? He's been tight with Pelly. We've got the cabbie's word on that. He's gone AWOL since Pelly binned the boat. Since Pelly got rid of the Volvo. Since Pelly got out the emulsion and painted every bloody thing that moved. And why didn't he ring in when his mum told him we were looking for him? She must have mentioned it. You really think all that's a coincidence?'

Imber had had enough of coincidence. It was coincidence, he pointed out, that had suggested a link between Pelly and the body at the bottom of the cliff. And it was coincidence, for that matter, that had put Unwin's name in the frame. Wasn't it about time that *Congress* started dealing in fact?

Faraday wasn't having it. In every investigation there came a point when you had to bite the bullet. Unwin, he was convinced, was key to whatever had happened back in October. No one had a clue where he'd been. No one knew why he'd so suddenly disappeared. Now, thanks to the sudden death of his precious nan, he was just round the corner. The man was there for the taking. Was Imber seriously suggesting they pass up this invitation?

'Disappearing isn't a crime,' Imber pointed out.

'Of course it isn't. But playing this by the book would be criminal. And I mean that.'

Michaels threw his head back and laughed. He loved the word 'criminal'.

'Sean Castle.' Imber was looking thoughtful. 'That night he chartered his boat to Pelly . . . what did he have to say about whoever took the Tidemaster to sea?'

'He said it was a young guy, tall.' It was Faraday. 'He didn't get a proper look but a description like that would definitely fit Unwin.'

'Or a thousand other blokes.'

'Sure. But who else have we turned up that might have had any connection to Pelly? The man's a loner, Brian. He doesn't have friends. He's not that type. Unwin was as close as anyone got to him. If you were Pelly and you suddenly had a big problem, something you couldn't sort on your own, who else would you rope in?'

Imber nodded. It made sense, he agreed.

'So we're sticking with Pelly?' he asked. 'We're really saying he killed someone? And that someone turned up at the bottom of the cliff? Four months later?'

'Yeah.'

'OK.' He leaned back. 'So who was that someone?'

Faraday himself went to the hotel, taking Dave Michaels with him. Tracy Barber and Darren Webster were parked up across the road. Faraday paused beside the unmarked Fiesta, bent to the window. He knew he owed them both.

'Nice one.' He smiled.

The Ryde Haven was a substantial Edwardian building disfigured by fire escapes and an ugly neon sign that promised en suite and TV in every room. A UPVC conservatory at the front served as an extension to the lounge bar and Faraday lingered a moment on the steps, wondering how full the hotel might be. Dave Michaels stepped past him and opened the door.

'This way, guvnor.'

The girl behind the tiny reception desk was plainly expecting them. The Unwins were up on the third floor, Rooms 32 and 33. She'd sent a pint of Carling up to Room 33 maybe an hour ago but hadn't heard a peep since.

Faraday thanked her for her help and headed for the stairs. Room 33 lay at the end of a low-ceilinged corridor at the top of the house. Faraday could hear the blare of a television from the top of the stairs. Passing room 32, he told Michaels to wait. If Mrs Unwin emerged, hang on to her.

Outside Room 33 Faraday paused. From the TV came the wail of a police siren, then a series of shots. Faraday knocked on the door. Nothing happened. He knocked again, tried the handle, but it was locked. Finally, at the third knock, the volume dipped on the TV and he heard the pad of footsteps. Moments later the door opened. Unwin was taller than Faraday had expected from the photo. Jeans, T-shirt, mop of blond hair, silver earring. Beyond him, propped on the bed against a nest of pillows, was his mother.

'Detective Inspector Faraday.' Faraday offered his warrant card. 'Your name, sir?'

Unwin stared at him a moment. His mother was up on one elbow. She looked startled. She wanted to know what was going on. Faraday glanced back towards Michaels, gestured him into the room.

Unwin was backing towards the television, barefoot on the pink carpet.

'Turn it off, please.' Faraday nodded at the TV. 'Mum?'

Mrs Unwin had the remote. Silence flooded the room. By now she'd recognised Faraday. She looked at him for a long moment. Since they'd met at the Lewisham Health Centre, she'd coloured her hair.

'What is this?' she said again.

'It's nothing, Mum.' Unwin appeared to have recovered his wits. 'I can explain.'

'Explain what?'

He had no answer. Faraday asked him again for his name. When he confirmed that he was Chris Unwin, Faraday asked whether he was prepared to return with him to the police station. Unwin shook his head.

'No fucking way.'

His mother was sitting on the edge of the bed now, staring up at her son.

'What's going on?' she said. 'Why doesn't someone tell me?'

Unwin was eyeing the door. Faraday heard Michaels shifting position behind him. A bolt for the stairs, thought Faraday, might solve a lot of problems. Finally, Unwin decided against it.

'I don't have to come,' he said. 'You can't make me.'

Faraday knew already that his instincts hadn't let him down. In these situations it wasn't difficult to recognise guilt. Unwin had a great deal he didn't want to talk about, least of all in front of his mother.

Faraday stepped towards him. Unwin stiffened, a frightened man expecting the worst.

'I'm arresting you on suspicion of murder. Anything you say may be taken down and used in evidence against you. Do you understand?'

'Murder? What do you mean, murder?' Unwin's mother was on her feet. 'This is outrageous. You can't just barge in like this. Murder? What are you talking about?'

Michaels stepped past Faraday. Unwin offered no resistance to the handcuffs. Mrs Unwin watched her departing son, unable to believe her eyes. One moment she'd been drifting off on the bed. Now this.

'You might like to come down as well, Mrs Unwin.'

'Are you arresting me too?'

'No, but your son might need –' Faraday offered her a wintry smile '– a little support.'

Back at the police station Faraday had already settled on an interview strategy. He wanted Dave Michaels and Tracy Barber in with Unwin. It would be at least an hour before they could sort out a brief for him, longer if Unwin insisted on shipping over a Pompey solicitor, but that would still leave time for a worthwhile session before PACE rules returned Unwin to his cell.

His mother, meanwhile, was still sitting on one of the benches downstairs beside the front desk. Prudence argued for a WPC to keep an eye on her but in Faraday's judgement that wouldn't be necessary. Mrs Unwin, like any mother would be, was appalled at this bombshell. The last thing she'd do was a runner.

'Let's get her in.' Faraday was still with Tracy Barber. 'See what she's got to say before we start with the lad.'

Half an hour on her own had quietened Mrs Unwin. The shock and outrage appeared to have gone. Instead, she was wary, watchful. When Faraday appeared at the front desk and suggested they have a chat, she got to her feet and nodded.

'Why not?' she said.

Faraday and Barber accompanied her to the interview suite. One of the rooms was being readied for her son. Faraday opened the next door and let her pass. She stepped into the small, bare room and looked around. There were four chairs tucked beneath the single table. Cassette machines were racked against the wall. Rain drummed at the barred window. She shivered, her face pale under the neon light.

'This is horrible,' she said softly. 'Where's Chrissie?'

Faraday told her he was awaiting interview. He'd elected for the duty solicitor and they'd get under way as soon as the booking-in process was complete.

'How long will all this take?'

'That depends. If we're satisfied with what your son has to say, he could be out of here by tomorrow.'

'You'll keep him in? Tonight?'

'Yes.'

'Why? What's he done?'

'We don't know, Mrs Unwin. That's why we've had to bring him down here. Murder's a serious offence. Interviews take time.'

'But he wouldn't have killed anyone, not Chrissie; he's not like that. He's never been violent, never. It's just not in his nature.'

'Let's hope you're right.'

Mrs Unwin gazed at Faraday a moment, not believing what she saw in his face.

'You're serious, aren't you?' she said at last. 'You really think he's done it.'

'Done what?'

'Murdered someone.' She shook her head, still bewildered, then let Imber pull out a chair for her. 'This is surreal,' she said finally. 'I can't believe this is happening.'

The formal interview began minutes later. Faraday established that she was free to leave at any time, then read her the formal caution. Anything she said could be used as evidence in a court of law.

'Against Chrissie?'

'In proceedings, yes.'

'Then why should I talk to you?'

'Because we're trying to get to the truth, Mrs Unwin. Somebody died. We have to find out how and why. Your son may be able to help us. So may you.'

Mention of a body appeared to surprise Mrs Unwin.

'Who is this person?'

'We don't know. That's another reason we have to talk to your son. To tell you the truth, we thought it might be him.'

'Really?' The thought startled her. 'And you had this . . . corpse?'

'Yes.'

'So why didn't you get me down? Show me?'

'It hadn't got a head. And the rest of it, to be frank, wasn't much to go on. Put a body in the sea for four months and there's not a lot left.'

'How ghastly.'

'Yes.' Faraday glanced at Tracy Barber, gestured for her to take over. Upstairs they'd discussed a strategy. In essence it boiled down to a single question.

'Mrs Unwin, you saw Mr Faraday and myself last week. Up in London. You remember?'

'Yes. At the health centre, yes.'

'And you told us then that you'd no idea where your son—'

'My stepson.'

'– your stepson had got to. In fact you hadn't seen him for months.'

'That's right.'

'You had no address for him, no mobile number, nothing. Not even a postcard.'

'Yes.'

'Then your mother, Mrs Mary Unwin, dies. That happened on Saturday night.'

'Correct . . .' Her answers were beginning to slow.

445

She's sensed where these questions are heading, Faraday thought, and she knows she's in trouble.

Barber hadn't taken her eyes off the face across the table. She leaned forward, puzzled.

'So how come your son gets to find out about his nan's death?' she asked. 'When no one has a clue where he is?'

There was a long silence. Someone was whistling out of tune in the corridor. Then came the distant bang of a cell door. Mrs Unwin physically flinched.

'Chrissie phoned up,' she said.

'Just like that.'

'Yes.'

'Out of the blue.'

'Yes.'

'The day after his nan had died.'

'Yes.'

'So where was he?'

Another silence, longer this time. Mrs Unwin was studying her hands.

'You'll talk to him, obviously; that's why he's here.' She nodded to herself. 'And you'll compare notes as well, won't you? That's how these things work. It's obvious.'

She looked up, desperate for support, for some way out of this nightmare. Tracy Barber said nothing. Silence, except for the soft whirring of the cassette tapes.

Finally, Mrs Unwin sighed. She hadn't told them the whole truth back there in the health centre. Chrissie had gone away in October. He'd left the place he had in Southsea and jumped in his van and gone abroad. She hadn't known why and yes of course it had bothered her but after a while she'd stopped thinking about it.

'And then what?'

'He got in touch.'

'When?'

'Before Christmas. He was living in France. He wouldn't tell me where but he said he was fine, OK, no problems. He'd got himself a little job, he said. He'd even found a girl he liked.'

'So why didn't you tell us?'

'Because he made me promise I wouldn't. Not just you, everyone. He didn't want anyone to know where he'd gone. He said it was nobody's business what he was up to. He was adamant. Like I said, he made me promise.'

'Didn't that strike you as odd?'

'Of course it did.'

'Weren't you worried?'

'I was out of my mind, especially with Christmas coming on. Then . . .' She shook her head. 'It was hopeless. What could I do? He sounded OK. He said everything was – you know – cool. So in the end I left it at that.' She tugged at a loose thread. 'Then you two turned up.'

'Didn't that –' Barber was choosing her words with care '– make you think at all?'

'Of course it did. Chrissie's never been an angel.' She looked from one face to another. 'But not this. Not *murder*.'

Faraday wrapped up the interview minutes later. Dave Michaels' face had appeared twice at the square of wired glass in the door and in any case he sensed that Mrs Unwin had nothing left to say. Profoundly apprehensive, she sat at the table looking up at Faraday as Tracy Barber wound back the tapes.

'He's in trouble, isn't he?' she said finally. 'And what have I done to help?'

Faraday offered her a lift back to the hotel but she shook her head. She wanted to stay here while they talked to Chrissie. She just hoped to God it wouldn't go on too long.

'It'll be twenty-four hours at least,' Faraday said. 'A night's sleep might do you good.'

'No.' She shook her head. 'Not while he might need me.'

'He's in a bit of a state.' Dave Michaels had followed Faraday into his office. Faraday shut the door.

'How do you mean?'

'He's in tears. He's like a kid. Flat out on the mattress. Face to the wall.'

'Anyone talked to him?'

'Not so far. The brief's due any minute. Might be tricky, eh?'

Faraday nodded. The last thing he needed was the duty solicitor claiming that Unwin was the victim of undue pressure.

'Take his mum along,' he said. 'Leave them in peace for five minutes.'

'Really?' Michaels shot Faraday a look. Potential co-defendants were rarely given the opportunity of time alone together.

'Yes. If anyone can sort him out, she can.' He paused. 'Why the tears, do you think?'

'I'm not sure. Trace thinks it's down to his nan. They were really close. Maybe he can't bear the thought of missing the funeral.'

Faraday nodded. Something similar had already occurred to him. He raised an eyebrow, the possibility of extra leverage unvoiced.

Michaels nodded.

'Exactly,' he said.

The interview started at 20.41. Faraday had spent ten minutes with the duty solicitor, who was insisting on full disclosure. Detailing the case against Unwin, Faraday was all too aware of how circumstantial it was but something told him that pressure from Unwin's mother might prove more influential than legal advice from a total stranger.

Dave Michaels and Tracy Barber were already in the interview suite. There was a speaker feed to the adjoining room and Faraday settled down to monitor what happened next. Michaels had agreed that Barber should lead. Five minutes' whispered conversation in the holding cell with his mum appeared to have restored a little of Unwin's self-confidence. Now he sat beside the duty solicitor, moist-eyed, his hair a mess, picking at his bitten fingernails. At Michaels' suggestion Tracy had brought in a box of tissues. When she offered him one, he shook his head.

'No thanks.'

Michaels started the tape, repeated the formal caution, added the date and time and names of those present, then gestured for Barber to take over. A situation like this often played badly in court many months later. Chris Unwin was hardly a vulnerable witness but she needed to protect the *Congress* team from allegations of harassment.

'You're sure you're up for this, Mr Unwin?'

'No problem.'

Tracy glanced at the solicitor. Late middle-aged, he was carrying far too much weight. After an exhausting day at the office he plainly wanted to be anywhere but here. Tracy returned to Unwin. Gently, she told herself.

'Rob Pelly . . .' she began. 'Tell me how you first got to know him.'

Unwin seemed surprised by the question. He thought for a moment, tipped his head back, evidently wondering where he might start.

'Couple of years back,' he said at last, 'my nan went into the home over there. I was already driving by then, deliveries mainly. Some of the jobs were on the island. Whenever I could I dropped in.'

'Why did your nan choose the island?'

'She lived here for a bit after the war. Somewhere round Ventnor way. She loved the place. It was Granddad who brought her back.'

They'd lived for a long time in Haslemere, he said. Then Granddad had died and after a spell with Mum in London his nan had decided to go back to the island.

'She couldn't really look after herself and Mum was out all day. Rob's place was on the local authority list. Kushti.'

'So you met Pelly at the home?'

'Yeah. He owns it. It's his place.'

'And you became friends?'

'Not friends exactly.' For the first time his voice began to falter. 'He's not that kind of bloke. We got on OK, though, and it was good because I was able to do him the odd favour, know what I mean?'

'No.' Tracy shook her head. 'Tell me.'

The solicitor glanced sideways at his client. Unwin seemed oblivious. He's made a decision, Barber thought. He's going to cough the lot.

'Well . . .' Unwin tore off a splinter of nail and flicked it away. 'Some of it was legit and some of it . . .' he shrugged '. . . wasn't.'

'Like what?'

'Like the blokes he brought in from abroad. There were loads of them. He was forever going over there,

Bosnia mainly. He told me all the immigration paper-work was up together and the Old Bill never bothered us so I just assumed it was OK. Talking to some of the blokes later that wasn't quite the story but – you know – none of that was down to me.'

When Pelly asked, Unwin would ship vanloads of immigrants across to the mainland, mainly Southampton. From there he'd drive them north, to addresses in Birmingham and Manchester. Each time he did it, he got paid. Not a fortune, he admitted, but then Pelly wasn't the kind of bloke you'd argue the toss with. Not about something as silly as money.

Next door, Faraday remembered the informant, Gary Morgan. Morgan had talked of a row between Unwin and Pelly, the spark that had put the first flames under the bonfire that had become *Congress*.

Barber obviously remembered the same conversation. Now she was asking whether such a row had ever taken place.

'Yeah, it did. I wasn't happy about stuff that was happening to my nan. Rob went off on one. I lost it too. Turned out I'd got it wrong, though. He was treating her OK.'

'When did that happen?'

'Dunno.' Unwin frowned. 'Last year. End of the summer, as far as I remember.'

'OK.' Barber nodded. 'So tell me about Lajla. What's the relationship between her and Pelly?'

Mention of Lajla brought Unwin to a halt. He looked from one face to the other. Michaels gestured for him to go on.

'They're married,' he said at last. 'Man and wife.'

'Married married? Or pretend?' It was Michaels this time.

'Dunno what you're talking about.'

'Married as in kipping together, screwing, or married as in getting the paperwork straight, getting the lady a passport, putting a roof over her head – all that?'

Unwin blinked. He was out of his depth. He leant towards his solicitor, conferred in a whisper. Finally, he shook his head.

'He says I don't have to answer that question.'

'But you'd know, surely?'

Another conference. Then the solicitor confirmed that his client was making no comment about this woman's exact status.

'How well did you know her?'

'I knew her a bit.'

'What's she like?'

'She's nice. Younger than him. But nice enough . . .' He nodded. 'Yeah.'

Barber brought the interview back to the end of last summer. Unwin had rowed with Pelly about his nan. The argument had been resolved.

'You were still going over there? Still dropping in?'

'Yeah.'

'How long did that go on for?'

Unwin stared at her. His hands disappeared into his lap. There was a long silence.

'I . . .' His mouth was dry. He licked his lips.

'Yes?' Barber warmed the question with a smile.

'Nothing.'

The silence deepened. Even the solicitor was getting uneasy. At last Unwin's head went down.

'This isn't fucking easy,' he muttered. 'The guy's going to kill me.'

'Who's going to kill you, Mr Unwin?'

'Who do you think?'

'I don't know. Maybe it would be easier if you told me.'

'Easier how?'

The sudden quickening in his voice was the give-away. He's after a deal, thought Barber. She glanced at Michaels. He'd obviously come to the same conclusion.

Tracy leant forward, sincere, concerned.

'It would be better if you just told us,' she said.

'Told you what?'

'Told us what happened.'

He nodded, considered the proposition, looked over at his solicitor.

'It's not just Rob,' he said at last. 'It's my nan. I need to see her. I need to be at that funeral. That's the only reason I'm back here. Don't you understand that?'

'OK.' Michaels nodded. 'Then why don't you just tell us what happened and then we'll make a few decisions of our own.'

'About what?'

'About whether we believe you, for a start.'

Unwin stared at him for a moment, then began to laugh.

'You think I'd make a thing like that up?' He shook his head. 'That's fucking mad.'

'A thing like what?'

Unwin's eyes flicked left again. He was looking at Barber. He wanted someone to get him off this hook, tell him everything would be sweet.

'Dave's right,' Barber said. 'Unless you get it off your chest, we can't possibly help. You have to trust us, Chris. There's no other way.'

There was a long pause. When the solicitor touched him on the arm and murmured something in his ear, Unwin ignored him. Finally he looked at Barber again.

'OK.' He swallowed hard. 'Why not?'

The last time he'd been over to Shanklin, he said, was back in October. It had been a Thursday, pissing down with rain. He'd dropped by the home to see his nan. They'd talked for a bit and had a pot of tea, just like always, and he'd been on his way out when he ran into Pelly.

'He was in a bit of a state. He looked like shit. I'd never seen him that way. I was amazed, tell you the truth.'

'What was the matter?'

'He wouldn't tell me, just took me upstairs, out the back, where he lives. I'd been up there a couple of times previous. Lajla was up there too. And the kid, the little girl. I'd never seen that before.'

'What do you mean?'

'Them up in Rob's place. You're right; I should have said. They don't live together. She's got her own place. Down below.'

Pelly, he said, wanted a favour. He told Lajla and the girl to go downstairs. Then he explained about a parcel he had to get rid of, big thing, heavy. It was out the back, in the garage. He needed a hand.

'What was it?'

'I didn't ask. Not then. I just said yes, why not. I had the van. No problem. I could dump it at the tip on the way back to the ferry. But then it started getting weird because he said the tip was no good. It had to be tonight, once it got dark. And it meant taking it out to sea on his boat. That got me thinking.'

'What did you say?'

'I wanted to say no.'

'But . . . ?'

'He wouldn't let it go. He said a hundred quid. Then

he doubled it. Coming from Rob, that's a fortune. Got me more worried than ever. I knew something was up.'

'But you agreed?'

'I had to. It wasn't just the money. It was . . . like . . . I knew. And once I knew he made it obvious that I had no choice. Either I helped him or . . .' He shook his head, looking away.

'Or what?'

'He's mad. You should see him sometimes, the things he does to blokes who cross him. You never want to go there, believe me. Man's a fucking animal.'

There was a long silence, finally broken by Tracy Barber.

'So what did you think was in the parcel?'

'A body. What else could it be?'

'And were you right?'

'Yeah . . . Turns out I was.'

Unwin disappeared into Shanklin for a couple of hours. When he came back it was dark. Around seven he helped Pelly bundle the parcel into the back of his Volvo. It was wrapped in black polythene, he said, and roped. It was soft as well as heavy. At one point he felt a knee.

'What about a head?' It was Michaels.

'Wrong end. He made sure I had the other end.' He frowned. 'Why?'

'Nothing.' Michaels scribbled a note. 'Go on.'

They'd driven in convoy down to the water at Bembridge Harbour.

'Whereabouts in Bembridge Harbour?'

Bent over his notes next door, Faraday nodded in approval. The edges of Bembridge Harbour were littered with boatyards, flats, houses, business premises, even – at the southerly end – a line of houseboats.

So just where would you find the privacy to risk something like this?

Unwin was talking about an area known as the Duver. You got there, he said, down a narrow road. There was a small car park surrounded by bushes. A path led up onto the dunes. A hundred metres or so and you were on a quiet stretch of foreshore, outside the harbour itself. There were beach huts there. The tide was up on the shingle below.

'So what happened?'

'We got the body out of the Volvo, carried it up over the dunes. Bloody thing weighed a ton.'

Concealing the body in scrub behind one of the beach huts, they'd driven back up the road and round to the harbour. Pelly had a boat of his own, a thing he called a Tidemaster, but he'd already done a deal with some guy about another boat. Pelly was going to be in charge of this other boat. Pelly's own boat was down to Unwin.

'Did you know anything about boats?' It was Michaels.

'Not much. I'd been out with Rob a couple of times. Mackerel mainly. I can steer OK. He knew that. He'd let me have a go.'

'So what happened?'

'It was crazy. The tide was up so we had to use another little boat to get out to his, a dinghy thing. We tied the dinghy to his boat and then went out of the harbour. The place where we'd left the body is down to the left. Rob dropped the anchor and we took the dinghy onto the beach.'

Getting the body into the dinghy, he said, was a nightmare. Rowing back out, he thought the bloody thing was going over.

'Was it rough?'

456

'No, not really. It wasn't that. It was still pissing down but it wasn't rough. It was just the situation. Something like that, it's just bizarre.'

When they finally made it alongside the Tidemaster, Pelly climbed on board. Unwin chucked him a line from the parcelled corpse and together they'd started to heave the body out of the dinghy. At this point, to Unwin's horror, the parcel had begun to leak and as they manhandled it onto the Tidemaster Unwin had found himself covered in various bodily fluids.

'Blood, piss, all sorts. My face, neck, chest, hands – fucking everywhere. I stank for days. I couldn't get rid of the smell.'

Next thing he knew, Pelly had pulled too hard on the rope and the whole parcel came undone. The poly-thene ended up like a tent, all over Unwin. By the time he'd fought the thing off, Pelly had bundled the body into the wheelhouse and then got it down below, into the tiny forrard cabin.

'You got out of the dinghy in the end?'

'Yeah.'

Unwin clambered aboard and then Pelly started the engine. With the anchor up, he'd motored back into the harbour and hopped across to the boat he'd borrowed from some mate or other.

'What happened to the dinghy?'

'We left it on the mooring.'

In the darkness the two boats had left the harbour, Pelly in the lead, Unwin at the wheel of the Tidemas-ter.

'I was shitting myself by this time. Pelly had obviously topped this bloke and here was I cruising along with the fucking body down below. So who holds his hands up if we ever got caught? Eh?' He looked at the two detectives, seemingly unaware of the irony.

Barber told him to carry on. Where did they go with the two boats?

'Miles out. Took forever. We went round the corner of the island, then across the bay and just kept going. I wanted to talk to Rob on the radio but he'd said there was no way. He gave me some cobblers about the radios being fucked but really I knew it was about other people listening in. He didn't want that. Too fucking right he didn't.'

'Did you ever go below? Have a look at the body?'

'No fucking way. I didn't want to know.'

'Didn't you ask who this person was? What Pelly was up to?'

'No. I just wanted to get it over with.'

'Get what over with?'

'Whatever was going to happen next.' He shook his head. 'Unreal it was. Complete fucking nightmare.'

A couple of hours out, they stopped. Pelly circled and came up alongside. He said he was going to bin the Tidemaster and then hop onto the one he'd borrowed. After that, they could both go home.

'Bin?'

'Sink. He had an axe with him, big thing. He showed it to me.'

Pelly made sure he had a couple of lines between the two boats so he could get back on board, then he disappeared below while Unwin got himself onto the other boat. There'd been a couple of minutes of crashing around with the axe, really heavy blows, and then Pelly came out of the wheelhouse again, said the Tidemaster was starting to fill. He'd opened some valve or other as well but the bastard refused to sink.

'In the end he had to go down there again and make

458

a bigger hole. That did the trick. The boat started going down by the bow, really quickly, and he was back out by now, trying to get the door of the wheelhouse locked. The real problem was the ropes that tied us together. The weight of Pelly's boat was dragging mine over. In the end he had to give up on the door and come back on board. The only way we saved my boat was by using the axe on the ropes. Just released us in time. Shit . . .' He shook his head again.

Listening next door through the speaker feed, Faraday remembered Sean Castle's indignation at the state of his boat when Pelly had returned it. Fucking great gouges on the starboard gunnels, he'd said. No wonder.

In the interview room Unwin had finally come to a halt. The story, as far as he was concerned, was over. He'd nothing left to say.

Tracy Barber wanted to know what he'd done that night, once they'd made it back to Bembridge Harbour. The last ferry back to the mainland would have gone. Had Pelly offered him a bed for the night?

'Are you fucking joking? There's no way I wanted to be anywhere near that guy again.'

'So what did you do?'

'I waited for him to go. Then I took everything off and washed myself in the harbour. You can't describe the smell. I just couldn't stand it. Problem was I hadn't got any other clothes so in the end I froze my arse off for nothing. Made fuck-all difference. I kipped in the back of the van. Or tried to.'

Next day he took the ferry back to Pompey. With Pelly's two hundred pounds and some debts hastily recovered from other sources he bought himself a ticket to Le Havre. From the French coast he drove south for a day, only stopping when it got dark and he discovered he'd blown one of his headlights. For the next week he slept in the back of the van and tried to get work. In the end he found himself working for a farmer in the middle of nowhere. Nice enough bloke but pissed out of his head most of the time.

'Perfect,' said Barber drily.

'That's what I thought.' Unwin nodded. 'Until Mum phoned.'

Next door, Faraday had drawn himself a map. Somewhere south of the Isle of Wight a cross represented the spot where Pelly had scuttled the Tidemaster. Faraday tried to imagine it going down, the wheelhouse filling, the unsecured door opening and closing in the underwater currents. On the seabed expanding gases would have lifted the swollen corpse. In time, maybe a shift in the current, it had floated free. Months later it must have lodged in rocks at the foot of Tennyson Down and – thanks to a diligent birder – earned itself the attentions of the Major Crimes Team.

Faraday rubbed his face and sat back. Tracy Barber had appeared at the door.

'Message from Unwin, sir.' She was smiling. 'Wants to know when he can see his nan.'

Twenty-three

Wednesday, 3 March 2004

Faraday and Dave Michaels arrived at the nursing home at 08.00. Pelly was in the kitchen, cooking scrambled eggs for eighteen breakfasts. He carried on stirring milk into the big saucepan while Faraday told him he was under arrest on suspicion of murder, only breaking off to ask Michaels to rescue the toast from the grill pan on top of the oven. The old ladies, he said, hated burnt toast. Played havoc with their dentures.

Before he accompanied the two detectives out to the waiting car, Pelly climbed the stairs for a change of T-shirt. Faraday went with him. Outside the door to his apartment Pelly paused. If anything, he seemed amused.

'I see you had the sentries back last night.' He nodded out towards the road. 'Shame. I wasn't going anywhere. You should have given me a ring, saved yourself the expense.'

Faraday was back at Ryde police station by 08.45. The Custody Sergeant booked Pelly in and organised a phone call to his solicitor in Newport. Under the Police and Criminal Evidence Act an early-morning arrest effectively gave Faraday two days in the interview suite. PACE permitted him to detain a suspect for twenty-four hours. With a twelve-hour extension from the local Superintendent, there'd be no need to release Pelly until tomorrow evening.

Willard, still in Portsmouth, wanted to know about the interview strategy. Faraday proposed to ask Pelly for a full account of events around the end of September and beginning of October last year. This was ground they'd already covered the night that Pelly had turned up drunk, but this time Faraday wanted a great deal more evidence about the buyers Pelly had allegedly found for both the Tidemaster and the Volvo. Only as the interview moved into the challenge phase would DS Michaels and DC Barber begin to feed in last night's allegations from Unwin.

Willard had seen the problem at once.

'The stuff from Unwin is uncorroborated, isn't it?' he said. 'Or have you got something else?'

'Only Sean Castle. He's got something called an Aquabel. Chartering the boat to Pelly checks out with Unwin's story, and we'll certainly put Scenes of Crime aboard, just in case he brought DNA over when he shipped back from the Tidemaster. But it's nearly five months now, so I'm not holding my breath.'

'What did Pelly have to say about Castle when you talked to him last?'

'He admitted hiring the boat, no problem. Just said he fancied it.'

'No other explanation?'

'None.'

'Doesn't care, does he?'

'Not in the slightest.'

'And you think he's lying?'

'Without a doubt.' Faraday told Willard about a conversation he'd had with the Crime Scene Manager. After three days' solid work at the nursing home Pelly was still bringing them tea, still pretending he couldn't remember who took sugar, still taking the piss. Given Unwin's story about the body at the back of the garage, Pelly must have spent weeks removing every last trace of DNA.

'And the body? The victim? Any thoughts on ID?'

'None. Unwin says he never saw it, just felt it through the bin liner. We can't even evidence it was a bloke.'

'Great.' Willard was sounding gloomier by the minute. 'So what's your feeling?'

'About Pelly?'

'Yes.'

'He's still not bothered. I don't think he's even surprised. Irritated would be closer to the mark. We gather he's got lots to do today. I'd say that was optimistic, wouldn't you, sir?'

Winter returned to the neurologist alone. Maddox had offered to drive him up to the hospital and wait in the car park, just like last time, but Winter said it wasn't necessary. He'd slept fitfully, aware of Maddox awake beside him, and on the one occasion when he'd managed to fool his battered brain into closing down, he'd woken minutes later, drenched in sweat, convinced that something grey and shapeless was lying in wait for him, indescribably horrible.

He paid the taxi fare and found his way to the neurologist's consulting room. Since he was last here, someone had nicked the most recent copy of *Homes and Gardens*.

The wait went on and on. A series of patients disappeared through the door at the end of the waiting room. One of them emerged with a small, shy smile, consulted his watch and hurried away. Another, with her husband waiting by the water cooler, broke down in tears. Winter watched these people come and go much in the way that he might cast a casual eye over a TV programme in which he had little interest. The fact that the man behind the door seemed to have acquired the power of life and death Winter viewed as a personal affront. Faced with the certain knowledge of what was to come, he'd decided to bluff it out.

'Mr Winter?'

Winter answered the summons. For once, all too typically, his head didn't hurt. No bubbles. No pressure behind the eyes. Just the faintest curiosity about what the next few minutes might hold.

Mr Frazer got to his feet to shake his hand. Evidently he'd already called up the CT scans from the hospital's intranet. He swivelled the PC monitor in Winter's direction. No messing, thought Winter.

'This is a lateral slice through your head. And so is this. And so is this. As you can see, we've used a dye to sharpen the image.'

Winter found himself looking down on the contents of his head. The bony white egg cup of the skull was clearly visible. Inside, one area of grey was clearly darker than the rest. Frazer fingered the mouse again. The perspective changed abruptly and Winter cocked his head, trying to adjust.

'These are vertical scans. Here's the top of your spinal column, and that bit there's your nose. Now then, just here is what troubles me. It's a tumour, I'm afraid. It has absolutely no business to be there.'

This time the darker mass was much more clearly defined. Winter stared at it, fascinated. It lacked the coils and fissures that badged the rest of his brain. It looked dense, evil, an intruder that did nothing but grow. When Frazer reached forward and helpfully adjusted the contrast, it even acquired a slight sheen. The cuckoo in the nest, thought Winter.

'How big's that, then?'

'Size of a golf ball, maybe a fraction smaller. To be frank, I'm amazed you haven't had the symptoms earlier. Our real problem is here.'

'Where?'

'Here.'

Frazer had produced a pencil. He pointed at an area immediately adjoining the tumour.

'This is the main vein that drains blood from the brain. It runs through the sinus. The tumour appears to be pressing on the vein, which may be why you're experiencing so much pain. Tumours growing *inside* the sinus are mercifully rare.'

Winter didn't like the word '*inside*'. He took a closer look at the image on the monitor.

'So what are you going to do about it?'

'We have to get rid of it. It's very probably what we call a benign meningioma. It won't be growing very fast but if we don't do something about it, it'll kill you.'

Winter nodded. It all seemed perfectly logical.

'So what happens next?'

'We find you a surgeon. I have to warn you, Mr Winter, this isn't everyone's cup of tea. Blood flows through the sinus at the rate of a litre a minute. Surgery will be . . .' he frowned at the screen '. . . tricky.'

'How tricky?'

'Very. You'll need a vascular neurosurgeon, chap who knows his way round the plumbing. There aren't too many around. In fact there are very few. I've already had a word with one of them. I'm afraid he declined.'

'And the others?'

'I've yet to talk to them.' He swapped the pencil for a pen. 'We'll need to know your movements over the next couple of weeks. There'll be a consultation first, of course, probably in London. The surgeon may elect for a course of radiation before he goes in. That should shrink the tumour. So . . .' He smiled. 'We can get you on the mobile number?'

Winter took his time. He gazed at the tumour, tried to imagine it chopped out, wondered what would happen to the hole it left behind. Then his hand went up to his forehead, tracking slowly across, trying to match the cranial bumps beneath his fingertips to the image on the screen. Finally he closed his eyes, squeezed hard, tried to trick the pain into returning, failed.

'Mr Winter?'

'Sorry, yes. You mentioned surgery.'

'I did. I just need to know where to find you.'

'Of course.' Winter smiled at him. 'We're here for a week or so. I've got some tidying up to do, then I think my girlfriend's got some other plans. She thinks Africa might be good.' The smile widened. 'What do you think?'

The first interview session with Rob Pelly started at 10.56. DS Michaels and DC Tracy Barber had been through their notes from last night's interview with Chris Unwin and had timetabled the exact sequence of events he'd described. First, though, they wanted Pelly's version of the night he'd chartered Castle's fishing boat and set off in convoy with the Tidemaster.

Monitoring the conversation from the adjoining room, Faraday knew at once that Pelly wasn't interested. Sober this time, he simply repeated what he'd already told Faraday. A mate had wanted a trip out, skippering the Tidemaster. Pelly himself had always had a fancy for helming Castle's Aquabel. A night's fishing had been the perfect excuse. They'd caught sod all, but who cared?

Michaels treated this account with derision. Pelly couldn't offer the name of this mate of his, didn't know where he lived, hadn't a clue where to get hold of him. Was he big? Small? Fat? Thin? White? Brown? Black? Green?

'Yeah, all of that.' Pelly was enjoying himself. 'Whatever you fancy.'

'This isn't a joke,' Michaels reminded him. 'We're talking murder, not some jolly.'

'*You're* talking murder. Me? I'm just telling you what happened that night. We went fishing. Fishing isn't a crime, not yet anyway. Then we came home.'

'And sold the boat.'

'That's right.'

'Who to?'

'French bloke. Nice as pie. Saw it on the mooring, went for a tootle round the harbour, made me an offer, took it away.'

'How much?'

'Can't remember. Three grand? Four? We're talking euros here.'

'What did you do with it?'

'Put it in a bank account in Bosnia. You want to see the paperwork? That could be difficult.'

There was a murmured conversation as Pelly consulted his solicitor, a plump, pleasant-looking woman from a big island practice in Newport. Finally, Pelly decided he might have left the money with a friend in Sarajevo. Strictly for safe keeping.

Dave Michaels, unusually, was running out of

patience. When Pelly's amnesia extended to the sale of his Volvo, Michaels accused him of lying.

'Can you prove that?' Pelly's voice had hardened. 'Only lying's a big word.'

There was a long silence. Michaels wasn't an easy man to wind up. Tracy Barber intervened. Between them, thought Faraday, they must have decided to go for broke.

'Chris Unwin's back on the island,' she began. 'Are you aware of that, Mr Pelly?'

'Yeah. He dropped by yesterday. Came up with his mum to sort out young Mary's stuff. Nice to see him again.'

'You know we've been looking for him?'

'Yeah?' Faraday could picture Pelly's dismissive shrug.

'Well?'

'Don't understand the question, love. What's any of that got to do with me?'

'I just thought you might have got in touch.'

'About Unwin?' He laughed. 'Listen, you blokes are supposed to know your business. If you choose to spend thousands of pounds looking for a guy who's been away for a while, good luck. Me? I've got a list of jobs as long as your arm. Doing yours for you isn't one of them. OK?'

'Do you know where Unwin's been?'

'He said something about France.'

'That's right. And do you know why he went over in the first place?'

'Haven't a clue.'

'Then let me tell you.'

Faraday bent towards the speaker. This was the crunch, he thought. This was the moment when *Congress* played its one and only court card.

468

Barber was detailing Unwin's account of the night he helped Pelly dispose of the body. From time to time she paused, asking Pelly whether he had any comment.

'Go on,' he said. 'Tell me the rest of it.'

At length she got to the end of Unwin's story. He was back in Bembridge Harbour, back in his van, freezing cold, waiting for dawn. Eighteen hours later he was driving that same van and a handful of possessions onto the Le Havre ferry.

'It checks out,' Barber warned. 'P & O have confirmed the booking.'

'Fine.' Pelly sounded totally unruffled. 'What's any of that got to do with me?'

'Unwin says you had a body to dispose of.' Michaels this time. 'It's not an unreasonable supposition to suspect that you might have had some connection with this person's death.'

There was a long silence. Faraday reached for a pad, waiting. Finally Pelly began to laugh again.

'It's bollocks, isn't it? Unwin lives in a world of his own. Always has done.'

'You're denying it?'

'Of course I fucking am.'

'There was no body?'

'Not that I ever saw. The guy's made it up. Like he makes everything else up.'

'Why would he do that?'

'We had a row, like people do. He tell you about that at all? He thought I was short-changing his nan. Happens he was wrong but I don't blame him for having a go. Maybe he took it personally. Fuck knows. Maybe he can't resist making stuff up. Some people are like that. They're kids. Prefer make-believe to the real world.'

'And Unwin's like that?'

469

'Course he is. You just have to look at the guy. He's a child. He makes it up as he goes along.'

Another silence, longer this time. Then Dave Michaels came in. His appetite for Pelly's brand of bullshit was exhausted.

'This is the way it goes, right? It's summer. You're trying to raise money to buy a new boat but this seems to be a problem because the fact is you're skint. We've talked to Cheetah Marine, the people down in Ventnor. We can evidence that. Come October, though, you're suddenly rolling in dosh. Lots and lots of it. We can evidence that, too. Mysteriously, at exactly the same time a witness comes forward and says he helped you get rid of a body. The next day your boat disappears. You haven't got a clue who bought it. Then the Volvo estate gets sold to some other stranger. Meantime you're redecorating fit to bust downstairs at the back. New carpet, new curtains, new chair – total blitz. Five months later we find a body at the bottom of a cliff. And now we discover you're selling up and getting out. You're telling me none of that suggests a pattern?'

'Like how?'

'Like you killed a guy? Took his money? Emptied his bank account? Covered up after you?' It was Michaels laughing this time. 'Isn't that the way it happened? Or am I missing something here?'

Pelly didn't answer. Michaels repeated the question, blunter this time.

'You killed him, didn't you? You killed this person?'

Pelly's sigh was all too audible. Here was a man, it suggested, whose patience had been stretched to breaking point.

'You want to prove that?' he said at last. 'Only you wouldn't believe how busy I am.'

*

It took the briefest phone call for Cathy Lamb to make time in her schedule to see Paul Winter.

'You're supposed to be resting,' she scolded him. 'The idea is to get better.'

'Nice one, Cath. I'll be down in half an hour.'

Winter drove himself into the city. It was a beautiful day, early spring sunshine gleaming on the wide bright spaces of the upper harbour. In the distance the grey bulk of Portchester Castle. As a kid Winter and his gang had ridden their bikes across and played on the foreshore beneath the castle walls. One time, a fat kid – Richard – had found a human thigh bone. He'd taken it to the police station and months later he'd got a letter saying the bone had probably belonged to one of the French prisoners banged up in the hulks during the Napoleonic Wars. Winter, slowing for the exit to Kingston Crescent, smiled at the memory. We all cop it in the end, he thought.

Cathy Lamb was even more stressed than usual but one look at Winter made her push the paperwork to one side. At least DIs qualified for an office, she muttered. Thank God for a bit of privacy, eh?

Winter took the hint and shut the door. He and Cathy Lamb went back years. She'd had her share of troubles, both private and professional, and it wasn't in her nature to waste time on small talk.

'You look shit,' she said. 'What's happened?'

Winter told her about the morning's visit to the hospital. He had a brain tumour. It was already the size of a golf ball. He filled her in on one or two details, remembering what he could about the ghostly grey shapes on the CT scan, and ended with the consultant's frank assessment of Winter's chances under the surgeon's knife. Telling her this way was oddly detached, he thought. He might have been describing the early stages of a particularly challenging inquiry. There were a number of pathways forward but none of them, to be honest, looked particularly bright.

Cathy nodded. She was a sturdy, big-hearted woman who'd spent half a lifetime trying to keep her emotions under control. Now she looked away. Her eyes were moist.

'That's terrible.'

She got up. There was a fold of tissues in the pocket of her anorak. She blew her nose and then sat down again.

Winter, embarrassed, wanted to talk about *Plover*.

'Fuck *Plover*.'

'I'm serious, Cath. You'd be doing me a favour.'

'The answer's no. You're sick, Paul. We have to get you better.'

'Then listen. I need to box this thing off.'

Ignoring her protests, Winter summarised his progress over the last couple of days. An informant had passed on the whisper about a black 4×4. Wishart's wife had a black 4×4. Wishart himself had been driving the vehicle the week of Lakemfa's death. Within days, after a couple of hours with the steam cleaner and the pressure hose, he'd traded the vehicle in for a brand new model.

'Not a contract at all then?' Despite herself, Cathy Lamb was interested.

'No. He did the job himself. That way, no one else is in the loop. Stands to reason, Cath. This is a guy who trusts no one.'

'But why would he do it? Why take the risk?'

Winter told her about the way he'd tucked Lakemfa up. Meals. Probably money. Definitely Camber Court.

'Lakemfa was on a freebie?'

'Several.'

'You can evidence that?'

'Yes.'

'How?'

'Maddox.'

Cathy looked at him, wanting more. Winter changed the subject. Jimmy Suttle, he said, had been on to ILET at Segensworth. The International Liaison Enquiry Team had links into all the London embassies and had made inquiries about a contract put out to tender by the Nigerian navy.

'They were after inshore attack craft, Cath. This is Wishart's game. They wanted a dozen. That's around twelve million quid. Wishart thought he had it in the bag.'

'Because of Lakemfa?'

'Exactly. He'd done the research. Lakemfa knew all the big players in Lagos, had the ear of the man with the chequebook. Game, set and match.'

'And?'

'The contract went to the Norwegians. Firm up in Stavanger. Maybe they bunged Lakemfa more than Wishart. Maybe he was crazy about Scandinavian women. Either way Wishart wasn't having it. This is a guy who's not into losing, Cath.'

'So he *killed* him?'

Winter held her gaze for a moment, then nodded.

'Dying's no big deal, Cath.' He offered her a weary smile. 'Believe me.'

The second interview session with Pelly lasted nearly two hours. Michaels and Barber went over the sequence of events time and again, testing every join, requesting clarification on this detail or that, constantly trying to provoke Pelly into a contradiction or a silly mistake. Not once did Pelly give them the slightest indication that he was prepared to shed precious light on areas of his story that remained bafflingly obscure. His life was his own. He led it the way he led it and he was under absolutely no obligation to share the details with anyone. If they really believed this nonsense story of Unwin's, then it was down to them to prove it. And for that, as he was only too aware, they needed corroboration.

'He's stitched us up.' Michaels was on his second coffee. 'And he knows it.'

Faraday listened to Michaels' thoughts on where a third interview might take them. He'd been in and out of the second session, monitoring it from next door, only too aware of Pelly's ever-lengthening silences. The clock was ticking. Soon he'd have to drive over to Newport and explain his case for a twelve-hour extension to Pelly's period of detention. He knew and liked the uniformed Superintendent who'd have to make the decision, and anticipated no real problem keeping Pelly in for another day's questioning, but more and more he was asking himself what else they had to throw at the man. It was only too clear that Pelly was beyond intimidation. After surviving Bosnia, as he was so fond of pointing out, there were precious few things in life that really bothered him. So just how could they prise open this absurd story of his?

Michaels, uncharacteristically, had fallen silent. Tracy Barber was staring into space. It fell to Faraday to move the process on.

'We need to take a hostage,' he said.

The third interview started an hour later. Faraday himself had replaced DC Tracy Barber. DIs rarely conducted interviews, but on this occasion Faraday believed that the gamble was amply justified. He was beginning to get a sense of where Pelly's weak spot might lie, and if his instincts were right then the next few minutes would be crucial.

Pelly and his solicitor were already seated at the small, bare table when Faraday and Dave Michaels walked in. According to the Custody Officer, Pelly had refused the offer of lunch, opting instead for a roll-up and a copy of the *Guardian*. He was, he'd told the turnkey, a vegetarian. No way was he going to trust a lukewarm burger from the microwave upstairs.

Faraday settled himself opposite Pelly. Michaels joined him. Pelly looked from one face to the other

'Where's the lady?'

'Otherwise engaged.' Faraday was leafing through a sheaf of notes. 'We've arrested your wife. We need a bit of a chat with her. I thought DC Barber was best suited for the job.' He looked up, his finger anchored in the middle of a page. 'Now then, where were we?'

The transformation in Pelly was remarkable. The languid composure, the air of slight boredom, had gone. There was anger in his eyes.

'You've done what?'

'Arrested your wife.' Faraday looked mildly surprised. 'Do you have a problem with that?'

'Too fucking right I have a problem with that. You've got me. Here. What else do you need?'

'A few sensible answers would be nice. Just for starters.'

'And Lajla?'

'I'm sure she'll oblige.' Faraday smiled. 'I gather she's a bit upset just now but I suppose that's understandable. You don't get arrested for murder every day of your life.'

'*Murder?* Laj? You're off your head.' He looked

sideways at his solicitor. 'I don't have to put up with this, do I?'

The solicitor told him he didn't have a choice. Lajla would herself be entitled to legal representation. Her rights would doubtless be respected.

'Of course,' said Faraday lightly. 'The duty brief should be here any minute.'

'The duty fucking brief?' Pelly's face had reddened. 'What would someone like that know about what Laj's been through, eh?'

He let the question hang between them. Faraday sensed that Michaels wanted to dive in, wind Pelly up a little more, but Faraday extended a restraining hand. His eyes hadn't left Pelly's face.

'I'm afraid I don't understand.' He smiled again. '*Been through?*'

'Yeah, been through. You people have no idea, do you? You're clueless. Worse than that, you've no fucking interest. Just imagine. You're eighteen years old. You've lived in the same village all your life. You've gone to school with the same bunch of kids, boys, girls; they're like one family, moving on through. Then one day it all kicks off and suddenly you're back at school, back in that same classroom, except now there are dirty old mattresses on the floor, and a bunch of hairy-arsed soldiers getting their fucking kit off, just gagging to dick you. And you know who some of those animals are? Yeah . . .' He leaned forward, stabbing the air between them. 'The blokes you grew up with, the blokes you called fucking brothers. Can you imagine that? Can you imagine how that must *feel*? Can you?'

He slumped back in his chair, shaking his head, disgusted. His solicitor inched her chair sideways,

476

widening the gap between them. Even Dave Michaels looked impressed.

Faraday permitted himself the beginnings of a smile. The softness of his voice brought Pelly's head up.

'Fascinating,' Faraday murmured.

Winter was exhausted by the time he made it back home. A meet with Jimmy Suttle had left him feeling helpless and grumpy. Like Cathy Lamb, Suttle had taken one look at Winter and told him he was mad to even think about continuing his pursuit of Maurice Wishart.

DI Lamb was due for a conference with Willard on the direction that *Plover* should now take. A possession charge had been laid against Singer, and the solicitor had also been made aware of his indiscretions on the DVD. The fact that he'd helped his clients fabricate evidence for use in court put Singer in deep, deep shit and celebrations had already started in CID offices across the city. As far as Wishart was concerned, on the other hand, Willard seemed to be cautious about committing too many resources. Available evidence was circumstantial in the extreme. With *Congress* bogged down once again, the Detective Superintendent didn't want two enquiries that might last months and then dead end.

Dead end, thought Winter, pretty much summed it up. He struggled out of the car, wrapped his coat around himself and then pushed in through the garden gate. The lights were on in the bungalow again, and Maddox met him at the door. He hadn't phoned her all day. The three calls she'd made, he'd ignored.

'Where've you been?'

'Work.'

'*Work?*' She kissed him. 'You look worn out.'

Winter nodded, lacking the energy to argue. He'd spent all day building a dam against the real implications of his conversation with the neurologist. Now, with his head beginning to throb again, he felt miserable. The medics, in the end, were right. When the system failed, what's left of your body took charge. You could try and fight it, of course you could, but what – in the end – was the point?

Maddox wanted to know how the session at the hospital had gone. Winter told her. She stared at him.

'Shit,' she said finally. 'How do you feel?'

Winter shook his aching head and sank into a chair. The last thing he wanted to discuss was the prospect of his own mortality.

'Tell me something cheerful.' He was looking up at her.

'You want a drink? Scotch?'

'No.' He shook his head and then winced. 'You have one for me.'

Maddox disappeared into the kitchen. Winter heard one *glug-glug-glug*, then another. She returned with two sizeable glasses.

'Here.' She gave it to him, kissed him again, turned off the harsh overhead light. Winter looked at her in the semi-darkness. She'd been on the net, hunting for deals. There was a flight leaving early next week, Egyptair. They'd have to change planes in Cairo but the price was a steal. Up in the mountains, she said, they could start to sort things out. A change of continent, and anything might be possible.

'I'll make you better,' she said. 'Promise.'

Winter gazed at her. Next week sounded a wildly optimistic proposition. Just now he'd be lucky to make it to the bathroom. She was talking about Rimbaud, about Harar, about the camels they could rent for expeditions into the mountains, about the local guides who'd show them the best places to camp. In the evenings, back in Harar, there was a wonderful souk, merchants selling carpets and brassware, and a thousand spices. Winter's eyes began to close. For the second time in days he was close to tears. He could see this place of hers. He could almost smell it. But it was never going to happen. Then came the sound of a mobile, Maddox's distinctive call tone.

Winter lay back in the chair, nursing the Scotch. There was a pause while Maddox read the number, then she was on her feet, padding across the living room into the privacy of the hall. Winter caught a muffled conversation, then Maddox's throaty laugh. A minute or two later she was back beside the chair.

'A friend.' She bent and touched his glass with hers. *'Fais-moi confiance, mon chéri.'*

Twenty-four

Thursday, 4 March 2004

The weather obliged Faraday to meet Willard off the hovercraft. An area of low pressure had been deepening in mid-Atlantic for a couple of days and now the leaden swirl of cloud was pushing up the Channel. All night the wind had been strengthening, and Faraday had awoken to a hard, driving rain lashing at the window of his tiny hotel room.

An hour later, virtually alone in the transit lounge at the Hoverspeed terminal, he waited for sign of the approaching hovercraft. Barely a fortnight ago he'd struck exactly the same pose in the Southsea terminal across the Solent, gazing out at the churn of waves and tatters of wind-torn bladderwrack. This was the twin brother of the gale that had so nearly halted services to Ryde that stormy morning, and Faraday glanced back towards the enquiry desk, wondering whether they hadn't bothered to announce a cancellation.

Then, very dimly, he saw the approaching hovercraft, a low squat shape wallowing in through the murk. The nearby pier normally offered shelter from the prevailing westerlies but today the wind tore between the rusting supports, lacing the heaving sea with spume. The bigger waves were smashing against the pier itself, huge explosions of creamy brown surf, and Faraday watched the hovercraft dipping and rolling as the captain clawed his way towards the concrete ramp.

Willard, who'd spent a month last summer on a sailing course, was first off. He ran the twenty metres to the terminal building, bent against the howling wind, then shook himself like a dog once he'd managed to get inside.

'Brilliant,' he announced. 'You pay a fortune at Alton Towers for a ride like that.'

Faraday's car was parked outside. Willard wanted an update before they went into conference at the police station.

'We released Pelly last night, sir. Half eight. Bailed him for six weeks. I didn't try for the extension in the end. Not worth the hassle.'

'A night in the cells?'

'No point.' Faraday shook his head, waiting for a break in the traffic. 'This is a man who just doesn't care. He's telling Dave Michaels this is kids' stuff compared to some of the things he's been through. Problem is, we're starting to believe him.'

'Nothing?'

'Zilch. You could drive a bus through the holes in his story, but the longer Dave points that out the less interested he becomes. We've never managed to shake him, not as far as his story's concerned, not once. Eerie, really. It's like the man already knows he's home free. How would you explain that?'

'Christ knows.' Willard was watching an elderly woman battling her way across the road, oblivious to the traffic. 'What about his wife?'

'She went no comment. I put Tracy Barber and the lad Webster in with her. They didn't get further than her name and address. Tracy said she was really upset, but we can't do her for that, can we?'

Lajla, he said, had been released last night without charge. She and Pelly had taken a cab back to Shanklin and Faraday himself had watched them drive away. Lajla had been in the back with her husband, her head buried in the folds of his anorak, sobbing.

'Unwin?'

'I bailed him as well. We got a full statement. He and his mum took the first hovercraft out. Didn't even go and see his nan. He's terrified Pelly's going to come after him.'

'He's probably right.'

'I doubt it. Pelly's turned the page. New chapter. New life. We checked with the estate agent this morning. Pelly's pushing for completion by the end of the month.'

'What about the bail date?'

'Good point, sir. But to be honest I can't see him hanging around for us.'

The formal conference began half an hour later in the office used by the investigation's DCs. Faraday was in the chair, with DS Dave Michaels offering an overview of statements gathered to date and DS Pete Baker reporting on the ever-diminishing tally of actions still awaiting the attention of the Outside Enquiry Team.

Willard wanted a thorough review of every LOE and was merciless about the small print. Brian Imber, who held the intelligence file, took the Detective Superintendent through each line of inquiry. Forensically, the SOC team had drawn a blank. Nothing in the home, nothing in the garage out the back, nothing in the outhouse Pelly used as a makeshift workshop.

'What are we trying to stand up here?' The pad at Willard's elbow was still blank.

'We're thinking Pelly did the guy in the flat downstairs. That's the one that's been redecorated. The CSM says they tried everything, the lot. If we're talking a cleaned-up crime scene, he says Pelly deserves a medal.'

'We're saying he took the guy's head off in there?'

'Hard to say, sir. The scale of the redecorating tells me there was a lot of blood.'

'What about disposal of the carpet? Wallpaper? The chair you say he replaced?'

'We've talked to the council people in Newport. There are three tips on the island. Rubbish goes for landfill. Five months later is a hell of a time to start digging, and in any case I'm not sure Pelly would have taken the risk. A bloke who covers his arse the way he's done might well have stuffed it all in the Volvo and taken it over to the mainland.'

'And the Volvo?'

'He says he's sold it. Bit vague about the new owner.'

'PNC?'

'No new details logged.'

'How does Pelly explain that?'

'Says he forgot to get the info off the buyer. Told us the guy looked a bit dodgy. Paid cash; shot off. It's bollocks, of course, but when we challenge him, he just shrugs. Isn't that right, Dave?'

Michaels nodded. Pelly, he said, was denial on legs. Any more prime suspects like him and he'd be looking for early retirement. The comment raised a ripple of laughter round the table. Willard wasn't amused.

'This guy's taking the piss. Shouldn't we be doing something about that?'

Faraday could only agree. He asked Imber to take Willard through Pelly's financial transactions. Imber

483

had prepared a timeline tracing the various sums that had so suddenly appeared in Pelly's bank account. Over the last couple of days he'd managed to relate the deposits to cross-Channel ferry bookings for which Pelly had retained the receipts. These receipts had formed part of the haul of paperwork seized from his flat and Imber's painstaking analysis had revealed that each deposit had been made the day after Pelly's return from abroad.

'The deposits were in cash?'

'Yes, sir.'

'Sterling?'

'Euros.'

'Any indication of where he might have got them?'

Imber shook his head. Pelly had excellent contacts in the Balkans. He'd been going there, off and on, for the last ten years. By his own admission he made money from bringing in asylum seekers – individuals with a genuine case to plead. Some years, he was flush with funds. Other times, like more recently, he was pushed. Maybe the cash deposits were a windfall from a couple of particularly successful trips. Maybe he'd called in long-standing debts or raised a loan from local backers in Bosnia. Or maybe the paper trail – if Imber ever managed to establish such a thing – would lead directly to the headless corpse at the foot of the cliff, but without a firm ID it would be impossible to check. Once again, by either luck or design, Pelly had fenced off yet another line of enquiry.

Willard stirred. Watching him, Faraday could sense the frustration his boss was beginning to share with the *Congress* team. No inquiry should be this much of a wind-up. Ever.

'We need a name, don't we?' Willard sat back,

tossing his pen onto the pad. 'That's where this thing begins and ends. The body.'

Imber began to speculate again about Pelly's possible links with people smugglers. Checks on the status of the lodgers in his Shanklin and Ventnor properties had drawn a blank. They were all legit, either asylum seekers awaiting adjudication or – in the majority of cases – individuals who'd been granted indefinite leave to remain. Nonetheless, it was perfectly feasible for Pelly to have brought in other refugees who were promptly shipped over to the mainland and driven north. Why else would he have wanted a £70,000 boat with forty-five knots on the speedo?

'Sure. But a spot of people smuggling suddenly earning him this kind of money?' Willard gestured at Imber's figures. 'You have to be joking.'

There was a long silence. The wind was rattling a loose frame in one of the windows, and Faraday caught the sound of the train that clattered along the pier to the station at the seaward end. Berthing alongside in this weather would be a nightmare for the regular cross-Solent Fast Cat, he thought. Banged-up on the island with the frustrations of *Congress*, there seemed no escape.

There came a knock at the door. Expecting a tray of coffee from one of the Management Assistants, Faraday glanced up. It was DC Tracy Barber. She was beckoning Faraday into the corridor. She needed a word.

Faraday excused himself. Barber was looking unusually tense.

'I've had a call from Lajla,' she said. 'She wants a meet.'

'When?'

'Now.'

'So what's the problem?'

'There isn't one, except it might be wise if you came too. She doesn't want to talk at the home. It has to be somewhere else, in Shanklin. I've suggested the caff we went to the other day. What do you think?'

Faraday glanced back at the group around the table. Imber was talking again, doubtless giving Willard yet more ammunition for a halt in proceedings. At this rate, *Congress* would be dead in the water by lunchtime.

Barber was waiting for a decision.

'She asked for you by name?'

'Yes. She says she won't talk to anyone else. I thought you might come as back-up, sir. Stay in the car for a bit. Maybe join us once she's settled down.'

'And you think it's important?'

'Yes.'

'She's not pissing us around?'

'Definitely not.'

'OK.' Faraday reached for the door handle. 'Give me five minutes.'

Winter awoke late. To his astonishment he felt wonderful. The steady *thump-thump* of the headache had gone. The queasiness it brought had vanished. He rolled over to break the good news but found a note on Maddox's pillow. 'Gone into town,' she'd scribbled. 'Back later.' Winter smiled at the line of kisses beneath and then reached for his watch. Nearly half past ten.

He shaved and dressed, resisting the temptation to tiptoe round the edges of this sudden transformation, to disbelieve the evidence of his nerve ends. He'd no idea what governed the complex biochemistry of his brain, what made for good days and bad, but the sight of yesterday's CT scan had persuaded him that time was precious. The last thing he intended to do was waste it. Cathy and Jimmy Suttle were right. There were more important challenges in life than Maurice Wishart.

He found a couple of eggs in the fridge and half a loaf from Maddox's last expedition to the supermarket. Twenty minutes later he was looking for his heavy raincoat and his car keys. The rest of the morning nosing round the shops, he thought, then a pie and a pint and fingers crossed that Maddox would make it back in time for a leisurely afternoon between the sheets. Maybe they'd find time to discuss travel arrangements. Maybe not.

He drove down to Portsmouth, exhilarated by the weather. A lid of low grey cloud had clamped itself over the city, ragged at the edges, and the Subaru rocked in the blast of wind as he crossed the harbour on the motorway. Looking out at the nose of Whale Island, he marvelled at the contrast with yesterday. Boats were heaving at their moorings. The motorway itself was ribboned with seaweed. Even the gulls were having a hard time.

The shopping precinct in Commercial Road was virtually deserted. A scatter of shoppers were battling the wind and the rain but in the city's centre, thought Winter, it might have been an old-style Sunday. Heartened by this new mood of his, he looked for a present for Maddox. Ottakar's was the obvious place to start but the longer he spent looking at shelf after shelf of books, the more he realised he was out of his depth. Winter's taste had seldom extended beyond Robert Ludlum and Dean Koontz. The woman who read him poetry in the small hours wouldn't be impressed.

He abandoned the bookstore and ducked into the shopping mall beside it. He wanted to get her something she'd remember him by, something that belonged in the space they'd made for each other. His first thought was perfume, or body oils, or maybe a scented candle, but nothing he found seemed to do the trick. A succession of bored shopgirls suggested potpourri or little fancy bags of lavender, shrugging dismissively when Winter wagged his head. Finally, gone midday, he found himself in HMV.

Music, he knew at once, would be a no-no. Maddox was unlikely to share his passion for Tom Jones and the Everly Brothers. Neither was he confident enough to make any kind of stab at classical music. Lately, he'd found himself listening to Beethoven, surprised by how easy it was to surrender to the music, and there were half-decent bits of Rachmaninov, but he knew that neither was quite right. It had to be something else, something that would bring a smile to her face.

In the section devoted to DVDs, inspecting a rack of all-time classic movies, he knew he'd found it. Only days ago he and Maddox had watched *The Bridges of Madison County* together. Then she'd sorted out a couple of French films. A movie, therefore. Had to be.

He began to browse through the titles, enjoying the short cuts they offered to half-forgotten moments in his own youth. He'd been in his teens the first time he'd seen *The Dam Busters*, and he remembered sitting in the flickering darkness with his first girlfriend, bullshitting her with tales of joining the RAF. *Klute* was another favourite, a seventies cop movie with Jane Fonda and Donald Sutherland in the lead roles. Watching *Klute* was the moment which had first planted the thought in Winter's brain that he might become a cop himself. Sutherland had played a detective who'd fallen for a hooker, and with a slight shock Winter realised just how closely real life now mirrored the plot. He smiled to himself, browsing through more titles, wondering if *Klute* might have made it onto DVD. Then he paused. *Casablanca*. Perfect.

Winter felt for his mobile and put a call through to Maddox. Her phone was switched off so he thought for a moment or two, then sent her a text: 'This afternoon? Usual place? Usual time?' He added a couple of kisses and took the DVD to the counter. A minute or so later Maddox's reply arrived. 'Out with a friend,' she'd written. '*Chez toi*, four o'clock? *A bientôt*.' Winter read the text, beamed at the girl behind the counter, then checked his watch. He still had three hours before getting back for Maddox. He had no DVD at home so he'd borrow Maddox's flat for a couple of hours of Bogart and Bergman before heading back to Bedhampton. He produced his mobile again and sent a follow-up text. 'Here's looking at YOU kid,' he wrote, tucking the DVD in the pocket of his coat.

Faraday sat in the Mondeo, perfect line of sight on Munchies Café. Lajla had arrived minutes before, a small, thin figure cocooned in a big quilted anorak. Now she sat in the window, half hidden by condensation on the cold glass, deep in conversation with Tracy Barber. When Tracy judged the time to be right she'd come to the door and give Faraday a wave. Faraday settled down for a long wait.

On the eastern side of the island, Shanklin was protected from the worst of the weather, but out in the bay whitecaps were rolling towards a scatter of moored cargo ships, sheltering from the storm. It had stopped raining now, and barely feet from the boiling surf black-headed gulls were hanging motionless in the teeth of the wind, surveying the debris thrown up on the beach, looking for likely morsels. Faraday watched them for a moment, marvelling at the way they could ride the strongest gusts with seeming ease. If only, he thought.

On the drive over he'd been aware of Tracy Barber pumping him for the direction that *Congress* might take next. He'd fended her off with a shrug, telling her the truth – that it wouldn't be his decision – but he knew she hadn't really believed him. He'd watched her closely over the past couple of weeks, impressed by her diligence and her determination. Faraday himself had never served in Special Branch, never been obliged to deal in the currency of political intelligence, but he was aware of the extra perspective a posting like that could impart.

Barber, it turned out, had spent nearly half her service in SB, and it showed. She had a good analytical brain, a natural flair for making connections that others might miss, and – more to the point – she was excellent in tricky face-to-face situations like these. Faraday watched her now, a blurred figure behind the glass, bending into the conversation, making a point, relaxing, then extending a reassuring hand. Lajla must like her, Faraday thought. More than that, she might trust her.

Faraday turned on the radio, found himself some music. Ten minutes or so later Barber appeared at the café door. Faraday got out and locked the car. Hurrying into the café, he was grateful for the warm fug after the chilly blast of the wind.

Lajla was still sitting at the table in the window, her sodden coat hanging on the back of her chair. She barely spared Faraday a glance as he sat down, and Faraday had the strong impression that he'd wrecked something intimate.

Barber returned from the counter with two mugs of tea. Lajla's was barely touched.

'Lajla and I have agreed some rules.' Barber sat down. 'I've told her that what she's got to say is better said in front of both of us. She knows you're in charge of the case. Pelly's told her that too.'

'He thinks you're a good man. Wrong but good.' Lajla's voice was low, barely a whisper.

'Who does?'

'Rob.'

Faraday raised an eyebrow. A compliment from Pelly was the last thing he'd expected.

'He knows you're here?'

'No.' For the first time she looked up. 'I didn't say anything.'

'Tell Mr Faraday what you told me.' Barber reached for her hand. 'I think that's important.'

Lajla nodded, bit her lip, ducked her head again. Even like this – cornered, uncertain – she had a definite presence. Faraday could sense what an impact she must have made on the young Corporal Pelly, visibly pregnant, struggling through the snow with her plastic bags while the jeering Serb soldiers looked on.

'You have to understand,' she said at last. 'It's important you understand.'

'Understand what?'

'Understand how such a thing can happen. There was no choice. We had no choice. We didn't want him here. We told him that. Rob told him that. He wrote. He phoned. Email. Everything. He wouldn't listen. Rob shouted at him on the phone. Said not to come.'

'Who?' Faraday was leaning forward across the table. 'Who are we talking about?'

He waited for an answer but Lajla said nothing. Tracy Barber caught his eye and signalled for him to back off. In her own time. Slowly.

Faraday nodded, easing away from the table. Mention of email took him back to the cluttered basement room in Southsea – Wowser Productions, the thin, pale, bearded youth who'd quarried his way into Pelly's hard disk and emerged with fragments of a six-month-old correspondence. Lajla had never sent a single reply, he thought. Not one.

'You know about the Balkans? The war? Bosnia?' Lajla again, her voice stronger.

'I know you were a refugee.' Faraday reached for a lump of sugar. 'I know you had to flee from the Serbs.'

'They stole everything. They stole my life.'

She nodded, her chin tilted in Faraday's direction, a sudden blush of colour in her face.

'Some of them I knew, the soldiers. They were boys. People I knew from the village.'

'Serbs?'

'Yes. We Muslims stuck together. Some of our men the Serbs killed. Not all of them. My father, one of my brothers, Muharem ... they survived. Except my father was like me. Dead inside.' She touched her heart then her head. 'He's mad, my father, crazy. You can mend a broken leg but the mind stays broken for ever. The Serbs made him that way.'

Faraday nodded.

'Were there no good Serbs?'

'Of course. Of course there were. There are good people everywhere. But in war bad people take what they want.'

'Rob?'

'He was a good person. He still is a good person. That's why I come here today.' She gestured round at the empty café.

'You want to tell us something about Rob?'

'I want you to understand.'

She ducked her head again, began to play with a plastic spoon. Long, thin fingers. Beautiful nails. A single silver ring. Then her fingers tightened briefly on the spoon and she talked about the day the soldiers came, the faces she recognised from her youth, faces she'd grown up with. Afterwards, she said, girls of a certain age were taken to the school. Because she had her period she was spared the first few days but watching was even worse. She felt what her father must have felt. Madness.

'We stayed at the school most of the summer. It was very hot. The soldiers came most nights, often different faces. I remember every one of them. I have a camera in here . . .' She touched her head again. 'You never forget.'

By the end of the summer she knew she was pregnant. It made no difference. Only when she started to put on weight did the soldiers lose interest. By then it was much colder. She thought the soldiers would kill them all. When, months later, they put the women on the coaches, she thought it was the end.

'They even sold us tickets,' she said. 'Eighty Deutschmarks to be pushed out of my own country.'

The coaches dumped them at the border. They walked to Travnik, to the refugee camp. Soon, her baby came. Older women helped her, did their best. She met Rob. He spoke a little Serbo-Croat. She could manage OK in English. He looked after her – brought her blankets, rusks for the baby, even some books. Angry with the army, angry with the war, he came to

493

the camp one day and said he was leaving, going back to England. She remembered crying, the baby too; then he said he'd be back, as soon as he could. And that's what happened. He came with a beaten-up old truck. He wasn't wearing a uniform. He asked her to come back to England with him. She said yes.

'You understand this? You understand my English?'

Faraday nodded. 'You came here? To Shanklin.'

'Yes. Rob made a home for us. The old people's place belonged to his mother. She was sick. Then she died. I helped him all I could.'

Fida got older. She went to school. She learned English. She made friends. She put the war behind her.

'And you?'

'It never goes away. Never.'

For years, she said, she thought she'd be able to forget. But then came Kosovo, and more refugees, and Rob went back, a better truck this time, and did what he could. He brought lots of people out, men and women, some of them young mothers like her. With the money he made he bought houses, gave them shelter, found them work. Lajla offered to help as well, but Rob would never let her.

'Why?'

'Because he's a brother to me. Because he knows the way I feel about it all. Just to hear the language again . . .' She shuddered.

She paused for a moment. Barber offered tea. She shook her head. Last year, she said, a friend got in touch with her brother in Berlin. She and Muharem had known this man since he was a little boy. He came from the same village. Lajla had always liked him. But he was a Serb.

Dragan, thought Faraday.

'What did he want?'

'He was still living in the village. He's a good man. He became a priest, a Serb priest. He knows everyone; he wants everyone to be friends, to forget, to forgive. Such a thing –' she shrugged '– how can he know it is impossible?'

Dragan was close to another Serb from the same village. His name was Branko. Branko was a Serb also. He'd been the clown in class. He'd made everyone laugh, including Lajla. Then the war had come, and the soldiers, and one of them was Branko.

'He came to the school?'

'Many times.' She looked up, her eyes burning. 'Many, many times.'

After the war, according to Dragan, Branko had become a builder. He'd made lots of money mending houses, selling them to local Serbs. Many of the houses had belonged to Muslims. One of them had belonged to Lajla's family.

'The village now is full of Serbs. And Branko is a rich man.'

But Branko also had a conscience. Dragan said he wanted to make amends, to say sorry. He had money he wanted to give to Lajla. He wanted to explain, to tell her that it was all a long time ago, that things were different now, that maybe she could even come home, back to her own village.

She looked up again.

'This man thinks he is the father of my daughter. Who knows? Maybe he's right.'

Through last summer Dragan kept in touch with Lajla's brother in Berlin. Then, somehow, Branko got hold of her telephone number, of her email address, maybe through Dragan or maybe through Muharem. More and more Branko wanted to come. To explain. To say sorry. Lajla never replied, not once. Rob, she said, was the one who told him it was impossible, that he was to stay in Bosnia. But he never listened.

'You understand now? You understand why?'

'Why what?' This time Faraday couldn't resist the question. Tracy Barber was watching Lajla.

There was a long silence. Outside, the wind seemed to have fallen a little. Then came a sharp crack, and Faraday looked down to see the plastic spoon snapped neatly across the handle.

Lajla was on her feet, reaching for her anorak.

'Come,' she said simply.

Winter parked on the seafront opposite Rose Tower. He could hear the thunder of surf on the nearby pebble beach, and the wind still tasted of salt, but the racing clouds were punctured by shafts of livid sunlight and the downpour had eased to occasional flurries of rain.

Winter locked the car and crossed the road. The cleaners had been at work recently because there was the scent of air freshener in the lift and someone had run a cloth over the mirror. He got out at the tenth floor and paused for a moment beside the window. The view down the Solent was curtained by a line of advancing squalls, soldiers marching to the slackening drum beat of the morning's gale. Closer, one of the big P & O ferries was negotiating the dogleg in the deep-water channel off Southsea Castle. Winter watched it for a moment as it heeled in the turn, trying to imagine the crossing those people must have had. Then he checked for the DVD in the pocket of his coat, and wandered down to Maddox's apartment.

The moment he stepped inside he knew something was wrong. He could hear a stir of movement from deep inside the flat. Then he saw the big cashmere coat discarded across the occasional table where Maddox normally left her keys.

Winter froze, chilled to the marrow. Softly, he closed the door behind him. He could hear the murmur of conversation now, then a yelp of pain or perhaps pleasure. He crept along the hall. The big lounge was empty. Beside the champagne bottle on the low table in front of the sofa, two glasses.

Back in the hall Winter stood motionless. The nearest door led to the kitchen. The two doors at the end belonged to separate bedrooms. The spare bedroom door was open. He moved towards it, knowing already that the room would be empty. The voices were coming from Maddox's room. And they weren't interested in conversation any more.

For a moment Winter hesitated, reluctant to put his feelings to the knife, to hazard the temporary truce his body seemed to have declared, to shatter everything Maddox had brought into his life. Then, with a terrible certainty, he knew there wasn't a choice to be made. He was, in the end, a detective, the guy who had to find out.

He turned the handle and opened the door. Maddox was straddling a figure on the bed, easing herself up and down, a string of pearls round her neck. The naked body beneath her belonged to a middle-aged man. He was lying on his back, his head hanging over the end of the bed, his face contorted in a snarl of pleasure. Winter looked at him a moment, knowing that life had brought him full circle. First Steve Richardson's DVD. Now the real thing.

'Mr Wishart,' he said softly.

Maddox's rhythm slowed. Finally she stopped altogether and slipped off the bed. She paused beside

Winter, kissed him on the lips. Winter studied her a moment, totally lost.

'The drawer beside the bed,' she murmured.

Wishart's eyes followed her out of the room. Anger had given way to something else. Uncertainty.

Winter told Wishart to get dressed. The drawer in the bedside cabinet was open. Propped inside was a small cassette recorder. Winter took it out, checked the cassette. Forty-five minutes.

Down the hall, from the bathroom, came the hiss of the shower. Wishart had recovered himself. He sat on the edge of the bed with a towel over his lap, a big man, overweight, his chest and lower belly matted with curls of greying hair.

'What's this about?' He nodded towards the door, towards the splash of falling water, towards Maddox.

Winter didn't answer. He'd rewound the tape and now he pressed the PLAY button, the tiny cassette machine still in his hand. A moment's silence, then Wishart's voice. He sounded suspicious.

'What are you doing down there?'

'You want some of this?'

'Ah . . .' Wishart's tone softened. *'Is that what I think it is?'*

'You want to try?'

'Silly question. Come here.' Winter's first thought was a toot or two of charlie. But then came Maddox's soft command – *'Roll over, spread your legs'* – and Winter's gaze began to roam over the wreckage of the bed, looking for whatever appliance Maddox had come up with.

'Here? Is that good?' She was taunting him now. *'Deeper? Quicker?'*

Wishart was eyeing the cassette. From the tape came a long groan of pleasure and a flurry of movement.

Winter was trying not to visualise what Maddo̶̶̶̶
up to, satisfying Wishart's insatiable appetites. A job,
he told himself. She's doing a job.

There was a movement in the hall behind Winter.
He glanced round. Maddox was barefoot on the carpet
in a long silk dressing gown. She had a towel in her
hand. Water was still dripping from her hair.

'It's further on.' She nodded at the cassette machine.
'About fifteen minutes in.'

Winter pressed FAST FORWARD. The cassette
whirred. He pressed PLAY again.

'*You could, you know.*' Wishart's voice – reflective,
satisfied, rich.

'*I know. You've told me before.*'

'*I'm serious though. My pleasure. Cheque, cash –
whatever. Just name it.*'

'*What about your wife?*'

'*She'll never know. It just comes out of the business
account.*'

On the tape Maddox began to laugh. It was a
taunting laugh and whatever she was doing to Wishart
made him laugh too.

'*Everything comes out of your business account,
doesn't it? What about me? Do I come out of your
business account? What about this? Do you like this?
Come here. Talk to me. Pretend I'm real for a
moment.*'

'*That's nice ... Slower ... Yeah ...*'

'*Well?*'

'*Forget it. Come here.*'

Maddox began to dry her hair. The sound of her
own voice had put a smile on her face.

'It's the next bit,' she said. 'Just listen.'

On the tape her voice had lowered. She was

whispering something to Wishart, sharing a confidence, telling him a story. Wishart, still on the edge of the bed, was staring up at her.

'Whore,' he said softly. 'You fucking whore.'

Winter was enjoying himself now. He caught Wishart's eye, gave him a smile, then turned to Maddox.

'What were you saying to him?'

'I was telling him about Victor. How big he was, how strong, what he liked to do to me.' She nodded down at the cassette machine. 'It's coming up now.'

On the tape the sound of Maddox's throaty laugh.

'*Twice,*' she murmured. '*Twice in a couple of minutes. And me a working girl. Can you believe that?*'

'*Shame.*'

'*Shame? I loved it.*'

'*Shame about Victor. Shame he had to go.*'

'*Go?*'

More laughter, Wishart this time.

'*You should have seen him. He knew he was in trouble. The man had screwed me. Silly thing to do, really. He knew exactly what was coming. I could see it in his eyes every time he turned round on that silly bike of his. The man might have had balls the size of melons but it doesn't matter in the end, does it? Not in a situation like that.*'

'*Situation like what, darling?*'

'*Nothing. Dick around in business and you should expect consequences.*'

'*You were jealous.*'

'*Not at all. I was settling accounts.*'

'*My account.*'

'*Yeah? Is that what you believe? You think I'd kill a man because he fucked you witless?*'

'*Yes.*'

'*You're wrong.*' The laugh again, harsher. '*Come here. And remember who paid you to screw that monkey.*'

Winter's finger found the STOP button. There was a moment of silence. Then came the sigh of the wind and the faraway keening of a ship's siren. Winter was still gazing down at Wishart. Then he felt Maddox's hand on his arm. She wanted to know what to do. Winter gave her his mobile and told her to phone Jimmy Suttle.

'Tell him to come round. His number's in the directory. Tell him to bring some handcuffs.'

Maddox stepped into the hall. Both men listened to the soft pad of her footsteps as she retreated into the living room. Then came the beginnings of a murmured conversation as she got through to Suttle on the phone.

Wishart had his head in his hands. For the first time Winter caught sight of the huge purple dildo, abandoned on the carpet beside the bed.

'You know something, my friend?' Winter slipped the cassette into his pocket. 'You're fucked.'

The rain had stopped by the time Faraday arrived at the nursing home. He got out of the car, opening the back door for Barber and Lajla. Neither woman had said anything on the drive up from the cafe. Now Lajla led the way round the side of the house towards the garage. Beyond the garage was an outhouse. Lajla opened the door and disappeared briefly inside. When she came out again, she was carrying a garden fork.

'Please . . .' She gestured towards the garden.

Barber and Faraday followed her across the sodden patch of lawn. A cinder path led between patches of vegetables. Faraday recognised sprouts and a row of onions. Towards the back fence, set aside, was a small flower garden. The carefully turned soil was edged with pebbles and there were stands of daffodils nodding in the wind. Amongst the daffodils, a clump of tulips. The tulips were a deep red, newly flowering, the boldest of flags, impossible to miss.

Lajla paused for a moment, eyeing the flowers, then drove the fork into the wet soil. She began to dig, turning the soil aside, plunging deeper and deeper. Finally she hit something solid. She glanced up at Tracy Barber, wrinkled her nose, then squatted amongst the wreckage of the tulips. With her bare hands she began to scrape the soil away. Slowly the shape of a skull began to emerge, the pale whiteness of the bone matted with hair and a grey slime that must once have been flesh. Faraday could smell it now, the sweet stench of death, and he took a tiny step backwards as Lajla's fingers dug beneath the skull and pulled it clear of the hole.

She stood up, her thin hands cupping the soiled head, inviting Faraday to take it.

'Branko Grujic,' she said.

Faraday stared at this hideous trophy.

'Pelly killed him?'

'No.' Lajla smiled. 'I did.'

Faraday glanced across at Tracy Barber but she was looking up at the house. Faraday saw nothing for a moment, then he too noticed the watching face in the upstairs window. Pelly stood motionless, staring down at them. Then he was gone.

Epilogue

It was a week before Terry Alcott drove down to Portsmouth for a hastily summoned conference on *Congress*. Willard, as puzzled by this sudden visitation as everyone else, convened a meeting in his office. At the ACC's insistence only Faraday attended from the *Congress* squad.

Alcott, unusually, was late. When he finally appeared he had a guest in tow.

'Robin Philpott.' Alcott did the introductions.

Philpott accepted a seat beside Faraday. He was a pale man in a nicely tailored suit, close to middle age, with thinning hair and carefully buffed nails. The contents of his briefcase, Faraday noticed, barely extended beyond a single file. He put the file on the table in front of him. On the front cover, a single word. *Congress*.

Willard took Alcott through the closing stages of the case. After exhumation of the skull Pelly and Lajla had both been arrested on suspicion of murder. DNA tests had matched the head to the body from the foot of the cliff, and further samples had been requested from the appropriate authorities in the Republika Srpska. Lajla had volunteered not only the name of her village but the address of Branko's house. She knew it well, she said, because she had once lived there.

In a formal interview Lajla had repeated what she'd told Faraday and Barber in the café. Branko had fought and fought to come over and see her. When he'd finally arrived, he'd given her money, lots of money, insisted she take it. He'd come into her flat, sat in her armchair, tried to explain. He'd had a lot to drink, she said. He was laughing one minute, very nervous the next. He wanted to say sorry. He wanted her to understand. He needed to know that she'd forgiven him.

Lajla had been polite – she'd listened, she'd nodded. Then she'd sent her daughter away to the shops and, when the man had become sleepy with the drink, she'd taken a kitchen knife, stepped across to the back of the armchair, pulled his head back and cut his throat. There'd been a lot of blood and she'd panicked and gone running for Rob. Branko was dead. Rob had cut through the rest of his neck with a saw and wrapped up the body in black polythene. Then he'd started to clean everything up.

While he was still lifting the carpet, old Mary Unwin had come in. Lajla said she did that sometimes – just wandered around. Lajla had taken her back to her own room, told her it was nothing, just a game, and until Tracy Barber had started asking questions it seemed that the old lady had believed her.

Back in the flat Branko's head had gone into a big Tesco bag. Lajla had sealed the bag and wrapped it in another one, and then hidden the package under an old wooden box in the garden. At first she'd planned to add the package to all the rubbish collected by the dustmen every week. Then, without telling Rob, she decided to bury it in the flower bed. She'd done it one afternoon while Rob was out and afterwards she'd planted tulip bulbs on top. That way, she said, she could see it from her window. That way, she'd try and make a kind of peace.

As for Pelly, said Willard, the man had opted for virtual silence. He admitted disposing of the body, smiled at the suggestion that his sudden financial windfalls might have come from the dead man's bank accounts, but had given very little else away. Challenged to explain his wife's actions, he'd simply shaken his head. Only later, after the tape machines had been switched off and he was en route back to the cells, did he volunteer an opinion. 'You blokes –' he'd said wearily '– haven't got a clue.'

Now Willard handed over the meeting to Alcott. Already, the Major Crime Team were busy on a domestic killing in Petersfield. After two results – the New Forest and now *Congress* – squad morale was sky high.

Alcott was pleased to hear it. Then he turned to the stranger at the table. Philpott, he said, was from Six. And he had a couple of things to say.

Faraday and Willard exchanged glances. MI6 handled foreign intelligence.

Philpott began with a mild word of caution. What they were about to hear would be by no means welcome. They might even resent this intrusion and, if that were to be the case, he wanted them to know that he entirely understood. They lived in an ever more complex world. And they were therefore obliged, on occasions, to make difficult decisions.

Willard scented trouble. In situations like these he was famously territorial. My turf. My team. My responsibility to get a result in court.

'Who are we talking about?' he growled. 'Who are "They"?'

'HMG.'

'And what's your point?'

Alcott laid a restraining hand on Willard's arm.

'Easy,' he said. 'Hear him out.'

Philpott opened his file, flipped through a page or two, found what he was looking for, then closed it again.

'Mr Pelly has led a colourful life. Some of the people he deals with are of interest to us. Not simply that but we need them.'

'Like who? Who do we need?'

'Serbs chiefly, but some Bosnians too. Pelly has excellent contacts on both sides. Without him, to be frank, our job would be a great deal harder.'

'You're telling me he's a spook?'

'I'm telling you he gives us a great deal of help. We've been dealing with Mr Pelly for a number of years and we've always given him . . . ah . . . a degree of latitude. I know you don't expect me to go into details but it wouldn't, I'm afraid, be in our interests to pursue any kind of prosecution against him.' His hand found the file. 'The CPS will not be proceeding on this case.'

Willard stared at him. He couldn't believe it. Not here. Not in his own office.

'What about her? Lajla?'

'I understand Mr Pelly has plans to emigrate. Under the circumstances, we believe that might be an appropriate outcome. Naturally we regret what happened to the unfortuanate Mr Branko but the quarrel, to be frank, was never ours.'

'She killed him,' Willard pointed out. 'Murder's an offence.'

'Indeed.'

Philpott was looking at Alcott. Clearly he believed the meeting was over.

Faraday sat back, understanding at last why Pelly had been so unmoved as the inquiry had tightened around him. He knew, Faraday thought. He knew from the start that we were wasting our time. He knew he had immunity. He knew that *Congress* wouldn't end in a court of law but here, around a table like this, listening to a stranger from London explaining the political facts of life.

Willard had got to his feet, his coffee untouched.

'This,' he grunted, 'is a fucking outrage.'

Two days later Faraday made time to drive up to Bedhampton and pay Paul Winter a visit. Word about the DC's state of health had spread to every squad office in the city. Reactions were mixed but there was general agreement that no bloke in his middle forties deserved to wake up and find himself on the end of a virtual death sentence.

Faraday himself had been the fall guy in a number of Winter's wilder investigative scams. As a divisional DI he'd spent three uncomfortable years trying to explain the judicial rules of gravity to someone who plainly never listened, and on a number of occasions he'd been close to referring Winter to the Professional Standards Department for a spot of serious career advice. At the same time, though, Faraday had a sneaking regard for Winter. Here was someone who had an absolute determination to nail the bad guys. And if – in a complex world – that meant bending the odd rule, then so be it.

Winter's bungalow lay in a cul-de-sac on the lower slopes of Portsdown Hill. Faraday had never been here before but knew that Winter's wife had treasured the place. When Joannie had been losing her own battle against cancer it was to Faraday that Winter had briefly turned. They'd spent a night talking about it, sunk a great deal of Scotch, and never once mentioned the evening again. Maybe now, thought Faraday, was the moment to revive that sudden intimacy.

Winter answered the door in his pyjamas. Faraday had phoned ahead to check it was OK to drop by, and Winter seemed pleased to see him. The bungalow, to Faraday's surprise, smelled of joss sticks. In the lounge at the back he found the reason why.

'Maddox.' Winter introduced a tall, striking-looking woman in her mid-twenties. Bony, slightly angular face. Eyes the colour of emeralds.

Maddox had been down the road for a cake. Faraday felt strangely touched.

He sat down, made himself at home. Winter wanted to get the medicals over and done with. He had a brain tumour. They were going to do something about it. He had a consultation booked with a London neurosurgeon later in the month but in the meantime he and Maddox and a bagful of painkillers were off to Ethiopia. Christ knows what they'd find there but it was Maddox's idea and Winter was in no position to argue.

Maddox was back with a pot of tea. She sat cross-legged beside Winter's chair, her head propped on his knee, smiling to herself as Winter shared the bare bones of Operation *Plover* with Faraday. A local businessman had topped a Nigerian naval officer. Had he not been such an arrogant bastard, he might have got away with it. As it was, the man had dug himself a huge hole and then fallen in.

Maddox grinned up at Winter. She objected to the word 'hole'. Faraday gazed at them both, bewildered. He'd never heard of *Plover*.

'You've arrested this guy?'

'Yeah.'

'Got the evidence?'

'You're looking at her.'

'I am?' Faraday wondered quite what was coming next.

'Yeah. The guy's name is Wishart. And you know what he said when we arrested him? He told me to get a life.' His hand found Maddox's bare shoulder, then he peered up at Faraday. 'Nice, eh? Under the circumstances?'

At the weekend, Faraday at last had a couple of days to himself. He spent Saturday morning cleaning the house, sorting his laundry, catching up with the post and a couple of dozen emails. Eadie Sykes, he learned, had been offered backing for her latest movie project and would be staying on in Australia for at least a couple of months. This, it seemed, would be good news for J-J, who was still occupying Eadie's top-floor apartment overlooking the beach on South Parade.

To celebrate, Faraday took his son to lunch. They walked to a pub on the harbourside in Old Portsmouth. J-J was as voluble as ever, his hands a blur of sign as he briefed Faraday on his career plans. For the time being he was still working for Ambrym, Eadie's company, but a production house in London had seen some of his editing show reel and had been impressed enough to offer him a six-month contract. They'd just won a Channel 5 commission, *Beyond the Beyond*, a documentary series billed as a major inquiry into spiritualism.

'Spooky or what?' J-J signed.

Faraday nodded, happy to be back in the giddy enthusiasm of his son's world, thinking quite suddenly of the Corey family.

He phoned Karen Corey the following morning. He

was, she said, lucky to find her in. It was her turn to take Madge to the temple but she had a bit of a cold and her mum had gone instead.

Faraday told her he had a bit of free time. He'd love to get out in the country, get some decent air in his lungs, maybe climb a hill or two. Did she fancy coming along?

Karen said she'd love to but there was something she'd been meaning to say to him. All the fuss and bother about Harry had made her feel guilty. Not just because she'd bothered Faraday when he was obviously busy but because he'd probably concluded that they were all crackers, the whole family, every last one of them.

Faraday told her not to worry. He'd been happy to read the letters, happier still to offer what little advice he could. He was just sorry there was so little they could do.

'He's in a home,' she said. 'In Southsea.'

'Who?'

'Bob. Harry's oppo.' She paused. 'Sundays, they always take him out along the seafront. I just wondered . . .'

Faraday was propped against the chest of drawers on which he kept the phone, gazing out at the harbour through the big French doors.

'You want me to meet Bob?'

'Yes, I do.'

'Why?'

'I just . . . I don't know. A favour, maybe? Just to prove he really exists? That we're not all bonkers?'

Faraday smiled to himself. Another war, he thought. Another ever-lengthening shadow.

'OK,' he said. 'Give me a time.'

*

They met on the seafront in Old Portsmouth an hour and a half later. Karen was wrapped up against the bitter wind, offering a cold cheek when Faraday bent to kiss her. Bob and his carer would be along any minute, she said. They kept to the same schedule every Sunday, the old man tottering the half-mile from the distant muddle of the funfair to the Square Tower, which overlooked the harbour entrance. After that, she promised, they could climb whichever hill Faraday fancied.

Faraday warmed to the prospect, eyeing the procession of strollers out for an afternoon in the bright, chilly sunshine. Within minutes Karen had spotted Bob and his carer.

'There he is.' She pointed to a bent figure beside a plump woman pushing a wheelchair.

Faraday watched them as they approached. Bob must have been in his eighties – thin, stooped, flat cap, glasses, one arm thrust into a cheap windcheater, one arm half out. He shuffled towards them across the paving stones, his head down, determined to make it to the end of the promenade. For a second or two Faraday tried to imagine him in the dock, answering to a jury for a moment of long-ago madness. The image, he decided, was bizarre.

The carer had answered Karen's wave. She steered the old man in Faraday's direction, stopped beside them. The old man struggled with the windcheater in his confusion, finally stiffening his body and knotting his big-knuckled hands in the small of his back. He might have been on parade, thought Faraday, answering to the sergeant's bark.

'Bob?' Karen was shouting. 'This is a friend of mine. Joe.'

'Joe?' He turned his head towards the voice. His

nose was running and a thread of saliva dribbled from the corner of his mouth.

'Joe Faraday, Bob. He's a friend of Madge's. He said he wanted to meet you.'

'Friend of who?'

'Madge. Madge Corey. You remember Madge?'

'Ah, Madge . . .' The vaguest of smiles creased the old man's face. 'Harry's girl.'

Monday, 11th July 2005, 04.30

Every driver's nightmare.

Assigned to the first train out of Portsmouth, he'd checked in at the Fratton depot before dawn, double-locking his Suzuki 900, stowing his helmet in the crew room, and then making his way upstairs to glance through the emergency speed restrictions and confirm his station stops. This time in the morning, the five-car set would be virtually empty. A handful of staff hitching a ride to stations up the line, maybe a dozen or so City-bound commuters, occasionally a drunk or two, slumped in the corner of the carriage, unconscious after a night in the Southsea clubs.

He was two minutes late off Portsmouth Harbour, waiting for a lone punter off the Isle of Wight Fast Cat, but made up the time before the miles of trackside terraces began to thin and the train clattered over Portsbridge Creek, leaving the city silhouetted against the fierce spill of light to the east.

The station at Havant looked deserted. Coasting to a halt, he waited barely fifteen seconds before the guard closed the doors again. Picking up speed, heading north now, he wondered whether the promised thunder storms would really happen, and whether his partner would remember to close the greenhouse door in case the wind got up.

Beyond the long curve of Rowlands Castle station,

the gradient began to steepen. Ahead lay the dark swelll of the South Downs. He added more power, watching the speedo needle creep round towards seventy. These new Desiros knocked spots off the old stock. German kit, he thought. Never fails.

Minutes later, deep in a cutting, came the sudden gape of the Buriton Tunnel. He slowed to 40 mph and sounded the horn, raising a flurry of wood pigeons from the surrounding trees. Then the world suddenly went black, the clatter of the train pulled tight around him, and he peered into the darkness, waiting for his eyes to adjust. Moments later, still enfolded by the tunnel, he had a sudden glimpse of something ahead on the line. In the dim throw of light from the front of the train, the oncoming shape resolved itself into a body spread-eagled on the nearside rail, then – for a split second – he was looking at a pair of legs, scissored open, and the unmistakable whiteness of naked flesh.

Instinctively, in a single reflex movement, he took the speed off and pushed the brake handle fully forward, feeling his body tensing for the impact, the way he might on the bike, some dickhead stepping out onto the road. Thenn came a jolt, nothing major, and he knew with a terrible certainty that his eyes hadn't betrayed him, that what he'd seen, what he'd felt, was even now being shredded to pieces in the roaring darkness beneath the train.

The cab began to shudder under the bite of the brakes. The tunnel exit in sight, he pulled the train to a halt and reached for the cab secure radio that would take him to the signalman back at Havant. When the signalman answered, he gave him the train code and location, asked for power isolation, declared an emergency.

What's up then?' the man wanted to know.

The driver blinked, still staring ahead, aware of the guard trying to contact him on the internal coms. 'One under,' he managed, reaching for the door.

One

This time, Faraday knew there'd be no escape.

He'd taken to the water an hour or so earlier, finning slowly out of the bay, scanning the reefs below, enjoying the lazy rise and fall of the incoming swell. An evening with a reference book he'd picked up in Bangkok let him put a name to the shapes that swam below.

Beneath him, he could see yellow-ringed parrot fish, nosing for food amid the coral; half a dozen milky-white bat fish, stately, taking their time, slowly unfurling like banners; even, for a glorious minute or two, the sight of a solitary clownfish drifting over the underwater meadows of softly waving fronds. The head of the clownfish was daubted with a startling shade of scarlet but it was the huge eyes, doleful, disconsolate, that had Faraday blasting water from his snorkel tube. The little fish reminded him of an inspector he'd once served under in his uniformed days. The same sense of tribulation. The same air of unathomable regret. Laughing underwater, Faraday discovered, wasn't a great idea.

Further out, the colours changed and with the blues and greens shading even deeper, Faraday became aware of the schools of fish beginning to thin. He'd never been out this far, not by a long way, and a lift of his head told him that he must have covered nearly a mile since he'd slipped into the water. He could see the tiny wooden bungalow clinging to the rocks above the tideline. A line of washing on the veranda told him that Eadie must have finally surfaced. Shame.

Adjusting the mask and clearing the snorkel again, Faraday ducked his head. It was hard to judge distance underwater but twenty metres down, maybe more, he cold just make a tumble of boulders on the seabed. This, he imagined, would be the point where the coral shallows suddenly plunged away into something infinitely deeper. In the beachside bar, only yesterday, he'd heard a couple of French lads describing a dive they'd just made. Faraday was no linguist but his French was adequate enough to understand *profondeur* and *requin*. The latter word came with a repertoire of gestures and had raised an appreciative shiver in one of the listening women. *Requin* meant shark.

Floating on the surface, barely moving, Faraday was overwhelmed by a sense of sudden chill. A mile was a long way out. There were no lifeguards, no rescue boats. Trying to slow his pulse rate, he scanned the depths below him. A thin drizzle of tiny particles was drifting down through the dapple of surface sunlight, down towards the inky-blue nothingness. Then, way off to the right, he caught a flicker of movement, the briefest glimpse of something much, much bigger than the carnival of cartoon fish he'd left in the shallows.

Faraday shut his eyes a moment, squeezed them very hard, fought the temptation to turn in the water, to kick hard, to strike for home. This is exactly what you shouldn't do, he told himself. In situations like these, panic was the shortest cut to disaster.

He opened his eyes again, watched his own pale hand wipe the toughened glass in the facemask. He'd been wrong. Not one of them. Not two. But half a dozen. At least. They were circling now, much closer, sleek, curious, terrifying.

All too aware of the quickening rasp of his own breath, Faraday watched the sharks. Every nerve end told him that something unimaginable was about to happen. He hung in the water, his mouth suddenly dry, feeling utterly helpless. He'd never seen creatures like this, so perfectly evolved for the task in hand, so ready, so close. The water rippled over the gills behind their gaping mouths as they slipped through the shafts of dying sunlight, and as they circled closer and closer he became mesmerised by their eyes. The eyes told him everything. They were cold, unblinking, devoid of anything but the expectation of what would happen next. This was their territory. Their world. Trespass was a capital offence.

Faraday had a sudden vision of blood in the water, his own blood, of pinked strips of torn flesh, of jaws closing on his flailing limbs, of line after line of those savage teeth tearing at the rest of his body until nothing was left but a cloud of chemicals and splinters of white bone sinking slowly out of sight.

One of the biggest sharks made a sudden turn and then came at him, the pale body twisting as it lunged, and Faraday felt himself brace as the huge jaws filled his vision. This is death, he thought. This is what happens when you get it so badly wrong.

Another noise, piercing, insistent, familiar. The shark, he thought numbly. The shark.

His heart pounding, Faraday turned over and groped in the half-darkness. The mobile was on the chair beside the bed. For a second or two, listening to the voice on the other end, he hadn't a clue where he was. Then, immeasurably relieved, he managed a response.

Buriton is a picturesque Hampshire village tucked beneath the wooden swell of the South Downs. A street of timbered cottages and a couple of pubs led to a twelfth-century church. There were 4x4s everywhere, most of them new, and Faraday slowed to let a harassed-looking mother load her kids into the back of a Toyota Land Cruiser. Buriton, he thought wearily, is where you'd settle if you still believed in a certain vision of England – peaceful, safe, white – and had the money to buy it.

He parked beside the pond at the heart of the village. Already, there was a scatter of other cars, most of them badged with the familiar chequerboard of the British Transport Police. Faraday was still eyeing a cople of BTP officers pulling on their wellington boots, wondering quite why a suicide had attracted so much police attention, when there came a tap at his passenger window.

'Jerry . . .'

Surprised, Faraday got out of the Mondeo and shook the extended hand. DS Jerry Proctor was a Crime Scene Manager, a looming, heavyset individual with a reputation for teasing meticulously presented evidence out of the most chaotic situations. The last couple of years, he'd been seconded to the British effort in Iraq, teaching local police recruits how to become forensic investigators.

'How was the posting?'

'Bloody.'

'Glad to be back?'

'No.' Proctor nodded towards the parked Transport Police cars. 'These guys have been here a couple of hours now. They've got a DI with them and it needs someone to sort him out.'

Faraday looked away for a moment. Proctor had never seen the point of small talk.

'You're telling me the DI's a problem?'

'Not at all, sir. But they haven't got the bodies, not for something like this. You want to come up to the tunnel?'

Proctor was already wearing one of the grey one-piece discardable suits that came with the job. While Faraday pulled on the pair of hiking boots he kept in the back of the car, Proctor brought him up to date.

The driver of the first train out of Pompey had reported hitting a body in the nearby tunnel. The power had been switched off, and control rooms in London alerted. Calls from Transport Police HQ in St James's Park had roused the duty Rail Incident Officer who'd driven over from his home in Eastleigh. By then, the batteries on the train were running out of juice and the twenty or so passengers aboard would soon be sitting in the dark.

'No one got them off?'

'No, sir.'

'Why not?'

'The driver didn't think it was appropriate. Young guy. Cluey.'

'Cluey how?'

'He'd taken a good look underneath the train, gone back with a torch, brave lad.'

'And?'

They were walking round the pond by now, following the narrow lane that wound up towards the railway line. Proctor glanced across at Faraday.

'He found the impact spot, or what he assumed was the impact spot. Bits of our man were all over the bottom of the train but the torso and legs were still in one piece.' Proctor touched his own belly. 'Chained to the line.'

'*Chained?*'

'Yeah.' Proctor nodded. 'We're talking serious chain, padlock, the works. Our driver friend thought that was a bit over the top, made another call.' He shot Faraday a bleak smile. 'So here we all are.'

'And the train's still in the tunnel?'

'Yes, sir.'

'Impact point?'

'About fifty metres in. That's from the southern end.'

'How long's the tunnel?'

'Five hundred metres. Transport Police are organising a generator and a lighting unit. Plus they've laid hands on half a dozen or so blokes to check out the tunnel. Don't get me wrong, sir. The DI knows what he's doing. It's just resources. Not his fault.'

Faraday was doing the sums, trying to imagine the size of the challenge that awaited them all. At worst, he'd assumed they were looking at some kind of complicated suicide. The fact that this body had been physically tied to the line changed everything.

'The DI's established a common path?'

'Yes, sir. Down this lane, under the railway bridge, along a little track, then up the embankment and itno the tunnel. The train's maybe forty metres in.'

'And that's the way we get the passengers off?'

'Has to be. The Incident Officer tells me the rest of it's fenced miles back in both directions. We've got no option.'

Faraday pulled a face. In these situations, absolute priority lay in isolating the crime scene. If Proctor was right about access to the track, then whatever evidence awaited them was about to be trampled.

'We need Mr Barrie in on this.' Faraday fumbled for his mobile. Martin Barrie was the new Detective Superintendent in charge of the Major Crimes Team. If it came to any kind of turf war, then Barrie was the man with the ammunition.

Proctor watched while Faraday keyed in a number, then touched him lightly on the arm.

'That's another problem, sir.' He nodded towards the nearby embankment. 'This is a mobile black spot. Either end of the tunnel, there's no signal.'

The train was visible from the mouth of the tunnel. Faraday stood on the track, peering into the darkness, trying to imagine what five carriages would do to flesh, bone and blood. Like every policeman, he'd attended his share of traffic accidents, successful suicide bids, and other incidents when misjudgement or desperation had taken a life, but thankfully he'd never witnessed the cooling remains of a human body torn apart by a train.

Other men, less lucky, spoke of unrecognisable parcels of flesh, of entrails scattered beside the track, of the way that the impact – like the suck of high explosive – could rip the clothes from a man and toss them aside before dismembering him.

The image made Faraday pause. Only days ago, three tube trains had been ripped apart by terrorist bombs in London and some of the media coverage of the consequences had been unusually candid. Was his incident, in some strange way, a twist on that theme? He let the thought settle for a moment, then he was struck by another image, altogether more personal, and he found himself fighting a hot gust of nausea, remembering the oncoming shark of his nightmare and that moment before consciousness when he knew for certain that he, too, was a dead man.

'Sir?'

All Orion/Phoenix titles are available at your local bookshop or from the following address:

Mail Order Department
Littlehampton Book Services
FREEPOST BR535
Worthing, West Sussex, BN13 3BR
telephone 01903 828503, *facsimile* 01903 828802
e-mail MailOrders@lbsltd.co.uk
(Please ensure that you include full postal address details)

Payment can be made either by credit/debit card (Visa, Mastercard, Access and Switch accepted) or by sending a £ Sterling cheque or postal order made payable to *Littlehampton Book Services*.

DO NOT SEND CASH OR CURRENCY

Please add the following to cover postage and packing

UK and BFPO:
£1.50 for the first book, and 50p for each additional book to a maximum of £3.50

Overseas and Eire:
£2.50 for the first book plus £1.00 for the second book and 50p for each additional book ordered

---

BLOCK CAPITALS PLEASE

name of cardholder .... *delivery address*
.... (*if different from cardholder*)
address of cardholder ....
....
....
....
postcode .... *postcode* ....

☐ I enclose my remittance for £ ....

☐ please debit my Mastercard/Visa/Access/Switch (delete as appropriate)

card number ☐☐☐☐☐☐☐☐☐☐☐☐☐☐☐☐

expiry date ☐☐☐☐ Switch issue no. ☐☐

signature ....

prices and availability are subject to change without notice